Archangel

Archangel

MIKE CONNER

TOR

A Tom Doherty Associates Book • New York

ARCHANGEL

Edited by David G. Hartwell

A Tor Book
Published by Tom Doherty Associates, Inc.
175 Fifth Avenue
New York, N.Y. 10010

Tor ® is a registered trademark of Tom Doherty Associates, Inc.

Design by Liney Li

ISBN 0-312-85743-8

First edition: February 1995

Printed in the United States of America

0 9 8 7 6 5 4 3 2 1

This book is for Megan Conner and for Shelby Conner,
who are as brave as heaven *and* hell.

Oh, it's been a long time
Since I had my shoes shined
Now that Porters are driving the trains.
It's lucky, I guess,
I ain't sick like the rest—
But I'll never see White Folks again!

—"Where Did All My People Go?"",
from *Hooligans*, Broadway, 1928

Any disease that is treated as a mystery
and acutely enough feared will
be felt to be morally, if not literally, contagious.

—Susan Sontag, *Illness as Metaphor*, 1988

Archangel

1

he Archangel was broadcasting from Chicago tonight. Danny Constantine had set up his view camera and strung an aerial wire from the windshield of his Ford to a section of rusted out chain-link fence and he had been listening to her program, beamed from the deserted Blackstone Hotel in the heart of that dead, cold city, as she put it, for three hours, until his B batteries had gone dead. He cursed himself for not having charged the batteries before coming out tonight, because he loved the sound of the Archangel's voice, and loved the things she said. She was a wise guy and a cynic, but she was sweet, too, and she told the truth about the way things really were: here in Milltown, Minnesota, and now down in Chi, too.

Danny took down the aerial, checked his travel alarm clock, got back in the car, pushed the seat back as far as it would go, and sat with his feet up on the dash. Rising above him were the flour mills that had built Milltown. Danny's Ford was parked on a rail siding that lay between the mills and the river. There was a wall of them that ran for four city blocks, each mill six or seven stories tall, built of limestone or whitewashed brick that seemed to glow in the pale moonlight. They had been built that way purposefully, one against the other so that they hid the river, and the falls that powered them, from the rest of the city. The flour barons who had ground wheat into money at the turn of the century were jealous of the source of their power. On the downtown side of First Street they had built a power canal that diverted the river and fed the wheel pits and turbines that powered all the machinery on the work floors of the mills. They had covered this canal with a rail trestle. Water still ran through the canal, but above it, the rails were orange with rust, and milkweed plants poked through the cinders and grew high between the cracked ties.

Once, that canal and the river had meant everything to the city; the mills worked twenty-four hours a day. Now, in the summer of 1930, all of them stood dark and abandoned. In the middle of this miller's row stood the ruins of what had been the largest flour mill in the world: the Crockett A mill. Two years ago last January, Crockett A had exploded and burned, launching a pillar of fire fueled by flour dust, and the timbers and floors inside the limestone shell, that shone like a candle for fifty miles around the frozen prairie. It had been fifteen degrees below zero that night, and when morning came and the fire brigade had given up, the walls of the Crockett A were clad with fantastic blue-white stalactites of ice that glittered in the weak sunshine, warmed, and fell off to shatter at the base of the wall.

Danny Constantine had taken pictures of all of that. When the fire raged at its peak, Danny had sneaked through the lines and stood on the spur between the mill and the grain elevators and taken shot after shot as pieces of burning timbers rained down on him. He had been up for a Pulitzer for his picture of the flaming rooftop monitor sagging over the wall, power shaft still turning and whipping the flames. But there had been no Pulitzers given that year, nor any since, just as there had been no effort to rebuild the mill. The ruins of Crockett A stood ghostly over the river. And every so often, when the moon was full, Danny liked to come out with his view camera and shoot them. He would bring a cot and an alarm and make long time exposures, lulled to sleep by the sound of the water slipping through the power canal.

Now it was summer, early Sunday morning; Danny slept while he made his third plate of the evening. He had set up near Portland Avenue, at a spot where a line of young willow trees had grown up along the spur. Their branches touched the mill walls and made a tunnel over the tracks. His tripod stood just inside the tunnel, shaded from the moonlight, looking out toward the ghostly white bulk of the walls to the north.

Portland Avenue ended at First Street. When the mills were open there had been a string of taverns on Portland between First and Washington Avenue. The taverns had been officially closed by the Volstead Act in '19, although most of them had continued to operate as social clubs or blind pigs. By the time Prohibition was repealed, however, there were no more thirsty mill workers coming out of the gates. Now only one of the old taverns remained in business. It was called Vern's, at the corner of Second Street and Portland.

Around three A.M., a man and a woman left the tavern, pushed through the broken mesh of the fence at the end of Portland Avenue, and walked unsteadily along the tracks over the power canal. After a few steps they stopped to take in the view. Toward the river, the big full moon was just touching the tops of the mills and the grain elevators. Ahead was the tunnel formed by the willows, a cylinder of darkness with silvery light at the end where the moonlight cut across the tracks.

"Oooh, it's ever so dark in there!" the woman said. She had a husky voice and platinum hair that was also very bright with the moon shining on it.

The man examined his companion.

"You talk like a Brit!" he said.

"You just figgered that out, did you?"

"I thought you talked funny. But I ain't talked to any Brits since the war."

The woman smiled up at him and took the lapels of his jacket and stroked them. "What's the matter, Charlie?" she whispered. "Don't you like the English?"

"Ain't supposed to be any here. They spread it, you know."

"Spread what?" the woman said, twirling her finger in his hair. "What is it we spread?" She smiled at him and pulled him close and kissed him. He kissed her back, and kissed her back good. A Brit! She could infect him with Hun just with one kiss, but he didn't care anymore. In fact, the danger made him even more excited. He kissed her harder, but she pushed him back and turned her head away.

"Wha's wrong?"

"Well, you know, Char, I've always been a bit frightened of trains."

"Hasn't been a train down these tracks in five years!" Charlie said with drunken confidence.

"But maybe they might send one tonight. They could, couldn't they? You drive a streetcar. Couldn't a train still use these tracks?"

"I guess it could."

"Wouldn't that be something. To be kissing so hard you didn't even feel it hit you."

"You're teasing me—"

She took his hand and pulled him toward the willows. "Aw, I never was! Come on down this way, where it's nice and dark."

They walked, scuffing cinders, until she caught her heel on one of the ties and stumbled, her beret falling off. That was the end for the man. He gave up any pretext of reserve. He forgot about his job and his family, and whether she might be sick with Hun or not, and whether she might give it to him if she was. All he could see was her hair in the moonlight. She hadn't been that pretty in Vern's, but now she was the most beautiful thing he had ever seen.

Halfway inside the copse, the woman stopped, laughed softly, and put her arms around his waist. They came together and kissed again.

"I'm crazy to kiss you," Charlie said.

"Yeah, and why's that?"

"Shut up," he said and kissed her again. He could smell her and feel her against him and taste her, all of it a vapor that filled his head and reached down to the inside of his chest. His fists tightened into the silk of her dress, and he pulled up on it and pressed closer, kissing her neck now.

"You can't get sick, luv. I know you can't, you got some of that black blood in you. Don't you, luv? Who was it? Was it a granny, Charlie? Was it your grandmother?"

"Yeah," he said, and the thought of *that* got him, too. Only it wasn't his grandmother, it was his father, something Charlie never talked about. Nobody knew; it was a secret and he was light enough, and living in this town, nobody ever even considered the possibility, because there had been so few coloreds before the war. They couldn't stand the winters. Hell, Charlie hated them, too. But how did she know? He tried to remember what they had talked about at the tavern. There had been an awful lot of talk. Maybe he'd got drunk enough to tell her. Well, so what. He wasn't ashamed of it now. She liked that. She wanted him because he was that way.

The dress she was wearing, a green silk print, buttoned up the front. He put his hand between the buttons and pulled, trying to unfasten them, but instead he popped one, and the sensation of it coming away so quickly pushed him past all thinking and he ripped the whole front of her dress open.

"Charlie," she whispered as he put his hand down the front of her slip, felt the warm soft skin and a breast that seemed awfully small, but hard, with a hard nipple that pressed like a coat snap against the palm of his hand. She squirmed and kissed him back hard, shoving her tongue deep into his mouth.

"Charlie," she said excitedly. "Let's lie here on the tracks. Look, there's plenty of grass here, it's good and soft. Let's lie here and pray the bloody train don't come and cut us in half!"

"There's no fucking . . ." he was saying as she knelt, unbuckling his belt.

"What's that?" she said, kissing him again.

"No fucking *train.*"

"Yeah, there is, Charlie. Lie down here with me. Let's lean our heads against the rail, where the wheels can cut 'em clean off!"

"You're crazy," he said, but he did it. The top edge of the rail felt sharp against the back of his skull, so he pushed with his feet and slid up, so that the rail was underneath the top of his neck. She knelt over him. Her slip glowed silver in the moonlight.

"You want it, don't you, luv?" she said, unbuttoning his trousers. "Close your eyes. I don't want you watching for that train."

He closed them, waiting, feeling his whole body tremble and the world starting to spin. Too fast, he thought. He might get sick if he didn't open his eyes. But just as he started to, he felt something cold press against his neck, and heard a strong puff of air, like a BB gun firing. Something jarred his neck. And then everything below his head went numb. He tried to move and couldn't. He tried to move his arm and couldn't, either. She was still smiling down at him,

pulling tubes from her purse, letting the straps of her slip slide down
her shoulders. He could see all of her now, and grimaced in horror.
She was pushing the tubes into a pair of black nipples that stuck out
of the rib cage of her lower right side.

"Close your eyes, luv," she said. "It'll all be over soon. Give us a
last kiss. And make it good."

She pressed her lips against his. Then something scraped against
the side of his neck and she bent and kissed his neck and stayed there
kissing it, making low moaning sounds, moving herself up and down
on her knees. Then the dizziness took Charlie and flung him off far
away above the trees and the river, spinning in the darkness toward
the silvery moon.

2

t three-thirty the little travel alarm clock burred softly in Danny Constantine's ear. He gave a start and sat up, blinking his eyes. He had been dreaming hard, talking to someone. No, he corrected himself, not someone. He had been talking to *her* again. They'd been sitting together and she put her head on his shoulder and talked softly, right into his ear. God, how he loved it when she did that.

Except his wife had been dead for three years.

Danny rubbed his eyes resentfully, feeling the dream fade. Why couldn't he keep that happiness he'd been dreaming about? Sonja had this way of filling up the empty places inside him, smoothing everything out. You could be sour and looking at things all screwy and just by leaning her head on your shoulder and talking to you she could make you let it go. And he *had* let go, in his dream, but now his neck hurt, and there were cinders stuck to the palm of his hand, and the inside of his mouth tasted like shit, and she was gone for good.

He stood up, brushed off his hands on his trousers, went to the Dierdorff, picked up the shutter release dangling at the end of its cable, and closed the shutter. He put the slides in, pulled the exposed plate into the plate box, closed it, and then pumped up his gas lantern and lit the mantel. "*#3,*" he wrote in his notebook. "*ASA 25.*

Orange filter, 10 in. lens, f 8.5, 1 hr., 15 min. Full moon, slight haze. 2:15 am."

Danny put the notebook into his coat pocket and went back and had a look at the alarm clock. Three-thirty-five. If he opened the lens another stop and a half there was plenty of time for another shot or even two before the sun came up. He turned the lantern down and had a look down the rail spur. The moon had gone down behind the trees now and everything was in deep shadow. He envisioned the shot in his mind, but then he lost heart. He couldn't stand the thought of going to sleep and having that dream again.

Danny took the lens off the Dierdorff, racked in the bellows, put the travel alarm and the lens inside his accessory case, collapsed the tripod, bundled it together with the cot, tipped the camera over his shoulder, picked up the lantern and the plate box, and started down the tracks. It was a big load, and he'd made two trips coming in to set up, but he was willing to carry the stuff because he didn't feel like sticking around there anymore.

It was disheartening, because he'd been doing okay lately. Sometimes he went all day without thinking about her. And maybe he wasn't his old self anymore, but he'd been all right, going on as some kind of new self, and it had been okay. He knew Sonja wanted him to go on living. Not for her, she'd said, but because he owed it to himself. What had happened to her, and to the rest of the world, this horrible plague, was just bad luck. Tanya had left a letter for him to read after she was gone and in it she had told him he must never let luck convince him to do something or not because that was superstitious and wrong, that was not using your brains. But still, there he was, having those dreams. Just when he was feeling okay. It was so goddamn discouraging . . .

Danny stopped. Just ahead a dark shape lay across the tracks. He had walked down these tracks from Portland coming in and this thing, whatever it was, hadn't been there. He came closer and saw it was a man. Passed out, Danny thought at first, holding the lamp over the man's face. It was bone white. He lay there with his mouth open and his eyes staring up at nothing.

Danny put his equipment down and knelt alongside and pressed two fingers to the side of the man's neck. The skin was still warm.

There were a couple of wounds on the other side of the neck, puncture wounds. Danny straightened, and saw that the dead man's trousers were undone. Then he turned away. The penis had been cut off.

"Shit," Danny said, getting a breath. "Shit."

He opened his camera box and took out his Speed Graflex and his flash bar, loaded the bar with powder, set the lens to f.16, backed off five feet. It was always different when he had the camera in front of him. He could stand looking at things through the finder. Then it was a story. He fired, and the powder went off with a *whoosh* and a burst of light that exploded in the dark tunnel and disappeared into a rising ball of magnesium-white smoke. Then, looking at the body again, Danny, thinking he would never want anyone to find him dead that way, buttoned the dead man's trousers. He picked up his stuff, went out to Portland, put everything into the back of his Ford. Then he went into Vern's. There were a couple of people drinking at the bar. The owner, Vern Smith, né Schmidt, was washing glasses.

"All done, kid?" he asked, glancing back at Danny.

"Yeah, Vern. Listen, is the phone working tonight?"

"Not now. Nobody's at the exchange this time of night."

"I gotta call the cops."

"Cops right there, if you want 'em," Vern said, jerking his thumb toward the end of the bar where a couple of big men sat hunched over beers. "Hey, Dooley. You got a customer."

Dooley Willson turned his head slightly. He was a big, dark Negro whom Danny recognized as the sergeant of the major crimes section of the detective division. Willson was one of the first black cops the city had ever hired. Now he was the only sergeant left in major crimes. He looked Danny up and down.

"Off duty," Willson said, looking away.

Danny went over to him. "My name's Constantine. I work for the *Journal.*"

"Yeah, I know. So what."

"I just found a body on the First Street trestle."

Dooley Willson screwed his lips together. "A body, huh. Hear that, Francis? There's a *body* out behind the plant."

"Ask him is it a dead one," Francis Lingeborg said.

Willson turned on his stool and looked Danny over slowly.
"Well?"

"Never mind. I'll go down to Central and make a report myself."

"Hold on, Constantine," Willson said. He finished his beer in a
long gulp, and turned on the barstool. "What the hell are you doing
out at this hour?"

"Taking pictures," Danny said.

"In the middle of the night?"

"I do it all the time. Ask Vern."

"That right, Vern?"

Vern shrugged. "He's been in for coffee a couple of times tonight."

"It wasn't there the last time I went out," Danny said. "The
murder must have happened between two-fifteen and three-thirty."

"And why's that, Sherlock?"

"That's when I made my plate."

"I mean why's it a murder?" Willson said with a cold, disdainful
stare. *Show me*, it said, with the knowledge behind it that there was
nothing anybody could show him, anywhere, that would ever make a
difference to him inside, where it counted.

Danny held his gaze steady. He could feel Willson's disdain.
Willson was trying to get him to look away, to step back, to leave him
alone, but Danny held on.

"Somebody cut the guy's cock off," Danny said.

Willson glanced back at Lingeborg.

"How about it, Swede? You want to walk out there with me?"

"Fuck yes," Lingeborg said. Willson took his hat off the bar,
pulled it low over his eyes, and got up. He was huge. Half a head
taller than Danny, and Danny was six feet tall. He must have
weighed at least two fifty, too.

"Let's go, Constantine."

The three men went out to Portland Avenue. It was darker now
that the moon had set. "I've got a lantern," Danny offered.

"Get it."

He got it out of the trunk, lighted it, and they walked through the
hole in the fence onto the tracks. The shadows stretched and pivoted
ahead of them as they walked.

"Busy tonight?" Danny asked Willson to make conversation.

"Hear that, Francis? He wants to know if we're busy tonight."

"Maybe he's worried about us."

"Maybe he should worry about himself." Willson said. Danny felt a flush of resentment. "Maybe he don't know what we've been doing all week."

"Sure he knows. He's a reporter, ain't he?"

"You boys don't have to give me a hard time. I know what you go through," Danny said, and Willson stopped.

"What I go through? You know what I did all night? Rode with the coroner's van. We pulled in maybe three dozen fresh, white bodies. Don't even have time to write up a proper report. Percy Satin's got stacks of death certificates all filled out. All I do is put in the name and the date. Cause of death is always the same. Maybe I feel bad and maybe I don't, but whatever I go through is my business. You got that, Constantine?"

"Yeah, I got it."

"Don't you 'yeah' me, boy! If it wasn't white folks dying I wouldn't be loading your dead white asses into a county van."

"Look, Willson. It's late. I'm not trying to start anything. I just want to show you where the body is."

"That's starting something right there."

It wasn't any use, Danny thought. He had dealt with Dooley Willson before. The sergeant was a good cop, but he never hid the fact that he had no use for white people. But he was funny about it. It was white people's law he was enforcing, but there was nobody on the force who went by the book more than Willson.

"There it is," Danny said, swinging the lantern up. Willson went to the body and crouched down, pressed the corpse's cheek with his thumb.

"Gimme the light," he said. Danny gave it to him and Willson moved it close to the dead man's head.

"Look at that, Francis," he said, lifting the tab of the man's celluloid collar. "Lipstick." He bent closer and took a deep sniff. "And perfume." Gently, he turned the man's head. "Two puncture wounds on the side of the neck." He scooted over, put the lantern down, and unbuttoned the victim's trousers.

"Fuck!" he said softly.

"His fly was open when I found him," Danny said. "I buttoned him up."

Willson stood. "This bastard's drained," he said.

"What do you mean?"

"I mean, if we took him to the morgue they wouldn't find a drop of blood in him. Look at his linens. Hardly any blood at all. You get a wound on your pecker it's like cutting your tongue." He stood up and looked around. "You say you were out here taking pictures when this happened?"

"Yeah. I was making time exposures. I bring a cot along and sleep."

"How long were you sleeping?"

"Maybe an hour. I had the lens stopped down pretty far. I keep a notebook with the exact times."

"Where were you set up?"

"That way. Just where the trees end."

"You didn't see anything?"

"I told you. I was asleep." Danny took the travel alarm out of his pocket. "You can see I set it for three-thirty."

"What were you taking pictures of?"

"The tracks."

"You take pictures of railroad tracks at night?"

"It's a moonlight shot," Danny explained. "I'm trying to capture the light, and this wall, and the way the trees come over."

"What the fuck for?"

"Art."

"Art," Willson repeated disgustedly, showing the whites of his eyes. "What the fuck is that?"

"My hobby. I use a view camera. One of the big ones."

"I know what a view camera is. You were making a time exposure, right? That means you could have taken a picture of anyone that walked into the frame."

"That depends how long they were standing in one place, what color clothes they were wearing."

"When are you going to develop those plates?"

"Tomorrow, probably."

"You know my name?"

"Dooley Willson."

"*Sergeant* Willson. You get in touch with me downtown. Let me know if you got anything on those plates."

"All right."

"I'm going to finish going over the scene. Swede, see if Percy's still downtown. Have him send the wagon if he is."

"Sure, Dooley."

"Could I help you with anything?" Danny said.

"Lend me the lantern. I'll leave it with Vern when I'm through."

"Sure, Sergeant."

Danny started back along the tracks with Detective Lingeborg.

"He sounded like you guys have seen this before," Danny said.

"What ain't we seen," Francis said.

"Have you, though?"

"It's the third one. One last month. One the month before that. Both still open."

"What about the blood?"

"All three dry as a bone."

Danny went through the fence. "Sounds like we've got a vampire."

"What we've got," Francis said, "is one sick bastard." They went back into Vern's. "Got to call the coroner, Vern," Francis said, going behind the bar to use the phone. He held the receiver to his ear and waggled the cradle with his finger.

"Son of a bitch is dead," he muttered.

"What, the guy?" Vern said without much interest.

"No, the fucking phone." He put it down. "You see any new customers tonight, Vern?"

"Maybe."

"Who?"

"Charlie Hayes was talking with a blonde all night."

"Yeah? What she look like?"

"I just told you. Blonde."

"What was she wearing?"

"How the hell would I know?"

"Maybe you'll know when Dooley talks to you."

"My memory's the same, if I'm talking to a white man or a nigger," Vern said stiffly.

Lingeborg decided to let that go. Vern was all right. Anyway, Dooley Willson had made it clear to Francis a long time ago that he didn't want anybody sticking up for him. In the race department, Willson could take care of himself. Francis was more worried about the fact that they were going to have to haul the victim downtown themselves. Number fifteen for the evening.

At least it was clean, though, he thought. At least it was murder. He came back out from around the bar.

"Looks like we're hauling him down ourselves. See you, Vern."

"How's your mother?"

"Getting along."

"Say hello to her for me," Vern said.

"Okay."

Danny followed him outside. The sky was brightening up now in the east. It was still pleasantly warm, which meant it would get damn hot today.

"You want some help?"

"Yeah. But Dooley'll want to secure the scene himself. Regulations."

"Okay," Danny said, waving. Francis waved back and stepped through the hole in the fence. Danny watched him step through the weeds. Vampire claims third victim, he thought. That might play.

He decided to run it by Walter tomorrow.

3

*D*anny went home and slept until it was too hot to
sleep anymore. His window was wide open, and the
curtains hung motionless in front of it, as if they had
been soaked in plaster. Danny swung his legs over the side of the bed
and got up and took a look outside. Everything was still. The sky
was milky and there were big thunderclouds piling up in the west. It
was going to rain, all right, but that wouldn't help. Rain would only
make it steamy.

He sat down on the bed again, lighted a cigarette, and picked up
the clock from the bedside table. Just after noon. He'd slept pretty
good. No dreams this time. He put the clock down and put on a robe,
and went down the hall to the bathroom to shave and clean up. When
he came out Mrs. Lund called to him from downstairs.

"Is that you, Dan?"

"Yes, Mrs. Lund, good morning," he said, sheepishly. He was
always the last one in the house to get up on Sunday.

"Dinner's ready. Will you come down?"

He could smell her roast chicken now, and it finished the job of
waking him up. All he'd had yesterday was toast downtown at the
Pantry and a hard-boiled egg and a couple of pig's knuckles at
Vern's.

"I'll get dressed and be there right away, Mrs. L."

"You have some time. I'm just bathing everything under the lamps now."

Mrs. Lund had just bought a set of violet-ray lamps. Putting cooked food under them for five minutes was supposed to be a cure for Hun. Danny wished he'd been home the day the salesman called, because he would have poked the lousy crook in the nose for trying to take advantage of her. Maybe it was okay, though. Having the lamps did seem to make her feel better.

Danny put on an undershirt and a shirt with a new collar, gray gabardines, and tied on a dark blue bow tie. Mrs. Lund liked her boarders to dress for Sunday dinner. He slipped the straps of his hairbrushes onto his hands and ran them rhythmically along the sides of his head. He made his bed, put his clothes from yesterday away, closed the curtains, and went down to the dining room. The other boarders had already sat down. The food—a big capon, mashed potatoes and giblet gravy, peas with pearl onions, dinner rolls, and cole slaw—sat along the sideboard glowing weirdly purple in the light of the violet-ray tubes. Kal Hromatka looked at it all with growing impatience. Kal was a practical man who didn't believe in letting good hot food sit around, Hun or no Hun.

"Lucille," he said, "it's been five minutes."

"Three and a half. And you know very well the salesman said at least eight, and preferably ten, especially when there's this much food."

Kal rolled his eyes in exasperation. He was a Slovak with iron-gray hair, a strong nose, handsome and very trim for a man of sixty-five. Like Danny, he indulged Mrs. Lund. You couldn't blame her much for trying the lamps, trying anything, when you knew that her whole family had died of the bleeding—everyone except her twelve-year-old grandniece, Shirley. She was a bleeder, too, though chronic. Today she sat at the table in a nicely starched summer dress that showed arms and legs swathed in pressure wraps.

"Morning, everybody," Danny said, sitting down quickly.

"Morning?" Kal said. "What do you know about it?"

"I was up 'til five last night, Kal."

"Doing what?"

"Took a few shots of the old Crockett Mill."

"*I* think he's got a secret life," Shirley said. "*I* think he's meeting someone."

"Yeah?" Danny said, grinning at her. "And who do I meet?"

"We know. Don't we, Kal?"

"Sure," Kal said, staring longingly at the purple food on the sideboard.

"Kal!"

"Oww! What're you kicking me for, girl!"

"Shirley," Mrs. Lund began.

"It's not polite to pretend to answer someone when you haven't the slightest idea what they've just said. Is it, Auntie?"

"No. But kicking is not the way to correct them."

"Oh, pooh! It's the whole reason they invented tables."

"Well, you've got my attention now," Kal said. "What is it?"

"I think Danny's meeting a certain someone he interviewed last February."

"Oh, the *Archangel,*" Kal said, interested now.

"Remember how she made him wait inside the Ice Palace? And there he was, smoking one cigarette after another, because the paper told him they'd let him go if he couldn't do more than just take pictures. And he'd somehow swung an interview with her, but she made him wait and wait, and then, just when he was sure she wouldn't come, *ohhh!* It's her, right next to him, breathing into his ear, 'Daniel, I've been wanting to meet you so very, very, *very* much!'"

"Honestly, Shirley! Where on earth do you get these notions?"

"It's true! They were together three hours in that Ice Palace. Think of it. The moonlight all pale and green-blue coming through the ice. The Archangel's wrapped up in her beautiful silver fox coat. Danny's shivering, but not because he's cold. He keeps smoking and smoking and smoking, and trying to make her face out through her veil. And the veil getting frosted from her breath. Danny scribbling down notes he couldn't read after because his head was spinning so. Why, he's been queer ever since!"

"Shirley Lund, we do not say queer at the table!"

"But he *is* queer. Aren't you, Danny?"

"As a three-dollar bill," Danny said, grinning.

"Look at him," Kal laughed. "He's the same color as Lucille's chicken!"

Danny, who had been sitting there trying to keep his face from turning red, lost the battle and felt himself flush all at once and so thoroughly that even Mrs. Lund began to laugh. Of course, he was secretly pleased when Shirley teased him about that interview he'd done with Milltown's famous radio angel. He'd thought of her often since that winter night, and really, Shirley wasn't that far wrong. Danny had thought about her for weeks after their interview. But the real reason he was embarrassed was that it was all so useless. The Archangel *had* been perfectly sweet, and maybe, if he interpreted the flirtatious way she'd talked to him in a certain way, there had been some kind of spark between them. But the Archangel, whoever she really was, had made it clear that she intended to continue living her secret life alone, and never had responded to Danny's attempts to arrange an interview for a follow-up piece later that spring. Anyway, whatever he'd been feeling inside that night, he'd forced himself to be businesslike and ask good questions and get straight answers. Walter Burns, his editor at the *Journal,* had made it plain: either write a decent piece or lose his job at the paper. The way things were, the *Journal* needed men who could do more than one thing. That meant Danny couldn't just take pictures anymore; he had to write copy, too. And, as hard as it was for him to do that, and as bad as he was at writing, he'd managed, somehow, to pound out a half-decent story and keep his job.

Maybe all that intense concentration that night had put the Archangel off. Or maybe he'd just been imagining that attraction he'd written about in the article: *"In person she pulls you in the same way she pulls in her listeners all over the state,"* he'd written. *"You hear that voice with such pleasure that you want to hear more, until the voice turns into something soft and warm and clear that almost, but not quite, melts inside your head. That 'almost,' of course, is her secret, and the main reason for her success, because it keeps all her listeners, and this interviewer, wanting more and more and more, while leaving them still capable of appreciating her message . . ."*

Danny winced inwardly, remembering what Walter had said about that line. "Jesus Christ, Constantine, that stinks! 'Leaving them still capable'? Do you know one person who's ever been left *still* capable?"

Danny's questions had been good, though. There'd never been any doubt about that. He might be a lousy writer but he knew what a story was and how to talk to people. He'd learned that chasing pictures. Sometimes he'd have to do lousy things, like the time he worked the police desk and they sent him over to the wife of some poor Hun victim and he impersonated the county coroner, asking the widow for a photo of the dead man "for our records." He could do that all right. The writing, six months later, was possibly getting better.

"I know you met her last night!" Shirley insisted. "You must have heard her. 'Floating through the still, dead town, free of everything . . .' Including her clothes!"

"Now, that really is enough, young lady!" Mrs. Lund said sternly. "Another word and you're off to your room."

"But Aunt Lucille—"

"Don't sass! You know I don't approve of what that woman's doing. She's an outlaw. I'm crazy to let you go out to that radio shack with Kal. *He* can do what he wants, but you're another matter."

"She's not an outlaw. She's the only person in this town who tells the truth. She's an *idealist!*"

"Idealist? How on earth would you know who and what an idealist is?"

"Danny told me. Isn't that right, Danny?"

Mrs. Lund turned and looked at him severely.

"Well?"

"Well . . ." Danny said. "I may have said something like that. I mean, she is considered to be a reformer."

"By whom?" Mrs. Lund said coldly.

Just then the bell of the lamp timer went off, and the violet beams above the food slowly faded.

"Thank God!" Kal exclaimed.

"Help me with the platters, will you, dear," Mrs. Lund said with a sigh, giving Danny one more look before getting up. Shirley carefully pushed her chair back and moved with a slight limp over to the sideboard, winking at Danny as she passed him. She was such a lively, quick young girl, and so direct with her speech, that Mrs. Lund felt she had to be stern with her, and rein her in; but she was impossible to keep down, and anyway, it was impossible to stay angry with Shirley for long. It had just about killed Mrs. Lund last year to find out that Shirley had caught Hun, too. It made a person indulgent when they loved somebody who, sooner or later, would start the bleeding that nobody could stop.

Together, the landlady and her niece brought the food to the table.

"Maybe it'll turn my insides blue, but my, that chicken smells grand, Lucille!"

"Thank you, Kal," Mrs. Lund said. She stood behind Shirley's chair as she sat down, and smoothed the girl's hair affectionately. "Now, Kal, would you please say grace?"

Kal put his browned, strongly veined hands together and closed his eyes. "Dear Lord," he began gruffly, "bless all those who gather here today to receive your bounty." Danny felt a kick at his ankle, opened his eyes, and saw Shirley making a face at him. "We thank you for the kindness you have given us and beseech you to protect all those near and dear to us. Amen."

"Amen."

"Beseech," Shirley said. "Isn't that an awfully strange word?"

"Don't blaspheme," Mrs. Lund said, as the screen door banged open in the kitchen. Mrs. Lund's other tenant, young Lou Ravelli, came into the dining room. He looked at everyone, flushed, then headed for the stairs.

"Louis? What's wrong? Why aren't you at the ballpark?"

"'Cause the game's been canceled!" Lou said in a stricken voice.

"Wait," Kal said. "Come here. What's going on?"

Lou's face was very red. "Four Toledo guys came up sick yesterday. Four! So they canceled the game. Then Kelly gets us together and says the league might have to suspend the season and re-form with guys they knew were okay. They're talking it over right now."

Mrs. Lund got up. "I'm sure everything will be all right, Louis. They're just taking precautions. They have to, because the public's involved. You're a strong, healthy boy; you've got nothing to worry

about. Why don't you sit down with us and have some dinner?" She
took a plate from the china cabinet.

"Aw, Mrs. L., I don't feel like eatin'. I'm sick to my stomach!"

"That's exactly why you need to eat. Sit!"

She bustled over and took his arm and led him to the table, then
set a place setting in front of him. Meanwhile Kal left the table, went
upstairs, and came back with a bottle of whiskey. He poured a
couple of fingers into a tumbler and gave it to Lou.

"The boy needs it, Lucille," Kal said, anticipating her protest.
Lou took the glass with both hands, stared at it a moment and tossed
it down. Kal poured him a second, smaller drink, then put the cork
into the bottle. The smell was tempting, but he knew it would be too
much for him to take a drink himself on Sunday, in Mrs. Lund's
dining room. Lou drank the second whiskey more slowly. Finally he
looked around.

"I'm sorry, everyone. I didn't mean to come in and bust up your
dinner. I oughta be out there at third right now!"

"Don't be silly, Louis. This is your home. Have some chicken."

Lou sat down, and the rest of the house passed around the platters
and began to eat. The food was wonderful. Danny ate two helpings
of chicken, and made himself some gravy bread. All the while Lou
sat staring over his plate.

"Is there something else bothering you, Lou?" Kal said.

"The old man said we might consol . . . consol . . . something."

"Consolidate?" Danny said, mopping his plate with a crust of the
bread.

"That's right."

"Who with?"

"The goddamn nigger league, that's who!"

"Louis!" Mrs. Lund cried in horror, but Lou had let it out and
now the rest came in a gush.

"I'm telling you, it ain't fair those colored bastards don't get sick!
Oh, hell, you don't understand what it's like, none a ya do!" With
that, Lou threw down his napkin, left the table, and went out the
front door.

"Well," Danny said, "that was either one shot short or one too
many, Kal."

Shirley started to laugh, but Mrs. Lund froze her with a single icy look.

"That's not funny, Danny. You go talk to him. Bring him back."

"I think he probably just needs to cool down a little, Mrs. L."

"Yes, he'll only come back here and curse, Aunt Lucille!"

"You be quiet! Please, Danny!"

"Okay, I'll see what I can do."

As he went out to the front porch, Danny wondered how much he really *could* do. Lou Ravelli was generally angry and miserable anyway. He was only twenty, living away from what was left of his family out in San Francisco for the first time. He was a hotheaded Italian with dark eyes and curly black hair, and a lithe body that could do practically anything on a ball field. But he was also not the brightest man Danny had ever met.

Lou sat out on the porch steps holding his head in his hands. The street was quiet. On this block, all but four of the houses had been boarded up, and only one of the four had a real family living in it. The other three places were rooming houses, like Mrs. Lund's. It was the same up and down all these residential blocks on the south side of town. Danny went and sat down next to Lou. It was hot as hell out in the sun.

"That's a tough break," Danny said. "About the season, I mean."

"What else can they do? Nobody's got any fucking ballplayers."

"Knock off that talk. It doesn't impress me. And it sure isn't any good talking like that in front of Mrs. L."

"It ain't got nothing to do with her."

"It's Sunday, Lou. You can't curse in a nice lady's dining room on Sunday. And Shirley sitting right there, too. Don't you have more sense than that?"

"You don't know how I feel. I worked all my life for a shot at the big club. I'm off to a great start. Kelly said it was a cinch the Giants were gonna buy up my contract this season. Now that's all shot to hell. How can they pick me up when they can't see what I can do?"

"You said yourself they're not canceling the season. They're just reorganizing, getting everything back on a sound basis. That's the way things are now, Lou. People get sick, but the ones that are left, they still need baseball. The thing is not to get discouraged. You have to keep on as though none of this stuff was happening. Otherwise what's the use?"

"That's what I keep thinking, though."

"Yeah, I know. But the thing is, Lou, you're not sick. And the longer you don't get sick, the more chance there is that you won't. Just like me. I was in the army, I came back here, and I'm on the paper, I'm all over town all the time, and I haven't got it yet. I don't even worry about getting it anymore. And even if I did, well, that's tough and all, but you can't go around living like you're afraid of Hun."

"I ain't afraid. I just wanna play ball."

"Well, you will. They're reorganizing the league, aren't they? You're gonna play ball again soon, and that's the main thing. And I've seen some of those Negro ballplayers. Some of them are pretty damn good. Why not play with 'em? Forget about who they are. When you're up there swinging you don't think about whether the pitcher's an Irishman or a Polack or a Hebe, do you?"

"It ain't the same thing and you know it!"

"Look, Lou, maybe it isn't, but you're still thinking about this all wrong. Negroes didn't start this. They didn't do it to us. It's not their fault they don't get sick, any more than it's your fault that you're not sick right now. See that? All you have to do is pretend it's still like it used to be. Pretty soon you won't be thinking you're playing against Negroes. They'll just be the other guys."

"I ain't playing with niggers," Louis insisted sullenly.

Danny sighed, reached into his pocket, and got out a silver dollar. "Look, Lou, why don't you go to the movies on me? There's a swell picture over at the Minnesota, and it's air-conditioned."

"Yeah?"

"Yeah. It's a Louise Brooks. I might go see it myself a little later. She's a swell-looking doll. Go watch her, and try to forget about all this stuff for a while."

Lou looked at him. "You think that's what I oughtta do?"

"Yeah. That's what you oughtta do. Get out of the damn heat."

Lou nodded, took the dollar, and punched Danny lightly on the shoulder as he got up. "Okay," he said.

"I'll square things with Mrs. L. for you."

"Thanks, Danny," Lou said, and headed off toward Lyndale. Danny watched him for a while to make sure he would not change his mind, then went back inside. Kal Hromatka was cutting out slices of rhubarb pie.

"Where is he?" Mrs. Lund said.

"I sent him off to the movies."

"If I curse at the table can I see a picture, too?" Shirley asked.

Mrs. Lund ignored her. "Is he all right?"

"He's just worked up. He's worried he won't be able to play ball this year. But he's sorry for cursing like that."

Mrs. Lund pressed her lips together in a sad smile, and squeezed Danny's arm. "You're a good boy, Danny. It's good for Lou to have you around. And Kal. He needs good big brothers like you."

Danny's face reddened. He always felt embarrassed when Mrs. Lund fussed over him like that.

"Sit down and have a piece of pie!" Kal said.

CHAPTER

4

After dinner, Danny helped the women clear dishes and wash up. Then, as they did every Sunday, Mrs. Lund and Shirley got ready to call on the sick and bedridden of the neighborhood. Kal went out to the backyard and fell asleep in the hammock. Danny, who hated the slowness and inactivity of a Sunday afternoon worse than anything, took his plates and film pack and went downtown to the office.

He took the parkway along Lake of the Isles, driving in the shade of big elms and willow trees. There was hardly anyone out. Even a few years ago, on a hot day like this, the velvety lawns would have been crowded with picnickers, the water full of boaters and swimmers. Today there were only scattered groups, mainly Negro families. A lot of the white people who were left were afraid to go outside for fear of catching the disease, even though, twelve years after the start of the epidemic in the trenches of Europe, public health officials were still unable to discover exactly how Hun was transmitted.

In the early days, when the epidemic raged in the barracks of the Expeditionary Force, then on the buses, trains, schools and factories of the cities, it was thought that Hun spread through the air, like influenza. Strict quarantines had been established, and all public buildings were shut down. But that hadn't made any difference. The epidemic continued to spread. The next target was the water supply: people used only bottled water, or boiled everything they drank or cooked or even washed their clothes with, but that hadn't stopped the disease either. As Hun killed millions year after year, and one public health strategy after another was put into place only to fail, officials finally gave up trying to keep the institutions and public places shut. People were advised to go about their business, at their own risk.

And they had. It had been twelve years, and no one could stay terrified that long. After twelve years, terror had worn away to a kind of dull dread. Meanwhile Hun seemed to come in waves, every two or three years. Until recently, Milltown had been in a lull, trying to rebuild. That was why the news of the Toledo ballplayers wasn't good. People began to drop that way whenever Hun started up again. And now it was hitting the survivors, people like Danny, who had been through all the waves and now believed they were immune.

It carried away the people who hid in their houses and the ones who ate nothing but spinach and kale; the people who prayed and the ones who cursed; people who exercised, who bathed in lime-water, who ate nothing but oranges and lemons, who tanned in the sun, who avoided the sun, who practiced meditation and hypnosis; people who attended health lectures or swallowed magnets; and ones, like Mrs. Lund, who paid money to quacks selling violet-ray machines, carbolic misters, radio-frequency transmitters, holy cards, germ-tight Lister suits, herbal cigarettes, iron pills, radium lozenges, and tonics made from the blood of any animal that had not suffered from Hun.

None of it made any difference, of course. There was only one sure way to be protected from the devastation of Hun, and that was being black. If you were a Negro, you did not get hemorrhagic fever. And there was no way to become a Negro except by being born one. Although people did try. Afri-Tonic was especially popular, advertised as a preparation made from sixteen different African fruits and vegetables. There were pills that darkened a man's skin, shampoos that curled the hair, preparations made from elephant bones, and even plain old African dirt. These you could find in any drugstore, but there were others available from bootleggers and dope pushers, elixers that were purportedly made from real Negro blood, or semen, or urine, all guaranteed to stop any bleeding attack cold. All of these remedies were a waste of money. The ones that contained alcohol, opium, or hashish might provide the purchaser with, at most, a few hours' drugged peace.

There was still only one thing that could stop a bleeding episode once Hun had struck, and that was a blood transfusion. Fresh blood, either from a Negro or a healthy white person, if you could find one, made the body stop leaking. Naturally, real blood was at a premium. You could make a lot of money giving blood these days. The going rate for a pint of blood from a healthy person was fifty dollars, twice as much as Danny made per week working for the *Journal.* Danny gave his blood away for free, though, once a month at the Red Cross, donating the credit to Shirley so she could get a transfusion if she needed it. They had worked out a way of storing whole blood, or blood plasma, which contained the factors that caused blood to clot, and when you gave a donation, they "banked" it and credited your account, which you could then draw on later. So far, Shirley had been lucky. There had been enough blood credits in her account the two times she'd needed a transfusion.

At Franklin, Danny cut away from the lake and took Hennepin the rest of the way downtown. As he passed Loring Park and the Basilica he could see the half-built Foshay Tower, topped by a rusted crane and bare steelwork that bled rusty streaks down the completed lower floors of the building. Construction had stopped last year when Irwin Foshay, the real estate magnate, had jumped from the skeleton of the nineteenth floor. Now the building that was to have been the tallest north of Chicago was known as the High Dive.

Danny turned right on Fourth Street, and parked in front of the *Journal* building, a narrow, white, four-story building with an arched entryway. He opened the trunk, took out his camera box with the exposed plates and the film pack from the Graflex, and went inside. Old Reno Jones, the watchman, got up from his desk to unlock the inner door for him.

"Well, Mr. Constantine! What you doin' here on such a fine day?"

"Work, Reno," Danny said, signing the register. "Anybody in?"

"Mr. Burns is. So's Mr. Lockner. Rest o' the boys'll be in

by-and-by. Still a little early yet. Thank you, sir." He blotted
Danny's signature carefully and closed the book. Reno was seventy-
five years old, born free in the Minnesota Territory. He'd held the
watchman's job for the *Journal* since 1902. Nothing that had
happened in the years since the war had really changed him. He was
always courtly, polite, and cheerfully respectful to the remaining
white folks on the paper. If you asked, he would tell you he did not
approve of all the new Negro settlers coming up to Milltown from the
South, and from other northern cities where things were not so good.
He was one of Milltown's Negroes; when you talked to him, you
sometimes came away with the impression that you did not know
what he was really thinking.

"You take care, Reno," Danny said, and went up to the city room
on the third floor. It was hot, because the windows were closed, and
dim because the shades were pulled. Everything was quiet, except
for the syndicate tickers in the back. There Bing Lockner, the
Journal's sports editor—and sports staff, what with the shortage of
writers on the paper—sat with his feet up on the machine, reading a
tape. Danny went back to see him.

"Hullo, Bing," Danny said. "Who's playing?"

"Yanks and Indians." The paper subscribed to a wire service that
provided scores, accounts, and statistics of simulated baseball games
from the American and National leagues. No actual league play
existed anymore, although teams barnstormed between cities where
there were enough people to sell tickets to. "What brings you to the
salt mines?"

"I've got some shots to develop. Is Burns here?"

"Walter's here, but I don't think you want to talk to him."
Lockner ran tape through his fingers—he was a small man with
delicate hands, who always kept his nails perfectly buffed—and
winced. "Ouch," he said. "Averill hits one for the Indians."

"What's the score?"

"Seventeen-ten."

"Yanks?"

"Indians. I'll make it Yanks if you want, though." He tore out a
section of the tape. "See?"

"I don't want any lost bets on my conscience, Bing."

Lockner shrugged. "It's a swing either way. Hear about the Millers?"

"Yeah, that's tough."

"How's young Lou taking it?"

"He's pretty broken up about it."

"Well, you can't blame him. He went three for four yesterday and swiped a foul ball out of the third-base seats besides. Did everything but sell peanuts and sweep up."

Danny grinned at him. "Is that how you wrote it up?"

"Connie, the weather is too damn hot for those kinds of remarks. What did you get last night?"

"Oh, nothing much. Maybe a murder."

"Story?"

Danny patted the film pack. "On film."

Lockner whistled. "That's all right. A good clean murder's something this burg could use. Nice, normal crime."

"I don't know how clean it is. This killer drinks blood."

"And you've got it on film."

"Maybe. I'll know in a little while."

"Come see me when you get through," Lockner said, and went back to his tape.

Danny went to the darkroom, got his developer and fixer ready, locked the door, turned on the safelight, and started working. He developed the sheet film from the Graflex first, setting the timer for ten minutes because the heat in the room would speed everything up. Next he used the developer box for his three glass plates, lifting the plate hangers every minute or so to agitate the solution. At ten minutes he pulled the sheet from the tray with tongs and put it in the stop bath. Then he switched the safety light off and a dim green inspection lamp on, removed the hanger holding plate number three from the box, and held it up to the light. Danny was interested in the least exposed area, along the tracks in the shadows beneath the overhanging tree branches. These places would be the first to react with the developer. He could see something like dark streaks, decided to risk another minute or two in the tank, agitated, and took another look under the green. There was definitely something there, so he took out the plate and put it in the fixing box. The other two

shots he waited on. They were art and he wanted them developed
properly. Meanwhile the sheet film was fixed, so he washed it and
hung it up to dry with the fan blowing on it, then rinsed the plate
and dried it the same way. A few minutes later he exposed two prints
in the contact box, developed them, and dried them with the blotter.
He hung his two remaining plates to dry, switched on the light, and
had a look at the prints.

There was the body lying on the tracks with the trouser front open
and the stub of severed penis framed by his shirttails. The victim's
mouth was wide open, and his skin was shockingly white in the
magnesium glare of the flash powder. One look and Danny knew
Walter Burns would never agree to print it. Walter didn't like news
shots to begin with. He liked portraits, and woodcuts.

The eight-by-ten contact print from the view camera was something else. Because Danny had stopped the negative so soon,
everything in the print was pale and ghostly. The only strong forms
in it were the converging lines of the rails and the shadowed leading
edges of the ties. But there were faint figures above the rails in the
middle of the shot. In the foreground, the dark mound of the body
lay across the tracks. Above it, in white, there was something that
could be another person, but very faint and blurred. Farther back,
and clearer, was black and white swirled together. Danny stepped
back from the print and let his eyes lose focus, and the image
snapped into meaning. It was *two* people embracing: dark sleeves
wrapped around a white body, one head silver and lifted up, the
other bent. They had to have been standing like that for a long
time—at least five minutes at the f-stop Danny had been shooting.
But there was another figure, too, standing farther back and to the
side. Tall, taller than the figure in the embrace, gray-haired. Danny
took the magnifying glass. The paper was fine-grained enough to
show some details of a face: sunken-in eyes, a thin-lipped mouth.

"Oh, kay!" Danny whispered, and took the print up the short
flight of steps to Walter Burns's mezzanine office. He rapped on the
glass. Burns was talking on the telephone, saw Danny, and motioned
for him to come in.

"I don't give a damn what she says she was doing. Don't you know a lie when you hear one? What? Yes, you're damn right she's not going to that party tonight. She's staying home. Well, how the hell else do you keep someone from going somewhere? Lock her in her room! Dolores . . . Dolores! By God, if you won't do it, I'll send the cops over and have her arrested! You, too! Yes, by God, see if I won't!' "

With that, Burns jammed the receiver into its cradle and pushed the candlestick, which was mounted on a scissors arm that swung over his desk, away from his face so hard that it made a 360-degree swing back in front of him again. He snatched a blue bottle of bromide from his desk, poured two fingers of the crystals into a glass that had some amber liquid in it, rose as the foam climbed the inside of the glass, turned his back on Danny, and gulped it down as he looked out the window at the view of the city toward the river.

"Let me give you some advice, Constantine," Burns said in a dire voice. "Don't have any female children. They will absolutely kill you."

"I can come back later, Walter."

Burns kept going. "Of course, in her mother's eyes, she can do no wrong. That woman lets her do anything she wants. Then when something goes wrong, when she's in hot water because she's got no self-control, no regard for authority, no goddamn common sense, well, then, by God it's my problem! Do you know what my wife says?" Burns raised his voice a notch. " 'She rebels because you are so harsh. She thinks she can never do good in your eyes, and so she does just the opposite. You must pay attention to her psychology!' *Psychology*, by God! Not, 'Follow the rules we have made because seventeen-year-old girls don't know their ass from a hole in the ground!' "

Burns broke off. Gradually his breathing returned to normal. He turned around and sat down again.

"You got sisters, Constantine?"

"I had two—" Danny began.

"Of course," he said. "Sorry. I suppose we're lucky Cloe's still with us. By God, that's what she counts on!" He smoothed the hair above his ears—the only hair he had on his head—with the palms of his hands, then showed his teeth. Burns had two expressions, a grimace and a snarl, and while he showed variations of both, they were pretty much alike.

"It's probably a rough age," Danny offered.

"Try being my age sometime."

He opened his desk drawer again, took out a little box.

"Sen-sen?"

"No, thanks."

Burns tossed down a handful, crunching them loudly. Danny could smell licorice. The anise in Sen-sens was supposed to be protection against Hun.

"Now, where the hell were we?"

"Look at this, Walter." He laid down the print from the view camera plate in front of him.

"What the hell's this?"

"It's a murder. I was out last night taking shots behind the old Crockett A mill. I took a nap while I was making the last one, and somebody got murdered on those tracks while the shutter was open. You can see the body there," Danny said, pointing. "Then standing over it are the two people together. You can see where they walked in by that streak. They stood like that for a while. The woman's a blonde."

"She's the victim?"

"Uh-uh. Killer."

"Who's the dead guy?"

"Cops think it's a streetcar motorman named Charlie Hayes. And look, right here's another figure. Standing back in the shadows? Our killer might have had an accomplice."

"What else you got?"

Danny put the other shot down and watched Burns's face tighten and turn red first, then white.

"Jesus fucking Christ! Is that what I think it is?"

"She cut it off. And get this—there was no blood left in the body."

"Get that off my desk!" Burns said. "Now."

Danny took the top print away.

"Who's the cops?"

"Dooley Willson and his partner. You know, Lingeborg, that big Swede."

"Dooley Willson, huh. So what we've got is three blurs, a cut-off dick, and a nigger cop."

"What we've got is a female, bloodsucking maniac," Danny said. "It's one hell of a story."

"One hell of a story?" Burns said. "One *hell* of a story? All right. Let's assume, for the sake of argument, that a picture-chaser like you knows what a story *is.*"

"Hey," Danny said, smarting.

"Hey what?"

"You keep sending me out on assignment, Walter. And all I ever hear is what a lousy writer I am."

"You *are* lousy! And if everything hadn't gone completely to hell I'd get a court order against your coming within a hundred feet of a typewriter!"

"Why keep printing my stories then?"

"I'm not printing this one."

"I haven't written it yet, Walter."

"Do me a favor, Constantine? Have a look at that ad copy. Yes, right there in front of you."

Danny picked up a tear sheet. At the top of the ad was an engraving of a man and his wife standing with their back to the reader, their arms around a boy and a girl, looking out over a lush farm valley, with the sun just rising over the fields. "The Great Northwest," read the headline. "A Land of Health, Prosperity . . . And All the Future One Could Hope For." The copy promoted Milltown as "the center of a self-sufficient region safe from the epidemic, with a sturdy population of immigrant stock from the healthiest nations of Europe—combined with a growing number of the strongest, healthiest, and most intelligent of the New Negroes, raised not in the backward South but in the enlightened Northwest, where they have been prepared to take their proper place in the building of a New, Strong, Eternally Healthy Northwest." Danny put the tear sheet back on Burns's desk.

"That ad was taken out by the Greater Northwest Development

Company," Burns said. "Of which Mr. Crowley is chairman. I don't suppose I have to go on, do I?"

"Since when have you let the advertising department edit the paper, Walter?"

"Crowley isn't the advertising department, he's the goddamned publisher! And he wants us to run these full-page, Monday through Friday, plus Sunday's rotogravure, for the next six weeks, starting tomorrow. And you want me to print that, that *cock* story right next to it!"

"Walter? Is that *you* talking?" Bing Lockner said, standing in the doorway.

"Lockner," Burns said, waving him in. "Good, come in here. Maybe you can help me straighten Constantine out."

"Oh, I think you're doing just fine, Walter."

"Shut up. Have a look at these pictures."

Lockner settled into the other chair, crossing his legs and whistling softly as he looked the picture over. "So this is your murder, huh? Not much detail, is there?"

"Give him the other one, Constantine."

Bing sat forward. "Wow," he said.

"Constantine tells me some nigger cop claims a *vampire* did this."

"Which cop?"

"Dooley Willson." Danny said.

"Hmm! You know, he was one hell of a heavyweight in his army days. I saw him outpoint Dempsey once. An exhibition at Fort Keough. Would have knocked him out, too, except the ref kept picking Jack up off the canvas. When the fight was over the quartermaster pulled all us writers in and said if a word of what we'd just seen ever got printed, he'd make sure every last one of us would be lining the bottom of a trench in France." Lockner took a look at the second print. "What's with this one?"

"That's the murder victim on the tracks. Possible killer standing over."

"Blonde?"

"Yeah. Vern Smith told me the dead guy'd been drinking a couple of hours with a blonde."

"Did you get a description?"

"Vern just saw the hair."

"Some girls might take that as a great insult," Lockner said, putting the photo down. "I don't know, Walter. I think Connie's got something here."

"You two can afford to be romantic about the newspaper business," Burns said, getting up from his chair to pace with his hands held behind his back. "Well, I can't. You'll notice I said *business*. Twenty years ago when I was starting out, there were seven dailies in this town. Seven! You did anything you could to sell a paper. Well, now there's one left, and it's us. I don't have to do a thing to get more readers. I've *got* all the readers I'm ever going to have. We're saturated. What I've got to do now is increase advertising. Do you boys understand that? Advertisers pay the bills around here!"

"But there's a killer out there!"

"So what? People don't care about murder anymore. It doesn't thrill them. Everybody's been dying for the last twelve years! People are sick of it! They don't want to hear about more death. They want *this!*" Walter flicked his thumb at the ad copy. "They want to read about normal things. Hopeful things!"

"Aw, Walter, what's more hopeful than murder?" Bing said. "You say you want a normal town. Ten years ago you would have jumped on something like this. It'd be smeared all over the front page. You'd be writing editorials pressing the cops, and you'd run Connie's picture, with a black strip over the groin. That'd make it even better. Sensational photo of the mutilated corpse! Then you'd have those diagrams you used to love, Walter, remember with the crime scene all numbered out. One! Bloodstained area of tracks! Two! Bloodstained coat found on scene. Three! Footprint of the lady vampire in the cinders! You would have been *thrilled* to have a cock-sucking vampire on the loose."

"That was then," Burns said sourly. But he knew that Lockner was telling the truth.

"Maybe people do miss that stuff, Walter. Maybe if you gave 'em some of that now, instead of always trying to handle everything with kid gloves, it'd make 'em feel better. And you should think about the poor maniac killers, too."

Burns gaped at him. "What?"

"How do you think they feel, getting bumped off page one by *health* statistics!"

Burns sat down again and pushed the photos back at Danny. "I won't run these now. But find out what you can, Constantine. Maybe if there's another one of these murders, we'll do something with it."

"You promise?" Danny said. "'Cause I've got a witness."

"I'm not promising a damn thing. By the way, Constantine. Tomorrow noon at the Interlachen Club there'll be a lecture by Dr. Simon Gray."

"No, Walter. Please don't say it."

"Crowley wants someone there, and it's you."

"You know I hate that garden party stuff!"

Burns's eyes narrowed. "You giving me an argument?"

Danny sighed. "No."

"Good. Now get the hell out of here. I've got work to do!"

On the way back to the city room Bing said, "There's Walter for you. Consolidate and conquer."

"What are you talking about?"

"You will not be alone, son. Dorrie Van der Voort will be there."

Bing had been writing the Van der Voort social column, "Let's Poke About Town," for about a year now, ever since the real Dorrie had come down with chronic Hun. At first, Danny had found it hard to believe that Bing, who mixed with gamblers, saloonkeepers, ballplayers, and jockeys, would endure the luncheons, teas, and society evenings that were the meat of Dorrie's column, but Bing had taken the job with enthusiasm and three times a week put out a "Poke" column that put the old one to shame. For it turned out that Bing mixed with the rich, particularly with rich women, as well as he did with anyone else. "I love the rich!" he told Danny more than once, explaining how he had learned in Paris, after the war, that the rich were no different from anybody else, except perhaps more frightened of the epidemic, because money couldn't protect them from Hun the way it protected them from most other unpleasant things.

Gertrude Stein had told him that the rich were stunted now. "Money can build a fortress," she'd said. "But you cannot eat it." The thought that the rich were vulnerable endeared them to Bing, and made him want to write well about them. And when Bing Lockner was writing well, nobody on the paper, maybe nobody in the country, could top him.

"What will Dorrie be wearing?" Danny asked.

"The official uniform of the *Journal,* naturally. Chintz!"

Down in the city room, things were starting to pick up. Reporters and rewrite men and copy boys were starting to come in to put the early Monday edition together. Above, Danny could hear the clatter of the linotype coming from the composing room on the third floor. There was a deeper rumble, too. The presses were running ad sheets up in the plant above that. The *Journal* carried only a fourth of the staff it had before the war, but in another hour, and for the rest of the week until the Monday edition was put to bed, the old building would be a noisy, busy place. Everybody worked hard, and fast, and did two or three things now instead of one. Bing Lockner, for instance, besides writing the sports copy and the social column, also reviewed books and filed an occasional humorous short story for the Sunday features page. Somehow he found time to get drunk every night, and to write other stories for *The Dial* and *Smart Set.* Lockner was a friend of Mencken's. Supposedly, he was helping Mencken put a last book of essays together, now that the great man had gotten sick, too.

"Say, Connie," Lockner said. "Could you find me an empty-stands shot of the ballpark?"

"You're writing about the season being suspended?"

"Yessir."

Danny went down to the photo files. There were quite a few of Nicollet Field, but no empty-stands shots except for one aerial that had been taken from a balloon thirty years ago. He didn't think Bing would like it, but he brought it over anyway. Lockner laughed when he saw it.

"Not poignant enough. Would you mind running over and shooting some for me?"

"Okay. But I don't get it."

"What don't you get, Connie?"

"You're gonna write it about the Toledo players getting sick, right?"

"Sure am."

"So how come Walter doesn't think that's alarmist?"

Bing grinned sympathetically. "Walter knows I'll give it the right angle, that's why. I'll put our fair city in a good light. We canceled the game because we're *prudent.* We put those sick Toledo guys on the first train out of town. That's what you should have done. Play up the prudent."

Danny grabbed his Graflex. "I'll be back in a little while."

"Hey. Cheer up, Connie. Maybe you'll get lucky."

"Yeah."

"Yeah. Maybe she'll kill somebody else *tonight.*"

5

After supper and washing up, Kal Hromatka and Shirley Lund went out into the backyard. The sky was turning a funny green color.

"Thunder bumpers," Kal said. He was looking at the new antenna he had strung up last week between the roof of his radio shack and the telephone pole in the alley. The wire passed through the branches of an old box elder tree, and though Kal had gone up on a ladder and sawed out a few limbs to give it room, he was worried about what would happen if that box elder started dancing around in a storm.

"Maybe we ought to free up the lower end and just let it hang till tomorrow," Kal said.

"But it's almost eight, Kal. Can't we listen for a little while?"

"Don't want to lose my mast, Shirley."

"You won't. We'll hear the static anyway before the storm gets here. Then I promise I'll climb up on the roof for you and unhook it." She knew how much Kal hated climbing anything, especially since he'd taken a fall off the roof last winter chopping ice out of the gutters of Mrs. Lund's house and got laid up for three months with a broken hip. It had taken him a couple of days to work up the nerve to put that new wire up.

"I don't know, Shirley," Kal said, rubbing his chin, "your aunt would boil me alive if I let you up on that roof."

"Oh, pooh! She doesn't know half the things I do! Can't we listen for a little while? Please?"

"Okay, okay. But if I hear one pop, that mast is coming down."

"Thanks, Kal!"

They opened the shack and Kal lighted the kerosene lantern and hung it from the hook on the rafter. The front half of the shed was full of gardening equipment and tools, a lawn mower, and Kal's boat and trailer. The back half belonged to his radio rig. He had a piece of an old rug on the floor, a coal stove for the winter, a table for his A battery, and then, against the back wall, his pride and joy, the four-tube Ultradyne he'd made from a kit. It was shaped like a long shoe box, had three tuning dials, a counterbalancer, tone volume and tone quality controls, and jacks for two headsets. It was hot in the shed, and Kal threw open the windows, and lighted another lamp for the radio table. Its glow illumined a U.S. map fastened above the desk that bristled with colored pins showing all the stations coast to coast that Kal had picked up with his rig.

"Throw the switch. Let's warm her up," Kal said, screwing down the posts of the A battery to the leads. Shirley did, and sat down and put her headset on, listening anxiously for the hum to start coming up. Kal had been complaining about his B cells the last time she'd been out here, and she hoped he'd done something about replacing them. But the hum came, and that was followed, as soon as Kal put his own headset on, by a big crackle of static.

"That doesn't count, Kal!" Shirley cried, giving him a pleading look and pointing to the curtains that hung straight down and motionless beside the window.

"I shouldn't have opened that door," Kal groused.

"Oh, you know you wanted to listen. Let me try to find her?"

"There'll be nothing but static."

"Oh, hush!" Shirley opened the logbook. All last week, June 7 through 14, the Archangel had broadcast at 213 meters—right around 1430 kilocycles. "Did you catch her last night, Kal?"

"It cut off, but she was there."

Shirley checked the log for the dial positions. Number one at three, number two at seven, number three at zero. Her earphones whistled and buzzed as she moved through the wavelengths, and once or twice there was a quick swell of music or talking as she passed stations that were broadcasting programs. Shirley didn't care about those. She could listen to them on the set in her aunt's living room anytime. What she wanted to hear was that sweet mystery voice that came on at nine, three and sometimes four nights a week. She wanted to hear the Archangel.

She was notorious—a pirate broadcaster with no call letters and no license, who played thrilling records from places that didn't exist anymore, Harlem and New Orleans and Chicago, and told the grandest, most spine-tingling stories Shirley had ever heard about what life had been like in those places during the first years of the epidemic. She told those stories with irony and humor, and a grand sense of tragedy, while laying the blame for what had happened on the complacency of government and business and organized religion and the failure of almost everybody else to admit that there really was an epidemic at all. In this vein, the Archangel saved her most scathing commentary for the Milltown city government and the efforts of the Greater Northwest Development Company to somehow "stabilize" the situation in Minnesota—again while ignoring the disease.

Such comments made her a sensation, the subject of newspaper editorials decrying the spread of false cynicism and defeatism, and a woman wanted by the law. There were rumors that the governor had put a fifty-thousand-dollar reward on her head, and that a radio-detecting truck loaned to the city by the Treasury Department prowled the streets every night trying to locate the source of her transmissions. But Shirley knew the Archangel was too clever to ever be caught like that. She was too smart and too tough. And too rich. Her family had all been killed by Hun, but she had taken her inheritance and bought, from the Soviet government, a new kind of powerful, portable transmitter that was small enough to fit inside an ordinary makeup case and was capable of reaching from Alaska to Mexico. She intimated that she made her broadcasts from secret locations all over the city, and sometimes, when things got too hot, she even left town. In March and April, just after Danny's interview with her had appeared on page one of the Sunday *Journal,* she had taken a vacation to Chicago, broadcasting from the ruined ballroom of the deserted Blackstone Hotel.

Of course, Kal said that was a lie. He insisted to Shirley that the Archangel had never left town. There was no such thing as a radio transmitter that fit into a makeup case, or even a steamer trunk. Why, Kal's own rig was as compact as they came, and with the batteries and all took up a third of the shed. Shirley hated when Kal talked practical like that. He always pretended to know things about the Archangel, but they were stupid things, things that, if you believed them, made her seem so *ordinary.* Kal would say that the Archangel was really sponsored by the Red Cross, or that he had helped install her transmitter, though he had signed a contract that forbade him from telling anyone where he had done the work. He always hinted, though, that the Archangel's lair was really in the basement of the main library at Tenth and Hennepin, that big, ugly sandstone fortress of a building. Why, the Archangel would never set foot in a place like that! Kal didn't know anything. Shirley was sure he made those claims because, like most people, the Archangel made him feel uncomfortable about the way things were. Even though he liked her, he was really trying to bring her to earth somehow, spoiling the mystery the same way it would spoil your idea about what angels were, if you knew what they really looked like.

Anyway, Shirley thought, the Archangel would never broadcast from the basement of some musty old library. If anything, her lair was on the roof garden of the Metropolitan Building, with its twelve-story light court and its glass-floored arcades. That was the place for an angel!

"This has got to be it," Shirley said, wincing as the static popped sharply once more in her ears.

"Storm's coming," Kal said. "I ain't ever seen the sky look so green before."

"Shhh!"

"I'm telling you, Shirley, I'm taking that mast down—"

"Listen! Turn it up!"

Faintly, just faintly, came the strains of the Archangel's theme. The Archangel theme! It was fading in and out and cut through with whistling and lightning bursts, but there it was. Kal reached for the compensator and balanced the battery voltage, and the signal cleared. There was the Archangel singing over the end of the verse:

> *We meet in an alley*
> *'Cause we can't meet at home*
> *Stealing moments*
> *We can't call our own*
> *There in the darkness*
> *I hold you tight*
> *Minute by minute*
> *We use up the night*
> *And I'd stop time, if I had the power . . .*
> *Love by the hour*
> *Love by the hour*

"This is the Archangel calling. This is the Archangel calling. Can you hear me? You don't know how much Archangel wishes, sometimes, that you could talk right back to her. Sometimes I talk and talk and I have to remind myself that I am not really in an empty room, at the top of an empty building, in the middle of an empty city at all. No, Archangel, I tell myself, you look into the darkness and you'll see them, huddled round their radios, listening to you. The boys in the treehouses with their crystal receivers, and the family men who wait for the children to be put to bed before lighting their pipes and pretending to read the newspaper, while all along it's me in the headsets. You husbands do use the headsets, don't you? Meanwhile Mother's rocking under the lamp, doing the darning or the knitting. Or maybe there's just a chair where Mother used to be.

"I wrote a poem like that and sent it in to the Post *not long ago. I haven't seen an issue of the* Post *in almost a year, of course, but I hear it's still coming out, that the problem is only a distribution problem, and we all know we have so many of those. So I finished the poem and sent it in. It went:*

> *There's a chair where my Mother used to be,*
> *There's a chair where my Mother sang to me.*
> *Oh, she's gone up above,*
> *That dear mother I loved,*
> *Leaving nought where her—well, I can't say it—used*
> *to be.*

"I wonder. Do you think the Post *would publish such a poem? Leaving nought where her nought used to be?*

"This is the Archangel calling, where my Mother used to be.

"Do you know, I am considered a morbid person by at least one of my listeners. I know this because just this morning I was having my breakfast at a diner that I frequent because it is the only place left open. There are nine of us left and we all eat breakfast at this particular diner, run by a colored gentleman from Kentucky, fit as a horse, a wonderful cook, too. He says he can make chicken taste like anything, including chicken, and he does. But I was sitting at the counter drinking my coffee, and the two gentlemen to my right were discussing the fact that I had read an account the other evening of what had happened on a farm outside Jamestown.

"I'm not going to repeat all of the details, but it was a sensational story of an honest-to-God case of spontaneous combustion. Now, I did not witness this conflagration, nor did I write the description, nor did I even comment on either the possible veracity of the tale or the style and skill it was written with. I just repeated the story right out of the paper, and this man strongly objected to my doing so.

" 'She ought to realize that she is spreading panic and defeat,' the man told his friend somewhat pompously, as though he was some kind of alienist specializing in the public morale. You might imagine, my ears certainly pricked up to hear someone speaking of me! And of course, it is so delicious to sit in on conversation having to do with one, while the people conducting it have no idea of the depth of one's interest! It was as if I were invisible. It was as if I were, well, an angel!

"At any rate, this man claimed that I had read the account of spontaneous combustion with a certain amount of irony. He was especially critical of one sentence in particular, the one having to do with the head and hair of the unfortunate victim of this supernatural

occurrence. He said that I had laughed at the notion of one's hair standing on end, trembling like cornstalks before a storm, and then erupting into a pillar of flame! Laughed!

"Well, you can imagine that I examined my conscience to see whether I had indeed laughed, and I could not remember, but as the man repeated himself, saying 'Cornstalks! Erupting cornstalks!' I began to bite my tongue, and tried to drown it down with a large sip of very hot coffee, but even that couldn't work, and I started laughing then! I suppose I had fooled myself into imagining that I really was invisible!

"So there I was, laughing, and of course, as proper gentlemen, they had to pretend at first that I was making no sound, and then, failing that, that I wasn't really laughing, and when that didn't work, that I wasn't laughing at what they had said. But finally I succeeded in completely exasperating them and the gentleman looked over at me and said, icily, 'Might I ask what you find so amusing?'

"I am sure he expected I would be mortified, but by now things had gone too far. 'Sir,' I told him, 'I'm sorry, but you see your own hair is, well, sticking up just now, and I'm just trying to decide whether it is safe to sit here next to you or not—' "

There was a huge roar of static now. Kal pulled his headset off as thunder rolled in fast from the west.

"That's it, Shirl," he said.

"But, Kal—"

"If you give me any more trouble, little girl, you won't listen out here for a week!" The curtains were starting to stir.

"But she's so good tonight, Kal! Everybody's going to be talking about her tomorrow and I won't know a thing because you're worried about some old piece of wire!"

Kal was getting the ladder down off its hooks on the shed wall. "Lightning travels right down a wire. Through my receiver, then out the jacks and headsets and right into *you.* That's what I'm worried about, missy!"

"She *was* good. She was really saying something tonight. About how people pretend, and look the other way—"

"Okay, she was good." Kal said, leaning the ladder against the gutters. "And maybe your aunt's gone to bed. If she has, we'll try to pick her up on the set in the parlor."

"Aw, Kal, you're swell!" Shirley said, taking hold of the ladder.

"Uh-uh," Kal said. "I'll do it."

He went up and unhooked the mast wire himself.

C H A P T E R

6

*A*ll afternoon and evening it had got hotter and hotter as the clouds piled up to the west. Now day was about to turn over. The sky looked a corroded, copper green, and even though sunset was still a half hour away, it was dark. In the Glenwood switching yards of the Great Northern Railway you could see a scattering of cooking fires of the tramps who had settled in for the night.

They were bold about it. In the old days, because of the yard bulls, they would have camped without fire, or gone to the jungles north of the yard to camp. But these days there weren't many bulls left to blast 'boes off railroad property with two barrels of rock salt, or knock them out with saps or lanterns. Not that there were many tramps left, either. Ten years ago, in the first wave of Hun when the hysteria was at its peak, railroad bulls killed any tramps they found in the yard. Any who made it out of the yard into the town looking for a handout or a sitdown were liable to be shot by the cops, or by regular citizens who feared that tramps spread the epidemic from town to town.

Now things were different. There weren't many road kings anymore who rode the rails because they preferred life on the main line. Now the tramps were mostly dubs trying to get from one place to another. Usually, they were running from Hun, and so the tactic of the roads and the towns had changed. Most good-sized cities surrounded their yards with high fences, spotlights and guard towers like those around a prison. And many times a security perimeter extended several miles along the right-of-way leading into the yards. Once a tramp was inside, he owned the yard. He could stay as long as he wanted, and ride whatever train he pleased, so long as he did not try to come out into the town.

Milltown was good now. They fed the men and sent social workers out to interview them. There was always a good percentage of healthy tramps, whose strength and vigor were valuable. Here, if you passed muster, and wanted to leave the yard, they would process you out and put you in a halfway house for six months. Then if you were still free of Hun, you were set. They'd get you a job, a place to live, even a new family if you wanted it. Because of that, the Milltown yards filled up all summer long. Some men got sick, some went out to live in the town; the real tramps kept riding, though they stayed in Milltown longer because they could eat for free, which wasn't true in some of the other towns on the high line. Then, before the population got too large, winter always came and cleaned the place out.

This evening, a man named Dakota Pete walked up to a fire tended by two men. He smelled beans and boiling coffee, and wished they smelled good to him, because he hadn't eaten anything since yesterday morning. But he wasn't hungry. He walked into the circle of light from the fire, slung his bindle down, and sat on a tie. He recognized one of the men.

"Hello, Wall-Eye," he said.

"Pete. Where you come from?"

"Chi," pronouncing it *shy*.

"How is it?"

"Real bad. They was having trouble making up the trains and getting 'em out. All the shacks is niggers now, an' there ain't no bulls." Shacks were brakemen.

"No bulls," said the third tramp, whose name was Sailor Jack. "Imagine that. Somehow it don't seem right."

"Put your feet under," Wall-Eye said, spooning some beans into a can for him. Dakota Pete swallowed thickly. The food scared him.

He was plain scared of everything now. But if he didn't eat, these two would know there was something wrong with him. He'd been doing okay in the afternoon, riding in a boxcar with the doors closed. But now with that breeze starting to stir, he shivered hard, and hoped the other 'boes hadn't seen him.

"Anybody seen Lum Johnson?" Pete asked, stirring the beans.

"Not since March, April."

"I saw him in the yard at Havre," Wall-Eye said.

"It's hot there now. Whole high line's no damn good anymore."

"I got shot at last time I was there."

"Got you right between th' eyes, too," Jack said, laughing.

"We was supposed to hook up," Pete said. "We were gonna leave the yard and go into town together."

Sailor Jack spat contemptuously into the fire. "What the hell you want to live outside for?"

Pete closed his eyes. His head felt like it was pumped up with ice water. It was swollen so tight he thought it would bust any second. "I got . . . I got a daughter up in Fargo I ain't seen since '24. She's got kids I ain't ever seen, either."

"Tomorrow afternoon the ladies'll come from the Lutheran Mission," Wall-Eye said. "They'll mail a letter for you. They set up a kitchen and put on a good spread, too. You can stay on here 'til your daughter writes back. They come in three times a week."

"I don't know if I can wait that long."

"There's places you can get through the fence, but man, you'd be takin' a chance. It ain't worth it. Not when they treat you royal in the yard."

Dakota Pete tried to think about the letter he would write. Dear Dorothy, he thought. Dot, he used to call her. She was getting married in June 1925. He was going to give her away. In a few weeks. He frowned. He had just seen her, hadn't he? Little Dot and big Dot, his wife. They got married in ought-seven. He felt warm for a moment, remembering that day. Then he shivered again, hard this time. His eyes hurt so damn bad. They'd been hurting all day and he was trying to ignore it but now it felt like ice picks going in. It was more than he could take, and he groaned and let the can of beans drop to the ground.

"Hey!" Wall-Eye said, jumping up. "What the hell's wrong with you?"

Pete couldn't answer. He was doubled over, trying to wish the pain away. Telling himself his daughter was going to be married tomorrow, and that tomorrow was tomorrow and not seven years ago.

"He's sick, that's what's wrong," Sailor Jack said. "Look at him. He's a fucking bleeder!"

"Bullshit!" But Wall-Eye saw that Pete was bleeding bad. Brown blood with clumps in it slid out of Pete's mouth. He was bleeding out his ears, too.

"Son of a bitch!" Jack said, kicking at him. "Hey. Hey! How long you been sick, you stupid son of a bitch?"

"He can't talk, his mouth's all full o' blood," Wall-Eye stammered. "We got to get the hell out o' here!" He started off, but the other tramp pulled him back by the arm.

"Where you going? This is a good camp. We'll drag him off and dump him someplace."

"I ain't touching him!"

"We'll be all right. We'll handle him by his clothes. We can put him on that handcar. Come on."

"I ain't doin' it!"

Sailor Jack slapped Wall-Eye hard across the mouth. "You'll do it, all right!"

"Okay, okay! Let's get it over with."

Wall-Eye tucked his hand inside the sleeve of his coat and grabbed the back of Dakota Pete's jacket. Jack took him by the back of his pants, and they dragged him over the gravel. Pete's body was limp, and the tramps pulled him over to the next spur, and got him up on the platform of the handcar.

"God, look at that son of a bitch leak," Wall-Eye moaned.

"Shut up and help me."

Reluctantly, Wall-Eye got aboard. He released the brake and pulled on the handle, and the car started to move along the spur. The wind was coming up now, and lightning flashed and seemed to make everything jump. Wall-Eye winced when the thunder hit. He didn't like thunder. Out in the open like this you felt it like a punch. Pretty soon it was going to rain like a son of a bitch, too. He had a nice dry

bedroll inside an orange car that didn't leak, and he wanted to go
back there. He had the awful feeling that the longer he stood over
this poor, bleeding son of a bitch, the more chance he had to catch
Hun himself.

"Ain't this far enough yet?" he cried. There were a few bright
patches of sky left in the west, but the lightning forked again in front
of the downtown buildings and washed them out. They had turned
the yard lights on.

"I'll tell you when it's far enough!" Sailor Jack yelled, pumping
on the handle. Crazy son of a bitch, Wall-Eye thought. The first
drops of rain—big, cold ones—splatted against the back of his neck.
"Over there!" Jack yelled, pointing to some cattle cars on a siding.
"We'll toss him onna one o' them slat-sides."

A blast of cold wind knifed along the siding. Rain pelted them as
they dragged Dakota Pete over to the cattle car. They slid the door
open, and hoisted him up halfway. Then Wall-Eye saw a lantern.
Yard bull! he thought, the old instincts taking over, and got ready to
beat it. He'd been cold-cocked by lanterns way too many times.

But then Jack whistled. "Will you look at that," he said. It wasn't
a bull holding the lantern. It was a woman in a dress. She lifted the
lantern so the two men could see her face. She had platinum blonde
hair that looked like cold silver. The wind blew the hem of her dress
up above her knees.

"Who the hell are you?" Sailor Jack said.

"Someone 'oo's been watching you for a little while, that's 'oo,"
the woman said, in some kind of Brit accent. She swung the lantern
toward the cattle car. "What'd you do 'im in for?"

"W-we didn't do nothin'!" Wall-Eye said. "He got sick. We're just
taking him away from our camp so we don't get it, too."

The woman smiled, and touched Jack's arm. Slowly, she ran her
fingers down his sleeve. "Don't tell me a couple of big strong boys
like you are 'fraid of getting sick, now!" She was looking Jack in the
eyes, not caring that wind made her dress snap like the sails of a
ship.

"We ain't afraid of nothin'," Jack said.

"Really. Not even me?"

"Not on your life, lady."

"Prove it," she said, tugging on his coat so that he bent his head down. He kissed her. Then he straightened and looked back over his shoulder at Wall-Eye.

"Beat it. I'm gonna visit with this nice lady."

Wall-Eye stared. What the hell was going on here? No women ever came into the yard, except for the ones from the mission. He didn't like this. He didn't like it at all.

"I said beat it!" Jack said, as lightning seared the whole yard white, with the thunder right behind it loud as a quarry blast. The rain came down in heavy sheets that beat the grit while Jack and the woman stood there pawing each other. Somewhere far off came the wail of a steam whistle. It was like a signal to Wall-Eye. He bolted and ran off a ways and took shelter inside an open boxcar. From there he could still see them in the glow of her lantern and in the flashes of lightning that came faster and faster. The wind tore through the yard, bringing with it more rain, and hailstones, too. Then the lantern blew out, but the lightning was coming so fast now Wall-Eye could see them moving in flickers, like figures on a cinema screen. They were wrapped around each other, the rain plastering the woman's dress against her body. Wall-Eye licked his lips. It had been one hell of a long time since he'd had a woman. He couldn't even remember how long. Sometimes you ran into a female tramp, but you were never tempted, not really, because every one Wall-Eye had ever seen was a real hellcat, tougher than any of the kids and ready to rip you to shreds if you even tipped your head the wrong way.

He began to think that maybe there'd be some left for him once Jack got finished with her. Then he saw her put her hand up to the side of his head. Jack went down like he'd been shot and lay still. She jumped on top of him, crouching low in the pounding rain. Jack never moved.

"Hey," Wall-Eye said. "Hey, what the hell did you do to him!" He ran out fighting the wind and the rain and came up on her from behind. She was bent over, bobbing up and down on her haunches, and even through the wind he could hear the low, hungry moans she made as she—what? Jack lay there on his back with his eyes wide open, and his eyes moved to pick up Wall-Eye as he came up. They locked on him, and Wall-Eye could see how scared he was. But he never moved.

"What's wrong with Jack?" he shouted. "What'd you do to him?" He pulled her away and she looked back and *snarled*, red blood streaming from both corners of her mouth, the rain hitting it, spreading it in a pink wash down her neck and the open front of her dress. Wall-Eye backed off, looked around on the ground, and picked up a coupling pin.

"Get away from him!" he yelled, as Jack's eyes moved from him to her, and back again. He raised the pin, ready to cave her fucking head in with it. But something hot tore at his shoulder, whirling him around and knocking the pin from his hand. He saw a man in a long dark coat walking toward him. The man's eyes were locked on his. They were pale gray, and cold, the coldest eyes Wall-Eye had ever seen. Wall-Eye groaned and stumbled back. A second shot exploded in the wet cinders at his feet. Wall-Eye turned and ran, dove into an open boxcar and tumbled out the other side, ran up the spur, crossed a flatcar the same way and then ran straight toward the orange car at his camp. He got back to it, closed the doors, and stood, breathing hard, while the hail beat down like rocks on the roof. After a while he felt something wet on his arm. He touched the spot and looked at his hand.

He was bleeding.

CHAPTER

7

*T*he next morning, in a private room on the third floor
of the Interlachen Club, a meeting of the steering
committee of the Greater Northwest Development Company
was held. No minutes were taken, as was the practice of the steering
committee, whose work was mainly the informal discussion of
policies that would later be taken up by the entire board of directors.
Attending this morning were Alexander Crowley, publisher of the
Milltown *Journal*; Daniel Evald, head of the Milk Producers'
Cooperative; Jason Whitney of Northern States Power; the Reverend
Amos V. Ellington of the African Methodist-Episcopal Church; and
an invited guest who was not a board member: Theo Rostek, a Negro
businessman who owned Rostek's, a popular restaurant on the city's
North Side.

Addressing the meeting, which was being held just prior to the
benefit luncheon at which he would also give a speech, was the head
of the Hematological Institute of North America, Dr. Simon Gray.
His subject was a new project of the institute, for which Gray hoped
to obtain GNDC funding, the construction of an emigré facility in
the town of Savage, along the Minnesota River southwest of
Milltown.

"Let me understand this," Reverend Ellington said. "You want to
build a camp large enough to hold ten thousand of our people."

"I think, Reverend, that 'camp' is the wrong term. We intend to build permanent structures."

"Barracks?"

"Bungalows," Evald said, with a touch of impatience. "Two families per building."

"But some of these people are coming up from the South with all their relatives," Ellington pointed out. "Fifteen or twenty people."

"The design of the bungalows takes that into account, too, Reverend. We've gone over this before."

"I'm just saying that these folks must be provided for properly. And why can't they be settled into town as we've been doing?"

"It is a question of efficiency, Reverend," Gray said in his smooth, patient voice. "We must concentrate the services required by the emigrés which presently are provided by a patchwork of institutions and agencies, including my institute. Obviously, Negroes born and bred in the rural South will require a considerable period of adjustment and training before they can take the place of our former populace. Before, when we were able to recruit educated, urban Negroes from other cities, such problems were not so serious." Gray smiled smoothly. "Sometimes, it was only a matter of providing a good coat and a pair of gloves for the winter."

"You got that right," Theo Rostek said.

Evald and Whitney laughed, and glanced at each other, and Whitney made a tiny writing motion on an imaginary pad. Evald nodded. It was no secret to these men that Rostek's business interests included numbers running.

"Nevertheless, we must be very careful. I don't want these people herded into a camp, the way the Turks did the Armenians. What did they call them? Concentration camps."

"There are no fences, Reverend," Gray said tolerantly. "The grounds will be pleasant. Work and education will be provided. And the community has the potential to earn vast sums as blood donors. The project will pay its own way, gentlemen. It will revitalize the city, and provide productive lives for people who faced only poverty and death where they were living before."

"Of course," Reverend Ellington said. "I'm only saying we must be careful about the accommodations."

"I think we better break this up, Reverend," Crowley said, glancing at his watch. "Dr. Gray's got another speech to make soon. Thank you all for coming, particularly you, Mr. Rostek, arriving on such short notice."

"I'm glad you boys realized you're wise to clue me in on these things," Theo said. "If it's right for the North Side, I'm only too happy to help you out."

"Let me walk you to your car, Theo," Gray said. "There's a matter or two I'd like to discuss with you."

"Sure thing, Doc. See you later, gents."

When the door closed, Ellington turned to the other three men. He was seething. "I don't know what you're thinking of, bringing that . . . *scoundrel* into our meeting. It's outrageous!"

"Reverend, please," Crowley said. "I know exactly how you feel. Under normal circumstances the man would not be allowed to set foot in this club. Not even as a porter! Unfortunately, we are not able to build this facility alone. We just don't have the capital."

"We would if Eddie were still alive," Evald said. He was talking about Edward Foshay, the financier who had begun constructing the fifty-story tower, whose unfinished skeleton loomed over the downtown loop. Foshay, discovering he had contracted chronic Hun, had leapt from the steelwork last spring, leaving a financial empire that collapsed like a soufflé without him.

"But he's not," Crowley said. "So we take Rostek's money instead. You know it is the better way, Reverend. We make him part of the club. Flatter him, make him feel white as we can. And that way we can turn him any way we want to."

"Your insults do not exactly reassure me," Ellington said, getting up. "Good day, *gentlemen.*" He stomped out of the room, slamming the door behind him.

"Touchy old bastard," Evald said, with a shrug. "What the hell's wrong with him?"

"He's jealous," Whitney said. "He wants to be the only nigger on the board."

The three white men laughed, and went downstairs to the dining room.

*   *   *

Down in the kitchen of the Interlachen Club, Danny Constantine shoved a fork through a mound on his plate that looked like gray scrambled eggs. He was grabbing a bite with the help before the luncheon began.

"What the hell is this stuff?" he said.

"I told you," the Negro cook on the other side of the plate warmer said. "It's lamb."

"It ain't lamb."

Just then Bing Lockner came in. He wore a brand-new straw hat tipped back on his head, and a bow tie. "Floyd!" he said to the cook. "What are you doing here?"

"They rounded up help from three clubs to put on this lunch, Mr. Lockner," Floyd said. "Minikadha, Brookside, and Oak Ridge." Floyd was from Oak Ridge, the restricted, Jews-only club out in Hopkins.

"This look like lamb to you, Bing?" Danny asked.

"Well, it's part of the lamb," Bing said. Floyd began to laugh.

"You know this man?" he asked.

"Oh, yes. He's a fellow wage slave of the dear old *Journal.*"

"You tell him that's a free lunch."

"You know there isn't any such thing."

"I just want to know what the hell I'm eating," Danny said.

"Lamb sweetbreads," Floyd said.

"Thank you," Danny said, putting the plate down.

"That's what the guests are having. Good for you. It's got tremendous amounts of iron."

"I got plenty of iron," Danny said.

"Plate in his head from the war," Bing said to Floyd, tapping his temple as he followed Danny out of the kitchen to the pantry. There, Danny got his Graflex and flash rig, loaded the bar with powder, and went out to the dining room, where the guests were mingling.

The dining room overlooked the velvety eighteenth green of the famous Interlachen course. Greenskeepers were picking up branches and pieces of bark that had blown down during the storm last night. Danny was glad to see the windows were open, and that the veranda door was, too. There was less chance of smoking the room out with his flash. He looked around for a likely grouping, saw Dr. Morton

Philips of the University Hospital, who was talking to his wife and some other people beside an architect's rendering of the new research wing about to be constructed at the Hematological Institute. Danny went over to them.

"Pardon me, folks. Shot for the *Journal?*"

"Not at all," Mrs. Philips said. She was wearing a candy-striped volunteer nurse dress. A lot of the women were. Volunteering at the institute was popular among the surviving wives of the rich.

"How would you like us?" Mrs. Philips asked.

What a question, Danny thought. How *would* he like these rich bastards?

"You're fine just like you are," he said.

As he composed the shot he realized that one of the women in the group was looking back through the finder at him. She was wearing candy stripes, too, but she was a lot better looking than Mrs. Philips. *Come on*, he thought, *lay off*. He hated being sized up like that. It happened all the time these days to any healthy-looking white man who looked unattached. Danny had been propositioned many times the past couple of years. Not because he was particularly handsome, although he wasn't bad-looking—but because many women who were still young and whose husbands were either sick or dead wanted to bear healthy children. In the beginning before he had figured out what was happening, Danny had indulged these women, and himself, a few times. But there had always followed scenes and demands, and once an irate husband had appeared at the *Journal* and threatened to blow his head off. Danny stayed away from it now. He made it a rule to keep his distance when he was working. He did not want to contribute to the disorder.

The woman continued to stare at him until finally, pushing the shutter release as though it were the trigger of a gun, he blew off the flash. The woman stood there, blinking. "Thanks, folks," Danny said, taking advantage of her momentary blindness to move off. The woman came right after him, though.

"That wasn't very nice," she said wryly.

"What wasn't?" He was sliding a fresh film pack into the camera.

"Why, you positively curled your lip when you took that picture."

"Facial tic," Danny said.

She smiled, looking up at him with big, brown eyes. "Goodness! You didn't strike me as being a surly person before, Mr. Constantine."

Danny snapped the camera closed and looked at her. "You talk like we know each other," he said.

"Don't you remember me?"

"No," Danny said. *"Have* we met?"

"Maybe," the woman said. Then without warning she cupped her hand around his neck and kissed him softly there, before smiling and turning away. Danny stared at her as she rejoined her friends. There *was* something familiar about her, but he couldn't think what it was. He went over to Bing, who was standing at the bar.

"Who were those people with the Philipses?" he said, opening his notebook.

"The Roald Petersens. And you've got lipstick on your neck." Bing took a handkerchief from his pocket. "May I?"

"Knock yourself out."

Bing dabbed the handkerchief onto the tip of his tongue and rubbed Danny's neck. "You're the one who's knocked out. You've just been kissed by the flour king's daughter. Selena Crockett."

"She's *that* Crockett?"

"The one and only. You know: she runs the Lutheran Mission at the old Milwaukee Road station, works with the tramps and settlers. Also does volunteer work for Gray at the institute. You never met her before?"

"No," Danny said, rubbing his neck. "But she thinks we have." He watched her walk across the room. "Maybe I should let her convince me."

"Forget it, Connie. She's devoted to her work. I've never even seen her out with a guy, unless it was making an appearance with Gray."

"Speak of the devil," Danny said, looking out through the veranda doors. "That's Gray, isn't it?"

"Yup."

Simon Gray was impeccably dressed in a dark blue linen suit. He had silver hair worn rather long and brushed back straight from his forehead. At the moment, he was speaking intently to a thin, light-skinned Negro with a goatee.

"He's a good-looking guy!"

"Tell me about it. Who else could get a roomful of women to wear those god-awful striped smocks?"

"You could, Bing." Danny said.

"Different kind of stripes, in my case," Bing said.

"And that's Theo Rostek he's talking to?"

"So it is."

Danny dumped his burned flash powder into an ashtray and reloaded the bar. "Be right back," he said, heading for the veranda. He walked through the doors, brought the Graflex to his face, composed the shot, and snapped it.

"For tomorrow's *Journal,*" he said as the smoke rose to the ceiling. "Thanks."

A couple more shots would do it, he thought, as he went back inside. Then maybe he could get the hell out of here. This institute was all about rich people, anyway. The rich couldn't go to Switzerland anymore, not since the European quarantine. So they had imported Gray to build them a fancy sanitarium where they could get their blood washed, and bathe under tanning lamps, and practice yoga and all the rest of that crap the rich did to protect themselves from Hun. Not that all their cures and mumbo jumbo did them any good. The rich had died off at the same rate as the rest of the population.

Danny noticed old man Crowley walking toward him with a scowl on his face. Crowley was short and dried up, eighty-three years old and hard of hearing.

"You're working for me, aren't you?" Crowley asked, coming up to him.

"Yes."

"What? Speak up."

"Yes, I am!" Danny said into Crowley's ear horn.

"Don't you know you ask permission before you shoot someone?"

"I thought I had."

Danny glanced up and saw that Dr. Gray had followed Crowley over, and stood behind the old man with a bemused smile on his face.

"Really, Robert," Gray said. His accent was faintly British. "It's quite all right. I merely meant he seemed rather . . . *aggressive.*" He looked at Danny, gazing at him with pale, almost aluminum-colored blue eyes.

"Do you want your picture taken or not?" Crowley asked peevishly.

"In connection with today's luncheon, I would prefer not. I wouldn't want your readers to get the wrong impression. After all, I am not here to socialize."

"You're kidding me," Danny said.

"Don't be impertinent!" Crowley snapped, his eyes glinting like those of an evil little bird. "Give me that film."

"But it's all my shots of the guests!" Danny protested.

"Take them again! That's what I pay you for, isn't it?"

"Oh, that won't be necessary, Robert," Gray said. "So long as Mr. Constantine promises to destroy the negative, his word is quite good enough for me. Mr. Constantine?"

"Of course, Dr. Gray," Danny said with relief. "I'll bleach it out first thing. You don't have to worry. And I'm very sorry. It's just I don't run across many people who don't like their picture taken. Public figures, anyway."

"That is where you're mistaken, Mr. Constantine," Gray said, continuing to stare coolly right into Danny's eyes. "Not everyone who is out in public is a public figure. I prefer to do my work behind the scenes. Quite frankly, I would be much happier in a world that had no newspapers. *Or* photographers," he added, a faint smile returning to his lips. "Well. I believe they want us to sit down. Robert?"

"You bleach that negative," Crowley said, shaking his cane. Gray extended his arm, and Crowley took it, and together they went behind the head table, the other guests taking their places at the round tables on the floor. Danny found Bing talking to the waitresses who waited in line with trays of salad at the entrance to the pantry.

"Look at these, Connie. Hearts of palm."

"Hands off," the waitress said, and started out.

"Ditto," said the next one in line.

Bing watched them fan out and put the plates in front of the guests. "So. What bee bit the old man?"

"The guest of honor doesn't want his picture taken."

"Not with Theo Rostek, anyway."

"You think that's what it was?"

"Oh, Connie," Bing said with a long, sad sigh.

Danny shook his head and looked around. "Jesus, Bing. How can you stand this lace-curtain stuff? How can you *write* about it?"

"Because I'm a sports writer! These afternoon gatherings are just as much a sport as baseball or the fight game. You got your heroes and your villains, your great performances and players that come a cropper. Every afternoon there's somebody trying to win something out here, and somebody trying to keep them from doing it. Then you've got your statistics, and your quotes, the standings change, the old ones start to falter and the new kids come up and get their chance, maybe 'cause somebody's out with a hangover. And I write it up, same as I always did."

"Dorrie writes it, you mean."

Bing grinned. "That's right. Miss Van der Voort. And right now she's got two columns to write."

"Won't you stick around for Gray's speech?"

Bing grinned at him and tipped his straw hat back. "Well, you know, Connie, I keep hoping you'll learn to appreciate the high life as much as I do. Have a drink. Play a little mah-jongg. Meanwhile"—he made a popping sound flicking the brim of his hat with his forefinger—"don't get any older, kid."

C H A P T E R

8

*D*uring lunch, Danny had a smoke out on the veranda and watched the club kids playing in the pool beneath the balcony. About half of them had pressure wraps around their arms or legs, and all wore leather helmets, even in the water. Watching them, along with the mothers and nannies, were two lifeguards and a nurse. The kids moved carefully, played carefully, and stayed pretty much spread apart. Unlike the other clubs in Milltown, Interlachen was mixed, meaning you could join if you were chronic, and that meant that most members had at least one bleeder in the family. Even so, the membership rolls were still pretty thin. According to Bing, rumor had it that Interlachen's membership committee had begun, discreetly, to consider Negro applications for membership. That was something, all right. Before the war, a Negro couldn't even *work* at a club like this.

Danny went back inside when he saw that Robert Crowley was standing up, tapping his water glass with a knife.

"Thank you all for coming today and eating this rather interesting lunch," he said. "What was this?"

"Lamb," someone said, getting a laugh.

"Yes. Lamb. At any rate, on behalf of the Milltown *Journal* and the members of the board of the Greater Northwest Development

Company, I would like to say how much all of us appreciate your support of the tremendous work being conducted by Dr. Simon Gray and his fine staff at the Hematological Institute. It is through your hard work and generosity that Dr. Gray—the top man in his field—has chosen our fair city as the home for his battle against the scourge.

"As you know, since 1918, no place on earth, no matter how remote or cut off from modern-day affairs, has been spared by the epidemic we know as Hun. Like every other American city, ours has suffered. But we were blessed with hearty pioneer stock here, toughened by the struggles of the last century, tempered by our harsh winters. How fortunate we are to have them! Those fierce winds and sparkling snows cleanse the air and melt into pure, health-giving waters. Our farms are the richest in North America. Our people are the healthiest. Yes, we have been decimated, but unlike so many other places, we can look to the future. We have survived! And, through the efforts of the GNDC, we are dedicated to building a new world here, with Milltown as its capital: healthy, strong, and secure in its future.

"Make no mistake, ladies and gentlemen, the man I am about to introduce to you will, in no small measure, become the guardian of the hope we have for that future. He and his institute have declared a holy war against this disease! Simon Gray is not like so many of the hand wringers in his profession who have given up against the pressure of Hun. No! This man faces the epidemic squarely, stares it down, and makes it yield! It is no accident, ladies and gentlemen, that the final battlefield of this war—a war truly to end all wars—shall be here in Minnesota, where such strong, brave, resolute people live.

"It is with great pleasure, then, that I introduce to you the chief of the Hematological Institute of North America, Doctor Simon Gray."

There was loud applause. Gray waited a moment, rose, shook Crowley's hand, and waited for the old man to sit before taking the podium. As the applause dwindled, he gazed over the dining room with that same cool expression Danny had seen in the finder of his Graflex. Danny got his notebook ready so that he could take down the main points of Gray's speech.

"Robert, members of the GNDC, members of this beautiful club, its guests and staff, my volunteers, members of the press. First let me say how much your warm, wholehearted support has meant to me. Someone once tried to convince me that your average midwesterner is a taciturn sort, prone to be dry, practical, fatalistic, even a little complacent. Let me say now that from my first contact with the citizens of this great city, I have found quite the opposite to be true. You have been passionate in your welcome, tireless in your efforts, and have made me feel like one of your own." Gray smiled. "This after years of feeling a bit like the proverbial Wandering Jew. Now this city has refreshed my spirit to an extent I could never have foreseen or dared to hope for. I am and shall be grateful to it, and you, forever."

They already love him, and he butters them up anyway, Danny wrote in his notebook. Gray smiled again, waited for the applause to die down. Then, slipping on a pair of silver-framed glasses, he bowed his head, and examined his notes. He took his time. The room was very quiet. When he looked up, the amusement had vanished from his face.

"1918," he began in a low, barely audible voice, "ought to have been known as the most terrible year in all the troubled chronicles of man."

He waited again.

"In 1918, after four years of war that decimated the best and brightest sons of the West, and with the hope of peace glimmering at last like a star in the red glow of sunset, the Spanish influenza swept through Europe, North America, and Asia and killed many who had been spared by the fighting.

"Influenza was a known disease, of course, which spread quickly and then took its course. This particular strain proved more deadly than most, and resisted many of the then-available stratagems of public hygiene. However, after six deadly months, it abated. Those who had contracted the disease and did not die of it were generally immune to further attacks. Doctors everywhere felt that at last they could begin to relax. The worst was over. Once again in the capitals of Europe and in Washington, the talk was not of illness, but of peace. And that is when the first cases of acute German hemorrhagic fever were reported in the trenches of the Western Front.

"It was the spring of 1919, and 1919 was to become a year so terrible that all the trials of the previous year, and of the four before, and of all the years that men had remembered and recorded, were forgotten forever. For 1919 was the year over ninety million people perished of the disease we now call Hun.

"Some of my colleagues, in trying to understand what agent could possibly kill such great numbers of people in such a short amount of time, have sought to identify the infectious agent and trace its history. Their efforts, while not complete, provide some clues. We know, for example, that the German high command had undertaken a secret program of medical research aimed at producing a weapon which could spread an infectious agent among the enemy. There were, for example, experiments conducted with the anthrax virus.

"In this case, we know of a German project to cultivate the germ responsible for a type of hemorrhagic fever known as Ebola. This disease is transmitted by mosquitoes, and affects monkey populations in east and central Africa, and also occasionally infects white settlers and missionaries. The natives of the region, probably because of centuries of exposure, show little ill effects other than slight fever, sore throat and an occasional headache. Whites afflicted by Ebola showed different, quite dramatic symptoms: Kidney failure. Internal bleeding. Spontaneous hemorrhage leading to death.

"We believe that the Imperial researchers brought both monkeys and mosquitoes from German East Africa with the aim of cultivating vast quantities of the infectious Ebola agent. An important aim of their research was to change the method of transmitting the disease from injection, as by the bite of a tiger mosquito, to aerosol, as the cold and flu viruses employ. In that way, the agent would be dried into a powder which could then be loaded into shells or aerial bombs launched against the enemy.

"We suspect, but cannot know for sure, that during the cultivation process, the character of the Ebola germ changed. It became more virulent, and, although I don't wish to anthropomorphize an organism which, after all, cannot even be seen under the microscope, the virus became more *opportunistic*. By this I mean that the germ now gained the ability to transmit itself by a number of different means. We know this because of the subsequent failure of all normal methods of public hygiene to quell the epidemic. Quarantine failed. So did water treatment, treatment of food, sterilization of clothing and cooking utensils. The same was true for mosquito abatement programs, laws mandating the destruction of tropical birds and monkeys, the destruction of zoos and the killing and burning of all zoo animals. Nothing worked. We believe this is so not because such stratagems were ineffective in themselves, but because the mutated germ, finding one avenue blocked, merely took another which it heretofore had not been required to employ."

Gray paused for a sip of water. There wasn't a sound in the room.

"Now, whether this opportunism was deliberately bred into the germ by its cultivators we do not know, nor can we ever know. We believe that, sometime in late 1918, when the German military position became desperate, and with revolutionaries in the streets of Berlin, the order was given to deploy this terrible weapon against the new units of American Expeditionary Force along the Meuse and in the Argonne Forest. However, before this order could be carried out, we believe that there was an accident of some kind at the germ warfare facility that exposed researchers and laboratory workers to the agent. Within three days, most of these people were dead.

"The disease spread to the surrounding towns, and soon became an epidemic along the Ruhr. But the agent did not discriminate. It took friend and foe alike. Within six months, more people died of what we now call German hemorrhagic fever than had been killed in all the previous years of the war. During this initial phase, the German high command ordered the germ warfare facility destroyed, along with all records of the experiments and procedures conducted there. This order was unfortunately carried out. The laboratories and buildings were shelled by artillery, and then bombed from the air with incendiary explosives. When the fires cooled, tanks driven by officers encased in rubber suits, presumably offering protection from any germs that survived the fire, were employed to plow the earth under. But it was too late. Hun began its raging course, with results we now know far too well.

"Perhaps I should recite the statistics, the grim litany of death that has been intoned in Europe, in Asia and Australia, in North and South America. Perhaps I should remind you that in twelve long, terrible years more than half the world's people have vanished. That in the United States, which had a robust population of one hundred twenty-five million people in 1912, now only thirty million remain. That France and Germany and the British Empire are no more; that Russia has become a frozen, empty land; that China is reduced to twenty squalid cities; that in Japan, the wind chimes *ting* across the gardens and ponds that have grown wild for lack of tending. And that, of all the world, only the Negro population of Africa has been spared.

"Who among us in this room has not been touched by all this horror and sorrow? I do not have to explain it to you, nor do I wish to remind you again of all you have suffered. Instead, I wish to tell you where we now stand, and what our hope is for the future.

"Hun infection classically takes two forms: the acute, which is sudden and violent, and whose victim quite literally loses his ability to hold his blood inside his body, and the chronic. A person with chronic hemorrhagic fever suffers from an affliction that is very similar to hemophilia. His blood clots very poorly, or not at all, so that any slight cut, or a bruise sustained in an accident, even one so trivial as bumping one's leg against a table, results in bleeding episodes which are very difficult to stanch, weaken the patient, and, eventually, prove fatal. Though the symptoms of chronic Hun and hemophilia are similar, there are important differences. First, hemophilia is a hereditary disease. Hun is not. Second, the genetics of hemophilia are such that the vast majority of its victims are male. We believe that in hemophilia, a defective gene is carried on the X chromosome, and that, in the case of women, a normal gene on the second X chromosome protects her, so that chances are very remote of a woman suffering from the disease. German hemorrhagic fever, on the contrary, is indiscriminate as to the sex of its victims. In fact, Hun is a particular scourge of women, for while it is possible to live with a chronic case if one is both careful and lucky, there is no precaution an afflicted woman can take against the devastating consequences of her menstrual cycle. Generally, a woman with chronic HF will perish with the onset of her first menses following infection."

Gray waited. Danny closed his eyes. Sonja had died of her period.

"But there is another important difference between the two. One that is puzzling, and yet perhaps offers us our greatest source of hope: the fact that the African racial type, in all its manifestations, from the Zulus of the Transvaal to the Creoles of the Caribbean and to the café au lait mulattos of New Orleans, tiny pygmy to the giants of the Sudan, has so far been untouched by the epidemic.

"This fact naturally brings up the question of how the racial characteristics of a person inhibit the full expression of hemorrhagic fever upon exposure. Is there, for instance, a genetic factor that prevents an acute attack but not a chronic one? And is there a relationship between this hypothetical factor and the severity of the chronic condition? Is it perhaps possible that Negroes are indeed infected, but that the disease in them expresses only the most minor symptoms? If so, what factor exists in the body of the Negro that protects him so strongly? And, most importantly, is it possible to isolate this factor, duplicate it, grow it, *manufacture* it, so that we may be able to produce a serum that will protect the entire world once and for all, allow it to heal itself and begin to grow again?

"The answers to these, and a hundred other questions, remain a mystery. Finding the answers to these questions is the raison d'être of our Hematological Institute."

Gray glanced up from his notes. It seemed to Danny that everyone in the room looked sick and afraid, but that the doctor was Strength. You could feel it. He was stronger than Hun, stronger than anything. Gray gazed out at his audience, as a smile returned to his lips.

"I pledge to all of you that for as long as this scourge walks among us, we of the institute shall dedicate ourselves to tireless, relentless, unstinting research conducted by the best men—yes, and women, too, for this crisis requires the participation and the talents of *all* people of the world—to pin down the foe and strangle it! And, in the meantime, we shall give all we can in the way of treatment, employing the latest techniques of blood transfusion, blood separation, and blood product storage, so that those chronic sufferers who so desperately require treatment have a fair chance of getting it.

Soon you will see our blood-collection vans patrolling the streets. The healthy will be asked to give, and give again, so that the health of one can be the life of many. But be assured, ladies and gentlemen, that I will never ask anyone to give more than I give myself."

Gray straightened to his full height, removed his jacket, and rolled up the sleeves of his shirt. People gasped.

"Brother, will you look at that," the waitress standing next to Danny said.

Both his arms were a battlefield of puncture wounds and purple bruises. His skin was pale and almost transparent, and Danny wondered whether Gray used makeup to add color to his face. Nodding, Gray rolled down the sleeve and put his jacket on again.

"That is how it is for me now," He said in a soft, sad voice. "But know this. I came here because this city is the healthiest in all of North America. I intend to make it healthier still. Working together, we shall become strong, and shall grow stronger, until this place becomes the fountain of health for the nation, and the nation becomes the fountain of health for the world. Thank you very much."

He sat down. Everyone else sat silently for a moment, and then jumped to their feet, clapping and cheering wildly.

Gray wows 'em showing off punctured arms, Danny wrote.

9

As soon as Gray finished his speech, Danny drove back to the office. He did his darkroom work first. When he got to the shot of Gray he watched as the image started coming up in the pan. There was the doctor standing a little apart from Rostek, looking tall and gaunt, his eyes deep and shadowy. He was staring down at Theo with—what? Contempt? Danny fixed the negative and had a look. What a strange guy! He got out an empty pan and reached for the bottle of bleach, then stopped. Why should he destroy the negative? It was his work, after all. He'd promised to destroy it, but if the shot never got published, what difference did it make? Danny hung it up to dry with the others, then went back to his desk and began writing up the story about the luncheon. He slugged it, "Doctor Gray at Interlachen," with a second head, "Famed Physician Promises His Hematological Institute Will Become Fountain of Health for Region." Danny played up the part where Gray showed arms "ravaged by the puncture scars of countless transfusion needles, the doctor being most generous giving his own precious fluids." Danny stayed away from the word "blood." Old man Crowley didn't like printing the word in the paper, and Walter Burns backed him up. The rewrite man would only wind up taking it out.

Danny was about to call for the copy boy when his phone rang.

"Constantine."

"This is Willson. Those shots you took the other night come out?"

"I got something, yeah. Why?"

"I think we've seen our vampire again. Bring your stuff to the Great Northern yards. Colfax Avenue checkpoint."

"I'll be right there," Danny said, reaching for his hat.

Danny parked his Ford across from the checkpoint and got his camera and a manila envelope with his pictures inside out of the box in the trunk. Dooley Willson stood in the shade of a ragged maple, chewing on the end of a cigar. A railroad cop stood behind him on the other side of the gate. "That's him," Willson said, and the guard opened up the gate.

"Hello, Sergeant. Thanks for the call."

Willson tipped his head, showing the whites of his eyes. They were yellowed like old ivory piano keys, good eyes for staring someone down, and Willson was one of those guys who liked to do just that.

"You bring the pics?"

"Yeah." Danny handed the envelope to Willson. He hardly glanced at the shot of the victim, but he shoved the cigar into the corner of his mouth and stared for a long time at the eight-by-ten. On the spur just beyond the fence, a switch engine pushed three boxcars toward the train shed. Finally Willson turned the photo around toward Danny.

"How many people do you make out in this?"

"I think it's three," Danny said.

"How come?"

"That figure off to the side? It's right on the edge of those shadows, for one thing, and for another, it's wearing dark clothing. It would have had to be standing there at least ten minutes for me to have got any kind of an image. In the meantime you've got the two people together over the body, then that streak going off—that would be from the blonde hair—and the body left lying on the tracks. That's the clearest image. You see his shirttails, and the profile of his face. I'd say it was three. The victim, the murderer— and someone else who was watching them."

"Come on down here with me," Willson said.

They went through the gate and down some weathered wooden steps to the yards. Danny followed Willson up over the platform between two coupled passenger coaches. Down the siding to the left was Detective Lingeborg, swinging his legs in the open doorway of a car. Below him on cinders that were still soaked from last night's storm lay a mound covered with a tarp.

"We got a call from the yard boss about an hour ago," Willson said. "Tramp came in and showed him this." Willson took hold of the tarp, and pulled it off.

Danny swallowed hard. Underneath were two dead men. One of them was covered with dried blood. Trails of it ran from his ears and his mouth, and eye sockets, too. The other man lay with his eyes open, as though he were still looking at whatever had killed him. His face was bone white.

"Go ahead, Constantine," Willson said. "Take some pictures."

Danny loaded the flash bar, climbed up next to Lingeborg, and took a shot. He looked through the viewfinder at the man's trousers, but they were buttoned. He got down, took another one from ground level. When he finished, Willson covered up the bodies again.

"Man on the left's a bleeder," Willson said. "And lying right on top of him's a man who don't have a drop of blood left in his body. What do you make of that, Constantine?"

"Maybe this is your vampire right here," Danny said, pulling the exposed film pack out of the camera and putting it into his pocket.

"How so?"

"Let's say he was a chronic who got it into his head that he could cure himself if he drank fresh blood."

"Maybe. Except this guy wasn't chronic. Look at the bastard. He's acute. Popped like a fucking tick."

Just then Francis Lingeborg came down the siding, holding a frightened-looking tramp by the arm.

"Look what I found, Dooley," the big Swede said. "This is the guy who tipped the yard bulls."

"Well, well, well," Willson said, shoving his cigar into the other corner of his mouth. "What's your name, 'bo?"

"You didn't tell me I had to talk to no nigger!" the tramp complained, looking up at Lingeborg.

Slowly, Willson took the cigar out of his mouth. He let it drop. "We don't have to talk, 'bo. We can do *this*—"

He stepped up and dug an uppercut deep into the tramp's gut. The tramp fell to his knees and began puking on the cinders as Lingeborg looked on approvingly.

"What the hell are you doing!" Danny said, stepping between Willson and the tramp.

"I'm working here, Constantine," Willson said, staring at him hard with those piano-key eyes. "You don't want to get in my way when I'm working."

"Don't hit him anymore," Danny said, trying to keep his voice even.

"Did you hear that, Francis?" Willson said, raising his voice to address Lingeborg, who had returned to his seat in the open boxcar, but all the time keeping his eyes locked on Danny's. "This pecker-wood says don't hit him."

Behind him, Danny heard Lingeborg let out a harsh burst of laughter. He knew that if he gave any ground now he'd never get anything from Willson again. Danny could feel how close Willson was to exploding, but he made up his mind to stand there and take it, whatever it was.

Then, abruptly, Willson smiled. "I don't have to hit him again. Do I, you trash-talking, rail-riding piece of shit?"

"N-no," the hobo said weakly, spitting on the ground.

"Get up."

As the tramp struggled to his feet, Willson pulled a pint of rye whisky out of his pocket, yanked the top off with his teeth, and offered the bottle to the tramp, who took a long drink and then wiped the side of his mouth with his sleeve.

"What's your name?" Willson said.

"Wall-Eye."

"I said your *name.* Not your moniker."

"Earl," he said. "Earl Larsen."

"Write that down, Francis. Earl Larsen. Is that s-o-n or s-e-n?" The tramp glared at Willson, who went on cheerfully: "I only ask because people make that mistake all the time with me. Hey, maybe we're related, you and me."

"I ain't no—" he began, but thought better of it.

"What was that?"

"Nothin'," Larsen said miserably.

"That's right. Nothin. Just like you are."

"Shot's what I am!" Larsen cried.

"Yeah?" Willson pulled on the torn fabric of Larsen's sleeve and had a look at the arm. "Grazed your shoulder."

"It's deep! An' it hurts like hell. I musta lost a quart o' blood."

Willson picked up the cigar, brushed the grit off the wet end, and busied himself relighting it.

"Ain't you even gonna ask who shot me?"

Abruptly, Willson's eyes bored in on the tramp. He leaned over and lifted the tarp off the bodies again.

"You know these two men, 'bo?"

"Oh, God—"

"Better answer quick, Earl," Lingeborg said from the boxcar.

"One of 'em's a 'bo I was riding with the last couple o' days. Sailor Jack. T'other fella came around last night. Dakota Pete's his monica."

"How well did you know them?"

"Jack was my pal. Pete I seen around th' yards."

"You with either of 'em last night?"

"Jack and me was staying here. Pete, he came up, so we gave out with some grub. Then we seen he was sick. He got it right there in front of us. I ain't ever seen it that bad before. Spitting blood out all over th' place. He fainted, or maybe he just died, but Jack said we had to get him out o' there. So we pulled him onto a handcar and took him out here to the edge o' the yard. We were gonna put him in that car."

"But you didn't get him on it?"

"No . . ." Larsen looked scared.

"Why?"

"Because a lady came out here, that's why."

"A lady? You mean another tramp?"

"No. A fine lady. Wearin' a dress! She came up to Jack and kissed him right on the mouth, an' Jack told me to get the hell out of there so he could f—"

"Watch that mouth, 'bo," Willson warned.

"Okay, okay! Just don't hit me no more."

Willson glanced at Danny and held his open hands up.

"This lady," he said. "What did she look like?"

"Small. Blonde hair, silver-like. To tell you the truth, I thought she was kinda horse-faced."

"Awfully discriminating, ain't you, Earl?"

"I know what I like, if that's what you mean."

"Okay, go on."

"I go off. But I was watchin' 'em, you know? And they's standing out in the rain kissin' and all of a sudden, she does somethin' to him, and he goes down like he was shot. One minute he's standin', next he's on th' ground."

"What did she do?"

"I'm not sure. Looked like she was holdin' something to th' back of his head."

"Gun?"

"I didn't hear no gun."

"Take a look at him, Francis," Willson said.

Lingeborg went over, crouched down, and lifted the tarp. "No bullet wound to the head," he said.

"Okay. Go on, Earl."

"I run up to see if he's all right and this lady—hell, you can't call her no lady—was bent over 'im, suckin' on his neck! I tried to grab her away and she turns around and growls at me like a cat what's got a chicken bone! An' I look down at Jack, and see his eyes is open, and they're lookin' up at me, I can see how scared he is, but he don't talk and he don't move. He's lyin' there the same as he is now."

"So he was still alive."

"Yeah. An' they's blood all down his neck. It was rainin' straight down and hard and some of it washed away. But it couldn't wash it all. Seein' him like that . . . well, it made me want to kill her, that's all. I pulled her off him and got my hands 'round her throat like this—" He formed a circle with his hands to demonstrate. "I was chokin' her, and chokin' her, 'til I squeezed blood outta *her* mouth! I woulda killed her all right, but that's when *he* shows up."

"Who showed up?" Willson asked.

"A man all dressed fine, like th' lady was. Comes outta nowhere, like a ghost. Looks me straight in th' eyes and says, calm-like, 'Come here.'" The tramp shook his head. "I'll never forget how he said that. Somethin' about 'im scared me even worse than that lady. Like he was the devil or somethin'. I beat it outta there. He took a couple o' shots at me, though, an' caught me in th' shoulder. I know I'd be dead for sure if th' good lady from the mission hadn't come for me today!"

"You know what I think," Lingeborg said, straightening up.

"What do you think?" Willson said.

"I think he done his pal in himself. Then winged his arm to make it look good."

"Come on, Swede. Nobody shoots himself in the arm," Willson said. "If this 'bo wanted to make it look good he woulda shot himself in the *mouth.*"

Larsen groaned then, and sagged. Danny caught his arm to keep him from falling.

"You boys ought to take a little better care of your only witness," Danny said. "Look at the blood on his coat. He's going to die on you if you don't get that shoulder looked at."

"There he goes again. Why don't you mind your own business—" Lingeborg began, but Willson cut him off.

"Shut up, Swede," Willson said. "Where we gonna take him? County's packed. There ain't a doctor or a bed."

"They have a doctor over at the Lutheran Mission," Lingeborg said. "Let's have him looked at there."

"Okay."

"Mind if I tag along?" Danny said.

"Don't you got nothing better to do?"

"Nope."

"Well, find something."

"Aw, come on, Sergeant. Give me a break."

"You got a hearing problem?" Willson asked ominously. Danny looked at the two cops. Willson and Lingeborg standing together made a wall.

"Okay, boys. Have it your way."

"Let him out," Willson said to the yard bull. The bull and Danny started back toward the gate.

Willson called after him, "Come 'round and see me with those new pictures, Constantine. We don't got a photographer anymore."

"Maybe I will," Danny said.

"I'll give you something when you do," Willson promised.

"Yeah," Danny said. "You do that."

CHAPTER

10

When the yard bull let him out, Danny started the
Ford, backed up half a block, parked in the shade,
and waited. He didn't have to wait long before Willson
and Francis came up with the tramp between them, supporting
himself with his arms around the two cops' shoulders. Willson let
the Swede hold on to him, got his car, and loaded them into the
backseat. They started off, Danny following them to Hennepin. As
soon as the cops crossed Fourth Street, Danny cut over to Portland,
crossed Washington, and drove around to the back of the Milwaukee
Road depot.

The depot had closed down two years ago, and last summer the
Lutheran Mission had taken over the waiting room and offices for its
relief operation. Part of the mission's work was under contract to the
Greater Northwest Development Company, assisting Negro settlers
who had been recruited from other cities. The mission also provided
medical care, food, temporary shelter for the needy, and, Danny
knew, transportation out of town for transients, as well as for settlers
who after evaluation by GNDC social workers were deemed undesir-
able.

Danny went in through a door under a peeling sign indicating this
was once the entrance to the freight claim room. As usual, the
mission was very busy. There was a line of people waiting for a lunch

of turkey soup, bread, and an apple, and another line waiting to be seen by the doctor and the two nurses who assisted him. Danny sat down behind a desk and waited for Willson to bring the tramp in.

"Whoever's in my chair get out of it now," a woman said, coming over with a big stack of file folders clamped in place under her chin. Danny got up.

"Sorry," he said, and took the folders from the woman, setting them down.

"Thank you," she said.

"You're welcome," he replied, his attention still on the doors. Then, glancing at the woman, he felt an instant of shock. If the hair had been a dark brown rather than auburn, this woman might have been a double for Sonja, his dead wife. But he *knew* her, and tried for a moment to think of how he could, and then remembered the luncheon at the Interlachen Club.

"Why, Mr. Constantine. You really *do* get around."

Danny flushed. It was Selena Crockett. He touched his neck involuntarily as he remembered her kissing him. She noticed him doing it, and laughed.

"Did I hurt you or something?"

"No," Danny managed to say, embarrassed.

"Good." Selena began looking through the file folders. Really, if she hadn't spoken, Danny might not have recognized her. She had changed to a green cardigan worn over a plain, pale green cotton dress, and her hair was gathered into a loose ponytail. Stray wisps of it hung damply over her eyes. It was stuffy in the waiting room, and the big ceiling fans beating slowly overhead weren't doing much good. Here at the mission, there was nothing of the heiress about her at all. She looked like an ordinary secretary or a teacher or a salesgirl.

Just then Willson and Lingeborg came into the depot with the tramp.

"Miss Crockett?" Danny said.

"Please call me Selena," she said, reading one of the files.

"There's a couple of cops who just came in with a tramp they arrested at the rail yards. I'd like to sit in while your doctor looks him over, if I could."

She closed the folder and looked up at him. "Why?"

"Well, they were a little rough with him and he's not in very good shape. He was shot—" he started to explain, but Selena was already on her way over to the clinic area.

"Hello, Sergeant Willson," she said.

"Miss Crockett."

"Who do we have here?"

"Tramp name of Earl Larsen," Willson said.

"Hello, Mr. Larsen," Selena said.

" 'Lo, Miss," Larsen said, glancing furtively at her.

"This man has lost a considerable amount of blood," the doctor said. He was cutting away the sleeve of Larsen's jacket.

"Oww!"

"Could you help me, please, Selena?" the doctor said. "Some hot water and gauze?"

"Of course, Dr. Cramer." She went to a counter and returned with an enameled pan full of steaming water. She clamped a gauze pad in forceps, dipped it in the water, and dabbed at the dried blood that was holding Larsen's sleeve to the wound.

"That's not too hot, is it?" Selena asked.

"Could be cooler," Larsen replied.

"Shut your mouth, Earl," Willson growled.

"Now, Sergeant. I asked the man a question, after all. There, is that better?"

"Yes, ma'am."

Carefully, Selena got the cloth away and swabbed the wound clean while Dr. Cramer examined the back of Larsen's shoulder.

"I don't see an exit wound," the doctor said, picking up a probe from a tray. "This is going to smart a bit." Gently, he inserted the probe into the wound. Larsen winced, but Selena took his hand and smiled reassuringly. There was a scraping sound.

"It feels like fragments," Cramer said. "They'll have to be removed. And they may have hit bone."

"Can you do it?" Willson said.

"Not here."

"Why not?"

"We'll need an X ray, for one thing."

"Can't you just clean it up as best you can?"

"There's too great a risk of infection."

"How about doing the job for us over at County?"

"Impossible," Cramer said.

"I could arrange something with the Institute," Selena said.

"Like what?" Willson asked.

"They've a fine hospital. I'm sure they'd dress his wound for you."

"Not on your life," Willson said.

"Why not?"

"He's in custody."

"He's a witness to a murder," Danny said.

"Who let you in here?" Willson said disgustedly.

"Which is it, Sergeant?" Selena asked. "Is he a witness, or your prisoner?"

"He's under protective custody."

"And does protective custody entail not having his wound attended to properly?"

"You heard the doc. Things are backed up at County."

"Then let me take him to the institute. He'll be looked after, and when he's been treated you can have him back."

"We can't do that, ma'am," Willson said.

"Nonsense. I'll take him there now. You've a car here, don't you, Mr. Constantine?"

"Sure—"

"Then it's settled. Mr. Constantine will drive us there." The doctor was wrapping Larsen's shoulder in a dressing; Selena went over to some bins that were filled with donated clothing, and came back with a jersey that she helped the tramp slip on over his head.

"Do you want a receipt, Sergeant? I'll be glad to write one out for you."

"No, I don't need no—"

"Where's your car, Mr. Constantine?"

"Right out back."

"Well, then, come along, Mr. Larsen. Sergeant? Good day."

"I'll see you later, Constantine!" Willson said, yanking his cigar out of his mouth and pointing it at him. "You got that?"

Danny grinned at him, lifted his hands helplessly, and followed Selena outside.

They helped Larsen into the car, then drove across the river on the Hennepin Avenue Bridge. As the tires thrummed over the grated deck, Danny glanced over at her. It was uncanny how much she looked like Sonja. She even sat back in the seat the same way, enjoying the feeling of the wind blowing her hair back.

"Damn," Danny said, starting to laugh.

"What's so funny, Mr. Constantine?"

" 'Do you want a receipt'," Danny said. "That's rich!"

"Well? I *would* have given him one."

"Do you have any idea what you just did? You pried a murder witness off Dooley Willson."

"So?"

"So?" Danny shook his head. "You really don't care, do you?"

"Not much," she said, and smiled. Her smile was like Sonja's, too. All of a sudden he began to feel a dull ache deep inside, one that he hadn't felt for a long time. Danny had locked the pain of his wife's death away, and had gone on with his life, doing everything he'd done before. Except that he stayed away from women as much as he could. Women stirred things up inside him. *All* of them, not just this one, reminded him of Sonja in different ways, and Danny tried to handle it like a dipsomaniac who allowed himself one drink a month. When he was around women and felt the old memories stirring, he would go home. There he steeled himself, and made sure there was nothing and no one else around who might distract him, and finally, when he was absolutely sure he was alone and could concentrate, *then* he would let himself remember.

Now, though, with Selena Crockett, there hadn't been any time to prepare. And yet here he was, riding in a car with a woman who looked so much like his dead wife, and *who had kissed him*—and it wasn't killing him. In fact, he was enjoying himself.

When Sonja started bleeding that awful March night, Danny had almost gone out of his mind. He'd always been crazy about her anyway—too crazy, some of his friends thought, and then many of the friends had died or moved away and only Sonja had been left, and then she had died, too. That had been in the second wave of Hun in '26. The wave that had knocked the whole world on its keyster for good. Back then there had been nights when he had almost decided to kill himself. Once he had gone so far as to open the oven and turn on the gas, but in the end it wasn't any good. It was in Danny Constantine's nature to try to hold on. If you were still healthy you had to go on living and try to do a good job of it, and that was what Danny had done. Getting worked up couldn't bring Sonja back. Anyway, all the experts said you were more likely to catch Hun if you went around worked up all the time. You didn't want your blood to boil. That's when Hun got you.

"What's this place we're going to, miss?" Larsen asked, looking out at the big empty houses that lined Riverside Avenue, south of the university. Many of the lawns had gone to scrub, and hedges had grown wild over the windows and dangling shutters. Squatters lived in some of these places now.

"It's a special hospital where they treat blood diseases. They'll take care of your shoulder, and watch you to make sure you haven't got sick yourself."

"Can . . . can they fix me up if I do?"

Selena glanced at Danny. "They're working very hard right now to find out how to do that, Mr. Larsen. The important thing is for you not to worry. You're a healthy-looking man. Weak ones wouldn't be able to stand up to a life on the road. I know plenty of road kids, and I think they're generally much healthier than townspeople, as long as they keep the drinking down."

"Pete didn't like to drink," Larsen pointed out. "He was full-blooded Sioux. Hooch didn't agree with him."

"Don't worry, Mr. Larsen. You'll live to be a hundred."

"If I'm all right, can I go back down to the yard?"

"Of course."

Wall-Eye nodded and settled back in his seat. Danny pulled to a stop at a four-way.

"Where to?"

"Down Oak, then right on Riverside Terrace."

Her voice, too, he thought. Pleasant and smooth, with a hint of her chest in it. It was the kind of voice that came from inside a person rather than just out of her mouth. There was something awfully familiar about that, too.

"How much do you work at the institute?" Danny asked. He wanted to hear her talk some more.

"Three evenings a week."

"What do you do?"

"Oh, I'm a nurse's aide. I was trained as a VAD during the war."

"Really? You don't look that old."

"Thank you very much!" she said, laughing.

Danny flushed. "I didn't mean—"

"I know what you meant. I'm twenty-eight, Mr. Constantine. To save you the trouble of looking up my debut in the back issues of the paper."

Danny drove along.

"Oh, dear," she said. "It seems I've got a positive knack for embarrassing you, don't I?"

"You're not embarrassing me."

"I did at the luncheon, though."

"Well. It's not often I get one planted on me by somebody I just met."

"But that's just it! I was sure you'd remember me."

"Remember you?"

She looked at him. *"Don't* you remember me?"

"You're the kind of girl who makes an impression on a guy."

"Maybe not," she said. "You're positive you don't remember?"

"Look, miss, I swear if I remembered you I'd say so!"

"Well, then! It was my mistake, and I'm sorry I was so forward."

"It was okay," Danny said with a grin.

She smiled back at him. Then: "How did you like Simon's speech?"

"He gives a good talk."

"It's the least of his talents," Selena said. "He's a great man. Simply one of the best surgeons who's ever lived, not to mention the foremost hematologist, and the recognized expert on hemorrhagic fever."

"But can he sing?" Larsen said, from the back.

"Say, that's pretty good, 'bo," Danny said, laughing.

"Well, as a matter of fact, he *can* sing. And play the piano beautifully. Why, he's got the most beautiful hands I have ever seen. If you could ever see him operate—"

"Sounds like you've seen plenty," Danny said.

"Why, Mr. Constantine. Is that a sour remark?"

"Sorry. It's just I had a little run-in with him today."

"About the picture, you mean? Well, everyone's entitled to his idiosyncrasies. If a man doesn't want his picture taken, isn't that his privilege?"

"You're asking the wrong guy."

"There's the gate," Selena said.

Danny pulled into a drive, and a uniformed guard stepped out of a gatehouse and looked into the car.

"Hello, Jerry," Selena said.

"Afternoon, Miss Crockett."

"I've got one patient and a guest with me today. This is Mr. Constantine and Mr. Larsen."

The guard wrote the names down on a clipboard, and handed out three metal badges. "Please wear these when you're on the premises. Good to see you again, Miss Crockett. Drive right in." He touched two fingers to his hat brim, and threw an electric switch that swung the heavy, spike-topped gates open, and Danny drove up the sweeping, graveled drive. The grounds were thick with trees; there was a pond covered with lily pads. Men in coveralls were spraying the water with oil to keep the mosquitoes down. At the crest of a slight rise, the drive came out of the trees and crossed a velvety lawn. Ahead of them was the institute. It was a big building, two wings of four gables each, and a five-story, central structure with bay windows that rose above a vaulted, steel and glass drive-through portico. Danny began to turn toward it.

"Go around to the back. That's where the hospital receiving is."

"Okay."

Behind the institute was a parking lot and a stretch of lawn that ran to the edge of the river. Beneath the line of trees that shaded the bank was a small, drum-shaped building topped by a cast-iron dome. He saw a sign indicating the receiving zone, and parked next to it.

"I'll take Mr. Larsen inside and get him admitted. Could you wait?"

"How long will it take? I've got to get back to the office pretty soon." Danny was getting anxious to write up the story of the latest murder. Burns had promised him some play on the next one and now he had it.

"Don't you want to have a look around? This is a wonderful place."

"Maybe some other time," Danny said.

She seemed disappointed for a moment, but then brightened. "I shouldn't be more than a few minutes. Perhaps you could drop me back downtown. Come along, Mr. Larsen." She opened the door for the tramp and helped him inside. Danny lighted a cigarette and sat smoking. It was a sticky day, and the air was heavy this close to the river. After he finished the cigarette he got out of the car, took his jacket off, and decided to have a look at the domed building.

It was made of ironwork columns with red stained-glass windows. Danny peered through them and saw candles burning inside. *Must be a chapel,* he decided, and tried the door. It was locked. There was a path leading from the door to a wall along the edge of the bluff. He followed it, and found a set of stairs leading down to a boathouse on the riverbank. Across on the west side were grain elevators and the Ford plant that had been constructed and then shut down without ever having built a car. Danny lighted another cigarette and watched a barge move slowly upstream, headed to the docks downtown.

Danny liked looking at the water. This time of day it was like a ribbon of liquid gold. It would be good to shoot the river from here, he thought, making some quick calculations for exposure times. He didn't have the Dierdorff with him now, but maybe he could do something with the Graflex and an orange filter. He went back to the car, opened the camera box in the trunk, loaded a film pack, and fit the filter on the lens. He was calculating the values, composing the shot. When he wasn't working a story, he always made the shot in his head before he ever reached for the shutter release.

As he walked back toward the river, a big man with a brush haircut and a collar that looked too tight for his thick neck stopped him.

"What do you think you're doing, pal?" the man said.

"Just looking around."

"You got a badge?"

"It's in the car," Danny said.

"Didn't you see the sign? All visitors must wear a badge."

"So I'll get the badge," Danny said.

"Not so fast," the man said, catching Danny's arm. "What's with the camera?"

"Get your mitts off." Danny yanked his arm out of the man's grip.

The man smiled. "Wise guy, eh?" He folded his arms and stood with his legs spread out right in front of Danny.

"Look, I don't want any trouble. I came with Miss Crockett. She's admitting a patient here."

"What's that got to do with taking pictures?"

"I'm a photographer. I just liked the way the river looked."

"Give me the camera."

"Like hell I will!"

"Nobody takes pictures here."

"I haven't taken any yet."

"How do I know that? Give me the camera."

"Go to hell!"

"That's right, wise guy. I was hoping you'd say that."

Danny made a move to the big man's right. He thought it would be easy to get around him but the man was quick. Quicker than Danny, anyway; in a flash he was right in front of him again, crouched low and smiling, his huge arms spread wide.

"Come on, wise guy. You can do better than that."

Danny went straight at him, then rolled off, sprinting toward the chapel. He heard a grunt behind him, and the big guy caught his ankle and tripped him up. Danny sprawled forward, hitting the ground hard on his chest, the Graflex tumbling ahead of him on the grass. He rolled over and tried to catch his breath again, but the big man was already standing over him.

"Now what are you gonna do, huh?"

"Horace!"

As Danny looked up, the security man straightened and pulled on the front of his coat. "Oh. Dr. Gray. I didn't know you were in there. I'm sorry—but I caught this guy taking pictures."

"So you decided to engage in a football match."

"No, Doctor. He was just trying to get by me, that's all."

"Help him up."

The big man reached down and pulled Danny to his feet. Danny brushed himself off. There was Dr. Gray, staring coolly at him, his eyes showing no sign that he remembered who he was. But then he said, "You're that photographer from the *Journal*, aren't you?"

"Yes, sir."

Gray picked up the camera. He turned it over in his hand, examining it as though it were a child's unusual toy. Then he gave it back to Danny.

"Might I ask what you are doing here?"

"Like I was trying to tell him, I helped Miss Crockett drop a patient off here."

Something like interest crystallized in Gray's eyes. "Selena's here?"

"Yes. I gave her a lift from the mission."

"That's pleasant to hear. Horace, thank you for your vigilance. I'll vouch for the young man."

"Sure, Doctor. I'm sorry—"

"Please don't apologize. You're doing your job."

Gray took Danny's arm. "Shall we?" he said, raising his hand toward the institute. "I apologize, Mr. Constantine. Our security staff has orders to challenge anyone on the grounds not wearing an identity badge. Unfortunately, boredom sometimes causes Horace to become rather too enthusiastic in the performance of his duties. He didn't hurt you?"

"Got my heart pumping a little, that's all."

"And the camera is all right?"

"Seems to be," Danny said.

"Good."

"You were inside that building?" Danny asked.

"Yes. The chapel."

"That's what caught my eye in the first place. It's quite unusual."

"Would you care to see it?"

"Sure, if it's not any trouble."

"None at all." They went to it. Gray took a key ring out of his pocket, and unlocked the door, holding it open for Danny. Inside it was dead quiet and cool, bathed in deep red light from the stained-glass windows. The space itself was simple: a polished oak floor, a stand for votive candles, and in the center a rosewood pedestal topped with a ruby-red vigil lamp. Spaced around the perimeter of the chapel were three padded benches.

"This is where I come to think," Gray said softly. "Every man has a place like this. Whether he knows it or not."

"It reminds me of my darkroom," Danny said. "With the red light and all."

"This was a Masonic chapel. The whole facility was originally built as a sanitarium for members of the Scottish Rite. Unfortunately for them, and rather fortunately for me, the membership rolls became too diminished to support it any longer. The institute negotiated the purchase and transfer a year ago last November. I must admit it was this chapel that ultimately influenced me to agree to their terms. The moment I stepped inside for the first time, I felt an utter calm . . ."

Gray closed his eyes, smiling slightly, his face soaking up the peace even as he spoke. Then he opened his eyes and looked coolly again at Danny. "When I come out, I am refreshed. Ready for what the day may bring."

Danny listened to him and felt an attraction, like the tug of a magnet, pulling at him. Sometimes you ran into people who seemed to be able to get inside you. Gray, he could see, was the sort of man who drew followers.

"Well!" Gray said after a moment. "Shall we see how Miss Crockett is faring?"

"Sure," Danny said, waiting while Gray relocked the door. "Thanks for showing me."

"Not at all." They walked back to the institute. "So, do you intend to write an account of my speech today for the *Journal?*"

"We'll give it some play. That was a good talk you gave. Very informative."

"It ought to be old news," Gray said. "But you would be amazed, even now, twelve years after this all began, at the amount of ignorance that persists about Hun. I've found that the first way people react to tragedy is simply to ignore it. That's become rather impossible, I'm afraid, but still, many people try to fool themselves. Then, they can't ignore the situation entirely, they refashion it into something else in their minds. The amount of superstition and fear in your average citizen is truly astonishing. In some ways it is harder to fight than the disease. I hope your paper soon starts to do a better job of reporting the reality of the epidemic."

"I'm all for it," Danny said. "But, we've got to work around certain things. For instance, old man Crowley—I mean, Mr. Crowley—had the style sheet fixed so we can't use the word 'blood.'"

"Really?" Gray seemed interested suddenly. "What word do you use instead?"

"Well, I don't write about it that often, but when I do I usually say 'fluid.'"

"Fluid."

"Yes. For instance, when I write about your speech, I'll say something like, 'Dr. Gray described the types of hemorrhagic fever, and the course of its attack on the fluids of the body.'"

"Good God," Gray said. "That won't do. I shall have to have a talk with Robert about this immediately."

"I wish you would, sir, because there's another story I'm working on right now, and it's going to be a little hard to write about without using the word 'blood.'"

"Really. What story is that?"

They were at the hospital receiving entrance now, and Gray held the door open for him.

"Well, sir, I feel kind of funny talking about it in a place like this. But there's been a series of murders that were kind of violent. Actually, the man we brought in here today was a witness."

"Say no more," Gray said. "But you are right. Those types of accounts should not be suppressed, either. I'm grateful to you for bringing this problem to my attention. Ah, there she is!"

Selena Crockett stood next to the tramp, who was sitting on an examining table, wincing as a nurse swabbed his shoulder with a sponge.

"Why, Dr. Gray!" she said, blushing. "I was told you were away for the afternoon."

"Merely resting." He smiled, and took both her hands and kissed them. "It's an unexpected pleasure to see you again so soon." Watching him do it made Danny feel flushed all of a sudden.

"Must be the smell," he muttered.

"What's that, Mr. Constantine?"

"Nothing. I'm sorry. I guess I don't like hospitals much."

"You ain't the one gettin' poked," Larsen said.

"Oh, Mr. Larsen, really!" Selena said.

"It stings, that's all!"

"Better a little stinging now than a case of gas gangrene later," Gray said, bending to examine the wound. "Passed clean through, did it?"

"I've probed the wound," Gray's nurse said. "I found a slug, and possible fragments. We'll x-ray him and make sure."

"Otherwise healthy?"

"He could use a bath," the nurse said.

"Then he shall have one. What's your name?"

"Wall—" the tramp began, then, self-conscious about using his moniker in a clinical setting, said, "I mean Earl. Earl Larsen, sir."

"And how did you come to be shot, Mr. Larsen?"

Larsen blinked his eyes and shifted on the table. "Yow! Whatchoo doin' ta me?!"

"You'll have to hold still. I'm just about through."

Selena said, "It apparently happened at the rail yards last evening, Dr. Gray. He told a rather incredible story about the whole thing."

"T'ain't no story. It's the God's truth! And you're done, too!" he cried, pulling his shoulder away from the nurse, who threw up her hands and dropped the forceps she had been using into a enameled pan. "I'll tell you what happened. There's a witch out there that killed Sailor Jack. Killed 'im and drank his blood!"

"And this witch also shot at you?"

"No. There was somebody else. A man in a coat. I didn't get a good look at 'im. But he shot me, all right."

"Did you tell this story to the police?"

"I told 'em. They don't believe me, either, but I don't care. I know what I seen. I'm shot, and Jack's lyin' dead and that's all I need to know, goddamn it!"

"Nurse," Gray said, "I'll need the hypo tray."

"Yes, Doctor." She went to a cabinet and came back with a tray that was covered with a towel.

"Let us have eighty cc's of Sodium Pentothal."

As she prepared the syringe, the tramp's eyes widened. "You ain't pokin' me with no needle!"

"It's to make you relax and feel more at ease, Mr. Larsen. We can't have you squirming around as we're trying to make an X ray."

"You ain't doin' it! Miss Crockett, help me, for God's sake!"

"Mr. Larsen, you mustn't fuss this way."

"I'm gettin' out o' here—"

Larsen jumped off the table and ran toward the entrance. At the same time, the nurse moved to the counter and pressed a button on a panel underneath it. There was a buzzing sound, and a loud click. When the tramp pulled on the door, it was locked.

"Thank you, Nurse." Gray took the hypodermic and held the needle up. "Now then, Mr. Larsen, are you quite finished?"

"L-l-leave me alone," Wall-Eye said, cowering against the glass.

"Come here," Gray said coldly. He stood next to the counter holding the syringe and staring steadily at the tramp.

Wall-Eye Larsen moaned and looked wildly at Selena. "Now I know him! I remember him now! Please, Miss Crockett, for God's sake! Now I know where I seen him." He pointed at Gray with a trembling arm. *"He's* the one what shot me!"

"Mr. Larsen!" Selena said, shocked.

"It's him, all right! I thought there was somethin' funny about him, and now I know, it's th' eyes. Nobody's got eyes like that but him!"

The nurse tried to hold him, but Larsen pushed her away.

"Mr. Constantine, if you would care to assist us—" Gray said.

Danny moved in and locked his arms behind the tramp's. He was shaking like a baby. "I tell you, he done it!" Larsen wailed. "He killed Jack, an' tried to murder me!"

Gray swabbed Larsen's arm with alcohol and gave him the shot. A moment later, Larsen sagged in Danny's arms.

"Why'd you kill . . . Jack . . ." Wall-Eye said thickly, and then his head slumped forward. Gray put the needle down, and then he and the nurse got the tramp up on a gurney.

"Are you all right, Nurse?" Gray asked.

"Yes, Doctor."

"X-ray, then, and have him cleaned up."

"Right away, Doctor," the nurse replied, wheeling the gurney through a set of double doors. When she was gone, Gray turned to Danny.

"Strong-arm medicine, I'm afraid. Thank you for your help."

"It's okay. I'm getting my exercise today, though."

Gray patted him on the shoulder.

"Oh, Doctor, I'm sorry I brought him here," Selena said.

"Nonsense! I would have been quite upset if you hadn't. We'll look after him. A few days' rest, proper food—and no drink—and he'll have an entirely new outlook. Well, then. Would you two care for tea?"

"I appreciate the offer, Doctor, but I've got to get back downtown," Danny said.

"What about you, Selena? It's not often we have the opportunity to chat, when we're both so very busy."

"Mr. Constantine's my ride."

"I can have Horace drop you anywhere you like."

"Well, it *would* be nice to talk a little. If Danny doesn't mind."

Danny, Danny repeated sourly to himself. *So now all of a sudden it's* Danny.

"Why should I mind?" he said.

"It's settled, then," Gray said, taking Selena's hands and pressing them. She blushed slightly and her eyes shone. So that was it, Danny thought. She had a thing for him. This whole business of taking Earl Larsen out here, and crossing Dooley Willson in the bargain, had been done on the chance she might run into Simon Gray.

"All right, then," Danny said, and went to the door. He pulled on it, but it was locked. When he turned around, Gray was staring at him, still holding Selena's hands, and there was something in his eyes that chilled Danny to the bone. Cold, heartless malice settled there a moment, making everything else in the room—even Selena Crockett—seem pale and transparent. Then, suddenly and deliberately, Gray replaced that expression with his ironic smile.

"Thoughtless of me," he said, releasing Selena and stepping behind the counter to press the button that unlocked the door. He came forward, hand extended, and Danny shook it.

"I will be talking to Robert about your story," Gray said. "It was a pleasure to see you again."

"You, too," Danny said.

Gray held the door open for him and Danny went out. When he got into his car, and looked back and saw the two of them together, laughing about something, he decided, once and for all, that it had been a mistake to think warm thoughts about a girl like Selena Crockett. Let her play Madame Curie to his Dr. Curie, or whatever other game it was she wanted to play with Simon Gray.

To hell with him *and* her, he thought as he drove down the long, shaded drive to the gate.

*A*t the clinic door, Simon Gray watched Danny's car turn out and disappear into the shadows along the drive.

"I find it rather odd, your bringing Mr. Constantine with you today."

"I needed a lift," Selena explained quickly. "That's all. He happened to be at the mission this afternoon when the policemen brought Mr. Larsen in."

Gray did not answer right away, but kept staring out the window. Selena could feel his disapproval, though—and tried to think what she might have done to deserve it. It was always that way when she saw Simon: he seemed to be able to understand things she did not, but ought to. Perhaps disapproval was putting it too strongly. Perhaps his reaction was closer to disappointment, but she hated it anyway, and tried always to avoid making him feel that way. He made that impossible, though. Sometimes Selena felt that Simon knew where all the obstacles between them lay, and led her toward them deliberately, knowing which ones she could see and which ones she couldn't—all for the pleasure of seeing her stumble. She felt her anxiety grow, and as she tried to think of another, better explanation for why she had come with Danny, Gray turned back toward her and smiled reassuringly.

"Shall we go upstairs? It's so much cooler in my office."

"Yes, of course," she said, hoping the relief in her voice wasn't obvious. But as they rode the private elevator, Gray seemed cheerfully unconcerned. The elevator stopped, and the door opened directly into his dim, high-ceilinged study. There he went to his desk and picked up the telephone. "Yes. Tea service, please. For two. Thank you." Gray put down the instrument, and indicated Selena should sit in one of the two armchairs that were arranged on either side of a low table by a bookshelf wall.

"Was I wrong to bring him here, Simon?" Selena said all at once, so suddenly that his eyebrows rose.

"Oh, my dear! Are you still worried about that? Please don't be concerned. I did not mean to question your motives. I only made the remark because I find Mr. Constantine to be rather . . . *curious* about me of late. Do you know him well?"

"Not really. I was only introduced to him at the luncheon."

"Well, if I may say so, he seems rather to have made an impression on you."

He's done it again, Selena thought, cursing herself for blushing. "Honestly, Simon, it isn't like that at all!"

Gray peered at her, and said, "But more to the point, you seem to me to be a bit feverish in general. May I?" He leaned forward and touched her cheek with the back of his cool, smooth hand, resting it there a long moment, then brushing it softly across her skin as he withdrew it. "Have you been feeling well?"

"Of course."

"And your last menses was normal?"

"Yes. Please, you mustn't worry about me . . . *Doctor,*" she added quickly.

"But I always worry about you, my dear. You are so active, and much too generous with your time. My constant fear is that you may . . . overstrain yourself." He gazed into her eyes. "Perhaps . . ." he said, letting his voice trail.

"Yes?"

"Perhaps it is time for another treatment."

"But the next one isn't scheduled for another six months!" Selena said, in alarm. Once again, he had surprised her completely.

"We've discussed this before, my dear. You know our schedule is merely a point of reference," Gray said. "All depends on the demands you place on yourself. I'm sure you'd agree they have been high of late." There was a knock on the door. "Yes, come," he said. A maid entered, carrying the tea service. She placed it on the table and began setting it up.

"I'll take care of that, thank you," Gray said, dismissing her.

As he poured out the tea, he said, "I know how important your work is to you, Selena. And, as unpleasant as the reality of your condition is, you must think of those you help every day. What would happen to them if you became . . . incapacitated?"

"But I told you. I feel fine!"

"And we must keep it that way. As it happens, I have some free time this afternoon. And there are several paid donors with your blood type living in the dormitory now."

"Oh, Simon, I really don't think—"

"You forget, Selena, how fortunate you are that we can keep your condition in remission with these preemptive treatments. Perhaps, strictly speaking, you don't require one at the moment. But we must take advantage of opportunity where we find it. If there is an emergency later, there may not be suitable donors available. I'm speaking now as your physician," he added sternly. "Not as your friend." He went to the cabinet behind his desk, unlocked the doors, and took out a large, soft-leather case and his doctor's bag. He opened the bag, found a dark brown bottle, and, added three droppersful of a thick brown-red liquid to Selena's teacup.

"Drink it, my dear," he said soothingly, offering her the cup. "Think: by doing it now, you spare yourself six months of dread."

"It's not that I dread anything, Simon. It's only the dreams I have sometimes, afterward."

"A side effect and nothing more. You drink, you sleep deeply, and I am able to treat you. If you dream fantastic things, you mustn't take them to heart."

"Sometimes . . ."

"Yes?"

"Sometimes it feels as if I'm drowning," she said softly, eyes wide.

"Not in water, but in something warm and thick, something that fills my throat and chokes me!"

"Dreams mean nothing," Gray said, lifting the cup to her lips. "This is what is real. And you must drink it to live. That is all that matters."

Selena closed her eyes and took the warm, sweetened tea into her mouth. She felt flushed, and ashamed of herself for thinking it tasted so good.

"There," Gray said, putting the cup down, and pressing her hands between his. "Relax and let it take you. I shall be here. You have nothing to fear."

"I know, Simon," Selena said.

"It's begun. I'll go prepare the donor myself. Promise me you won't worry."

"I promise," she said, managing a smile.

"Good. The next time you see me it will all be over," he said, and went out.

She sighed sleepily, and then, sinking back into the soft leather chair, slowly let her eyes close, and tried not to think of anything.

Especially not that she wished she had left with Danny Constantine.

Back at the *Journal* offices, things were busy as the staff worked to get tomorrow's first edition into shape. It wasn't like the old days, of course. In the city room, perhaps a fourth of the desks were actually used now, the staff working clustered together in the corner of the floor opposite Walter Burns's mezzanine office. It would have been too depressing to spread out. This way, you still had the illusion that the paper was up and running with a full staff.

Danny came in, parked his straw hat atop a cast-bronze replica of the Eiffel Tower that held a pencil sharpener in its base. He rolled a sheet of paper into the Remington, and started to write:

Vampire at Work in City?
Fourth Victim Discovered in Series of Unusual Slayings

—A transient found murdered near the Colfax Avenue North entrance to the Great Northern rail yards appears to be the latest victim of a killer whose methods duplicate those of the fabled vampire, Dracula.
—The victim, known among the yard tramps as "Sailor Jack," was discovered this morning alongside the

corpse of another man who had apparently succumbed to an attack of acute hemorrhagic fever. The murder victim's corpse was found to be completely drained of fluid. Two puncture wounds marked the victim's neck.

—Sergeant Dooley Willson, of the city police major crimes section, stated that the murder was similar to one which occurred early Sunday morning on the First Street spur just outside the ruins of the Crockett A flour mill. In that incident, a man identified as 37-year-old Charles Pierce of south Milltown was discovered drained of fluid and bearing a similar set of puncture wounds to the neck. Sergeant Willson stated that the first body also had suffered ritualistic mutilation that matched that committed on the bodies of two other murder victims discovered in January and in mid-March.

—"We feel certain all these murders are related," Willson said. "The victims were transient men between the ages of 25 and 45, and the murders took place alongside railroad property."

—Willson added that the police had questioned several potential witnesses to the latest slaying, and, although he refused to discuss any clues he might have gained concerning the identity of the killer or killers, cautioned citizens against patronizing after-hours taverns, or taking late-night strolls away from the lighted streets.

Danny read it over and thought it was pretty good. Low-key, told the facts—and he had written the entire story without using the word "blood." He pulled the sheet out of the typewriter and yelled "Copy!" Jackie, the copy boy, came trotting over.

"Hiya, Jack. Get Mr. Burns to okay this right away. Oh, and this picture, too." He gave him the picture from the view camera. The shot was captioned, "Murder of motorman captured by amateur photographer."

"Gee," the copy boy said. "We've got a vampire now?"

"Wise guy. Get going."

Jackie was a high school kid working this summer to help his family out. He had an answer for everything. A lot of the kids were like that now. Especially the Negro kids, like Jackie. You couldn't blame them, though. They had every reason to think they'd be in the driver's seat soon enough.

"Hey, Sullivan," Danny called to the rewrite man. "You seen Bing around?"

"In his office," Sullivan said, jerking his thumb toward the empty half of the floor.

"Is he in or out?"

"He didn't say."

Bing Lockner's "office" was an empty storeroom on the north side of the building. Bing liked to be alone sometimes when he was working, and he'd go there. If he said he was out, you weren't supposed to bother him. If he was in, you could knock and then he might talk to you. Danny went to the door and knocked.

"Bing?"

"Yeah."

"You in or out?"

"Out. But you can come in, Connie."

Danny checked to see whether Burns might be watching from the mezzanine, then slipped inside. The lights were off, and the windows were so dirty he could hardly see Bing, who was stretched out on the old sprung couch, smoking a cigarette.

" 'Lo, Connie. Whaddya know?" He reached down to the floor and picked up a bottle. "Have a snort?"

Danny swallowed a mouthful and winced.

"Jesus, that's awful, Bing!"

"You're telling me. Remember that blind pig Timmy Rice used to run over on Loring? He gave me a case of the stuff. God, I miss Prohibition!"

"You shouldn't get stewed, Bing. Walter won't like it."

"Fuck him. Anyway, how does he know who's stewed and who isn't? He's a teetotaler."

Danny sat down on the arm of the couch next to Bing's head.

"And, I am not stewed," Bing said.

"No?"

"No. I think I must have picked up something last night. I'm not feeling so good."

"Well, take off your coat, for Christ's sake. Open a window. It's hotter than hell in here."

"We Lockners don't open windows," Bing said. "And I sleep in this coat."

"How come I believe you?" Danny said with a grin.

"No reason not to." Bing took another swig from the bottle.

"That stuff'll help your stomach, all right."

Bing put the bottle down. After a moment, he said, "Connie, did I ever tell you I got a sister up in Michigan?"

"No, Bing."

"My kid sister, Edith. She's about your age. Got a swell husband named Arn. Arn's a grocer."

"No kidding."

"Edie called me long distance today. Actually got through all the way from Niles. She told me about a little weekend trip she made to Detroit a couple of months ago. Edie says she's having a baby."

"That's great, Bing!"

"Arn ain't involved."

"Oh," Danny said.

"See, she went to see one of those brokers. The ones who make arrangements between respectable ladies who want to have healthy babies, and certain gentlemen whose job it is to make them. So now I'm about to have a little coffee-colored niece or nephew."

"That's not so bad, is it, Bing? The way things are going. At least you'll know it'll never get sick."

"Arn is not happy about it. He told her he wants a divorce."

"Aww, that's tough," Danny said.

"She wants me to come up to Niles and have a talk with him."

"You going?"

"I don't know. It ain't so easy getting to upper Michigan these days. Probably have to drive, and I don't have anybody to cover for me."

"I'll do it."

"Will you write 'Let's Poke About Town?'"

"Maybe Dorrie ought to take a vacation when you go."

"Dorrie Van der Voort doesn't take vacations. She never sleeps. She's always on the poke, see?"

"Well, if you really want to go that bad, we can talk about it," Danny said.

"Thanks, Connie. You're swell. Now, tell me about you. Get in any mah-jongg after I left?"

"Actually, I wound up at the rail yards."

"How come?"

"There was another murder."

"Same kind?" Bing asked, matter-of-factly.

"Almost," Danny said. "This time the victim's anatomy was intact."

"That's too bad," Bing said.

"There was another difference, too. There was a witness."

"Who?"

"Some road kid named Earl Larsen saw the whole thing. Said there were two people on the scene. The blonde, and a tall man in a topcoat who took a shot at him."

"You believe it?"

"The tramp had a slug in his shoulder, however it got there," Danny said.

"Cops holding him now?"

"Uh-uh. We took him over to the institute to get patched up."

"We?"

"Me and Selena Crockett."

"Selena Crockett! You got your nerve, kid, after all that talk about the rich."

"Don't worry about it. She just happened to be working at the Lutheran Mission, which is where the cops brought the tramp to get looked at first. She wanted a ride, and I had my car. Anyway," Danny said, "she and I don't get along."

"And that lipstick on your neck proves it."

"Lay off, Bing. She's sweet on Simon Gray."

"Yeah?" Bing tipped his head back to look at Danny. "How do you know she's sweet on him?"

"For one thing, she pried that witness loose from Dooley Willson just so she could bring him down to the institute and just happen to run into him. You should have seen her when she did. Practically melted into a shiny little pool right at his feet."

"Connie sounds as if he does not approve."

"*I* think he's bugs!"

"Gray?" Bing said, pretending to sound shocked. "The man's a savior. A prince. A pillar of the community. What's left of it, anyway."

"He's a creep," Danny said flatly.

"Don't stop now, kid. What kind of a creep?"

"I don't know! There's something about the way he looks at people. It's only sometimes, when he thinks they're not watching, or if he doesn't care whether they catch him or not. He drops that front you were just talking about and shows his true self. And it ain't pretty, Bing. It's like he was born to live in this plague. He loves it. He loves the suffering, all that death. He feeds on it!"

"Whew!" Bing said. "And what the hell do you say about *me*?"

"I'm serious. There's something fishy about him."

"Are you sure this ain't just sour Selena-flavored grapes?"

"You knew Gray in Detroit, didn't you?"

"Yeah. He had a clinic there when I was still working for the *Free Press*. When there still was a *Free Press*. Or a Detroit."

"Why'd he leave?"

"Why don't you ask that same question to the other three million former citizens."

"What about Dorrie? Doesn't she have any dirt on the guy?"

"Well, Dorrie *does* know a little," Bing admitted.

"Let's have it."

"He graduated from Harvard. Played tackle and right end and gave transfusions to the football team. Once performed a cranial trephination on the forty-yard line. Transplanted a pig bladder into the fullback and saved his life. Now the wife has to blow fullback's head up every morning, but she doesn't mind. She's Catholic. She was Episcopalian before the operation. Gray takes credit for that, too. What else do you want to know?"

"Maybe I'll come back when Bing sobers up," Danny said. He got up from the couch.

"You going to the ball game tonight?"

"Tonight?"

"Yeah. This guy Willkinson, who owns that Negro team in KC, brought 'em up here to play the Millers tonight. He's got these portable lights that he carries around in a couple of trucks. They set up poles with floodlamps on 'em and light a whole field bright as day. They're going to stay in town a while, 'til the league figures out what it's going to do about Toledo and Louisville and the Blues, too. I guess things ain't so good down in Kansas City these days. Come up and sit in the press box with me?"

"You won't be at any game. You'll be sleeping it off."

"Watch me," Bing said. "I sleep it off *before* I start."

"I'll tell the boys you're out," Danny said.

"You do that, Connie. I'll see you tonight."

Danny went back to his desk. Lying there was his copy with the word *NO!!!* scrawled across it in blue pencil.

"Why, that no good son of a bitch!" he said, looking around for Jackie, and finding him over by the water cooler.

"Jackie, come here."

The copy boy came over.

"What's the big idea?"

"Burns took one look and blue-penciled it," the copy boy said, a little sheepishly.

"Did he read it?"

"Nobody reads that fast," Jackie said.

Danny grabbed the copy, went up the mezzanine stairs and straight into Burns's office.

"What's this 'no,' Walter?"

"Just what it says," Burns said, looking up over the top of his reading glasses.

"You promised you'd give me some play."

"I said I'd *think* about it."

"No, you said if there was one more murder. And now there's been one."

"Well, it came too damn quick. And what the hell do you mean barging into my office?"

"Walter, now we've got a witness who says our killer's a beautiful woman with platinum-blonde hair, possibly assisted by a tall man in a long coat."

"That wasn't in your copy."

"Dooley Willson wanted that part off the record. I'll call him and see if he'll let me put it in."

"The answer's still no."

"Why?!"

"You want to know why? I'll tell you! County Hospital reported thirteen new cases of acute Hun on Sunday. Eight so far today. It's starting up again, and I refuse to let this newspaper contribute to the panic. If we're going to get it again, by God, we'll take it and keep order at the same time. No riots. No lynchings!"

"This is murder, Walter. It's got nothing to do with people getting sick."

"Goddamn it, Constantine, it's blood! People have had it up to here with blood. They don't want to see it, they don't want to hear about it, and they certainly don't want to be reading about it over supper!"

"You said you want a normal life around here. If things were normal this would be all over the front page."

"If things were normal you'd be chasing pictures. You wouldn't be up here pressuring me about stories I've no intention of printing."

"It's not right, Walter."

Burns took off his glasses. "Don't you come up here and tell me what's right. I've got thirty men who depend on this newspaper for a living. If nobody reads it, they don't work, and that includes you. Just because I'm shorthanded does not mean you're indispensable. I got a call about you this afternoon from Crowley. He tells me you were rude and pushy at that luncheon today. He wants to know what I'm going to do about it!"

"What'd you tell him?"

"I told him you're a good man. But you've got to lay off, see? I can't afford to lose you. Forget about this vampire business! A lot of these sick killers only live for the ink they get, anyway. Maybe he'll quit if he doesn't get any publicity."

"*She* hasn't had any."

"Find a cat burglar, for Christ's sake. People always admire a cat burglar."

"Cat burglar," Danny began, then stopped. All of a sudden he had an idea. "What about a feature piece on Simon Gray?"

"Gray?"

"That's right. You say you want to reassure people. If they read a good piece about the institute, they'll have the feeling something's finally being done. Especially if they get the idea about the kind of man Gray is."

"I don't know," Walter said, rubbing his jaw. "I'll have to run that by Crowley."

"I was out at the institute today. They look like they're going pretty good. Maybe now's the time."

"Okay. I'll talk to the old man about it. I can't guarantee he'll want to do it, or want you to do it if he says okay. Like I said, he's not too happy with you right now."

"I'll make him forget all about that," Danny said.

"We'll see." Danny started out. "Oh, by the way, Constantine?"

"Yeah?"

"Do me a favor and tell Lockner to get his ass out of that goddamned closet?"

"Sure, Walter," Danny said.

13

*G*AME TONIGHT! HISTORIC FIRST!! BASEBALL UNDER THE LIGHTS!!! WORLD FAMOUS KC MONARCHS v. MILLERS!!!!" read the banner stretched above the gabled, tile-roofed grandstand box office of Nicollet Field. There were lines of curious fans at all the ticket windows. For the local baseball fans, this exhibition game was a reprieve after the depressing news about the suspension of the American Association season. It appeared that the novelty of Monarch boss Wilkerson's fleet of light trucks, and the first appearance of the Negro baseballers in Milltown in several years, would make for close to a sellout crowd. This despite the rumors that were sweeping through town about a fresh outbreak of Hun.

It was strange. In the first waves of the epidemic, people avoided the ballpark for fear of catching the disease. Now it seemed as if the desire to go out in spite of everything, and to sit together with as many people as you could, was stronger than fear of Hun. Maybe if you came to the ballpark and sat with a couple of thousand other people, you could forget about it for a few hours, anyway.

Danny waited in line with Shirley Lund and Kal Hromatka from the boardinghouse. Shirley looked nice in the new print dress and black tam Mrs. Lund had made for her. She was a little warm in her cotton stockings, but they did hide the wraps on her legs. And she was excited about the game. Danny had lent her his old catcher's mitt and she swore for sure, she'd get a foul ball tonight.

"They're good, aren't they, Dan?" Shirley said. "The Monarchs, I mean."

"Yeah, they are. They've got Bullet Rogan pitching for them."

"I saw him pitch for the Twenty-fourth Infantry team right after the war," Kal said. "Christ, he could throw! And hit."

They were moving up to the ticket window. The man in front of them bought a ticket, looked at it, and shoved it back through the grate.

"That's the colored section," the man said. "Do I look colored to you?"

"Sorry, mister, it's open seating tonight."

"What do you mean, 'open'?"

"It means there ain't any colored section tonight. Anybody sits anyplace they want to."

"Well, I don't want to sit in the colored section."

"That's what I got in bleachers, mister. You want to pay for the grandstand?"

"Hell, no!"

"Suit yourself," the ticket seller said, sliding the man's quarter back to him. "Next!"

"You don't mind about the seating, do you, Kal?" Shirley asked anxiously.

"Mind what?" Kal said. Danny smiled and clapped him on the back, paid for three field-level tickets, and took them in. Under the stands you could smell beer and steaming chicken dogs and roasted peanuts. They came up the ramp, and found their seats up behind the Millers' dugout. In the outfield, a crew was pulling on cables to hoist one of the light towers, which was mounted in the bed of a truck parked in the alley back of Lake Street and the left-field fence. Once they got it up, they secured it with guy wires attached to stakes pounded into the grass. In deep center, a noisy generator truck provided power, cables snaking around the warning track at the perimeter of the field. While the first crew finished pounding the stakes, another crew draped a white canvas backdrop over the whole outfield fence.

"What's that for?" Shirley asked.

"Probably to help the players see better once it gets dark."

"Hey, there's Lou. Lou!" she said, waving. "Louie, we're up here!"

The third baseman, who had been playing catch with one of his teammates, waved back and jogged over to the end of the dugout. He looked glum.

"How you folks doin'?" he asked.

"Okay," Danny said. "What's the matter?"

"I'm out fifty bucks, that's what. I got into it with Kelly before the game."

"What for?"

"Me and a few of the boys had a meetin' this afternoon. We don't like them bringing these coons into town."

"It's just an exhibition. You've played against a lot of these boys before."

"Yeah, I know, but it's different this time. They're sticking around. Us and them and the Saints are playing round-robin for a few weeks. After that, Kelly says, they're gonna fill up any slots open from players that get sick with Monarchs. They're gonna fill the whole circuit that way. Indy's already filling in with nigger players from the ABC's."

Danny hated to hear the kid talk that way in front of Shirley. Lou was a good kid, but he had a big chip on his shoulder when it came to the race question. A lot of people felt that way, especially the ones who had been hit hard by Hun. When you've had plenty of bad luck, it didn't seem right that it wasn't spread around equally. But he hated to hear it, all the same.

"Go easy, Lou. Just the other day you were crying because the league was going to shut down. This way, you're still playing ball, right? Maybe these night games'll catch on. People can come after work. The more people in the seats, the more chance you'll keep getting paid to play ball."

"I'll need a raise, to pay that fifty. Gee, Kelly let me have it!"

"Maybe he was right."

Lou's eyes flashed. "He ain't right. The whole thing stinks!"

"Ravelli! Stop yappin' and get out to third, we're takin' infield," the manager yelled.

"Just try to forget about it, Lou," Danny said.

"Yeah. Hit me a foul ball. Please?"

"Kelly charges us four bits every time we hit one out of play, Shirl."

"Here," Kal said, handing Lou a fifty-cent piece.

"Ravelli!"

"Yeah, yeah, keep your shirt on, I'm comin'! You folks enjoy the game. We'll murder 'em!"

Lou jogged over to third. His coach swung a long fungo bat and hit a sharp liner right at his knees. Lou knocked it down, pounced on it, and threw high over the first baseman's head.

"That's ten more, Ravelli!" the coach yelled, pointing with the bat.

"Maybe Lou ought to quit," Shirley said. "He can't afford to play, at this rate."

"He's taking the whole thing pretty hard, isn't he," Danny said.

"He never left his room all day. Not for breakfast or for lunch, and Aunt Lucille made chicken croquettes just to try and coax him out."

"He's just worried, that's all," Kal said.

"He's been acting awfully queer."

"Well, he's had it tough with his parents and all."

"So have I," Shirley said. "And I don't act queer, do I?"

Danny smiled. "No, I guess you don't."

They went back up to their seats. Kal bought some peanuts and beer, and a pop for Shirley. Danny sat back and watched the Millers' infield drill. They were a pretty good outfit this year, with Nick Cullop playing center and hitting them out regularly, and Carmen Hill showing plenty of stuff on the mound. Before the Association shut down, they'd been leading Louisville by four games and Columbus by six with just twelve contests left before the first half closed out.

Out in the infield, Lou settled down, and handled all his chances without a hitch. They finished with the double play, each man fielding a bunt and coming off the field after he threw to first.

Next the Monarchs came out for their drills, and they really made a show of it, lining up behind second as their coach hit alternate shots to the left and right of the bag, each man standing where he'd fielded the ball until all the players had taken one. Then the coach hit a fungo straight up in the air, and while it hung there, the Monarchs, on cue, ran out to their positions, and got there before the ball landed in front of the mound, where Frank Duncan, the catcher, grabbed it and threw to Newt Allen covering second, who fired it home to Rogan, Rogan pivoting and smoking a throw down to third that was caught right at the corner of the bag; Joseph wheeling and sidearming it to first on a rope about three feet over the grass to the first baseman, who relayed it home. For ten minutes, that ball never stopped moving. When they were through, the Monarchs left the field to appreciative applause and some boos.

"Those fellas know how to enjoy themselves, don't they?" Kal said, laughing. "I'll bet that got our boys good and steamed."

"Why would it get them steamed, Kal?" Shirley asked.

"Because they're showing the Millers up, that's why. They want 'em steamed. That way, they're not concentrating on playing ball. All they want to do is get even."

"Aren't you rooting for Lou's team?"

"I don't care who wins, so long as it's a good game," Kal said.

A brass band out behind the third-base line played the national anthem, the PA announcer gave the starting lineups, Ferdie Schupp went out on the mound for the Millers, and the game began. Right away he gave up a double to Allen, who then stole third and scored on a sacrifice fly to right by Giles. The fourth hitter, Newt Joseph, got up there, and on a 2–0 count hit a homer that bounced off the light tower in left-center. Schupp threw down his glove in disgust as the Monarch rounded the bases, waving to the Negro fans sitting behind his dugout. That prompted a chorus of boos from the whites sitting around them.

"How come they're booing?" Shirley asked. "Didn't he just hit one out?"

"They don't appreciate him waving like that."

"Why not?"

"Because you're supposed to be humble when you do something good in this game," Kal said. "You're supposed to run around the bases with your head down. Like you just found out your girl ran off with your best friend."

"That's a funny way of looking at something good."

"Otherwise they call it showboating. But I'd be laughing, too. That was a tough drop he just hit."

Schupp bore down after that and got the side out, and in the Miller half of the inning, Rogan walked the first two men on close pitches. That brought up Cullop, the big center fielder, who surprised the Monarch infield and himself by laying down a perfect bunt. The ball died on the chalk halfway between home and third, with Joseph, Rogan, and the catcher all standing over it. Then Rogan got down on his knees and tried to blow it foul. The umpire came out and told him to get back on the mound because it looked like he had his work cut out for him. Standing up there, yelling at Rogan to pitch to him, was Lou Ravelli.

"Oh, does Louie want to bust one!" Kal said. "Look at him pound the plate!"

Rogan pretended to argue with his infielders, then pointed at Lou and shook his head like he couldn't stand to go back to the mound. They had to practically shove him back there.

"Throw the damn ball!" Ravelli yelled.

"What you gonna do with it?" Rogan yelled back.

"Throw it and you'll find out."

"All right. Yes sir. Coming right up, sir!"

Rogan went into his stretch and threw a fastball right down the middle of the plate. Ravelli watched it go by.

"Never even saw it," Kal said.

"He wasn't going to take his bat off his shoulder," Danny said.

Rogan shrugged and threw another one just like it. Again, Ravelli observed it. Now Rogan turned to his infielders. "One more?" he asked.

"Sure," Joseph said from third. "All he does is look."

"Well, all right, then," Rogan said.

He looked back in, went into his stretch, and threw a rainbow lob that hung up there for what seemed like half a minute, then dropped down fat as a grapefruit. Lou swung right through it, yelling his head off, and headed for the mound with the bat in his hand. Frank Duncan tackled him from behind, and the players streamed off both benches like ants when you spaded out a nest. There was a lot of shoving and a few punches for show, and then some general milling around for a few minutes before the umpires could restore order. When the game started again, Rogan walked in a run, and then threw a sinker to Emmer that the shortstop grounded to second for a double play.

"Where's Lou?" Shirley asked when the Millers took the field.

"Oh, he won't be playing anymore today."

"Why not?"

"Because the ump threw him out of the game."

"Why'd they throw him out?"

"Because he ran down the pitcher with a bat in his hand."

"You can't do that?"

"You're not supposed to," Danny said.

"That Rogan," Kal said. "He knows what to do with a hothead!"

"I'm going to walk around a little," Danny said. "Do you two want anything?"

"Can I come with you? I want to look at how they work those lights."

"I'll keep your seats warm," Kal said.

Danny and Shirl walked around the front of the grandstand behind home plate. Then, on the Monarch side, at the top of the stands below one of the light towers, Danny spotted Dooley Willson sitting with his wife and two sons, and went over to him.

"Hello, Sergeant. Enjoying the game?"

Willson glanced at him. His eyes narrowed. Then he looked away.

"Dooley!" his wife said. "The man just said hello to you."

"I heard him," Willson said.

"I'm Danny Constantine," Danny said. "I work for the *Journal.*"

"*Ohh,*" Mrs. Willson said, suddenly understanding everything. Then, brightening, she stood and offered her hand. "I'm Della Willson. And these boys are Marcus and James."

"This is my landlady's niece, Shirley Lund."

"How do you do," Mrs. Willson said, smiling warmly. She had

kind, lively eyes and a nice smile. The two boys, who looked to be about five and seven years old, peeked shyly up from behind the bags of popcorn they held in their laps.

"Excuse me," Shirley said, looking at Della Willson's collar. "Is that a silver fox?"

"Sure is, honey."

"May I?"

"Go right ahead."

Shirley reached down to stroke the fur gently with the back of her hand.

"They still got teeth," Marcus said.

"No, they don't!"

"Yeah. Look." He pressed on the spring behind the fox's jaw so that the little mouth opened.

"Grrrr," Shirley said, and Marcus giggled.

"Write that story, Constantine?" Willson said.

"Yeah."

"I got a new ending for you. Larsen's dead."

"What?"

"You deaf? I called the institute about him and they told me he died late this afternoon. Heart attack."

"Forget about it, Dooley," his wife said, with a frown. "We're here to enjoy the game."

"That's right. Let's be like the white folks. Look the other way. Pretend everything is just *fine!* 'Course, while we're busy pretending, maybe something happens to Marcus and James."

"Now, that is enough! You're gonna scare these boys to death. Boys, you want a chicken dog?"

"Yes'm!" James said.

"You come on, then. How about you, Miss Shirley?"

"No, thank you, I think I'd rather stay—" she began, but Danny gave her a quick look, and she said, "I mean, sure, that'd be nice." She went off toward the concession stand with Mrs. Willson and the boys.

"She's got it, don't she," Willson said, watching Shirley walk carefully up the aisle.

"Yeah."

"How long?"

"Two years ago March."

"Two years. That's a long time to live with it."

"Yeah. And she's almost thirteen."

Danny did not go on. He saw that Willson understood. The two men were silent a moment.

"You took that witness off me," Willson said.

"That's not what happened."

Willson looked at him hard. "Cut the crap, Constantine. You were trying to show me up in front of Miss Crockett. Make me look bad." Willson took the cigar out of his mouth. "One way or another, that's what it always comes down to. You people still trying to hang on. Put us in our place while you still got the chance."

"You hit him," Danny pointed out.

"Goddamn right I hit him. But I sure as fuck wouldn't have _killed_ him. He'd be sitting in jail right now having his turkey and beans."

"Look, Willson, if it makes you feel any better, I didn't want to leave him at the institute, either," Danny said.

"Get the fuck out of my sight, Constantine."

"I'm telling you the truth. He wasn't in bad shape. They were cleaning up his shoulder and he was cursing and squirming. Then Dr. Gray came in, and that tramp went dead pale. He started yelling that Gray was the one who plugged him, and tried to run out. They grabbed him and gave him a shot of something to calm him down."

"Bullshit."

"That's what happened."

"You telling me a man with millions of dollars, lives in a mansion on the finest stretch of Riverside Terrace, goes prowling the yards looking to shoot him some 'boes?"

"I don't know. All I know is that tramp was terrified. And there's something about Gray, too. If you saw the look on his face when Larsen started yelling. It was like what comes out of a magnifying glass. White hot and aimed at one thing: Earl Larsen. Gray _hated_ him."

There was a crack of the bat and the crowd roared as Livingston of the Monarchs hit a high fly to right field. The ball disappeared into the lights and Elmer Smith stood looking up into the sky with a forlorn expression on his face. But as the ball came down, he saw it at the last moment, made a dive, and just managed to snag it for the third out of the inning. He got up, tossed the ball to the infield and his glove over his shoulder behind him, and trotted toward the dugout.

"Damn!" Willson said.

"Look, Willson. All I know is that this story's right up Walter Burns's alley, and he's killed it twice. Now your witness is dead. Then there's the way this killer's going about her business. There's something terrible going on, and I want to know why. I'll stay out of your way as best I can. But I have to try to find out what the hell's going on."

Willson struck a match and got his cigar going again. He blew smoke and watched it spread out under the glow of the arc lights. Then he started talking.

"After we finished at the yards, Swede and I went back and had a talk with Vern. This time he had a little more to say. Charlie Hayes came in that night after his shift. Hayes was a regular customer. Vern said that sometime around midnight that blonde came in, went right over to Hayes, and started drinking with him. They were there for a couple of hours, before they left together."

"You get a description?"

"Vern had a couple of hours to look at her. Not a lot of women who look like that come into his place. Mostly it's men from the car barns."

"And cops."

"And cops." For an instant, Willson showed a trace of a smile. "Our killer's a small girl, five-two, five-three. Platinum blonde with brown eyes. A mole just above the right collarbone. She came in carrying a big, soft-leather shoulder bag that Vern thought might have something heavy inside. And she was using an expensive-looking cigarette case, white gold or platinum. Engraved."

"What was she wearing?"

"Light green silk."

Danny nodded. "That fits with what I caught on film. And what Wall-Eye said he saw. What about the third person, though?"

"Nobody else came in other than the usual customers."

"So she's a good-looking doll, comes in, gets them interested."

"And from what Vern said, she ain't that good looking. She had to work on Hayes a long time. Vern didn't like to see it, either."

"Why not?"

"Hayes was a good family man. Six kids. When he first came in he was talking about what he and his wife were going to do on their anniversary. He'd rented a nice lodge up at Mille Lacs."

"Gee, that's tough."

"His anniversary's tomorrow," Willson said. "Same day as the funeral."

Della Willson came back then with Shirley and the boys.

"We saw Mr. Lockner upstairs," Shirley said. "I asked him how he liked the game and he said something back in French. Something that some general said after he watched the charge of the Light Brigade."

"Say mahgnyeefeek, maze etah pah la baseball," Marcus said in a soft, shy voice.

"He did? How do you know?" Shirley said.

" 'Cause I'm taking French in school."

"My boys go to Breck Academy," Mrs. Willson said proudly. "There's a lot of our young men out there now."

"Well," Danny said, "so what's it mean, genius?"

"He said, 'It's magnificent. But it ain't baseball!' "

*U*nderneath the grandstand, in the Millers' dim, humid dressing room, Lou Ravelli sat on a bench in front of his beat-up locker and slowly got dressed. He had stood under the shower for a long, long time, feeling nothing, trying to wash even that away. Finally the hot water gave out and he knew it was time to get dressed and go home. He didn't want to be around when the rest of the boys came in, and he especially did not want to listen to Mike Kelly jaw at him for what had happened on the field.

He didn't want to think about the game. He didn't want to think about baseball. Five years ago, when he was fifteen and tearing up the sandlots out in 'Frisco, the great Lefty O'Doul himself had come to his parents' house out in the Mission, the night after Lou collected five hits at Big Rec. O'Doul had a contract in his pocket. The manager explained that the Seals were going to be short of players that year, and though, usually, they would never consider signing somebody so young, under the circumstances, with the kid tearing up the local pitchers and making a name for himself, there was no point waiting. His parents had inked it for a three-hundred-dollar bonus, and the next day Lou was out at third base at Seals stadium in front of a packed house.

And then Hun had swept in the way the Fire had in '06, and now

San Francisco was back to where it had been a hundred years ago. Hills and blowing sand. A ghost town. Quarantined. They thought maybe Hun had come in with the rats that lived in the ships. They didn't know, though, not really. Whatever caused it, in the end there were maybe two, three thousand people left now, none of them Lou's people. All Lou's family—five brothers and two sisters, his ma and pa, his cousins, the priests at St. Paul's—everybody, all dead.

Lou had tried not to think about it. He put all his sorrow and confusion into playing ball. When the Coast League shut down he and what was left of the Seals moved to Salt Lake City and merged with the Mountain League club there. After that, Omaha, and now here in Millie. And always, it seemed like he was one step ahead of Hun, because everywhere he went got hit.

If everything had stayed the way it was supposed to be, Lou would have been called up to the big leagues two years ago. He had never hit less than .375 anywhere. At Omaha he clubbed 43 home runs and drove in an even 170. A fella couldn't hit any better than that and stay down, but two years ago, the big leagues stopped taking new players from west of the Mississippi. So Lou had come here to Milltown; only from the start, his luck here had been bad. He'd hit okay, but his head wasn't right. Halfway through the first year they stopped running eastbound passenger trains past Cincinnati. And rumor had it there wasn't any organized major league ball in the East anymore. That made it hard for Lou to keep up his old enthusiasm, which in turn put him at odds with Kelly, who had been with the Millers since 1912 and was a half owner now, and who preached that people went to ball games to forget about their troubles, and that he expected his players had to go out there like nothing was wrong. Lou still played spectacularly a lot of the time. But he had lapses. Swinging on a 3-0 count. Missing signs. Booting them at third. And, worse in Kelly's eyes, acting depressed all the time. That more than anything got him into hot water with the manager. For sure, Kelly would fine him the rest of the year's salary for that stunt he'd pulled, running at Rogan like that.

Lou sat there on the bench holding his socks and thought about quitting the game, but didn't know what else he could do. Ever since he could remember, all he'd done was play ball. He could read a

menu in a diner and endorse his paycheck, and recite the Latin from
the Mass, but otherwise everything he knew was out there on that
green field. What the hell else would he do if he couldn't play ball?

He'd have to take it, that's all. He'd sit there and wait for Kelly
and the rest of the boys to come in after the game and then he'd take
it, like he always did.

After a while he had a feeling somebody was standing behind
him.

"Beat it, Halsey," he said, thinking it was the clubhouse man. "I
don't need no shoe shine today."

"I can see that," came the reply. It wasn't Halsey. Lou glanced
back and saw a man standing near the door, holding his hat. He was
tall, with a vest that hung rather loosely on him, a farmer's haircut,
and two-toned shoes.

"Mister, you'd better get out of here. Ain't supposed to be nobody
in here but players, and reporters, after the game. You ain't a
reporter, are you?"

"Not on your life," said the man.

"Well, like I told you, this place is off limits. Better get back to the
grandstand."

"But I came to talk to you," the man said. "Do you mind? I'll just
take a minute of your time."

Insurance man, Lou thought. "Halsey!"

"Halsey's stepped out for a little while. He's the one that let me in
here."

"You know Halsey?"

"Sure. Halsey and I are old pals."

"You're wasting your time, mister. I ain't in the market for
nothin'."

"You got it all wrong, Lou. I came down because I saw what they
did to you out there. It's a crime they tossed you out of that game.
They should have let you whack that nigger good for showing you up
like he did. He didn't have any right to do that. You're a serious
ballplayer. They got no right to make you go out on the field with a
bunch of damn monkeys."

"Well, they did," Lou said uncertainly. The man came over and
sat down next to him on the bench and stuck his hand out.

"My name's Ed Pratt," the man said. "I've been a big fan of yours ever since you came on the ball club. Saw you play in Des Moines when you were with Omaha, too. I'll never forget the night I saw you hit a rope over the right-field fence that never got more than six feet off the ground. 'Damn!' I said to myself. 'That boy can sock 'em!' "

"Thanks," Lou said, shaking hands with him. "That was a good bunch down there. Although there ain't too much of Omaha left now, from what I heard."

"You're right about that. I used to sell printing supplies. My territory was here, Iowa, Nebraska, and the Dakotas. It's all pretty much gone now, except for old Millie. Hell of a thing to see. Fifty years ago we were spreading out across these plains, pushing the Indians out. Now it's all shrunk back to what it was. All in ten years. It's a good thing they built the railroads when they did. Couldn't build 'em now. The labor doesn't exist, except for the niggers, and they've got their sights set on more than swinging picks. They're waiting patiently for the day the last white man drops dead. Then they'll inherit everything he built. 'Course, I don't have to tell you that."

"Did you notice what the score was?" Lou said.

"Seven to two. And I've never seen such cheating and clowning in my life. They're blinding your boys with those lights."

"No!"

"It's a fact. They've got a man up on each of the towers whose job it is to shine a spotlight in the face of every Miller who comes up to bat. But hell, that's the way things are these days. We're down now, and they think they can do anything they want to us. Anything at all."

Lou hung his head. It was all too depressing to think about.

"Let me ask you something," Ed Pratt said. "Do you believe in the Christian religion?"

"Huh? Why, sure, I guess I do." He felt guilty all of a sudden, thinking of how many times he'd missed Sunday Mass the last three years. Although it wasn't his fault they always had a double-header on Sunday.

"Ravelli's an Italian name, isn't it? That means you're probably a Catholic, am I right?"

"Yeah."

"Let me get to the point, Lou. I'm Kleagle for the North Star Klan Number Two, Knights of the Ku Klux Klan."

"What the hell's a Kleagle?" Lou said. He would have laughed at the funny-sounding word, if not for the intense, serious way Ed Pratt was looking at him.

"In lay terms you might say a Kleagle's a recruiter. Though there's much, much more to the office than that."

"Recruiter? For the Klan?"

"That's right, Lou. And I'm here to let you know the Klan is very interested in young men like you."

"The Klan, huh." Lou thought about it, then remembered something and frowned. "Say! I thought you fellas were against Catholics. You were when I lived out in California."

"That was before this terrible plague, Lou. See, before the war the Catholic in this country always had a problem choosing between his natural allegiance to the flag and the allegiance to the pope that was drummed into him by the priests and nuns. But now, with the quarantine and all, your United States Catholic's cut off from Rome for good. Now he needs something else to look to, and when he thinks about it, what else can it be but the welfare of his own race and nation?"

"I never thought of that," Lou said.

"But the point is, you can now. Because all your illusions have been stripped away by the sickness. Your Catholic's now been *dis-illusioned.* See how it works? A Catholic's just something a white man's been made into, but underneath all the popery, he's still a white man, understand? And now's the time all white men have to band together. Not like before, to resist economic pressure or get the right kind of laws through Congress. Now it's a question of survival. The last of us, the ones that haven't got sick even though the plague's swept through four times across this land, have got to band together. Otherwise, this country belongs to the nigger and for good. And your nigger's got a long memory. Soon as he can, he'll do to the white man exactly what the white man did to him. All you have to do is see what happened in the South during Reconstruction."

"I don't know much about that," Lou admitted.

"That's when the Jew Lincoln gave the South to the niggers after the Civil War. White women pulled plows in the cotton fields while coons drank corn liquor in the governor's office. That's what gave rise to the old Klan, white men of honor and property who rose out of the ashes of the South, and drove the niggers and carpetbaggers out of the land."

"Lincoln was a Jew?" Lou said.

"You didn't know that, did you? You couldn't, because Jews used to control every printing press in this nation. Why, there never was a photograph of Lincoln published in his lifetime, and you know why? Because one look at him told you exactly what he was. Tell me something: You ever hear of *The Protocols of the Elders of Zion?*"

"No."

"Of course you haven't, because you were never intended to see them. The Protocols of Zion are a secret plan devised by the Jews to take control of the world. They intend to provide the brains, while their allies, the Negro race, provides the manpower and the market-place. Do you think it's an accident that this disease only spares niggers and Jews? No, sir! It spares them because *it was created in the laboratory by Jew scientists to do exactly that!*"

"No!" Lou said, feeling a chill at the thought.

"Of course you were never intended to know the truth. Because if you did, you wouldn't wait for your time to come, like so many others did before you, when the blood would burst from your eyeballs and the niggers would dance on your dead body while the Jews played the tune!"

"Jesus," Lou said. "Don't talk like that. It gives me the creeps."

Ed grabbed Lou's shoulders and looked deeply into his eyes. "It should do more than give you the creeps, Lou. It should make you want to do something about it. Look out in these stands tonight, at all those fools wearing masks, eating health food, taking blood pills, as if any of that could save them! There's only one cure for this disease, Lou, and it's a hard one to swallow, because it's truth, Lou, truth!" He took some pamphlets out of the inside pocket of his coat and pressed them into Lou's hands. Lou looked at the one on top. It was *The International Jew*, by Henry Ford.

"Is this Henry Ford the car man?"

"Sure is. Written on his deathbed, while he was stricken with Hun slipped to him by a nigger housekeeper. You read that. We meet Thursday night at eight at Foss Memorial Church. White America needs young strong men like you, Lou. You'll meet others who stopped believing the lies and stood up for the truth. There's more and more of us all the time. And we don't just talk." He lowered his voice and spoke into Lou's ear. "We *do* things."

"What kind of things?"

"Things you've thought of doing yourself, only you couldn't see how one man alone could accomplish them. You know what I mean."

"I guess I do," Lou said dubiously.

"You read that literature and call me," Ed said. "My number's stamped on the back cover." He stood up, smiling, and put on his hat. "I know you'll want to join us. And when you do, and learn how to recognize your brother Klansmen, you'll be surprised at how many of us there are all over this town. Why, there may be Klan brothers on your own ball club. Once you know them, and feel their strength all around you, you'll feel like a new man. You'll *be* a new man."

"That's what I want, all right!" Lou said eagerly.

"Then you read that and call me," the man said, putting on his hat. "Nice talking to you, Lou."

He walked out, the sound of the crowd swelling as the door opened and cutting off when it shut, leaving Lou alone to look at the pamphlets in his hand. Maybe this was what he'd been looking for all along, he thought.

Maybe it was time he did something besides take it.

CHAPTER

15

Two in the morning
It's you on the phone
You call from the corner
'Cause you can't call from home

Your voice starts to quiver
As the trolley rolls by
We whisper I love you
And can't say good-bye

And the clock keeps ticking louder and louder . . .
Love by the hour
Love by the hour

*G*ood evening, everybody. This is the Archangel calling,
and I really do give my love by the hour. It's rather cooler
tonight, isn't it? Almost lovely. No violent weather on the
horizon, fortunately. That storm last night knocked your poor angel
right out of the air, feathers and all. For a while, she was just a little
wet bird.

"In any case, it's good to talk to you again. I've been especially
anxious to come on the air tonight because, well, I suppose I mustn't
complain, but the fact is your Archangel has had a long and very
trying day.

"Have any of you read the* Journal *this evening? Well, of course you*
have! I've got a copy right here. Let me see. 'Tornado Deaths Mount to
Five.' That happened in Randolf on Friday. . . . 'Robbers Loot Three
Safes of $450 Cash.' This right below a picture of Miss Jocelyn Lee,

who was married Sunday in Hollywood to director Luther Reed. Do
you sometimes get the feeling that these Hollywood stories are
completely made up? Who is Jocelyn Lee? Or Luther Reed, for that
matter? The Archangel's Los Angeles friends tell her that Hollywood
is practically empty. Perhaps that's the reason someone like Luther
Reed got his chance to direct! Anyway, what else is here . . . Oh, yes,
'Chicago Police Chief Quits Under Reporter Murder Fire.' And finally
we've got 'Bandits Shot Near Anoka Cleared of Detroit Lakes Bank
Raid.' All very interesting, but of course, none of these stories has
anything to do with what is actually happening in this town. These
headlines are interchangeable with the headlines of a hundred other
days this year. They absolutely have nothing to do with reality.

"What I'm going to tell you is for your own good. You know the
Archangel would never lie to you. I'm afraid we all had better get
prepared, because the epidemic is with us again.

"I know. You would rather have me play records and tell amusing
stories, but tonight, you see, I'm feeling rather discouraged, and I
think, somehow, it's up to the Archangel's listeners to make the effort
to try to cheer her up. Could you send some cheerful thoughts my
way? Maybe if all of you just closed your eyes now—yes, that's right,
close your eyes and think any good thoughts you can and attach them
to my name. It's like addressing a telegram. Maybe if I feel all of you
out there thinking good things about me, I'll feel a little better about
telling you these things.

"They always kill the messenger, you see.

"There. Thank you. I think, yes, I actually do feel something good.
Oh, thank you all! I'm sure you probably think your poor Archangel's
crazy, talking about sending thoughts through the air like that. Well,
all I can say is that those of you who are a little older can probably
remember when the idea of sending the sound of an angel's voice
through the air without wires would have seemed equally absurd.

"At any rate, let me go on. I read you these headlines because they
are a screen that certain people have put up to protect you from the
truth. They do this because they don't trust anyone with the truth
other than themselves. They think it is their treasure, to twist and
play with as they think necessary.

"No doubt, listeners, these truth-tenders of the Journal, and of KMPS and WCCO and the other radio stations in town, believe they will spare our city the kind of civil strife and destruction that has brought so many other cities to their knees across the country. They feel that if they do not publish the facts about the numbers of people who have already died in the past two weeks, and the hundreds and probably thousands more who will die in the weeks ahead, that life will somehow go on as it always has, and that, when the outbreak has spent itself as it has done in the past, we will still have a city, and laws, and jobs, and homes to work with.

"But these men make a terrible mistake, because they represent the society they profess to protect. And by lying to save it, they call into question whether or not the society that turns away from the truth deserves to survive. Their stratagem has the opposite effect of that intended, because it causes people—people like me—to wonder whether there might not be some new form for society to take, since the old order has been destroyed anyway. Why not use the opportunity to build something new? The people whose houses were blown down in Randolf aren't going to simply build the same houses and barns over again. They'll try something different. Why not? There's nothing of the old left to hang on to anyway!

"I'm not going to be a grim reaper and tell you all the figures I have heard today. I just want you to realize what is going on. We've been through this three times now. We know how it goes. The important thing is that we must not ignore the Hun. We must face him. We must not cower in ignorance that which has been cultivated by those who seek to steal the one weapon we have to protect ourselves. This truth.

"Some of you may say, well, who is she to lecture us about truth? She won't say who she really is. Perhaps there is some justification for that charge, but I can only tell you that when I am on the radio, I am the Archangel, and when I'm not on the radio I'm someone else. And the two never really are the same. It is necessary for me to protect my privacy so that I can do the work of the Archangel without interference from the one or two men who still work for the Federal Radio Commission in this state, and so that I can do my other work, too.

"The Archangel wants to tell you that she loves those of you out *there who seek the truth: certain brave reporters . . . policemen . . . physicians, teachers, mothers and fathers. Today she tried to give some love to as many of these people as she could. Not everyone realized what she was doing, and sometimes they didn't want it when they did. But still, the angel must try.*

"I'm going to play some music now. This is a record I got from a friend who came back from Mexico recently, where the station XERC beams across the continent from just south of the border. The singer is Lillian Glinn, who is from Dallas, and the song is 'Cravin' a Man Blues.' There's one man I love, one man I crave, one man I'm wild about. The one man I crave, he knows what he's all about. Think of the Archangel when you listen, please, 'cause this is just how she feels now. Here's Lillian Glinn. Sing it, Lil!"

16

The next morning at the paper Jackie brought Danny down a note from Walter. The *Journal*'s request for an interview had been granted. Gray would see Danny in an hour, at the institute. He finished some prints of shots he had taken Saturday at Lake Calhoun, when it was so hot, then went out to the barbershop down on Fourth, had a shave, a haircut, and a shoeshine, then drove out to Riverside Terrace. They were expecting him at the gate and issued him another metal badge.

"Do me a favor and put in on this time?" the guard said.

"Sure."

"Drive through. The doctor will meet you in the main lounge."

Danny parked in the shade underneath the ivy-covered portico, got out, and then, on impulse, opened the camera box in the trunk and took out his folding Recomar. He took his coat off, slung the strap around so that the camera rested under his arm, and put the jacket back on. Then he went into the institute.

There was a reception desk looking out on a lobby with green leather chairs, thick wine-colored carpets, big-bellied table lamps in yellow and onyx. Tall windows gave a view across the shaded lawns. Opposite was a wide staircase, and farther back, two elevators. Danny went up to the desk.

"My name's Constantine. I've got an appointment with Dr. Gray."

"One moment," the receptionist said, smiling at him. She picked up a telephone and plugged a cord into the switchboard. "Yes, Doctor. He's here. Yes, I will."

"He'll be right down," she said, smiling again.

Danny sat in one of the green chairs and watched as a group of men and women came in, bellhops following with trunks and suitcases. One of the men looked very frail; a nurse walked with him, holding his arm.

Then Gray came down. He was in shirtsleeves, linen trousers with suspenders, and a narrow, raw silk tie. He greeted his guests, shaking hands all around. Everyone in the lounge watched him, the staff moving briskly to take care of everything while Gray listened to something the frail man was telling him, brushing his hair back as he did and then, turning his head slightly, looking at Danny. Gray still had his ear toward the man, and the man kept on talking as though he had Gray's full attention, but Danny could feel Gray boring in on him. It made him feel uncomfortable. Danny had never believed in the idea of personal magnetism. The most he would admit was that some people were inherently fascinating for reasons nobody could explain, but with Gray he felt some kind of ice rays shooting out of those pale eyes that had the power to freeze him, or anything, in its tracks.

Danny stood up. The doctor finished with the guests and came over.

"Good morning, Constantine," he said. "Good to see you again so soon. Thanks so much for coming on such short notice."

"Thanks for seeing me. Looks like you're pretty busy today."

"Well, when Robert told me you wanted an interview I could hardly refuse. I still feel rather awkward about what you saw yesterday. And then to have the unfortunate man die on my hands like that! To tell you the truth, I'm rather anxious to clear the whole matter up."

"We can talk about that if you like," Danny said, not wanting Gray to think he was all that interested. "But who were those people you were talking to?"

"They're some patients who have volunteered to undergo an experimental treatment with injections of fibrin."

"What's fibrin?"

"Merely what keeps you alive," Gray said.

Merely, Danny thought sourly.

"When you cut yourself, the blood supply triggers a mechanism that automatically forms a patch out of platelet cells, netted together by an insoluble protein called fibrinogen. Fibrin is soluble. Fibrinogen is not. Somehow, the body senses a wound and begins a chemical reaction that changes the fibrin in the bloodstream into fibrinogen. The mechanism is only vaguely understood. What prevents all of the blood from clotting, for instance, in the event of injury? And conversely, how does Hun inhibit the clotting reaction? If we can discover how this occurs chemically, we will be on our way to a cure."

"Is that what your institute is aiming for?"

"Nothing less than the complete elimination of this disease."

"And how do things stand now?"

"As always," Gray said, "crisis accelerates advances in a particular field. In the case of HF, we have made astonishing strides in a number of areas. For instance, we have learned how to 'bank' donated blood, and how to separate it into its components. Plasma is particularly important in this regard. We hope soon to be able to isolate specific proteins in the blood that may be destroyed by the HF virus, and thus treat victims with a single shot, rather than transfusions as now. And, of course, the strides we have made in the surgical field have been nothing short of remarkable."

"Why would surgery have anything to do with it?"

"I was trained as a surgeon, Mr. Constantine. Thoracic surgery is my specialty and true passion. I am a hematologist only by necessity and, some would say, luck and talent. I became interested in the management of blood during the course of my surgical work, particularly in the first years of the war. That, of course, was before this awful nightmare began." He paused. "Don't you take notes, Mr. Constantine?"

"I've got a photographic memory," Danny lied. Now that Gray had mentioned it, he wasn't about to bring his notebook out. Damn, it was unnerving, the way Gray kept those cool eyes on him all the time. "Knack I've got," he added.

"How interesting. Have you ever had your memory tested scientifically?"

"I've never had an interview take a swing at me later if that's what you mean," Danny said.

Gray laughed. "Well, I suppose that's as good an indication of eidetic memory as anything. Shall we go up to my office?"

Danny *did* want to see Gray's office. But he noticed the doctor kept glancing toward the desk as more of his patients came in. Whether he was concerned about the details of their arrival or simply did not want to be seen, here in the lobby Gray seemed slightly distracted, and Danny knew that sometimes a distracted man said things he might not otherwise intend to reveal.

"Here's fine," Danny said, sitting down. The coolness flicked briefly in Gray's eyes. He looked at his watch.

"All right. I should warn you, I've only twenty minutes or so to spare."

"Then let's begin. Some background first. How old are you?"

"I am forty-eight," Gray said, tugging on the knife-edged crease of his trousers as he sat in the chair opposite Danny.

"Now, that's something worth writing down. You don't look a day over thirty." Danny watched Gray's reaction. Nothing. Not even a hint of vanity. He simply waited for the next question.

"Now, I notice you speak with a bit of an accent."

"Yes. Well, I was born in Berlin. My father and mother both worked for a German pharmaceutical company. Bayer. When I was a little boy they were transferred to New York to oversee the company's American operations. So, I was educated here, first at Groton, then at Harvard, where I began my medical studies under Bigelow and Cheever. I interned at Massachusetts General, and then went to Vienna, where I spent two years in the cancer ward of the Allgemeine Krankenhaus with Professor Billroth. After that it was the University of Strasbourg. I took histology from Waldeyer, absolutely the top man in Europe at that time."

"What's histology?"

"Microscopic anatomy. The study of the microscopic structure of organic tissues."

"All right. Then what?"

"I worked in Berlin for two years. By then my parents had retired and come back to Germany to live. I was chief of surgery at the Charité Hospital. Then, of course, the war broke out. I was in the position at the time of holding dual passports, and therefore I chose to stay in Europe. There was a fascinating opportunity to study the pathology and surgical treatment of the many awful injuries caused by the weapons of war. That is where I first truly grasped the principles needed to deal with the problem of pneumothorax." He smiled, anticipating Danny's question. "By that I mean the collapse of the lungs caused by wounds to the chest, or surgically."

"You were all right until 1917," Danny said. "What happened when we declared war on Germany?"

"Then, of course, I had a most difficult decision to make. To remain in Berlin I was told I must renounce my U.S. citizenship. This I was unwilling to do. So, via Switzerland, I came to Paris, and joined the U.S. Army Medical Corps."

"Where did the hematology come in?"

"In September 1918 I was stationed at a field hospital in a place called Binarville. This was during the Argonne offensive, in some of the heaviest fighting of the war. Some casualties were brought into the station bleeding profusely from the ears and mouth. On the basis of past experience I assumed these men had suffered concussion injuries due to the explosion of artillery or trench mortar shells. This proved not to be the case, however. The men had been part of a reserve unit held several miles from the front. According to the ambulance driver, several gas shells had landed near the trenches a few days before. Other than that, there had been no shelling anywhere near their position.

"The shells had released a mist, or gas, and the unit was ordered to wear masks, but the cloud apparently dissipated without damaging effects. But then, the men in the unit began to suffer symptoms similar to influenza: headache, fever, chills. Many complained of a feeling of intense pressure behind the eyes. I myself witnessed two men begin to hemorrhage so violently there was nothing we could do for them. Shock was immediate and death followed. Now, of course, those poor devils are known to have been the very first documented cases of acute German hemorrhagic fever.

"More cases followed, of course. I immediately suspected the cause was a germ warfare agent. That in itself wasn't anything new. Both sides had shells delivering various agents. Actually, the practice has been going on ever since the fourteenth century. At the beginning of the Black Death, plague swept through a Tartar army that had laid siege to the Byzantine city of Caffa. At some point, one of the Tartar commanders had the brilliant, macabre idea of catapulting the bodies of men who had died of plague over the walls of the town. In short order, both the defending army and the town itself were destroyed.

"The accounts of those, like Petrarch, who chronicled the Black Death are the only reference we have for this disaster, Mr. Constantine. Then as now, the towns were emptied, fields left untended, wars suspended for lack of men to fight them. Here in this city we've gathered our survivors together, so we maintain an illusion of community. But take a drive around the countryside sometime. I have a house on Lake Minnetonka, a fine house built at the turn of the century for one of the iron barons who built the northern part of the state. Mine is the only house left occupied on the lake. It is twenty miles from here to there, and those twenty miles are practically abandoned. Houses covered with vines. Streets overgrown. Stands of young trees poking through what used to be lawns and gardens. The suburbs and hamlets are silent now. The disease has attacked us and beaten us back."

"But there are still people around," Danny pointed out. "One of the men at my boarding house strung up a long antenna for his radio. He listens to Chicago, New Orleans. . . ."

"Yes," Gray said with a smile. "But, you see, he proves my point. There are not more than two or three thousand people left in Chicago. They are the victims of bad luck and bad policy."

"What do you mean?"

"During the war, many Negroes migrated to Chicago from the South. When the epidemic hit, the political leaders made the mistake of blaming the new residents for the disease. Thus, they drove away, with great violence, their only potential source of healthy labor. Many came here, of course, where they were welcomed. Many returned South, where several states already are virtually populated entirely by Negroes. Alabama, Mississippi, South Carolina are that way. There are no white men or women at all.

"Here it is a little different, of course, and that is where luck has come in. The epidemic has spared a relatively greater number of people. There are more chronic than acute cases. And there has been migration from other cities as Milltown became known as the capital of health. Of course, it isn't really. This latest wave of HF is killing as efficiently as ever."

"So you believe there's another wave now?"

"It's a question of fact, not belief. I see more cases every day. Our wards are full of new chronic cases. The blood supply is dangerously low. We've had six months' reserve wiped out in three weeks."

"No kidding!"

"Of course, you won't be able to print that," Gray said. "Mr. Crowley's newspaper is completely dedicated to maintaining the illusion of a healthy community. Which, I suppose, is preferable to the approach taken in places like Chicago. There the newspapers played up the most lurid aspects of the epidemic. The result was riot, and panic." Gray checked his watch again. "Well, perhaps we should begin our tour."

They got up and went into an elevator. "Which floor, Doctor?" the operator asked, nervously, it seemed to Danny.

"Three, please."

The car began to rise.

"Here in six floors of the central lodge we have room for up to eighty guests. This place was conceived as a rest home, and so the facilities are quite nice. Most of the rooms are furnished with kitchenettes and full baths. We have added facilities, of course, to convert them for use as private hospital rooms."

"Are any patients here?"

"Not at the moment. Naturally, we try to generate as much revenue as we can, and so these rooms would be reserved for wealthier patients. At the moment, approximately a third of the rooms are occupied by our research fellows."

The elevator stopped and they got off in a pleasant lobby, with bay windows looking out over the tops of the willow trees toward the lawns and the wooded perimeter of the property.

"My office is here, if you would like to see it."

"Yes, I would, very much," Danny said.

Gray led him along the plush, gray and burgundy runner, and opened a door with a key. The room was very dark, and cool, and smelled of wool and furniture wax, with a hint of tobacco. So Gray was a secret smoker, Danny thought. The doctor turned on the lights. The walls were paneled in dark polished wood, the floor carpeted with a rich Persian rug. There was a fireplace with an arched granite mouth, and a painting hung above the mantel of a fierce-looking man with a dark beard and pointed mustache, who was dressed in academic robes.

"Who's that?" Danny asked.

"Perhaps the greatest surgeon who ever practiced anywhere, in any specialty. Ferdinand Sauerbruch. It was he who showed the way for all who wished to operate safely inside the wall of the chest."

"How do you mean?"

"Sauerbruch was the father of modern thoracic surgery. Inventor of the negative-pressure field method for operating on a man's heart or lungs. Also perfected the technique of positive-pressure anesthesia. I knew him in Zurich, before the war. Toward the end of it he was one of the first to investigate the pathology of HF. Unfortunately, during the course of his research he became infected and died of the very disease he was trying to study. Do you know, he once pulled an abscessed tooth for Vladimir Lenin?"

"Lenin?"

"You may not remember. He was the Bolshevik ruler of Russia after the tsar abdicated. Of course, when Moscow was ravaged, he fled to New York. That was just before the quarantine. The last I heard of him, he was running a tearoom in Greenwich Village." Gray shook his head. "When one thinks of what might have been . . ."

He went around behind his desk—an Empire-style campaign desk whose top was empty except for a pen set, blotter, and inkwell—and opened a door to the right of it.

"This leads to our research library. I daresay I have spent a fortune acquiring every monograph, every text, the results of every study possible on blood and blood-related diseases. The library is open to anyone who wishes to use it. And here, on the other side, is the scrub room for my amphitheater."

Danny looked into a green-tiled room. There were scrub sinks and lockers and, on the other side of the room, swinging doors. "We are right above the hospital receiving area, connected by a special elevator." Gray pushed the sliding doors open and Danny stepped into the top tier of an operating theater.

"Our surgery is the finest facility of its type anywhere in North America," Gray said. "It is equipped with ultraviolet lamps that make the operating field completely aseptic. We have a heart-lung machine that permits us to artificially oxygenate a patient's blood for up to three hours. With this equipment we can perform any type of repair to the heart or to the lungs. We also conduct experimental surgery on animals here. I myself have transplanted the heart of one dog into another, and kept the patient alive for nearly three months afterward."

Danny felt his skin crawl at the idea. He did not like knives or needles.

"Do you have any questions?" Gray asked.

"Is it always so hot in here?" Danny said.

Gray smiled. "It is kept a constant seventy-three degrees."

"It's a warm seventy-three, though, isn't it?"

"Possibly," Gray said.

"Tell me something, Doctor," Danny said in an offhand manner. "What happens when you lose a patient?"

Gray stopped and gave him the full stare. It was all Danny could do to keep from buckling, apologizing, and getting the hell out of there.

"What do you mean, exactly?"

All right, Danny thought. *This is what you came here to do.* "Sometimes patients die here, don't they?"

"Unfortunately, yes."

"What do you do with them when they do?"

"That depends. If there are surviving relatives, we notify them and leave the disposition of the remains to the family."

"And if there aren't any relatives?"

"Mr. Constantine, I assume this question is not a rhetorical one. Perhaps you should come out and ask your question directly."

"Okay. I'm wondering exactly what happened to that tramp."

Gray did not answer for a moment, but Danny saw his gaze flicker. Was that rage, flickering like the flame of a boiler seen through the small, dark-tinted glass?

"We performed an autopsy, of course."

"I heard he had a heart attack."

"That would be my guess. But until the pathology report is complete, I really can't venture to give you an exact cause of death. He was, however, extremely run-down. Malnourished and anemic."

"What will you do with the body?"

"If no survivors come forward, we'll make good use of it. He did not have HF, so his blood was bankable, and certain of his organs as well, the liver especially. We have found, for instance, that an extract of liver cells from an otherwise healthy donor can stop a bleeding episode."

"Is the body still here, Doctor?"

"Yes . . . in our morgue."

"May I see it?" Danny said.

Gray's eyes widened slightly in disbelief. Then he smiled. "Do you really intend to write about the morgue?"

"I'd just like to see the body. If you don't mind."

Gray checked his watch again. "Very well. But then I'm afraid we shall have to end our interview. I really must attend to my new patients."

"Of course."

"This way."

They went back into Gray's office, out into the hall, and downstairs to the second floor, through another locked door that led into a tiled room that was similar to the operating theater, except that there were windows high in the walls and instruments laid out alongside a stone dissecting table. There were not many of them, only a medium-sized scalpel, a pair of blunt-nosed forceps, blowpipes, and probes of various lengths, along with a sharpening stone. Above the door leading back to the morgue itself was a wreath made of woven sticks. Gray held this door open for Danny.

In the morgue was a bank of chrome-doored drawers. Gray pulled one open.

"Here's your man," Gray said, nodding at the shrouded corpse. He made no move to pull the sheet away from the head. It was clear to Danny that if he wanted a look at the dead man's face he would have to pull the shroud away himself. He swallowed hard, and did it.

It was Wall-Eye, all right, only now his skin was the color of soap. A puckered incision, closed with tiny catgut sutures, began at the collarbone and ran across the left side of the chest to the top of the abdomen. The hair had been washed and combed back and the face shaven.

"You say you took his liver?" Danny said, his voice sounding thick in the cold room.

"Yes, as well as his lungs, heart, kidneys, and spleen."

"Do you usually sew them back up again?"

"Generally not with sutures," Gray said in a voice that seemed to cover surprise at the question. "And now, unfortunately, Mr. Constantine," he said, reaching across Danny to pull the sheet over the body, then sliding the shelf back, "I really must end our talk."

"Of course, Doctor," Danny said.

They went back to the elevator, and Gray said, "Would you like one of our volunteer aides to take you around to the wards? To complete the picture?"

"That would be great."

The elevator doors closed and as the car descended, Danny said, "You say you performed the autopsy yourself?"

"No," Gray replied evenly. "I don't recall I said anything of the kind."

"*Did* you perform it?"

"Yes," Gray said.

"But you said before you were waiting for a pathology report."

"That's right."

"Why do you have to wait if you performed the autopsy?"

"Because I am not a pathologist."

"I assume you know what a healthy heart looks like, though."

"Yes."

"How did this man's heart look to you?"

"There was severe scarring on the left side of the heart brought about by the blockage of the circumflex branch of the left coronary artery. In addition, the pericardium was inflamed."

Now Danny took his notebook out. "You wouldn't want to tell me how to spell any of that, would you?" he said, smiling.

Gray smiled back. "I'm sure our aide will be happy to help you with that." The elevator opened onto the lobby, and Gray picked up a telephone at the desk to arrange for the rest of Danny's tour. "Yes, thank you," he said, putting down the receiver. "Mr. Constantine, someone will be with you in a few minutes, if you'd care to wait. Would you care for any refreshments? Coffee? Juice?"

"No, I'm fine, Doctor."

"I've enjoyed our talk very much," he said.

"I hope you didn't think I was giving you a hard time," Danny said.

"Not at all. I'm sure your article will not be quite so skeptical."

Not if Crowley has anything to do with it, Danny thought as they shook hands.

"Thanks for seeing me, Dr. Gray."

"My pleasure." Danny watched him go into the elevator, watched as the pointer above the doors stopped at four and stayed there. Then he looked around the lounge. There were more patients' guests here now standing around chatting in groups, drinking cocktails offered by several waiters who moved among them. No one paid any attention to him. He saw that the other elevator car was open, and went up to it and got in.

"Three, please," he said to the operator.

"Very good, sir," the operator replied, and took him upstairs.

He got out and looked down the hall he had just come from. Everything was quiet. Danny went to Gray's office door and put his ear against the wood. It was quiet. He tried the knob. Gray had not locked it when they had come out. Slowly, Danny turned the knob, pushed the door open, swung inside, and closed it behind him without making a sound.

It was dark except for thin blades of daylight where the heavy curtains joined over the window behind Gray's desk. Danny went to it, got out his spirit-match, and struck the flint. The desk drawers were not locked. He pulled open the large drawer on the lower right. It was full of files, the folders marked with the months of the year. Danny took out the one marked June and opened it. Glued inside was a sheet of ledger paper marked "New Inmates" and listing numbers for each day of the month. Danny closed the folder and put it back, and began to look through the other files, until the shaft of the spirit-match got too hot to hold. He blew on it to cool it, rubbed it between his hands, and struck it again, then looked again at the files. There were folders marked "mechanical specifications," "compressed air apparatus," "valve designs," and "p-p anesthesia/ pneumothorax." None of it except the last, which was a term Gray had used in their talk, meant anything to Danny.

He closed the file drawer and opened the middle one. Inside was a small device, two silver nipples connected by rubber lines to a cupped piece of metal that had two ports hooked up to woven fabric collars. Some kind of medical equipment, Danny thought. On impulse he shoved the gadget into his pocket, snuffed the match, and carefully closed the drawers.

He then went through the door leading to the theater scrub room, went down the tiers and across the surgery itself, pushing through the swinging doors that led through the surgeon's prep room and out into the back hall. Two doors down was the morgue.

Quickly, he opened Wall-Eye's drawer, pulled the body out and the sheet back, and, unfolding his Recomar, set the lens aperture wide open, and took some shots. He noticed then that there were metal buttons or nipples protruding from the corpse's abdomen, took the apparatus he'd filched from Gray's desk out of his pocket, and saw that the nipples were identical.

"I'll be damned," Danny said aloud, and pulled out another drawer. The first one he tried was empty, but the second held the corpse of a fat, middle-aged white woman whose body had the same sutured incision running from collarbone to solar plexus. Danny pulled the shroud down further and again found the metal buttons sticking out of the suture line at the top of her abdomen. He took another couple of pictures, opened a third drawer. In it was the body of a young boy, not more than twelve or thirteen years old. Shirley's age, and with the same cruel, red, carefully sutured scar ending in the metal buttons below the rib cage. Danny took some shots of the boy, then pulled a stool over, stood on it, and took three pictures of the whole group before covering all of the corpses up again and sliding their drawers back, one by one, into the cooler. Afterward he folded up the Recomar and slung its strap over his shoulder. He put his coat on, listened at the frosted-glass door that led to the hallway, then slipped out.

He was heading back to the elevator when Gray's security man, Horace, turned the corner, looking grim.

"There you are," he said. "What the hell are you doing up here?"

"Looking for the bathroom," Danny said.

"You were supposed to wait downstairs."

"Yeah? And aren't you supposed to be clipping hedges or something?"

The security man ground his fist into the other palm. "I'll clip something all right. Why don't I start with you?"

"Horace!" said a wide-eyed Selena Crockett, coming up the hallway. "What's going on? I asked you to find him for me, not decimate him."

"He's got a smart mouth, Miss Selena," Horace said, his neck turning crimson. "And this ain't the first time I caught him snooping around where he don't belong."

" 'Ain't the first time,' " Selena Crockett said, mimicking him in a dopey-sounding voice. "You go on. I'll take care of him."

"But Miss Selena—"

"I said go!"

Horace turned, got into the elevator, and saved one last murderous look for Danny before the doors closed. Danny filed the memory away carefully.

"What *are* you doing up here, Danny?" Selena asked him. "Simon told me he asked you to wait in the lounge."

"I get fidgety sitting around," Danny said. He noticed now how nice she looked in her red-striped volunteer uniform. Today she wore a matching red beret pinned to one side of her hair. "I didn't mean to cause any trouble."

"Oh, no," Selena said.

"Actually I was trying to locate a phone."

"Follow me," she said. They went back downstairs to the lounge, where Selena showed him a booth in the wall near the front desk. He sat in it and closed the door.

"Hello, operator. Give me Washburn-one-six-oh-oh. That's right, City Hall. Hello? Is this the switchboard? Let me talk to Sergeant Willson. Thanks."

"Willson," came the gruff voice over the line.

"This is Constantine. I'm calling from the institute."

"Good for you," Willson said blandly.

"Listen. They've got a morgue out here, and I had a look at the tramp. You've got to send someone down here right away to pick up that body."

"Like who? Percy's two weeks behind."

"You and the Swede come if you have to. Larsen was suffering from a gunshot wound. Therefore the coroner's got a right to the body."

"Don't quote procedure to me, Constantine!"

"I'm telling you you've got to get that body." Selena was looking in on him through the glass door. "Look, I've got to go. I'll explain later. Just do it, Willson!" He put the receiver back on the hook and pushed the door open.

"All set?" Selena asked.

"I hope so," Danny said.

17

I felt like I had to do something," Selena Crockett was saying as they headed for the children's ward, which took up the first floor of the institute's south wing. "And so I help here whenever I can. My family's always given money, of course. Tons of it. Tons more to come. But that's so boring. How hard is it to sit at a desk and write out checks?"

"Oh, it's impossible, all right," Danny said. Selena laughed.

"I'm sorry," she said. "I deserve that one. I only meant that money . . . Oh, I don't know. It just seems so passive, sometimes."

"It took something to make it in the first place," Danny suggested.

"That was Grandfather. He's the one who came and built the flour mills. He and his brother built the first one right above the falls with their bare hands. They ground up wheat and filled the sacks and loaded the wagons, and ran it like a real business. They got rich because they worked hard. I'll bet they never wrote a check in their lives. It's so much better to do things, don't you think?"

"It depends what kind of things you're doing," Danny said.

Selena stopped and looked at him quizzically. "I hope you don't take this the wrong way, but why do you pretend to be so hard-boiled all the time?"

"I'm not. I was just making a joke," Danny said, caught off guard.

"What is it you think I'm doing that you don't approve of?"

"Nothing," he said.

"You're not hard-boiled enough to be honest, obviously."

Danny stopped then. "You want honest? Okay, sister: I don't like Simon Gray. And it's pretty *obvious* that you do."

"Assuming that is true," she said, "What does that have to do with anything?"

"It means one of us is wrong about him. And I don't think it's me."

"Why does one of us have to be wrong?"

"Because," Danny said, "either he's the way you see him or he's the way I see him."

"Couldn't he be more than either of us sees?"

"Oh, I'm sure he is. I think he's fooling everybody. And I don't think he's making much of an effort to hide it, either."

Selena searched Danny's face. "Is that what you do?" she said. "Make up your mind about someone all at once and so completely?"

"I trust my instincts," Danny said.

"There you go being hard-boiled again. Every time you're afraid of something."

"Yeah? And what am I afraid of?"

"What you don't know. That's what you're afraid of. You dismiss it and pretend it's not important. You're doing it with me now. You do it with everybody."

"You sound like some two-bit alienist," Danny said.

"You say you've got instincts? Well, I've got them, too. But unlike you, I don't assume they're everything. You stand here, thinking you've got me all figured out, and the joke is, you really don't know me at all! You know nothing about me! And you know nothing about Simon Gray."

"All right. Forget him. And forget you for the moment. Let's talk about what I know about *me*. *I* know *I* don't like the way you look at him when he comes into the room. How he changes you."

"Changes me!"

"That's right. You change. Your voice changes. The way you stand changes, and so do the things you say."

"Don't be ridiculous!"

"You wanted me to be honest, Selena, and that's what you're

getting. All I know is that I like you very much, even now. But when he's around . . ." Danny shook his head. "Not a chance."

Selena's eyes dropped, and she was silent a moment. Then she said, "That sounded hard-boiled. But it really wasn't."

"Thanks for the compliment. I guess."

They started walking again.

"May I be honest now, too?"

"Shoot."

"I like *you* very much—when you're not afraid." She held the door open.

"Well. Maybe that's something," he said.

She smiled. "Here's the ward."

They went into a long, bright, pleasant room whose windows were shaded by elms and maples outside that filtered the light coming into the room to a cool, restful green. Selena explained that there were beds for fifty children. About half of the cases were confined to bed, some children hooked up to bottled blood that dripped slowly into their arms through rubber tubes. Most of the patients were very pale and bruised. The ones who could played carefully in the padded area at the end of the ward. There was also a sun porch, where some of the children splashed in a wading pool.

"These are bleeding cases that have been treated by transfusion and are responding," Selena explained. "Even so, it's just heart-breaking to come in here. When I think of how mean and selfish I was when I was only a little older than some of these kids. I didn't care about anything. Why, I've crashed at least five very expensive cars in my time. And a boat. My father paid plenty of money to hush it up and keep me out of trouble. One time the girl who was riding with me was badly hurt. Fractured skull. She got better, but I wouldn't have cared even if she'd died. I was a spoiled, horrible thing! Still am, I suppose. That's why it's good for me to see these poor kids. To remind myself how lucky I really am, and what my responsibilities are."

"Would you mind if I took some pictures?"

"Not at all. As long as you say I'm an unidentified volunteer." She stopped by one of the beds. "Hi, Jinny."

"Hi, Miss Crockett."

"How are you feeling today?"

"My tummy still hurts a lot. But I ate a turkey sandwich for lunch."

"All of it?"

"Half."

"That's good, sweetie."

Danny unfolded the Recomar. "Hold it right there, you two," he said, and made the shot.

"Is he a doctor?" Jinny asked.

"No, love. He's from the newspaper."

"Am I going to get my picture in the paper!"

"Sure you are," Danny said. "What's your last name?"

"Kinsella."

"Okay, Jinny Kinsella, you tell your folks to look in the *Journal* tomorrow afternoon. That's where you'll be."

"Thanks, Jinny," Selena said.

After that, Danny went out to the sun porch and took some shots of the kids playing in the water. Then he asked Selena about the other wing of the building.

"That's research facilities and labs."

"Could we see those?"

"I'm afraid not. They're off limits, to me at least."

"Who do I have to see to get in?"

Selena grinned. "Horace."

"Horace. You mean Horace, the mug who wants to flatten me?"

"I'm afraid so."

They left the children's ward and came out into the lobby again.

"Why do I get the feeling you're wishing I *would* ask him?"

"Because maybe a flattening would do you some good," Selena said, walking now with her hands clasped behind her back.

"You know Selena," he said suddenly, "You're okay."

She looked at him, and her expression turned serious. "There's someone else, though, isn't there," she said. "Someone you keep with you all the time. Someone who makes you feel self-conscious around me."

Danny began to blush.

"Don't feel ashamed. Everybody has things they hold inside. It's what people do when they've lost someone. Try and keep them near somehow . . . like an angel. It isn't such a bad thing to have an angel, Danny."

"It's strange," he said, "but when I look at you sometimes . . . I guess maybe I see her."

"What was her name?"

"Sonja."

"That's a beautiful name," she said.

"So's yours."

Selena beamed at him. "See? Sometimes you *do* say the right thing."

Now as the embarrassment took him completely, she burst out laughing. "Oh, this is *not* the place, is it!"

"I guess not," Danny said, laughing along a little.

"Listen, though. There's going to be a dance Saturday night, in the Elks hall above Rostek's, on the north side. Do you know it?"

"Sure. I used to eat there when I was a kid."

"Good. Why don't you meet me there around nine?"

"Meet you? You mean a date?"

"Yes, I mean a date! Will you come?"

"Okay. Yeah, I'd like that."

"Good."

"Good."

They stood looking at each other, and then suddenly, as she had the day of the luncheon, Selena kissed him quickly and softly on the neck.

"We'll talk then," she said. "And maybe I'll tell you about *my* angel."

18

*D*ooley Willson did not like punk, white-boy reporters—reporters who weren't even real reporters, but
picture-chasers who thought they could write, now that
the competition had all died off—calling him up and telling him
what to do.

Neither did he like the idea of that institute taking the law into its
own hands.

They'd swallowed up a material witness who then died on them.
Then they had failed to report his death to the county coroner as
required by law. That offended Willson. Hun had killed people, but
not the law, and Willson hated anybody who pretended it had.

Dooley Willson loved the law. Even though it had been written by
the white man and never applied fairly anywhere Dooley had ever
lived, the law, if you just read it straight and tried to think of it in a
vacuum, was a very good thing. It was the only way you could
organize people and let them know what was expected of them in
their relations with each other. And he, like any cop, was the
instrument of law. Without law, Willson didn't have a job. Even if it
was law he didn't agree with.

He lived to enforce the law.

Dooley Willson hated criminals. There were plenty of other things
he hated, too, but he always tried to put them aside when he was

working. The city had hired him to help keep order, and it was a damned hard job now, with Hun kicking up again, spreading that fatalism around along with the virus. That's when you got people doing crazy things just for the hell of it because they figured they had nothing to lose. Well, they did have something to lose. If they ran into Dooley Willson, they were going to lose their freedom, because he was going to do what he needed to do to keep order, so that even if every single white-bread motherfucker died, there would still be a town to live in. Milltown was a good place, the best he had ever seen. Willson wanted to stay here. He wanted his kids to live here, too, and grow up and raise their families here. Sometimes Willson liked to think how the world would be fifty or sixty or a hundred years from now. He was sure that America would rule. *Black* America. There wouldn't be no other kind.

But, for that to happen, there had to be law and order. Willson always came down hard on anybody he arrested, but he was especially tough on you if you were black. It wasn't that he had anything to prove. He just could not stand the thought of his people fiddling while Rome burned.

Dooley came from a military family. His father, Marcus Willson, was a sergeant in the 24th Infantry and had been decorated for gallantry in the charge up San Juan Hill. Dooley had been born in Mindanao, the Philippines, after the Negro 24th and 25th had been shipped there to quell the insurrection, and because no U.S. town wanted to billet any black regiments. Dooley had liked the Philippines. It was hot, and lush, and so green. That's what he liked about Milltown now in the summer. Everything had three months to grow and it just exploded, the way it did in the jungle all year round. He did not particularly care for the winters here, but he had to admit there was something about the snow and the twenty-below-zero January days that toughened a man up and made him think straight. *Or* drink. A lot of the surviving Swedes and Norwegians in Milltown were terrible drunks. Not to mention the Finns. And the Polacks and the Bohunks who used to work in the tractor factories. As for the Scotch-English—well, fuck the Scotch-English, they were the ones who thought they owned the fucking country in the first place, fuck them all, because now they were all going to die.

Sometimes, Dooley would try to remember when he had started to hate them like that. Was it when his family had to go back to Texas? His daddy had been sent to Mexico with Jack Pershing, to chase Pancho Villa, and Dooley, twelve years old now, found himself living in family quarters that were little more than a beat-up old shack at the edge of the base in Brownsville. There'd been some trouble in town one night; somebody had shot a Negro soldier and some of the boys in the regiment—pushed at too hard for too long and finding their place in the army sinking lower and lower despite a half-century of proud service since the Civil War, the Indian campaigns, and then in Cuba—went into Brownsville looking for revenge. There'd been a riot, a white man got killed, and Daddy had come back from Mexico just in time to see sixty-nine Negro enlisted men court-martialed in front of a panel of white officers. It was the largest military trial ever held.

After that, you couldn't go into Brownsville without getting called names. Nobody would wait on you. Kids who used to throw cinders at each other now threw rocks. Dooley remembered just walking down the street and feeling the hatred coming at him. At first, trying to sort out his hurt feelings, he blamed himself, and tried to go out of his way to be more polite, more respectful to the white folks. He was a conscientious kid who wanted to please, but there was no pleasing these people. Brownsville hated them. Their congressman—Daddy's congressman too, because Daddy had voted for him—introduced a bill to have all the Negroes fired from the army. He said it was a mistake for America to have blacks defending them, when there were more than enough whites to take on the job. That was the very thing that had brought down the Roman Empire, he'd said.

Then came the Great War. Even with all that had happened to the regiment, they were still professional soldiers and now here was a war, the big one, and everybody wanted action. Some of the boys resigned and went over as volunteers to serve with the French. Dooley was seventeen then and itching to go over too, but by then his daddy had suffered a heart attack and was lying sick in the post hospital, and he knew he couldn't leave his momma. Then Daddy took his medical discharge and moved them up to live with his brother in Chicago. Dooley never cared for that town, but he'd learned to fight, and started winning amateur bouts, sticking close to home because of his mother. And then finally the U.S. declared war on Germany, and Dooley refused to wait any longer. He volunteered, and got sent over to France with the 369th Infantry.

Of course, after all that had happened the last fifteen years, the army was only too happy to give the 369th to the French command, and the French were only too happy to use the 369th in the Meuse-Argonne. God, that was some fighting, though! And the French were glad they had, because the 369th kicked the Huns right back across the Siegfried line. Those Frogs had never seen fighters like the boys of the 369th. Dooley had won the *Croix de Guerre*. Hell, his whole *battalion* had.

And then had come that first leave, and those nights in Paris. Why, he'd been there when a shell from one of those Bertha guns had burst outside the Madeleine church. *Paris*, man! Back in Texas he'd been a nigger and he'd been the same in Chicago and then a nigger clod-buster in basic in New Jersey. To go to Paris where nobody looked at you except as a man, and better yet, as an *American soldier*, somebody who had come to help out: that had been the first time in Dooley's life he had ever felt free. Sure, if he thought about it, he wasn't free at all, he was a corporal in the fucking army, but he had been aware of being not free before the war, and this was just the opposite. When the armistice came he had a girl and the offer of a job for life working in her father's bakery.

Then she'd got sick, acute Hun. At the table during Sunday dinner she'd more or less exploded all over the tablecloth, and was dead before Dooley could carry her up to her bed. Just like that, her blood all over his arms and his hands. It had been a hot day and he'd felt it thickening up, like motor oil. Then he was on his knees out back, kneeling in front of the pump while her father yanked the handle up and down, the cold water blasting against his chest, both of them too stunned to cry. But then, with her blood thinned to a pink wash on the front of his shirt, her father had ordered him to leave. He screamed at Dooley and said it was his fault, that he had given her the sickness like a venereal disease. And Dooley had left crying, feeling his heart get thick and hardening the way her blood had.

Maybe, after all, *that* was when the hate had hardened for good.

She'd been one of the first civilian cases there, though of course it had been raging through the barracks on both sides, with the military authorities covering it up. All of a sudden the war had just stopped, mainly because there wasn't anyone left to fight it anymore. Half the soldiers had been killed in three months. Dooley had stayed in France until 1920, because the army was afraid to bring the survivors—including the half-million Negro soldiers who had never gotten sick—home.

But finally they did come home. Dooley went back to Chicago. The sickness was just starting there, but Dooley ignored what was happening and went back to fighting. In 1921 and '22 he had 130 fights, and he lost only ten of them, half that number on crooked decisions against white opponents. That was why, when they were white, he always tried to knock them out. They couldn't take it away from you when you had them laid out cold on the canvas. He was making a name for himself as a heavyweight, and then he broke his right hand and it never set right, not for punching, anyway. When Dooley realized he couldn't fight the way he wanted to, he quit.

Anyway, he'd been married two years by then, and had a couple of boys. That was in the beginning of '25. The year all hell broke loose in Chicago.

Hun was killing everybody that year, and there were riots, big ones, almost every night. People banded together and looked around for someone or something to blame, and went after it. The Negroes got it bad, back then. They were accused of being carriers, or worse, of deliberately poisoning the whites to get back at them. There was this preacher, the Reverend Omer Jonses—a motherfucking bughead name if you ever heard it—calling down fire and brimstone on the city, pretending that Chi was the only place Hun was hitting, and that it was hitting them because it had committed the sin of miscegenation. Jonses whipped the city up, and of course there had been the Klan, rising up after the war, and on the Negro side the fiery Muslim from Detroit who called himself Wali Farad who preached that it was not enough to let the white devils die on their own.

So many people died. You could smell the death even in the winter.

That's when the cows in the stockyards got it, and the pigs, too, the animals dying as fast as they brought them in. The companies packed them anyway, until the government made them stop. And then, in the summer of '26, the whole South Side burned down, and that was the end of Chicago. Willson wasn't around to see it happen, though. He'd been approached by a labor agent for the city of Milltown. They were recruiting army vets like him, for jobs in the factories, and out in the farm towns, too. They were getting organized up there, the agent said. They weren't about to let what had happened in Chicago happen to them.

So Dooley had moved Momma and Daddy and Della and his own kids up north. They'd found a cheap place down in Bohemian Flats, right on the river underneath the Washington Avenue Bridge. At the time the city fathers wanted to confine the Negro immigrants to the out-of-the-way places. Dooley had worked for North Star Flour in their mill just up the river from the flats. Then he heard there were positions for Negro patrolmen opening up in the Milltown police department.

Daddy had been a military policeman during the years in the Philippines, making an impression that his son had never quite forgotten, seeing him dressed so sharp with the gold-braid lanyard and puttees and camp hat worn just above the hard eyes so that his face had been all jaw and hat brim, with the eyes burning between. Dooley wanted his kids to remember him that way, too, and so he had joined the force in the spring of '27. At first his beat was restricted to the old colored neighborhoods in the flats, the North Side avenues between Plymouth and Broadway, and the tenements and cheap hotels of the Gateway. By 1928, though, reality had set in. The new colored residents of Milltown were healthy, and they were working for money. White people on the South Side and along the lakes were dying, and real estate prices dropped through the floor. Soon the Negroes started filling up those neighborhoods the way air fills up a vacuum, and Willson was patrolling Lake Street and the parkways around Lake Harriet and Lake Calhoun. He began to tire of walking a beat, though, and in '29 had applied for and got a transfer to the major crimes division. The homicide section needed men. All five detectives had died within a three-month span of acute Hun, the victims of the bursts the disease sometimes exhibited between its bigger sweeps. By default, Dooley Willson had taken over Homicide, and had got Lingeborg to work for him as detective.

Now his family was settled. His wife was a teacher and his kids were going to a good private school that would have been absolutely closed to them, financially and racially, only a few years ago. Willson, working hard, had won the grudging respect of his superiors on the squad. The white people who were left, having resigned themselves to their civic plan of making the city and the state survive in some form, for the most part treated him well. On Sundays Dooley took his family to the Bethesda African-American Church and listened to the preacher exhort the congregation to thank the Lord for its good fortune, though he never joined in on such prayers. As far as he was concerned, God was a white man's God who had turned away from his people. And, while he approved of that turning away, because the motherfuckers certainly deserved it, he did not think it was a good idea to remind Him of what he had done.

God might change His mind.

After taking the call from Danny Constantine, Willson collected Lingeborg downstairs, where he was playing dime poker with some of the boys in the radio room, checked out a Black Maria from the coroner's pool, and drove out to the institute. He had decided to take the reporter at his word and not wait for Percy's boys to get around to fetching the tramp's body.

"Christ, I hate this hot weather," Francis said, as they drove. "When the hell will it cool off?"

"It's all a state of mind," Willson said.

"The hell it is!"

"I'm telling you, Francis, there's a switch in your head. It's the heat switch. You pull it, and you don't feel hot anymore."

"You grew up in the fucking jungle. I came here so's I didn't have to live in weather like that."

"What did you do last summer, and the summer before?"

"I don't know. It ain't ever been this fucking hot before."

Francis Lingeborg, Willson thought, with a dash of affection, and said, "You dumb, fucking Swede. It's this fucking hot every fucking summer. And every summer you say the same fucking thing." The two men looked at each other and broke into smiles.

"It's still hot," Francis said.

"Shit," said Willson as he pulled up to the institute gatehouse. Then, "Look at that. It's King Michael of fucking Rumania."

He was talking about the elaborately uniformed guard who had stepped out of the gatehouse as the van approached. The guard was trying to look at Willson hard. They still did that sometimes, but somehow now it didn't have the old kick. The white motherfuckers had lost their inbred confidence, now that being white didn't mean shit except a ticket to a mass grave.

"What do you want?" the guard said.

Willson pulled his shield and held it out about an inch in front of the guard's nose. He kept it there, and said, "There's a body in your morgue that belongs to the city. We're here to collect it."

Francis nodded pleasantly and touched his hat brim.

"I don't know anything about it."

"We've got an order. The decedent's name is Earl Larsen. He checked in here Monday."

"Now he's checking out," Lingeborg added.

The guard went into the gatehouse and came back with a clipboard. "Nothing here, either."

"That ain't my problem, General. You gonna let us through? Or do I call dispatch and request a little help?"

The guard hesitated.

"I'd love to do that, you know. I'd love to rush this place and put my tire tracks right up the back of that John Phillip Sousa jacket you got on."

"I'll have to call somebody," the guard said.

"Make it happen, General. Make it happen quick."

"You're always so nice and pleasant, Sarge," Francis said as the guard went back to make his call.

"Brighten everybody's day, don't I?"

"Fuck, it's hot!" Francis said, pinching his hat by the crown and fanning himself.

"I'm giving this son of a bitch about ten seconds before I drive through." He gunned the motor, and felt disappointed when the guard suddenly reappeared.

"Drive 'round back to hospital receiving. Dr. Gray will see you there."

"Doctor Gray. *Doctor* Gray." The gate opened and Willson drove up the shaded lane and around the side of the institute. When they came to the back of the building, Gray stood in the shade of an awning watching coolly as Willson backed in and set the brake. Willson and Francis got out, Willson feeling his shirt sticking to his back.

"Sergeant Willson?"

"That's right."

"I'm Simon Gray." He offered his hand, and Willson shook it.

"This is my partner, Detective Lingeborg."

"Yes. Now, what can I do for you?"

"We're here to collect Earl Larsen's body."

Gray smiled. "I see. Well, it seems that Mr. Larsen is rather more popular dead than he was alive."

"Meaning?"

"Merely a joke, Sergeant," Gray said. "May I see the order, please?"

"There isn't one."

Gray's eyebrows rose. "Am I to take it you lied to my man at the gate?"

"Take it any way you want. Just give us the body."

"I don't believe I'm required to release it to you without an order."

"He was a material witness to a murder," Willson said.

"Oh, yes. The vampire," Gray said, sounding amused. "Mr. Constantine was interested in him for the same reason today. In fact, Sergeant, I must confess I *was* rather expecting you."

"Look, Doctor," Willson said, "material witness dies, it's my duty to get an autopsy performed."

"We've done one. I'll be happy to give you a copy of the pathology report."

"I don't give a damn about your pathology report. The body. *Now.*"

Back in the van, Francis Lingeborg swallowed hard. He could see that Gray was not used to being talked to this way. Gray stared at Willson, and Willson stared right back. Lingeborg was afraid of what would happen next if the doctor refused.

Then Gray said, "Of course, Sergeant. I'll have the body and the reports sent down right away."

Gray went back inside. Willson and Francis sat in the shade at the edge of the receiving dock and smoked, Francis a cigarette and Willson the stub of a cigar he'd been saving from last night at the ballpark.

"He don't like you, Sarge," Lingeborg said.

"Fuck 'im."

They sat and smoked. Willson thought about last night, sitting on the porch with Della after the boys were in bed and watching the glow linger in the western sky until almost eleven o'clock. They'd seen a couple of shooting stars streak across the sky, and Della had made a big deal about making a wish. Foolishness, Willson had told her, and she'd sat up from where she'd been resting in his lap and swatted the hat right off his head.

"Why, Dooley Willson, didn't I wish for you just that way! You'd better believe it's true."

"Don't talk crazy," Willson had said with a laugh. "People do what they gonna do, star or no star."

"Well, that night I decided I was going to tell Spencer Davis yes if you didn't start acting like you wanted to court me. And I made that wish, and didn't you come over the very next afternoon with those nice tuberoses and all."

"Wasn't my idea," Dooley said. "My momma made me take 'em. Lord, did they stink!"

"My favorite kind of flower, too," Della said, ignoring him. "And all because of that wish."

"You know what I wish now?" Dooley said, puffing on the cigar.

"What?"

"I wish you'd shut up!"

Willson smiled to himself, remembering how Della had jumped up and tried to go inside, and how he'd caught her, and the way they'd wrestled off the porch and onto the dewy grass. Of course, then he had to say he was glad she'd wished on that star, and how much he loved the smell of those tuberoses. They'd been married almost eight years now, and he loved that woman more than ever.

"Christ, it's hot," Francis said. He was watching a couple of men in coveralls who were washing dried mud off the fenders of a big Archer sedan. God, he wished he could get under that hose for a second. "I don't suppose they'd give a man something to drink here?"

"Why don't you ask Gray to make you a Bacardi?" Willson said, and started laughing.

Finally after twenty minutes an orderly appeared, unlocked the door from the inside, and pushed a gurney with a shrouded body on it out onto the dock.

"Dr. Gray says to give you these," the orderly said, handing Willson an envelope. "Sign here for the body."

"Sign, Francis," Willson said, shoving the cigar into the corner of his mouth as he lifted the sheet covering the corpse's head. He winced. There was a nasty, open gash that began at the side of the neck and ran down over the collarbone and across the chest. But it was Larsen, all right. Willson opened the back of the van, pulled out a stretcher, and he and the orderly transferred the body to it, and loaded it in.

"Thank you, brother," Willson said. "Tell your boss we appreciate the cooperation."

"Sure," the orderly said, exchanging a look with the sergeant, two black men taking care of business, with the white man off to the side having nothing to do with it at all.

"All right," Willson said when the orderly had gone back inside. "Now we got the fucker. You drive in today?"

"Naw, I took the streetcar. Why?"

"I'll drop you off at home." He knew Lingeborg had a couple of vacation days coming. They'd both been working long hours, and he wanted to give the Swede a break.

"Hey, that's swell, Sarge. Thanks."

They started off.

"Fucking hot, though," Francis said.

19

Thursday afternoon at Nicollet Field, Lou Ravelli went three for five, hitting one against the Walnut Hill candy bar sign in deep center, 435 feet from home that drove in two, as the Millers had gone on to beat the St. Peter's Saints 11-3. The Saints were down to twelve players. When the game was over, Mike Kelly had called the boys together in the dressing room and told them St. Pete would not be back.

"Those boys and Louisville are out of the league. So's Milwaukee and KC. So's Columbus," Kelly said. "Lord, I'm gonna miss Ohio."

"Who's left?" Cullop, the big right fielder, had asked.

"Us and the Monarchs."

So it was true! Lou had sat there feeling like someone had poured cold water down his back. It had all been rumors up 'til then, even though Lou had overheard a couple of the Monarchs talking about finding houses for their families.

There was a lot of muttering, and Kelly waited for it to die down before he said, "Willkinson's going to take over Parade Stadium and fix it up for baseball, but that's going to take about a month. Until he's ready, we're sharing the ballpark. They'll be home when we're away."

"We ain't ever *going* anywhere. Except Indy!" Jack Tate, the pitcher, said.

"They'll play nights when we're here days. It's only for a month."

"What about the facilities?"

"They'll dress in here."

"Niggers can't dress in here!"

"It's part of the deal with Willkinson. He's got money. He's got players. And we can't have a league without at least four teams. You want to keep playing ball and gettin' paid for it, you'll keep your mouth shut and do what you're told. It ain't gonna be any different than what you were doin' before. You go out and play. Instead of worryin' about how you're gonna shower after the niggers do, you'd better start thinking about how the hell you're gonna beat 'em. They whipped you twice in them exhibition games. You want to hit something, hit the fucking pill."

More muttering. Lou dejectedly started to unlace his shoes.

"And speaking of that, it seems our left fielder Ravelli has struck the Walnut Hill sign today, and so on behalf of the boys at the factory—" Kelly tossed a box at Lou, who barely looked up in time to catch it.

"Aw, Mike, I can't eat these goddamn things," Lou groaned.

"Then stick 'em in yer ear. Everybody report here at nine tomorrow for drill!"

Lou went home to lie down on his bed and think about things. Underneath his mattress were the pamphlets Ed Pratt had given him the night he was thrown out of the game, and copies of the newspapers *The Searchlight* and *Sgt. Dalton's Weekly*. Lou had tried to read them, but none of it made much sense to him, not that he was able to concentrate anyway. It all reminded him of catechism class back in grade school. They weren't trying to convince you. They were just drumming things into you that you were already supposed to believe in anyway.

He'd hated catechism, and to tell the truth, he hadn't liked the pamphlets much better. Ed Pratt had told him that the Klan did things. Well, that's what Lou wanted. He wanted to *do* something, anything to break out of that helpless feeling that held him so tight. He'd never had it this bad before. Not even when his family got sick.

Back then, everything had happened so fast, like an explosion or something that had kicked him free before he could think about what had happened to everybody he knew and loved. Lou had put that off to later.

Instead, he'd thrown himself into playing ball. Out on the field he could do things. He could stop the other team from getting anywhere, and then, when he was up at the plate with the bat in his hands, he could make them pay. Oh, how he made them pay!

Someone tapped at his door. "Louie? Are you decent?" It was Shirley.

"Just a minute!" Lou called, stuffing the literature back into its hiding place. He didn't know why he felt such panic about anybody catching him with the stuff, but he did.

"Now?"

"Yeah, now." He sat up on his pillows as Shirl came in. She'd been swimming at Lake Harriet this afternoon, and looked brown and fit, her hair still wet and combed straight back.

"Hey, good-looking," she said. "Why don't you open a window? There's a nice breeze." She went over and threw back the sash, then saw the box of candy bars on the dresser.

"Oh, Louie, you hit the sign!"

"Yeah, I guess I did."

"Can I have one?" she began, then frowned and stuck out her tongue. "Oh, ish! They're all melted, Lou."

"Put 'em down in the cellar. They'll firm up."

Shirley fished around and found a bar that wasn't too bad, unwrapped it, and started to eat. "You know," she said, bouncing down on the end of the bed, "you shouldn't oughtta lay around in here. You've got them worried."

"Who's worried?"

"Why, Aunt Lucy and Kal. They were talking about you while Aunt Lucy got dinner on."

"What did they say?"

"Well, *she* thinks you've got delayed shell shock. Like they had in the war? She was reading something about it in her *Redbook*. They say that sometimes, something so bad happens to a person that they actually convince themselves it never really happened at all. But to do that, they also have to convince themselves about a lot of other things that aren't true, either, and pretty soon they can't think straight at all anymore."

"Is that right? Well, where do you think those candy bars you're shoving down your face came from, Dr. Freud?" *Freud*, he thought. *Wasn't Freud a Jew?*

"Just telling you what she said, Louie."

"And you got chocolate on your mouth," Lou said.

"Yeah?" Shirley bounced off the bed and went to the mirror, pulling the hem of her shirtwaist up and touching it with her tongue, then wiping the chocolate away. "How's that?" she said, whirling around.

"Your aunt's gonna beat your behind for using your blouse that way."

"Maybe *I'll* get shell shock."

"Maybe," Lou said, laughing in spite of the way he felt.

"Are you coming down for supper?"

"What's the supper?"

"Turkey liver dumplings," Shirley said, making a face.

"I can't," Lou said. "I've got a meeting to go to."

"What meeting?"

"Just some boys I know. It's kind of a fraternal meeting."

"Are you joining the Odd Fellows, Lou?"

"Something like that."

"Aww. That's too bad, because Danny's supposed to be coming home, and Aunt Lucy was kind of hoping everybody could have supper together."

"I've got a day game tomorrow. Maybe I can make it then. You tell her I'm real sorry."

"Don't you want to tell her yourself? I'm sure she'd fix you a sandwich or something."

"Naw. I'm going to sneak out the back way. I hate it when she fusses over me."

Shirley sighed deeply. "Don't I know it!" She eyed the box.

"Take the whole thing, Shirl."

"Could I? Gee, thanks, Louie!" She rushed over and planted a kiss on his forehead. Then she grabbed the candy bars and left him shaking his head and wondering how anyone could possibly be so cheerful and energetic all the time when they were as sick as she was.

Foss Memorial Church was set back from the street, sandwiched between an old livery stable and the clapboard fence of a city corporation yard. Lou walked past it twice, then, seeing the lettering above the colonnaded porch, hesitated about going in. He wasn't sure he wanted to join up with any organization, no matter what it believed in. It was hard enough staying out of trouble in a ball club.

He had about decided to go home when a heavy hand clapped down on his shoulder.

"What did I tell you?" Ed Pratt said to the two men who were with him. "Here he is—and early, too."

Lou took a look at the men who were with Ed. They seemed respectable enough, wearing summer-weight suits, fresh collars, and hats that were not too old. They were almost *too* respectable-looking. Lou felt vaguely disappointed. Somehow, he had kind of expected them to be wearing sheets and hoods.

"We saw you out there at the game today," one of the men said. "You are one hell of a hitter."

"Thanks," Lou said.

There was a moment of awkward silence, then Pratt said, "We'd better go in and get the paperwork started." He had the keys to the church and unlocked it. Inside, the air was damp and very warm. "Throw open some of those windows, Arn. I'll get the lights." Pratt switched them on as the other man began pulling the tops of the windows open with a long pole. The third man went to a closet up behind the pulpit and brought out two furled flags: the U.S. flag and a yellow triangular ensign with a red scalloped border and a black flying dragon on it that had a barbed tail and a long, barbed red tongue. He put the flags into holders.

"The rest of the Klavern will be in soon, Lou," Pratt said, coming over with a manila folder. "While you're waiting, why don't you fill this out for us."

"What's it for?"

"It's just a formality. An application. The lodge rules say we have to check you out, make sure you're not a government agent."

"No G-man hits lefties like this boy," Arn said from the other side of the church. Pratt handed Lou a pencil and Lou put down his name and address.

"Just put down Christian for your religious affiliation. Remember, like we talked about?"

Lou read the questions. *Are you a White Male Gentile? Are you at least 18 years old, of sound mind and good Character? Do you believe in the Christian religion? Are you loyal to the United States Government and not to any Foreign King, Power, or Pontiff? Have you ever applied to any chapter, lodge, or Klavern of the Ku Klux Klan before?* Lou put down a yes for all but the last, which he figured to be a trick. They wanted to see if they could lull you into answering yes to that one, too. While he was working on the application more men arrived for the meeting. They looked like working-class people, and there was nothing remarkable about any of them. They chatted with each other and joked around. In a way they acted like the ball club did in the locker room before a game. One by one, they all took a peek at Lou, who was getting the impression he was some kind of celebrity here tonight. Nobody spoke to him. Finally, when around thirty people had filled the front pews of the church, Ed Pratt came over to him.

"You've filled that out? Good. Now, there's the matter of the Klectokon."

"The what?"

"It's the ten-dollar initiation fee."

"Ten dollars!" Lou exclaimed heatedly. "Hell, I just paid sixty for the privilege of going after that nigger pitcher."

"That's what it costs, Lou. If you don't have the money tonight, we'll take your note, of course. We trust you. Anyway, it's men more than money we're after."

"I haven't even said I'd join yet," Lou said sulkily. Ten dollars put this whole thing into an entirely different light. Why, that was a month's room and board!

"Why don't we talk about it later?" Ed said. "The Kludd's about to give the blessing and oath and read from the Kloran, and since you're not officially in yet, you're going to have to wait outside the Inner Door of the Klan."

He walked Lou out. There was a man in a hood standing in the vestibule, and another who stood watch outside. Ed grabbed Lou a folding wooden chair and opened it up for him. "You just sit tight, now, Lou. It'll just be a few minutes. You want a smoke while you're waiting?"

"I dip, if you've got some."

"Can't help you there. Don't go away. The Klarogo will open the inner door when we're ready to welcome you."

Ed went back inside and Lou sat down. The hooded man folded his arms.

"Who are you?" Lou asked.

"I'm the Klexter," the Klansman replied.

"What the hell's a Klexter?"

"The outer guard of a Klan."

"Well, quit looking at me."

"It's my job."

"Yeah?" Lou said, in such a way that the man shrugged, and turned away. Lou sat there and began to wonder what his father would have said about him joining the Klan. The old man would have had a fit, that's what. But things were different now. Anyway, the old man had his Knights of Columbus, and it was the same thing, all the costumes and secret meetings that turned into card games when they broke up, and then they'd get to parade up the aisle in their feathered hats on Easter Sunday and at midnight mass on Christmas.

This wasn't any different, Lou thought. Besides, he hadn't actually joined up yet. He was just here because he'd agreed with some of the things Ed Pratt had said to him after the game. Hell, the old man would have agreed with them, too. If Lou remembered right, his father had never had much use for niggers.

The prayers went on inside for a while, and Lou began to wish he had eaten supper, but then the door pushed open, and the Klarogo told him he could go in and listen to the Cyclops give a talk. Lou took a seat. This was more like it. Up behind the pulpit now were half a dozen men in white robes and hoods. One of them stepped up. He was a small man, and seemed frail, and walked to the pulpit carefully, holding on to the sides as he began to speak. Lou guessed that he must be the Cyclops.

"It is so good to see all of you," the man said. "And to know that our ranks are about to increase."

Everyone turned around and looked at Lou. Hungrily, Lou thought, putting an embarrassed half-smile on his face.

"In 1921, this lodge had nearly two thousand men on its roll. I'm sure I don't have to tell you what we could do now with two thousand men. With two thousand, we could scour this city clean! With two thousand men, we could grab the hands of time and force back the clock. No diseases! No adulteration! No mongrelization of every home and factory and office! Two thousand men could cauterize the effects of pestilence from our land!

"But there are not two thousand men now. In a sense, we have sacrificed the Two Thousand to hold back the waters of the flood. But man can hold fast only so long before the tide breaks him down and washes him away. Thus it was with the Two Thousand. But we must take heart! This Klavern, reduced as it is, has had all its soft parts worn away. All those that wavered, who lost faith, and who fell sick, are gone. What is left is hard. Hard as steel. Hard as *truth*, and with God on our side!"

The Klavern jumped up and applauded loudly. Looking at some of the bellies on the men in his row, Lou didn't think they looked all that hard. Some of the men were looking back at him. Lou got up and started clapping, too.

"One of the men who works for me came to my office the other day," the Cyclops went on. "He had a copy of an article one of his reporters had written. It seems there is a vampire in this city. A killer who slays and then somehow drains his victims of all their fluid. The man wanted to know whether we wanted to print such a story. Ordinarily I do not get involved in such decisions, but this is a sensitive subject, and he wanted my approval before going ahead with it. I asked him what he thought we ought to do. He replied that it was a good story, and that the paper ought to, in his parlance, 'give it some play.'

"Well, it was a sensational story all right, and certainly frighten-ing, something to worry about, something to prompt a man to part with his three cents, and I was inclined to give my permission without much thought. But then my man mentioned, almost in passing, that one of the last victims of this so-called vampire was a man of mixed Negro blood, and that another was an Indian. I asked him was this true, were there any white men among the dead, and he said he couldn't be sure. And you know what I did? I took the copy in my hands and I tore it to pieces, and I said to him, 'Let them die!' "

Men called out, "That's right!" and "Let 'em!"

" 'Let them die,' I said, because what are one or two or four of them compared to the flower of our race that has been wiped from the face of the earth! It is our children who are dying. It is our women who are killed each month by the very cycle nature intended to propagate the species with. And *they* who carry it and do not suffer, they who profit by our pain, they who dare to calculate the *increase* they will soon possess because of our destruction, *they* who alone of all the races on this earth have not been touched, I say *let them die*. If four of them die, I say let them, and pray to God for five hundred more. If, by next week, five thousand were to be murdered by this fiend, I will print no notice of it. Because I have learned, in the course of my long experience, that printing terror merely confines it.

"You have your when and where, and the reader believes that so long as he stays away from such and such place and such and such time, he will be safe. He is warned, and though it would be a sensation, it would also be a comfort to him. Because he would know where he stands in relation to the crimes.

"Much better," the Cyclops went on, after a moment of waiting, "not to publicize. Much better to let rumor take its course. Let the story be born and travel through their neighborhoods. Let the mothers fear for their children and keep them indoors; let the fathers arm themselves and walk quickly down the deserted streets, lest they be the next to fall. Let them fear for their blood, let them pray that nothing should happen to them! In that way, their confidence will be undermined. Fear will grip their hearts. And our work, which we shall continue, will by inference strike more terror than ever before!

"I do not know who the vampire is, nor do I care. If she is the avenging angel of our race, then so be it. We have no quarrel with her or her work, nor she with us. We both sow the same seeds, and harvest the same fear. To that end, we must help her where we can.

"All of you work with them. Your children go to school with their children. Your wives may chat with their wives at the market, or you may find yourself sitting next to them at the beach. Talk about this vampire. Tell how his victim was a young family man, found sucked dry behind the old Crockett mill! Say how he was found with his eyes open and his mouth twisted in a grimace of death that resembled a smile. That is God's smile, the reward for work well done! Tell how the police are baffled. Say that the vampire has vowed to kill and kill again until the people of this city are freed from the scalawags and carpetbaggers from Chicago and the South, the *aliens* who know nothing of our fine way of life, who merely degrade and turn it into a foul parody of civic life by their overwhelming, smug, untouched presence.

"Well, we shall touch them, all right. We have already, and will continue to do it. At last count we have removed almost two hundred, and we will remove more. We are going to step up our efforts. We are going to burst their families apart. We are no longer going to pick off the vagrants and the single men whom no one knows or mourns. Such missing people can easily be ignored, but our great work will be ignored no longer!

"We are getting sick again, but they shall pay. By God, we shall make them!"

He stopped speaking, and when the applause burst out, Lou jumped up with the rest of them. He had no idea what the hooded, frail old man was talking about, but it sounded good.

They were doing something here, and Lou wanted to help.

C H A P T E R

20

When the Cyclops got through speaking there was a business meeting that turned into an argument about whether the Klavern ought to spend some money putting on a fish fry the second weekend in July. In spite of how that speech had stirred him up, Lou felt himself getting restless. The truth was, he didn't care much for meetings, and he thought the Cyclops looked silly up there banging his gavel so hard it made his hood slip down over his eyes. But then Ed Pratt came and leaned into the pew and said he'd like to talk to him privately. Lou followed him through a doorway at the head of the side aisle, into a small meeting room. Ed's friend Arn was there, and a couple of other men Lou hadn't noticed before. Ed sat down next to Lou and pulled his hood off.

"Well, Lou. What did you think of that speech?"

"It was pretty good. Made me want to get going and do something."

"The Cyclops can do that, all right. You know, he was with the original Klan down in Georgia when he was a kid. He's been fighting the fight all his life."

"That's good," Lou said, wondering who the Cyclops really was.

"Now, Lou, you sat there patiently and listened to all that quibbling about the goddamned smelt fry, but I know that's not why you came. No, you came because you were hoping for some action, am I right?"

"I guess that's true."

"Good. Good. Now, like I said before, normally we'd have to look your application over real thoroughly, and then you would be instructed in the ways of the Klavern. You'd study the Kloran and so forth, then be tested, and finally initiated into the body."

"I'd learn the secret signs and all that."

"That's right. But we're in a war again, Lou, and wartime demands that we relax our rules a little and operate somewhat more informally. All of us here are considered pretty fair judges of character. We've nominated many new members, and all of them have turned out to be excellent Klansmen. And so—I'm speaking for the group now, Lou—we feel that tonight, we're able to offer you a certain opportunity you might not have otherwise."

"Opportunity?"

Ed leaned closer. "All of us like to put on the robes and make a public show of force. That's important, but there's another part of us the public never sees. That's where the real work is done. That's what the Cyclops was talking about. That vampire, she's killed a few. Well, that's just fine. But we've done more than that."

"About two hundred times more than that," Arn said.

"You've killed two hundred niggers?" Lou said.

"Let's just say that we have removed two hundred of them from the streets. Killing them's a waste when they've got something we need."

"What's that?" Lou asked, feeling panicky, like he always did when his ears seemed to be soaking up more than his brain could absorb.

Ed glanced at the other men. "One thing about the Klavern, Lou. You only know parts of the whole thing, only what you need to know. I don't know all of it. Arn here doesn't either. Even the Cyclops doesn't know everything. None of us do. We like it that way, understand? Look at it this way: when you're standing up there with the bat in your hand, you're not worrying about how many beers that vendor in the third base stand's got left in his case, do you? You're up there to do just one thing. Hit the ball. Am I right?"

"Sure, but—"

Ed Pratt put his hand on Lou's shoulder and gave it a squeeze. "We go on little hunting trips, Lou. We're looking to catch some young buck niggers. The younger and fitter, the better. Now, if it was just a matter of gunning 'em down, why, none of us has a problem with that. It's a lot easier than deer hunting, especially as they'll take any sort of bait. But we've got to catch these boys alive, see? And sometimes, they're just too young and too fast for us to handle."

"I ain't so good at running up the side of a fence anymore," Arn said.

"There's where you come in, Lou. We want to take you out tonight and see what you can do."

"You mean put me in a robe and all?"

"You don't need a robe. You just turn your collar up and pull your hat brim down. They'll never know what hit 'em. We all look alike to a nigger. All we want to do is drive around for a little while, and see what we can come up with. And if you catch one for us, why, then you're in. We'll waive the Klectokon, and the first year's dues, and throw in a swell satin robe set besides. We're having a Klonklave next week out in Chaska, and you'd look awfully good in it. We get the ladies out then, too. People act free at a Klonklave, Lou. It stirs up something in your soul that you never thought you had, and lets it loose out where it can do the world some good. I'll never forget how I felt that first time." Ed shook his head. "All I can say is I wish we could trade places with you for that one night!"

"When do you want to go?" Lou said. He was ready to do anything, so long as he did not have to listen to another speech.

"Right now. If we catch us one or two, we'll raise enough money to throw fifty smelt fries!"

"All right," Lou said. "I guess I will. But I got to be at the ballpark early tomorrow."

"You'll be back in your bed by eleven."

"Okay, then."

They went out a side door that led to the alley behind the church. There was a canvas-topped truck parked out there. Arn went to crank it, but had trouble turning it over, so Lou had to help him. He gave one yank, and the motor coughed and began running.

"It's my goddamned back," Arn complained, getting into the back with Ed, Lou, and another man named Mike Hansen.

"Last week you were blaming the magneto," Ed said. "Or was it the crank had oil on it?"

"Next time, you start it," Arn groused as the others laughed.

The truck drove downtown, and turned left on Washington Avenue, passing the Milwaukee Road terminal. Lou looked out the back of the truck at the empty streets. Only a few of the dark, crumbling buildings downtown had any lights on. A lot of the streetlamps were out, too, their bulbs burned out or broken. There was still a hint of a glow in the west—it was quarter to ten according to the clock tower on the depot, but it might as well have been three in the morning. There wasn't anybody out on the streets at all. They passed between the Nicollet Hotel and the Gateway Park pavilion, and turned right on Hennepin, where there was a stretch of bars and flophouses and chop suey joints.

"Say, look at that place," Arn said. "Jimmy Toy's. I heard the Archangel dresses up like a man and eats there sometimes."

"Big deal," Hansen said. "So do you."

"Lay off," Arn began, but suddenly Ed knocked on the back window of the cab.

"There's one!" he said, pointing to a man who had just come out of a tavern.

Lou watched a Negro look both ways along Hennepin, then cross unsteadily to the park, where he went into the pavilion.

"I'll get him," Arn said grimly, pulling a sap from his pocket and slapping it into his palm. "Once around the block."

He jumped out, and went into the park. The truck drove ahead slowly, turning the corner. Lou couldn't see much, and that made him nervous. What if somebody figured out what they were about to do? There had to be a cop or two around, especially with City Hall only two blocks away. But when the truck stopped again—directly across the street from the hotel entrance—there was no one, except for Arn waving from the pavilion door. Hansen grabbed a flour sack from the floor, jumped out, and joined him. A moment later the two of them dragged their limp victim over. "Come on," Ed said, and he and Lou helped pull the man inside. The other two jumped aboard; the driver gunned the motor, headed down Nicollet to First, turned north. No cars followed. A few blocks later they were in the warehouse district. Heart pounding, Lou looked at the black man. The flour sack, with four X's printed across it, was tied around his neck with a rope.

"That was a piece o' work, I'll tell you!" Arn said excitedly.

"Go on. He was sleeping it off."

"As a matter of fact he was taking a leak when I sapped him."

"Is that right? So who put his dick back in his pants?"

"Arn did," Hansen said. "Twice!"

They all laughed at that. Lou found himself laughing, too. Then, as the truck drove on, he kept staring at the Negro who lay limp on the floor.

"It's dead around here," Lou said after a while.

"Some nights it's that way," Hansen said.

"You guys are rounding up niggers, though, right?"

"What's it look like?"

"What it looks like is nothin'," Lou said. "Why the hell don't you go up to the North Side? That's where they live, ain't it? You could fill this whole truck with niggers up there!"

The others looked toward Ed, who tipped back his hat. "We've got to be careful, Lou. So we've got a couple of routes we follow, and we pick them off when we can. Alkies like this one are the best. They're less likely to have friends or family come for 'em later."

"Bullshit," Lou said. Something about these men was making him angry. It had seemed so dangerous before Arn had snatched the first one, but now he could see how safe they were playing it. "You're the Klan, aren't you? I thought the Klan did things. That's how it was out West. If the Klan rode out, all the niggers shut the doors and turned out the lights."

"What sort of action do you think we ought to take, Lou?" Ed said, trying to lace his voice with sarcasm, and falling flat.

"I say we drive up to Plymouth bold as you please and get us some."

"We'd have to run that by the Cyclops, Lou," Ed said.

"Didn't you listen to his speech? I say we go up there right now, tonight, and show them niggers the Klan means business in this town."

The others were all looking at Ed. Ed looked down at the unconscious Negro, poking at his legs with his toe.

"Okay," he finally said. "Hell, why not?" He leaned into the open back window of the cab. "Head north on Bryant, Tom."

Nobody said anything. The truck turned onto Bryant, and drove into the old Jewish neighborhood that had been taken over by the Negroes when they had first started coming in large numbers after the war.

"All right, Lou," Ed said. "You want action, you've got it. Things are real lively up in the North Side."

It was true. Lights burned in the houses up here, and there was traffic and people walking around on the street. Everyone looked nicely dressed. In fact, there seemed to be some kind of promenade going on. Driving past the doorways of the taverns they heard snatches of music. It all made Lou feel a little uneasy, but excited, too. He'd been out along Plymouth Avenue a couple of times with the boys, and he'd had fun playing cards or visiting some of the girls he and the boys knew. Those nights the North Side had been like a relief to him. People out laughing, having a good time. Lou hadn't thought about what color anybody was. Now, though, he could see it, all right. He couldn't see anything but.

"Okay, Lou," Ed said as the truck slowed just past Colfax. "Your idea, so you get first pick for yourself."

"Just grab somebody off the street? There's too many people around!" They passed a nigger cop, who walked slowly, twirling his nightstick.

"Ain't you ever gone huntin'?" Arn said. "You've got to figure things out and do them carefully."

"Like Arn did when he fell asleep in that tree last fall," Mike Hansen said.

"That's where he got that bad back."

"He did it carefully, though."

"Aww, shut up, all of you!" Just then the tied-up man groaned underneath the flour sack. Arn bent town and hit him again with the sap.

"Come on, Lou," Ed said in a taunting voice. "This is your chance to do something, just like we talked about. You're not turning yellow on us, are you?"

"I ain't yella!" Lou said, getting up.

"That's the way. We'll park up ahead and keep an eye on you."

Lou got out of the truck. He felt a little sick inside. He passed a tavern and thought, if he went inside and called home, Danny might be there. If the phones were working, that is. Some nights they didn't work. But there were taxicabs, he could call one of those. *Yeah*, Lou thought, *but that costs money. Yeah, but if I stay with these boys and don't catch anybody, they'll take two fins off me. They know I've got it on me, too.* The whole thing made him mad, and he remembered suddenly how he had felt paying Kelly that fine, and looked up and saw the whole street full of niggers and decided he would go through with it after all, just to show them. He pulled his collar up like Ed told him and tugged at the brim of his hat and walked past Rostek's on the corner of Plymouth and Emerson. It was crowded in there, the waiters were running around taking orders to their customers, and Lou smelled crisp potato pancakes and the sweet-sour smell of red cabbage and was suddenly homesick, remembering how it was to walk home from confession on Saturday afternoon and stop for cannelloni and prosciutto to take home for supper.

No, no, Lou, he told himself, *you're in with these fellows and you've got to prove yourself.* He began looking around, and his eyes rested on a man on the other side of the street, young and good looking, wearing a straw hat and a seersucker suit. He had stopped to light a cigarette and now he started walking north on Emerson, away from the crowds. Yes, that one, Lou thought, that one wasn't some drunk you could hit from behind like Arn had done downtown. If he caught that one these Klansmen were bound to be impressed. And he could do it, too. His heart started beating faster as he waited for a trolley to pass. He crossed the street and walked faster to catch up with the buck. Behind him he heard the truck grind into gear, and turn slowly up the street behind him.

"Excuse me, brother," Lou said. "You got a match?"

The man stopped, turned, and looked Lou up and down. He had a toothpick in one corner of his mouth. His eyes sparkled with intelligence and confidence, and he smiled at Lou.

"Why, sure I do—" he began, and then he saw the truck coming up. "You crazy motherfucker, you don't know who you're messin' with!" He swung his fist, smacking Lou hard on the jaw. Lou stumbled back and fell down, and the nigger bolted. Behind him Lou heard the Klan boys laughing.

"That's the last you'll see o' him!"

"Shut the hell up and follow me!" Lou yelled, getting up and running. The buck was fast, and had a good lead, but Lou knew how to run, and he was in shape, and he began eating up the distance between them. It was down to five yards and he could hear the nigger breathing hard, saw him take a quick look over his shoulder and then cut across a yard, into an alley, one dog barking down the street as Lou put on a burst. He could run like this all day, breathing regular and easy with his hat flying off his head. They were in the alley, both running as fast as they could, and then all of a sudden there was a high fence in front of them. The boy took a jump, got one leg over, but Lou caught him by the seat of his pants and pulled him down hard.

He turned around. Lou could see how afraid he was.

"Who the fuck *are* you?" he gasped.

"Maybe you heard about that vampire," Lou said. He wasn't sure why he'd said it, but seeing even more fear grip the Negro's face made him glad he had.

"You ain't killin' me!" he yelled, reaching into his pocket and pulling out a razor. "You try! I'll cut you, motherfucker! I'll cut you good." He swept at Lou, and Lou felt something catch against his arm. He looked down and saw blood, and the sight of it somehow filled him with all the rage that had been bottled up inside ever since he'd left Frisco. Behind him was a garbage can and he grabbed the metal cover for a shield, and when the Negro slashed at him with the razor again he smashed his arm with it, knocking the blade away. The Negro backed off now, eyes wide, Lou smiling as he stepped after him and putting all his weight behind his next swing, just like hitting a ball, bashing the Negro hard, watching as he moaned softly and collapsed unconscious against the fence.

The truck came into the alley, throwing Lou's shadow against the fence. Ed Pratt came up holding another flour sack.

"Look at that watch chain!" Arn exclaimed. Ed started going through the man's pockets, and came up with a thick money roll and a notebook. He opened the book, then frowned.

"Shit!"

"What's wrong?"

"This is one of Theo Rostek's boys. Here's his numbers book."

"Let's see." Arn took a look. "Christ, you're right. We'd better get the hell out of here."

"What are you talking about?" Lou protested. "The lousy son of a bitch cut me!"

"It's your bad luck, that's all. You did a good job, but this was the wrong nigger to jump."

"What do you mean?"

"I mean he's no good to us. He's protected. They wouldn't give us a dime if we brought him in. Dime, hell, they'd murder us." Ed put the money roll back. "Did you say anything to him?"

"I don't know."

"You didn't mention the Klan?"

"I don't know!"

"Come on. Let's get the hell out of here."

Lou dropped the trash can lid, got into the truck, and they drove out of north Milltown. He sat on the bench and held on to the handkerchief he'd wrapped around his arm. The cut looked pretty bad, but he didn't care. He said nothing. He felt like hell.

"Look, Lou," Ed said as they got on Washington again, "there's things we can't explain to you yet. We grab these niggers and take 'em to a place that pays a bounty. That's all I can say right now. Now, with what you did tonight, running that nigger down and all, you've proved yourself as far as I'm concerned. I'll just have to talk things over with the Cyclops. In the meantime—" He bent down and took the wallet out of the pocket of the first Negro, who by now had begun to snore loudly. "We'll take your Klectokon out of this. How would that be?"

"I knocked the son of a bitch cold," Lou groused.

"Yes, you did. I'll make a full report on it. I've never seen anybody run the way you did."

Lou thought about it, remembering how it had felt to gain on the nigger, arms pumping, shoes pounding the pavement. Sure, he was angry, but only because of the way things had turned out. He realized that he'd been more excited tonight than he'd been in years. Nothing in baseball could match it!

"As far as we're concerned, you're in, am I right, boys?"

"Sure he is," Arn said.

"Would you be willing to take an oath right now?"

Why the hell not, Lou thought. "All right, sure."

"Raise up your right hand. Do you swear that you will keep secure and to yourself the secret of a Klansman when same is committed to you in the sacred bond of Klansmanship?"

"I do."

The other men came around him, smiling and slapping him on the back. On the floor, the Negro snored loudly, and tried to turn over. The truck bounced over a hole in the road.

"We'll drop you home, Lou. Next time I promise you'll see the whole operation. Everything."

Lou nodded. "I'm on Lyndale an'—"

"You don't have to tell us, Lou. We already know where you live. We know everything about you."

"How—"

"Every Klansman's a detective, that's how. We keep our eyes open and our mouths shut. That's what you've got to do from now on, too. You can't let your brothers down, Lou. You've got to lock it in tight, except when it comes to the lodge. Understand? That way, we stay ahead of the enemy. That way, we can also keep 'em close. You're one of us now, Lou. We count on you. And you can count on us."

"Sure, I can," Lou said.

CHAPTER

21

Lucille Lund sat under the dim yellow light of the floor lamp and worked on her latest embroidery project, the head of a collie dog that Shirley had traced out of a magazine for her.

At one time Lucille had been quite fond of dogs, and her family kept several collies at the farm in Owatonna when she was a girl. Of course, hardly anyone had a dog these days. Nearly all of them had died in the first wave of the sickness in '19. That was the first really sad thing people had to face. Somehow it had been easier to ignore all the human death, and concentrate on the tragedy of the dying dogs. And you could think about them now and remember what nice animals they were. And Shirley had done a fine job with the drawing. That girl was a good artist. There was no telling what she'd be capable of, if only . . . Well, Lucille never let her thoughts about Shirley go beyond that. You had to make do with the present now, and that was good enough. She had nice boarders, and Kal certainly was very sweet, and what with Lou and Shirley, and Danny, who treated them like a good older brother would, it was almost like living with family, lots better, in fact, than plenty of families she'd seen.

She heard footsteps on the porch and then the screen door bang, everything sounding fast and too close together.

"Lou?" she said, peering out toward the stair landing. "Is that you?"

"Yes, Mrs. L.," Lou said from the darkness.

"Come here."

Lou moved to the edges of the lamplight. He was holding his arm.

"Did you have a nice time tonight?"

"Sure, Mrs. L."

"Did you get anything to eat? There's leftovers on the stove if you want them."

"I'm awfully beat, Mrs. L. I think I'm just gonna go to bed."

"What's wrong with your arm?"

"Nothin'. Nothin's wrong with it—" He backed away into the dark again but she was on him like a cat on a baby bird, and made him let go of the arm.

"Lou! That's a terrible cut! How in the world did you get cut like that?"

"I got spiked," Lou stammered. "Fillin' in at short an' a fella came into second with his spikes up. Halsey patched me up, but the bandage was bothering me tonight on account of how hot it was, so I took it off!"

"You come here into the kitchen," Mrs. Lund ordered. She made him sit at the table and turned on the weak electric lights, then struck a match and lit the white gas lantern she kept above the icebox. Lou's shirtsleeve was soaked in blood. So was the sleeve of his coat. She took it from him and folded it over the back of a kitchen chair, and wiggled her fingers through the place where the fabric had been sliced from the cuff almost to the patch on the elbow.

"I suppose you play baseball with your suit jacket on," she said, getting out the peroxide, cotton balls, and some gauze. She filled an enameled basin with water and took a scissors. "The shirt's ruined," she said, and cut the sleeve off. With a washcloth and water she cleaned the wound. Then, soaking gauze with peroxide, she dabbed it.

"Christ!" Lou yelped. "What are you doin' to me, Mrs. L.?"

"You don't want this to infect, do you?"

"It's just a scratch."

"You need stitches," Mrs. Lund said. "And there's no use taking you to the hospital, because you'd still be there waiting three days from now."

"You're not going to stitch me up, are you?"

"I grew up on a farm, Louis," Mrs. Lund said firmly. "Hold that."

Lou put his hand on the gauze pad. Mrs. Lund went out to the parlor and came back with a needle and heavy black thread, which she ran through a cotton pad soaked in more peroxide. She tied the ends, biting the thread off with her front teeth, and sat down next to him.

"Ten or twelve should do it, but it'll hurt a little. Ready?"

Lou nodded weakly.

"You should thank God you're not a bleeder," she said, jabbing the darning needle into his skin. "This would be more than enough to kill you."

"What would?" Shirley Lund asked, coming in through the back door. She and Kal had been out in the radio shack. Reception had been good tonight, but Kal's A batteries had run out of juice. He was going to have to charge them before they'd be able to use the radio again. "Ooohh!" she said. "What are you doing to him, Aunt Lucy?"

"Oww! Yeah, Mrs. L., what the hell are you doing?"

Mrs. Lund cuffed him gently across the back of his head. "If you curse again I'm going to give you three more. He's got a bad cut and I'm sewing him up."

"Why don't you use that nice satin stitch you were showing me, Aunt Lucy?"

"Why don't you mind your own business," Lou said.

Shirley stuck her tongue out at him. Then she took a good look at the cut. "Wow. How'd that happen?"

"He won't say."

"Looks like a knife got him. Were you in a knife fight, Louie?"

"Oh, leave him alone, Shirley. And stop right there, Kal!"

Kal Hromatka stood in the doorway, his face red from lugging one of his heavy wet-cell A batteries in from the radio shed.

"Don't you bring that thing in here! You burned holes all over my nice linoleum the last time you charged a battery in here."

"I've got to plug her in, Lucille."

"Take it outside and put it in a box first," she said.

"Told you, Kal," Shirley said, tilting her head to get a better look at the operation.

"You're in my light," Mrs. Lund said.

"Yeah, you're in her light!" Lou said. His arm hurt, but he was feeling better since he'd come home. Although not as good as he might have if he'd never gone out with those boys tonight. He was worried about the cut, but it was his left arm, so he ought to be all right. He hoped to Christ Kelly wouldn't see what had happened to him tomorrow. If he went down to the ballpark wearing his long sleeves, and stayed out of the shower, maybe he could get away with it.

"Did you hear the Archangel tonight?" Mrs. Lund asked.

"For a little while. She played some awfully good records. Then she read a poem about Wells Street in Chicago. Empty as a tomb, it was."

"Shirley, for heaven's sake, don't be so morbid!"

"It's not morbid. She's wonderful, up there all alone in her studio." Shirley made her voice sound spooky. " 'Calling out across the prairie from the ruins of a once great city, an invisible beacon of truth cutting through the darkness.' "

"Shirley!"

"That's just how she says it, too."

"Honestly!" Mrs. Lund said, tying off the thread. She lifted Lou's arm and bit the thread in two, her teeth making a sharp click as the ends came free. While Shirley watched in fascination, her aunt wiped the cut with peroxide again, and then wrapped Lou's arm with gauze. It was not bleeding at all now.

That's what was supposed to happen, Shirley thought. You got hurt and the blood came out, and then, somehow, it stopped leaking. It flowed around like water inside you but as soon as there was a hole it plugged the leak itself. Just like that stuff Danny had put in his radiator that time it got a hole and shot steam straight out the front. He'd bought a couple of little tubes of it, and Shirley had swiped one, pouring the little gray granules out on her dresser later when she was alone. She thought then that the next time she started bleeding, she'd swallow the whole tube, but she'd lost her nerve when the time came. Besides, if that radiator stuff really was a cure, they wouldn't be able to keep it on the shelves.

Lou was flexing his fist and turning his arm over. It didn't hurt too bad, he thought. Maybe it would be okay tomorrow. Kal returned with the battery inside a cardboard box, and took it to the place behind the sink where he could hook it up to the charger. He was getting too damn old to carry such heavy things. He sat down next to Lou and looked around. Here they all were.

"Where's Dan gone to?"

"He's still at work."

"He's always working. He'll never get married again so long as he's a reporter," Kal said.

"Maybe he doesn't want to get married," said Shirley.

Mrs. Lund gathered up the gauze and scissors. "And what would you know about it?"

"Because he told me. He said he'd wait to get married until *I* was old enough, because I'm his girl!"

"Aww, bugs is what you are," Lou said.

Mrs. Lund exchanged a look with Kal. It was heartbreaking to hear the child talk like that, when she knew very well . . . But you had to be happy with what you had, and here they were all together, so she smiled and smoothed her apron front as she got up from the table.

"There's peach crumble left from dinner," she said. "Anybody interested?"

22

*D*anny Constantine and Dooley Willson were down in the morgue in the basement of City Hall. Twice in one day, Danny thought, trying not to smell the air as he breathed it. The room wasn't cool. There were a couple of pole fans stirring the rotten-chicken smell around. He and Willson stood by as Percy Satin, the acting coroner, worked on the body of Wall-Eye Larsen.

Percy did it slowly, fighting his exhaustion. He'd been up for three nights in a row, and was about to go home when Willson had shown up with the tramp's corpse. *I don't need this,* he thought. He wasn't a medical examiner. He'd got the job on the basis of his immunity from Hun, and because he'd worked a couple of summers at his uncle's funeral home. But now he was in charge of what had become the biggest department in the city government. Tonight he was going on coffee and an occasional sniff of cocaine from the dispensary.

"Man," Percy said, "look at that. Whoever had him cleaned him right out. Cut through the pleura, folded it back, and scooped him out. Heart, lungs, part of the windpipe, too." Percy stepped back to give Willson and Danny a good look. Wall-Eye Larsen's chest wall was folded back like the doors of a cuckoo clock.

"What's that pink stuff?" Willson asked.

"Don't know. It ain't embalming fluid. He was pumped full of it, whatever it was. You can see it coagulated here on what's left of the pericardium."

"He was sewn up when I saw him this afternoon," Danny said.

Percy took a look. "Hey, you're right. There's still some sutures here."

"Why would they sew him up and open him again?"

"For a post-mortem? No reason at all," Percy said, rubbing his eyes with his forearm.

"You sure he was sewn up?" Willson asked.

"I got pictures, Sergeant. And before, when Gray showed him to me, he said he'd had an intern practicing his sutures on the corpse."

"Okay, okay," Willson said with annoyance. "Do people do that, Percy?"

"Beats me. If I have to sew 'em up I use common string. But, hey, come here. Come on, he ain't gonna bite you. Look at the area of the incision in this picture. See how the tissue's inflamed and swollen?" Percy poked the cut edge with a probe. A straw-colored fluid ran out. "That's an abscess," he said.

"So?"

"It's evidence of adhesion between the cut edges. Meaning, my brothers, that this gentleman had begun to heal after he'd been sutured."

"What you saying, Percy?" Willson said.

"I think this man had surgery performed on him, and at least twenty-four to thirty-six hours' convalescence after that. Takes that long to develop this degree of infection. I mean, can you see the difference here, where the trachea's been cut out, and the innominate artery? The edges are clean. Those cuts were made after death."

"Do you think they were trying to hide the signs of the previous operation?" Danny asked.

Percy snorted in derision. "Couldn't hide it from me. Any medical examiner would have seen it in a second."

"What about this?" Danny said, and showed Percy the device he'd stolen from Gray's office. "Any idea what it might be?"

"Who do I look like? Tom Edison?"

"I think it's some kind of medical device and I'm wondering what you think, that's all."

Percy rolled his eyes. "Medical device." He took off his gloves and took it from Danny, went to a tool bench, and worked on the metal dome with a screwdriver. "Hmm," he said, taking the top off. "There's a diaphragm in here. Rubberized silk." He refit the top of the dome without fastening the screws again, and blew into one of the nipples on the side of the housing. When he lifted the top, the position of the diaphragm had changed. "Looks like a valve or pump of some sort. Maybe powered by compressed air."

"Any idea what it could be used for?"

"Man, give me about three days' rest and maybe I could come up with something—" The phone rang. Percy picked up the receiver wearily and leaned against the mouthpiece as he talked. Then he hung up. "Three in one block up in Glenwood," he said. "I gotta go."

"You need some help?" Willson said.

"No, you boys got your jobs to do. You want me to keep this one on ice for you?"

"Yeah," Willson said. "Thanks, Percy."

"Here's your pump," he replied, rubbing his eyes and giving it back in pieces to Danny, who slipped it into his pocket. He and Willson left the morgue and took the stairs up to Willson's cubicle in the homicide division. There were few cops on the floor, and no other cops at all in major crimes.

"You want some coffee?" Willson asked, as Danny sat down.

"Thanks."

"All we got is that soy-cream shit to whiten it with."

"Black's fine."

While Willson went out to get it Danny looked around the cubicle. There was a picture of Della Willson and the two boys on the desk. Nailed to the wood frame of the frosted glass partition was Willson's diploma from the Milltown Police Academy, and a lithograph of Negro soldiers in battle. "Charge of the Twenty-fourth Infantry Up San Juan Hill," read the brass tag. He was looking at it when Willson came back with the coffee.

"That was my daddy's outfit," Willson said. "They broke the right side of the Spanish line and overran the trenches. He got a commendation from Roosevelt personally."

"That your father?" Danny asked, looking at the picture above the file cabinet of a black man in a field cap and a handlebar mustache. He was shaking hands with a youthful-looking T.R. Quite a contrast to the old man who had been elected president for the third time in 1928, suffered a stroke, and was serving out the rest of his term from his bed. Not that being president meant much anymore. It was all cities and counties now. There wasn't any foreign policy other than quarantine. There wasn't any army, either, except for local militias.

Willson sat down.

"Your father's a good-looking man," Danny said. "Is he in town?"

"He had a heart attack about six years ago. In Chicago."

"I'm sorry."

"It happens," Willson said. He opened his desk drawer, took out a bottle, and poured some brandy into his coffee. "Want some?"

"No, thanks."

He grunted and put the bottle away, took a sip holding the cup gingerly with two hands. Then he put the cup down.

"You and I," Willson said, "been following each other around on this thing. I want to know what you think you got here."

"I think Gray's involved with these murders."

"The killer's a woman."

"Yes. But the tramp saw a man, too. He said it was Gray, and I believe him."

"Why?"

"He had no reason to lie. I was holding on to him when Gray gave him that shot. He was scared to death."

"Gray," Willson said. "A respectable white man. Builds the biggest hospital and research clinic in the city. He's saved hundreds of lives. He's handsome and rich. And he's tight with the boys in the Northwest Development Company. You say I should bring him in? And what about you? Where's that story you were writing?"

"The paper won't print it."

"You can't print a story about Gray, and I'm supposed to *arrest*

him? On what evidence? I don't have a damn thing linking Simon
Gray to any of this other than that hobo yelling his head off."

"You've got my pictures from the mill."

"That's a *blob*, Constantine."

"Get a warrant, then. Tear his place apart."

Willson wheeled back on his chair, opened a file cabinet, and
brought out a stack of case jackets. "You know what these are,
Constantine? Missing persons reports. Two hundred thirty-three
of them. All colored folks who've vanished in the past year. Some of
'em we can account for, people running off, leaving town because
of problems and the like. But the rest are gone. No trace. Like this
one." He opened a folder. " 'Wife stated she asked husband to go
down to the grocery for a loaf of bread and some eggs approximately
seven-thirty in the evening; husband did not return. Grocer reported
he had seen the man; he bought groceries, a newspaper, and a tin of
tobacco approximately seven forty-five.' And this one: 'Subject went
fishing as was his habit along west side of Lake Calhoun. Tackle and
stringer of fish discovered near the spot frequented by subject.
Subject's daughter reported subject failed to return home from
work.' Or this: 'Following an argument with husband, subject went
out to walk around the block to cool off. Did not return.' "

Willson closed the jacket. "Two hundred thirty-three people, and
not a single body." Willson dropped the folder onto the pile in front
of him. "We don't have enough manpower in the department
anymore to follow up on a tenth of this number of cases. On the other
hand, just by law of averages, with so many cases, we ought to have
stumbled onto *something*. Four weeks ago we got our first body over
in Loring Park. Maybe it's been this so-called vampire all along.
Maybe I can tie the murders to all these cases. But I've got to have
some evidence."

"What about the body? Why'd Gray remove his organs?"

"I don't care if Gray cut him into *chops*, Constantine. The fact is,
Simon Gray's contributed almost a million dollars to help settle
colored folks here. He's one of the reasons this is an open town. Look
what happened in Milwaukee, for Christ's sake. They posted militia
on the highways and the railroads to keep us away. Now they got

nothing. That man's helped our people and he's helped yours. And you haven't given me a single good reason yet why I should suspect him of murder. Not just three murders, either. Maybe it's two hundred thirty-three murders."

"I'll find it," Danny said.

"Shit," Willson said, dropping the files back into the cabinet drawer. "You're a *reporter*. You don't know nothin' about police work. All you're interested in is making noise. And that's not all." Willson's gaze leveled and fixed on him.

"What?"

"You're *white*," Willson said.

"What's that got to do with it?" Danny said uncomfortably.

"There's two hundred thirty of *my* people missing in a year," Willson said fiercely. "Two hundred thirty that were reported. That's at least four a week. You never came around asking about it. Your fucking paper never printed a word."

"What are you saying? That I didn't care because they were colored? That's wrong, Dooley. I'm not prejudiced."

"Shit," Willson said, disgustedly.

"I don't hate anybody. I was brought up to respect people. Why, my father once washed my mouth out with soap because I said the word 'nigger'."

"He wash the inside of your head out, too? 'Cause I'll bet you *thought* it plenty of times."

"I'm telling you I'm not like that."

"I don't give a damn *what* you're like. You can't be any other way than what you are. A white man, loyal to his own kind. Oh, you tolerate us now because you're in trouble. But it's the same as it's always been. You *need* us, but you don't want us around. And when we get into trouble, tough shit."

" 'No man is an island,' " Danny said. "You ever heard that one? John Donne wrote it during the plague—"

" 'No man is an island, entire of itself,' " Willson quoted. " 'Every man is a piece of the Continent, a part of the main; if a Clod be washed away by the Sea, Europe is the less, as well as if a Promontory were, as well as if a Manor of thy friends or of thine own were; any man's death diminishes me, Constantine, because I am involved in Mankind; and therefore never send to know for whom the bell tolls; it tolls for *thee.* . . . ' Motherfucker."

"Sorry," Danny said, after a moment.

"Fuck you and the horse you rode in on," said Willson. "That's your true self just came out. Down in your heart, you don't believe I'm intelligent enough to read any pansy-ass English poetry. I see you looking around here. Looking for signs that I could actually organize an office. That I put up pictures, just like white folks do! You'd be scared if you came in here and saw a mess. You'd think, I'm sitting here with a real *nigger.* Well, you got yourself one, Constantine, and you know what? Niggers don't like white folks. Even the nice, *kind* ones."

"I'm sorry you feel that way," Danny said.

"How I feel is my own business," Willson said. "You so worried about what I'm thinking about you. Why don't you admit how you feel about *me?* Come out with it! At least then I'd know who the fuck I was dealing with."

Willson's cigar had gone out and he struck a match on his desk, leaned back, and lighted it. "Take the Swede. He hates niggers. Told me so the first time he ever saw me. I told him if I had to choose between a log and a big dumb Swede I'd take the log. Least I could make me a fire. But I don't have to worry about Francis. I won't fuck myself up relying on goodwill that ain't really there. Because I know that if he had his way, he'd set things back to the way they were in this town. How many colored folk lived here before the war? A thousand? Half of them railroad porters, so they were gone all the time." Willson blew smoke.

"I want to see that killer hang, Willson," Danny said. "If it's Gray, then I want him to drop. You should, too. No matter how much money he gave you."

"I don't have to arrest him. I don't have to hang him. All I have to do is *wait.* He's white. Sooner or later he'll be dead, just like the rest of you bastards. See, I'm *counting.* In the same year we lost two hundred thirty, you lost eight thousand. That's right. And every white son of a bitch who dies brings me that much closer to the day when I won't have to see any of your pasty faces again! But don't you worry. We all will do just fine. We'll run our own town, and we'll run it right. Maybe someday we'll put up a statue to y'all. Here's to the white race! Fuck 'em!"

"You know what, Sergeant?" Danny said, getting up.

"What?"

"Maybe you ought to think about that poetry you memorized. No man's an island, Sergeant. Doesn't say what color he is."

"Get the fuck out of here," Willson said.

rancis Lingeborg had learned how to sit for a long
time when he was a kid and went to the Swedish
Temple every Sunday to listen to Dr. Sendstrom's three-
hour sermons. The pastor had not been a hell-raiser, either. His
sermons were carefully reasoned and delivered in a monotone that
could turn a church full of people to stone. Sometimes, when he
finished, everybody would just sit there. If it wasn't for the choir
starting up at the end—and God knew how they did it; maybe the
organist had an alarm clock—everybody would have sat staring 'til
the next Sunday, by which time Dr. Sendstrom would have prepared
another paralytic lesson for his flock.

Now Francis sat parked behind a thicket of young birch trees
growing out of the cracked curb on the other side of Riverside
Terrace from the gates of the institute. He'd been sitting there a
couple of hours in the dark, all because of his mother's currant
coffee cake.

Francis had been getting ready to go to spend his day off at his
mother's house, and he'd been thinking about that cake. She put
cinnamon in it so that it was a nutty brown color studded with the
dark currants, and he'd thought of how it would smell and taste, and
how much he liked currants. And then, suddenly, he'd remembered
something he'd seen at the institute yesterday, when he and Willson

had claimed the tramp's body: those boys trying to wash the caked mud off the fenders and skirts of that deep-red Archer sedan. That mud had been cinnamon-colored, like his mother's cake. And in it were dark specks. *Cinders.* That car had been churning up mud that was heavily mixed with cinders. Francis had got that same mud all over his shoes on Monday morning, going over the murder scene at the rail yards.

Remembering that, Francis had gone out to the back porch and there were his shoes, caked with the stuff. With his pocket knife, Francis pried some off, and he could see the cinders inside looking just like his mother's currants, and clearly remembered those boys struggling to wash that same mud off that car without scratching the paint.

He'd stood there holding his shoe and enjoying that wash of excitement that always poured through him whenever he managed to catch something Dooley Willson had missed. Willson called him a big dumb Swede and maybe he was, but Dooley had his blind spots and there were times when Francis saw things Dooley didn't. He knew his boss was getting too worked up about this investigation, that he was taking it personally. That was why he'd ordered Francis to take a day off, so that he could bore in on it alone! Francis had telephoned his mother, got through after a couple of tries, and told her he'd be over on Sunday instead of Saturday. Then he'd driven to the institute and parked opposite the gates and waited for somebody to drive out in that Archer.

That was the trouble with niggers, he thought. They didn't know how to wait. Everything ran hot with them. They had to have everything right now. There were times during an investigation like this one where you had to stop and let things happen. Dooley Willson couldn't stand to do that. No nigger could, and that's why no Negro had ever worn a detective's shield before the sickness, and why they'd be helpless after all the white men like Francis were gone.

Feeling proud of himself because of how well he could wait, Lingeborg took a drink from the pint of gin he'd brought from home. He was awfully hot. The air was still and damp by the river, and it wasn't cooling off any, and he had to keep the windows rolled up most of the time because when he rolled them down the mosquitoes got wind of him and came inside in a cloud.

After a while, Francis started letting a few of them in. Then he'd hunt them down one by one. There was a mosquito bumping up against the windscreen in front of him. Moving slowly, he got a match out of the box in his coat pocket and struck it with his thumb, bringing it up from behind, wondering if mosquitoes could see fire or not and then *szszszszszszsz!* roasting it and watching it drop to the dashboard.

Then came the rumble of a truck, the first vehicle that had come down Riverside Terrace in two hours. He ducked his head down just before the headlights shot through the back window. Another mosquito buzzed past his ear and landed on the side of his face.

"Sum'bitch!" Francis growled, slapping himself hard, and feeling, with satisfaction, the moist dead body of the insect roll between his fingers. The truck turned into the institute drive. A man jumped out of the back, walked up to the guard, and said something to him. The guard hit the switch for the gate and the truck engine gunned, and drove through.

"EE three-six-two-one," Francis said aloud, licking the end of a pencil and jotting the license number of the truck. He put the piece of paper into his shirt pocket. That was something, anyway. Maybe he'd let Dooley bitch at him about sitting all night without a damn thing to show for it. Then he'd give him the number. He patted his shirt pocket. It was like having money in there.

He took another drink from the gin bottle and wished it was beer instead. Gin had a way of making a man feel awfully sticky when it was this hot. To hell with the mosquitoes, he thought, and opened the window, putting his feet on the dash, then suddenly perking up as he heard the low hum of an expensive motor, and saw the sweep of headlights, dipping as the sleek Archer came out through the gate. The top was down. There was a woman with her hair protected by a green scarf. Platinum-blonde hair. And driving was that sonova-bitch, Dr. Gray.

Francis got out of the car and fumbled with the crank twice before he got his motor started. By the time he jumped in and pulled away from the curb the Archer was far ahead, a couple of ruby-red pinpoints inside a conical light beam that was rimmed in green from the untrimmed trees that arched over the drive. Man, this was it! Francis thought, feeling that cop's instinct that always knotted up the top of his gut when he was onto something. Maybe he wasn't all that smart, but his instincts were dead on, the thing that got him promoted to major crimes, and the reason Willson kept him on in spite of how they felt about each other.

It was easy following the Archer in the dark like that. Milltown had always been a working man's town and everything shut down early, even before the sickness, and now, once you were out later than eleven or so the place was practically deserted. The Archer turned right on Fiftieth, crossed the bridge, drove west, and then turned left on Hiawatha and into Minnehaha Park. Francis waited a moment, took the same road, and then, cutting his headlights, drove over the lawn of the playground on the hill above the bandstand. From there he saw the Archer stop in the picnic grounds lot. Gray and the blonde got out, and walked together across the stone bridge that arched just above the falls.

"Shit!" Francis said out loud. This was it! This was going to get him promoted right out from under that goddamn nigger's nose. Maybe there was a lieutenancy in it for him. Imagine that: Dooley Willson, doing things the way Francis Lingeborg wanted. Yeah, that was one hell of a thought! But shit, Gray and the blonde had disappeared over the bridge. He'd better not lose them now, or Dooley would goddamned kill him for sure!

He checked his pistol and headed down after them. With all the rain lately you could hear the roar of the falls from a long way off, and it got very loud, everything cool and very damp and lush-smelling, as Francis crossed the bridge. On the other side was a paved footpath that led down stairs to a couple of terraces where visitors could look at the falls. There were also plenty of trails through the brush on both sides, including one that went along the cutout limestone behind the falls itself, but he had seen how the two of them were dressed and he doubted, whatever their reason for coming to the park this late, that they'd want to tackle the slippery clay tonight.

At the top of the stairs, Francis listened hard, trying to separate the sound of the water from voices that might be out there, or footsteps or branches breaking. Nothing. Okay. He didn't mind going down. He liked going down into dark places, and he'd been here plenty of times ever since he was a kid. Anyway, if Gray and the blonde stuck to the paved path there was only one way they could go, to a second bridge that crossed the creek some fifty yards downstream. From there you could take stairs up the other side of the gorge, or follow the stream for a while to a walled cul-de-sac that was popular with lovers.

There weren't that many lovers around anymore, and those that were around didn't go out. People stuck to home. They stayed out of the bars and the pool halls, and even up on the North Side there was hardly anybody getting murdered anymore. Not leaving bodies anyway, Francis thought, remembering Willson's Missing Persons jackets. These vampire jobs were the first in a long time, Francis thought, moving down. He knew he was onto something. People like the doc didn't come to a place like this to fuck, not unless they were perverted. Maybe that was it. Maybe the doc was queer somehow.

At the first terrace Francis turned and took a quick look at the falls. A half-moon was coming up and it made the water look like pale lace, or cotton. You could feel it pounding down onto the riverbed. Mist blew against his face. It was just a quick look to indulge himself. He hadn't been down to the falls in years, couldn't remember why, exactly. He'd loved it so much when he was a kid.

He walked down to the second landing, wondering why he couldn't pick them up, and making plans to go back to the car if he couldn't locate them soon. He didn't want to lose them. He decided that when they did come back to the car, he'd identify himself and question them, see if he could maybe shake something loose. It would be better if the sarge was there for that, though. People were scared of Willson. He had that way of fixing the whites of his eyes on you so you froze right where you were. Francis turned around.

The blonde woman came down toward him with a smile on her face.

" 'Ello, 'luv," she said.

Goddamn, Francis thought. It's fucking *her!* He flexed his shoulders back a little so that he could feel his pistol and holster pressing into his side.

"This park closes at ten," Francis managed to say. He was trying to sound like a cop, but his voice sounded faraway to him. He could not take his eyes off her. She had a red mouth and full lips. There was something about her face, though. It wasn't good-looking.

"Aw, luv, what do you care?"

"I'm a cop," he said.

"Ooh. A copper! And what's a copper doing all the way out 'ere so late?"

Francis swallowed. The air seemed heavy all of a sudden, and he felt trapped. He wasn't used to women. He had never been married and never fooled around with them much. She laughed lazily and took a step toward him, running her hand along the painted handrail as she did. She was wearing a filmy green skirt, and no shoes, and all the time kept her eyes on his.

"What's yer name, copper?" she said. Francis caught a whiff of lilac perfume, and pulled his gun.

"Oooh," she said. "What's that for?"

"Shut up."

"You're a queer one, hon. So tall and lovely looking. Can't we start over, you and me? There's something about all this water running down that gets me all shivery inside."

"I said shut up! Where's Dr. Gray?"

She came closer, eyes tipped upward to meet his, and brought her hands together slowly on the barrel of his pistol.

"You know what I think? *I* think you're afraid of me." She stroked the barrel, coming down the grip and over Francis's hands. "I think you know something about me. Don't you, luv?"

"You're under arrest," Francis said, reaching for the handcuffs on his belt.

"Is that all you can say?" She kept moving her hands up his arms, over the top of his shoulders, and then, softly, against his neck. "You don't really want to arrest me, do you, hon? You want to do something else. Don't you?" She pulled his head toward hers. "Don't you?"

She kissed him, pushing her tongue deep into his mouth. His eyes began to close, the sound of the waterfall seeming to cover both of them, his head spinning, his hand with the pistol in it dropping to his side.

He felt something cold touch the side of his neck, heard a pneumatic burst, like the sound of the water swelling up suddenly. His legs collapsed underneath him and he fell on his back, his head hitting a flagstone, stunning him a moment. When he came to, she was standing over him.

"I continue to marvel at the effect you have on these strangers," a man's voice said out of the darkness. "Though of course, he isn't a complete stranger." Gray looked down at him. "Hello, Detective Lingeborg."

Francis tried to speak, but nothing worked. He couldn't feel his body anymore. He could hear and move his eyes and that was all.

"Please spare yourself the effort," Dr. Gray said. "You're quite paralyzed. It's no longer a matter of willpower, so you might as well relax."

"Hook me up please, Simon?" She wasn't talking like a Brit anymore.

"Certainly." In the moonlight, Francis could make out Gray fixing a pair of flexible tubes to the front of the woman's stomach, between the buttons of her dress. Francis heard a hiss, like the one he had heard and felt just before he'd gone down.

"Mmmm," the woman said. Her voice sounded trembly and her eyes opened and fixed on him. She didn't make another sound. She pounced on him; he heard a click, and her ragged breathing in his ear.

"Wait, wait," Gray said from far off. "You have to wait and see if it's all right. . . ."

Her breathing settled down a moment. Then she screamed and stood up, spitting red clumps onto the ground.

"It's no good!" she cried.

"Yes. Wrong type. It's fortunate for you there's a filter in place. Otherwise, your red blood cells would be exploding at this moment."

"God!" she said, coughing and wiping her mouth. "It's never happened before."

"Because you've been extraordinarily lucky thus far. And though I'm sure you don't agree at the moment, you're lucky this evening, too. Lucky you don't actually need his blood."

"I need it!" the woman said. She sounded like a Brit again.

Gray's face tightened with contempt. "Look at you. Painted up, *acting!* You've convinced yourself that's the only way you can do what you have to do to survive. Make yourself into someone else. When are you going to understand? I've given you everything you need to be a magnificent predator, but your self-denial has turned it into something ugly."

"Shut up!" the woman said, covering her ears. Gray took her wrists and pulled her hands away.

"You came to me because you'd heard from your rich friends that I had a treatment for HF. And I operated on you because you were so desperate to live. And for years you've done what you needed to do to survive. Quietly. Properly. But now, what's happened to you?"

"Nothing's happened to me!"

"Oh, yes it has. You've become afraid of yourself. And worse than that: you've become ashamed."

"You've seen me! Have I been afraid of anything?"

"What you did to that man behind the flour mill is the result of fear. You're trying to deny what you are. You've made yourself into such a monster that you're no longer able to absorb the reality of what you've done! You cut that man's penis off."

"Stop—"

"You cut it off gratuitously, for no reason other than to finally outrage the authorities of this city. It's the reason these policemen and that damned reporter are after us now. You want us caught."

"No!"

"Yes, you do. Because your fear has twisted you. All you want now is to escape your essence. That's why I have to watch you. I have to make certain you won't go too far. That your personality won't become completely displaced!"

"Like yours!" the woman said bitterly.

"Not like mine. Long ago I acknowledged what I am. I embraced my impulses. I don't hide them from myself. I *glory* in them! I don't need to work myself into a state of hysteria that permits me to believe that I've 'blacked out'! As you will no doubt do later tonight, so that tomorrow morning when you wake up you'll be convinced that this evening has been yet another of your fantastic dreams!"

Gray took her by the shoulders. "Why can't you embrace it? Why don't you rejoice in what you really are? You have the disease, and yet you live. More than that, you *thrive!* That's extraordinary. You have the organs that permit you to survive and you must use them without any more shame or remorse than you would feel using your teeth or eyes or ears. That feeling of power inside you grows stronger all the time, doesn't it! That is what you are! Stop fighting it! *Stop pretending!*"

Suddenly Gray grabbed her hair and pulled. Francis saw a flash of yellow disappear into the brush along the bank of the creek. *A wig,* he thought distantly.

"What do you want?" Gray said.

"I don't know—"

"Yes you do! Say it!"

"I . . . I want more."

"Then pull the air lines away."

Francis heard a click and a hissing sound.

"Now you can drink. His blood can't mingle with yours."

Francis felt hands stroking his hair, and heard a distant voice. "You know everything now, don't you?" the voice said. "You were right to wait and follow us. And you know me. Blink your eyes if you do."

Francis blinked. He did. He knew who it was. The voice sounded very far away, though. He had been lying there bleeding from the neck all this time and everything was getting more and more fizzy.

He began to think of his mother's currant coffee cake.

24

*L*ate that night a front came through and by Saturday morning there was a steady rain with the temperature dropping into the low sixties. Danny sat at the counter of the Pantry, drinking coffee with Bing Lockner. Ahead of them two colored fry cooks, dressed in white coats and red bow ties, fried eggs and a turkey steak for Bing. The Pantry was a good place, a few doors down from the *Journal* building on Fourth Street, one of the diners downtown that still could draw a crowd. But now it was after the breakfast rush and Bing and Danny were alone at the counter.

Bing smoked quietly, pushing his cuticles down between puffs of his cigarette. He was terrifically hung over. The cook flipped the egg over in the pan, turned the steak, and made up the plate, pushing it down the counter to Bing.

"Turkey," Bing said with a sigh. "God, what I wouldn't give for a real steak. Just a *whiff* of big, juicy porterhouse." He cut his egg into strips, cut the turkey into strips, cut the hash browns into strips, then, with knife and fork, moved the strips around into an egg-meat-potato thatch. He chewed his first bite, swallowed it, and waited. Then he nodded, and Danny knew it was safe to talk to him. Once Bing found out he could keep his food down he was ready to start the day.

"Why don't you eat something?" Bing said.

"I'm not hungry."

"Rough night?"

"I spent it at the morgue with Dooley Willson," Danny said. One of the cooks heard and glanced back over his shoulder, but Bing merely took a sip of coffee.

"Lyndon, could you please toast up a couple of slices of gluten bread for my morbid friend here," he said.

"Sure, Mr. Lockner," the cook said, popping the bread into the toaster. Bing said nothing more until the toast was delivered along with a pot of gooseberry jam.

"There. Eat something."

Danny noticed there was egg yolk on the cuff of Bing's shirt. Bing's hands were shaking, too, as he brought his coffee cup to his mouth. Danny handed him a napkin.

"You've got egg on your cuff, Bing."

"Hmm," Bing said. Danny's eyes widened. He had thought the fastidious Lockner would have made a big production out of cleaning himself up. Steam from the kitchen and ice chips and maybe some boiled vinegar, too, but this morning Bing didn't seem to care about his shirt, or much of anything.

"You sure you're okay, Bing?"

"You know," Bing said, "maybe I'm not." He got a flask out from his pocket and poured a couple of fingers from it into his coffee cup. He didn't mix it, but sipped it straight off the top.

"Knew I forgot something."

Danny sighed. There were times he really felt like he and Bing were friends, that they understood each other. This wasn't one of them.

"Come on, Connie," Bing said suddenly, with a trace of impatience. "Let's have it. Why the hell have you dragged me out of my lair on a Saturday morning?"

"I want to know . . . Jeez, how can I put this? Oh, hell! Do you have anything on Walter Burns?"

"Why, *Connie*," Bing said, smiling for the first time all morning.

"You know everything that goes on at that paper, Bing. I know you must have something on Walter."

"Maybe I know a thing or two. Depends what you're looking for and what you want to do with it."

"You know what I want."

Bing speared a strip of turkey steak and chewed it slowly.

"What if I agree with Burnsie on that one?" he said.

Danny was incredulous. "You've never agreed with Walter Burns in your life!"

Bing pushed his plate away and got a cigarette out, tapping it on the counter, then lighting it. "I guess it seems that way. But Burnsie and I go way back. I knew him in Paris, right at the end of the war. He was working for the Hearst syndicate and I was still in the army writing for *Stars and Stripes*. I got out and was knocking around town and needed a place to stay, and he put me up. He was living in this big flat in the rue Cardinal Lemoine, right near the Jardin des Plantes. There was a bunch of the fellows living in that street."

"When was this?"

"Nineteen-twenty, twenty-one. There was this one kid from Oak Park. He and his wife lived across the street from us, over the dance hall. Walter was trying like hell to hire him. Christ, that kid could write! Ernie . . . what was his name? Hell, I can't remember. He was the only guy I ever met that I thought, maybe, could write a better short story than me. He used to show me this stuff all about what happened to him summers when his family went up to Michigan. It was all choppy, but Jesus, it packed a wallop."

"What happened to him?"

"What do you think?" Bing took a drag on his cigarette. "Paris was the first big town to get hit. Nobody knew what the hell was going on then, of course. They were trying to explain it away as delayed gas cases, or TB. Burnsie didn't believe any of that, though. He had some contacts in a French military hospital and got one of the doctors to talk. Walter found out that Hun was a new epidemic— and that it was man-made. Walter wrote that story."

"And then Hearst killed it."

"Nope. Walter never filed it."

"Never filed it? Why?"

"Because it got personal, that's why. See, Ernie had gone to the hospital with him, and, well, he must have picked up the bug somehow when he was there, because he got acute. One afternoon Walter went across the street to see him and found Ernie lying on the stairs. Blood everywhere. He told me it looked like somebody'd just squeezed the kid 'til he burst. Walter called upstairs for his wife, but she was out doing the marketing, and so he went down to the street and waited for her. He just had to tell her what happened. Now, this girl was crazy about Ernie. And this particular day she was going to make him a special dinner because she'd just come into a little money from one of her uncles. Burnsie had to stop somebody who was on top of the world and tell her something that ripped it apart. So, that night he went back to the office. He typed out a letter of resignation and then he burned up all his notes and the copy. He was on the next train to Calais.

"See, that's what you've got to understand about Burnsie. Ever since, he's dedicated himself to putting out a calm, steady paper. He doesn't want to be the one who tears people apart. That's why he's made the *Journal* the boring piece of shit it is today."

"Okay, that's Walter," Danny said. "What about you?"

"I've got my own reasons."

"Like what?"

Bing's dark eyes flashed. "Listen, Connie. I don't have to explain myself. I don't have to help you, or give you advice, or sit here in this crummy hole and have breakfast with you, for that matter. I'm a *writer*, for Christ's sake! I used to get telegrams from Mencken and Georgie Nathan begging me for material for the *Mercury*! Anything I cared to write! Now I should sit here and listen to you whine that I ought to blackmail Walter Burns to get stuff in print that reads like it was pounded out by a ham-fisted ape!"

Just then Lyndon the cook turned around. "You say what you like about your friend, Mr. Lockner. But don't you be calling the Pantry no hole!"

Bing closed his eyes a moment. Then, slowly, he stubbed his cigarette out in the ashtray.

"You're right, Lyndon. I'm very sorry. You know I don't mean it. This place is my favorite restaurant."

"Ain't no hole!"

"Of course not. I'm not myself this morning. Please forgive me."
He stood up and offered his hand, and Lyndon, after hesitating a
moment, wiped his own hands off on his apron and shook Bing's.

"You better say something to your friend, too," Lyndon said,
nodding toward the door, where Danny was collecting his hat from
the tree.

"Connie, don't go like that. Come back here."

"I never asked to be a *writer*," Danny said, turning around and
feeling the emotion in his voice as the words came out. "I just do the
best I can with that. But goddamn it, I *am* a reporter, Bing. I take
good pictures, and, damn it, I know a story when I see one! What the
hell am I supposed to do with this? Go over to St. Pete and sell it to
the *Globe*?"

"Suicide. They'd shoot you for a spy."

"Don't make jokes. Just tell me what you'd do if you wanted to get
it out."

"Do you care who reads it?"

"What do you mean, who reads it?"

"There's another paper in this town, you know. The *Defender*.
Yeah, I know you don't think of them like that, but the last I heard
their circulation's almost equal to ours. You should talk to the boys
in our advertising department. They're tearing their hair out about
the *Defender* right now. And some of the rough boys upstairs in the
plant have been making noise about putting them out of business the
hard way. You ever read it?"

"No," Danny admitted, and remembered what Willson had said
to him last night.

"Well, I do. They haven't printed a word about your vampire,
either."

"Maybe they haven't been tipped yet. Willson hates newspapers."

"Cops aren't the only source. Wives and grandmas call in when
their boys get killed. Just like ours do. Amazing, ain't it." He stood
and put a silver dollar down on the counter. "Thanks, Lyndon. I'm
sorry I said what I did."

"You coming back Monday morning's all the apology I need,"
Lyndon said.

"Let's go pay the *Defender* a call," Bing said. "Be ambassadors for our profession and our race." He looked at Danny, and added, softly, "I really am sorry, Connie."

"Okay," Danny said, and went out with him.

The offices of the *Twin Cities Defender* were in a storefront on Lyndale Avenue North, just off Plymouth. They were just like the offices of a thousand small-town papers that were written in the front room and composed and printed in the back. But the *Defender* had expanded so much that the original building was now the city room, and they had bought out the leases of the floors above and the buildings on both sides to accommodate their circulation and advertising departments and new, high-speed presses. People were running around and phones were ringing. Danny felt a pang, remembering how the *Journal* had been just a few years ago.

Inside, Bing shook out his umbrella and put it in the stand and leaned over the receptionist's desk, and asked to see Elisha Cooke, who was the managing editor. The receptionist seemed to know him pretty well; Bing kissed her hand and made her blush, and then, giggling, she buzzed Cooke and sent them on in.

"What do you say, Eli," Bing said, stepping into the lone separate office on the floor. "Looks like you've got a newspaper going here."

"Hey, Bing!" Cooke said, getting up to shake hands. He was pretty young for a managing editor, and was dressed very well in a satin-fronted vest and silk shirt. Unlike Walter, he still had most of his hair.

"This is a colleague of mine, Danny Constantine. He used to chase pictures, but now we've got him chained to a typewriter."

"You mean somebody actually writes that rag? Good to meet you, Constantine." Cooke shook Danny's hand and he and Bing sat down.

"Still living on Royalston?" Bing asked.

"Naw, we're down closer to the park now. Lottie had twins, so we needed the room."

"I'll be damned. Twins!"

"Martin and Monroe. They'll be two in August."

"Has it been that long since I've talked to you? Hell! Congratulations."

"Save it. She's pregnant again. The doc says we could have two more. There're twins up and down her damn family."

"You ought to leave her alone, Eli."

"Don't I know," Cooke said, and laughed.

"Listen, Eli, Danny here's been on a story, and he's got the goods. It's red hot! Only Walter won't print it, see, because he thinks Crowley will jump down his throat."

"And now you're coming to me with it?"

"Well, we thought maybe you could use it. Tell him, Danny."

"A week ago I was out taking pictures at that burned-out Crockett mill and I stumbled on a body. He'd been slashed, and there wasn't a drop of blood left in his body. I hooked up with the cop who was looking into it. Dooley Willson?"

"I know him," Cooke said with a frown.

"Willson's partner told me there'd been a couple of other murders like it. I've got an idea who's responsible, and, well, here's the copy."

He gave it to Cooke, who put on his glasses and started to read. " 'A moonlight tryst and the hope of a few stolen kisses proved fatal last evening to a Milltown motorman who stopped for a beer on the way home to his waiting wife.' " He looked up. "Christ, that's lousy! Don't they teach you white fellows how to write a lead?"

"Never mind that, Eli. I told you, he's a picture chaser."

"Uh-uh," Cooke said, pushing the copy back across the desk to Danny.

"What's the matter with it?"

"I've heard about this killer. And I ain't touching it."

"Funny," Bing said. "You don't *look* like Walter Burns."

"Call me all the names you want," Cooke said. "We're not touching it."

"Well, why the hell not? It's a hell of a story, Eli! There's a vampire out there and he's killed Charlie Hayes. He's one of your people, or half, anyway. Why, you could scare your readers to death! Hell, *I'm* scared!"

"Listen, Bing, do I walk into your office and tell you what to print?"

Bing didn't say anything. Danny had been listening to him first charm Eli Cooke, then put Cooke on the defensive, and finally tempt him, knowing all it would take would be another Bing quip or two to wrap up the whole deal. But now, suddenly, Bing clammed up. He was staring at the desk; Danny waited, and still Bing didn't speak. Finally Danny couldn't wait anymore.

"Look, Mr. Cooke, this is different," he said. "This story's dynamite! And there's another whole angle, about how my paper won't print anything because Crowley's taking orders from the Greater Northwest Development Company. And the cops are hushing it up, too! It's all because this murder has something to do with Dr. Simon Gray, who runs the Hematological Institute. Their biggest investor is the GNDC."

Cooke straightened in his chair. "The GNDC. You're saying these respected, civic-minded people are backing a murderer."

"Yes, I am."

Cooke swiveled around and put his back to Danny and Bing. "Tell me something, son. Do you know the names of the board members of the GNDC?"

"There's Crowley, Donaldson, Evald, Justus, Reverend Ellington . . . some others."

"Some others." Cooke wheeled to face him. *"I'm* on that board! You think I'm a murderer?"

"No, of course not—"

Cooke's voice rose. "But I'm covering up murder. Is that it?"

"No—"

Bing suddenly began to gather up Danny's copy. "Like I told you, Eli. He's a picture chaser."

"That ain't no excuse. You get him out of my office before I throw his sorry ass out!"

"We're gone, Eli. You come up to the press box next time the Millers play and I'll buy you a beer."

Bing hustled Danny out of the office. It was raining harder now. They stood under the awning as people walked past quickly with their coat collars up, some holding newspapers over their heads.

"What the hell's going on, Bing!" Danny said angrily. "You knew he was on the GNDC board, didn't you?"

"Yeah, I did," Bing said wearily.

"Then what the hell'd you bring me up here for?"

"Eli's always been an outsider. I thought even if he was on the board he'd still be independent. But as soon as he mentioned the twins and that new house I knew we were sunk."

"Then why'd you let me go on?"

"Didn't you see him? He wanted that story! For Christ's sake, he practically forced you to insult him, just so he could get mad enough to throw you out of there."

"Maybe he'll reconsider."

"Forget it, Connie. They *own* him. I'll bet you a C-note the GNDC financed his new plant. He's in too deep to break with them now."

Bing put his umbrella up and they walked under it together back along Plymouth. "Look," he said, "maybe I can slip something into the 'Poke' column. Walter never reads the copy. He hates it."

"Nobody's gonna pay attention to Dorrie Van der Voort!"

"What the hell else are you going to do? Pay to have your own broadsides printed?"

"I don't know!"

"Oh, Christ," Bing said. "Look who's coming."

It was Theo Rostek, trotting along in the rain with his hands in his pockets and his collar turned up. Bing held the umbrella up higher and Rostek came underneath it, taking his hands out and blowing on them.

"Gentlemen," he said pleasantly. "Ain't it a shame about this weather. It's cutting down on the visibility or something, because I just now found out from one of my boys that you two went in to see Eli Cooke. You know what I said to myself? I said *damn*, I wonder what these two want with Eli!"

"Just paying a courtesy call, Theo," Bing said.

"Is that a fact. Well, that's white of you, Bing. *Real* white!" Theo smiled with what looked like genuine good humor, and Bing laughed, but he seemed nervous all of a sudden. *Bing's afraid of him,* Danny thought.

"Listen," Theo said. "You mind if I borrow your umbrella a second and take a walk with your friend here? Danny Constantine, right?"

"That's right."

"I'm Theo Rostek. I own Rostek's restaurant, just around the corner from here."

"I used to eat there," Danny said, shaking hands with him.

"Yeah?"

"Yeah, all the time when I was a kid," Danny said. "Once a month on Sunday, my father would bring us up here."

"You remember a skinny little colored boy busing the tables?"

"Yeah, I guess I do."

"Well, that was me." Theo grinned broadly. "And believe it or not, I do remember your folks. Your daddy had carrot-red hair, didn't he?"

"That's right!"

"Well, hell, ain't but a small world! Wait for us here, Bing? I won't keep him long."

"Sure, Theo."

Bing handed him the umbrella, Theo held it over the car door until Bing got in, and then held out his hand, showing which way they were going to walk on Plymouth. He said nothing until they reached the corner where he nodded and they turned and started down Bryant. On the block ahead of them were two black coroner's vans. Their doors were open, and Percy Satin and two assistants were loading bodies sealed inside zippered rubber bags that had come from one of the houses.

"Look at that," Theo said. "Hun got the husband and the wife the same night. The Cermaks. Nice people, too. My step-pop knew 'em. They were the last white folks on the block."

They walked up to the van. "Morning, boys," Rostek said. They nodded back and continued loading the bodies. The rubber shrouds and the slickers of the coroner's assistants were shiny with rain.

"I heard they got sick about a week ago. They never came to me. Instead, they went down to St. Mary's Hospital and took a number and waited." Theo shook his head. "Number never came up. Never even got close."

Theo took Danny's arm and turned him back toward Broadway. "Point is, Daniel, they put their faith in the wrong people when they needed help. I hate to see you make the same mistake. Especially since your daddy was such good friends with mine. You going in to see Eli Cooke about printing that story. Without even stopping by to say hello to me first." He shook his head. "That ain't polite."

"You could help me?" Danny said.

"I'm the only one who can," Rostek said pleasantly.

"Up here."

Rostek stopped. "No, Daniel. In this *town.*"

The rain splatted hard onto the umbrella. Theo held it up, and started along toward Plymouth again.

"You don't believe me, do you?"

"I didn't say that."

"Maybe you don't *want* to believe it. I respect that, Daniel. I really do. I learned a long time ago working for my daddy that to get along as a colored boy in this town you had to make *allowances* for certain attitudes people been carrying around all their lives. They've had 'em so long that they don't even remember where they came from or why they believe in them. See, I always try, when I'm talking to people who are that way, to help 'em get past those feelings. I don't blame them for having 'em. People are what they're taught. The way I see it, the fault belongs to their parents and grandparents. You know? That's the way the world was when they came into it. And even though that world's dead, well, it makes some people hold on to pieces of it hard. Real hard. And I can always tell, when I talk to somebody the first time, *the very first time, I* feel like hanging on to those old ways, too. There's something comfortable about it. To this day, Daniel, when I'm talking to a white man like you, I have this overwhelming urge to be polite and respectful. Whether the man deserves it or not. 'He's a *white man,* Theo! You gotta look *down* when he speaks to you. You gotta say yes sir and no sir and you don't ever tell him what's on your mind, even if he asks! You put him off with some more shuffling and a thick layer of politeness. That's what it's for!'"

They were on Plymouth again. Danny could see Bing through the back window of his car. He was smoking.

"You come around to my restaurant tonight," Rostek said as they came up to the car. "Ask for me. We'll talk about what we ought to do about that bloodsucking bitch."

He opened the passenger side door for Danny, then went around to the other side, folded the umbrella, and set it on Bing's lap.

"Sorry we kept you waiting, Bing," he said. "Daniel and I had a nice talk. Didn't we?"

Bing started the motor. Theo stood up in the rain and smiled. Bing never looked at him. He jammed the car into gear, tossed the umbrella behind him, and started off. Danny turned and watched Rostek standing in the middle of the street, waving.

"He says he can help us," Danny said, when Bing had turned the corner.

"That's good," Bing said.

"That's *good?* That's all you can say about it?"

"What do you want me to say, Connie?"

"Tell me about this guy. You seem to know him pretty well. Does he really run the whole town?"

"You tell me."

What the hell's eating him? Danny thought.

Then Bing said, "Aw, hell, Connie, I'm sorry. Yeah, maybe he does. There's always been wise guys who ran this town. Most of 'em aren't alive anymore. That makes a vacuum. I guess Theo's filling it pretty good. Maybe in the old days he would have just run numbers or peddled dope. But that's the thing about vacuums, Connie. They make things expand."

"So he runs the town."

"If he says so, then maybe by now he does," Bing said.

25

At around eleven that morning, Mrs. Lund returned home with the day's marketing. The butcher had some nice Lake Superior whitefish today, and she thought she'd try making fish loaf. She took off her raincoat and hat and hung them to dry on the front porch, thought about whether or not it was too damp for baking, and went into the parlor. The house was quiet. Kal did odd jobs and plumbing at a couple of apartment buildings downtown every Saturday. The clock ticked slowly above the mantel; Mrs. Lund stopped a moment with her parcels to listen to it. She liked it when the house was quiet.

Too quiet.

"Shirley? Are you still in bed?" Mrs. Lund called. She had let Shirley stay up playing cards with Lou and Kal 'til well after midnight. Normally Mrs. Lund made sure the girl didn't overtire herself, but Shirley had been so lively and so much fun last night, and Mrs. Lund had been worried about Lou, who'd come in acting strange, never mind that awful cut on his arm, and she could see that Shirley was cheering him up, so Mrs. Lund had decided to let her stay up as long as she wanted to. She suspected that Kal might have given her some cherry brandy, too. There had been three of her cordial glasses carefully washed up and put away in the wrong spot in the breakfront.

"Shirley? Now, I've let you sleep long enough, young lady."

Mrs. Lund put her parcels down on the kitchen table and went up to Shirley's room. "Shirley?" She tapped on the door. "There's no use lying in bed, I've got plenty of chores for you today—" She pushed the door open and looked inside.

And screamed.

Shirley lay on the bed with her eyes open, clutching the top of the bedspread. The coverlet, and the blankets and all the linens, were soaked with blood.

"My God!" Mrs. Lund cried, rushing to her.

"Oh, Auntie," Shirley said in a weak, cracked whisper. "I've made an awful mess."

"When did it start!"

"I—I felt something when I woke up."

"Oh, you poor child! You lie still."

Mrs. Lund left the room quickly, but did not run. She did not want to frighten Shirley any more than she already was. Once she was out the door, though, she ran to the kitchen, pulling the block of ice from the icebox and dumping it into the sink, taking the pick and stabbing it to lumps so she could make an ice pack. She began to sob, stabbing and stabbing at the ice until the pick broke off at the handle.

Then she stopped, wiped her eyes with the towel draped over the pantry rack, went to the telephone, and called up the *Journal.*

"Here," Bing Lockner said to Danny, pulling the sheet from the typewriter. "How do you like this?"

" 'Certain of our best friends,' " Danny read aloud, " '*con* cash and *sans* swains, have taken over one of the best lodges on the shores of Pelican Lake, near Brainerd, and dressed it up to look like Biarritz on the Bay of Biscay, complete with twelve truckloads of pure white sand, potted palms, striped umbrellas, absinthe pitchers, and imported waiters whose first names are trimmed with vowels at both ends. The weather has been sunny, and though our friends now sport the most *impressive* tans, they still can't hope to equal the ones most of their new companions brought with them. Hot topic among the Biarritz-in-Paul Bunyan-land set: the mystery killer back home who shows a decided preference for the new friends of our old ones.'

"Jesus, Bing!" Danny said irritably. "Who the hell can follow this?"

"Dorrie's readers. All it takes is one seed. Plant it, water it a little in the next couple of columns, and a whole crop grows. You'll see."

The phone rang on Danny's desk. Danny let the copy drop and picked up the candlestick. "Yeah? What! Oh, God! Okay, you hang on, I'll get someone there. Yes, yes, right away!"

"What's wrong?" Bing said, sitting up. "Who was that?"

"My landlady," Danny said. "Shirley's bleeding bad."

"Oh, Christ!"

"Mrs. Lund called every hospital. They're all jammed. They won't take another bleeder—" He looked at Bing hopelessly. "What the hell am I going to do?"

Bing picked the phone up and clicked the cradle. "Yeah, get me the Lutheran Mission, quick."

"Oh, no you don't—" Danny began, but Bing cut him off.

"What do you mean the exchange is out? Since when? Hell!" He threw the phone down and put on his coat. "Hey, Jackie! You had a good breakfast this morning?"

"Three or four crullers," the copy boy said. "Why?"

"Never mind. You're going home with Mr. Constantine."

"Where are you going?" Danny said.

"You get home with Jackie and wait for me," Bing said. "I'll meet you there."

"If you're going for Selena Crockett, forget it," Danny said. "I don't want her coming anywhere near Shirley."

"Why not?"

"Because I think she's in with Gray!"

"Forget about what you *think*. You want Shirley to bleed to death?"

"No, but—"

"But nothing, Connie. Selena's got a doctor at the mission. And a whole depot full of blood donors."

"That's where I brought that tramp!" Danny said bitterly.

"Do you want me to stop?" Bing said. "Because if you really do, say so right now and I will. Maybe we can fix something else up."

Danny looked at him.

"It's up to you, Connie."

"Go!" Danny said.

"How is she?" Danny said, running into Mrs. Lund's parlor with Jackie five minutes after leaving the *Journal* offices.

"She can't talk anymore," Mrs. Lund cried. "She doesn't seem to hear anything."

"Is she still breathing?"

"Yes, thank God!"

Danny went into the bedroom. He felt his stomach twist as he took in the sight. She lay there breathing raggedly, on a bed that was completely soaked with blood. He went to her.

"Shirley? Baby, can you hear me? It's Danny."

She stirred a little and mumbled something. Then Danny heard the porch door bang shut, and footsteps on the stairs, and Bing coming into the bedroom. With him was Selena Crockett and Cramer, the same doctor who had first examined the tramp that day.

"Please give me some room," Cramer said, feeling for a pulse, and then opening his bag. "She's in shock," he said. "Does anyone know this girl's blood type?"

"She's a one," Mrs. Lund said.

"Good. That means she can receive from anyone. You," he said to Jackie. "Have you ever given blood before?"

"No, sir," he said, eyes widening as Cramer fit a long needle at the end of a length of rubber tubing. He fit two such tubes to the top of a receiving jar, and began wiping Shirley's arm with cotton.

"Sit down here," the doctor ordered. "We'll start with you, but we're going to need a lot to get this under control. Are any of you infected with HF now? Nobody? Good."

"Is it gonna hurt?" Jackie said dubiously.

"Walter Burns squeezes more out of you every day of the week," Bing said. "Keep quiet."

The doctor pushed the needle into the vein in Jackie's arm. He yelped, then watched as Selena wrapped a length of gauze around the arm to hold the tube in place. The transfusion bottle began to fill.

"Get me a pan of warm water, please."

Mrs. Lund went out and returned a few moments later. Pulling a second chair over, the doctor set the rapidly filling bottle into the water bath. "Sodium citrate, please, Miss Crockett. Five cc's in a hypo." Selena filled the hypodermic, and Dr. Cramer injected the citrate solution into the blood bottle. As soon as the bottle was half full, he used a hemostat to clip off the tube, removed the stopper, and fit it into a fresh bottle, releasing the clip so it continued to fill. He now put another stopper onto the first bottle, stuck the other needle into Shirley's pale, almost blue arm, and held the bottle up. The blood began to drain into Shirley's vein.

"Could you bring in a floor lamp or something we can hang these bottles from?" Dr. Cramer asked.

"I'll get it," Danny said, rushing out and returning with the one from the parlor.

"You were right to prop up her legs," the doctor was saying to Mrs. Lund. "It's probably what saved her. She was almost gone."

"How much are you gonna take?" Jackie said, wide-eyed.

"Just the rest of this bottle. Who wants to go next?"

"I will," Danny said.

"That other bag in the car has the rest of my kit, Miss Crockett," Dr. Cramer said. "Would you mind getting it? There're more bottles in it and we can get the other donors started."

By the time they were finished an hour later, Dr. Cramer had collected and given Shirley almost seven pints of blood. Everyone had contributed, even he—"to top her off," he'd said. He then asked everyone to go out to the parlor, keeping Selena and Mrs. Lund with him. Together, they sponged Shirley off, changed her nightgown, mattress, and bedclothes, and watched to see whether she was still bleeding. Danny and Jackie took the blood-soaked mattress outside. Finally the doctor came out to the parlor.

"It's stopped for now," he said. "She's sleeping. Heartbeat and blood pressure are okay. How old is she?"

"Thirteen," Mrs. Lund said fearfully.

"Onset of menses," Dr. Cramer said. "It's fortunate I got here in time, and there were people willing to donate. Many are afraid to, nowadays."

"We love her," Mrs. Lund said. "All of us here do."

"Love can do many things. But it won't keep this from happening to her again. She may not have a regular period at first, but she is pubescent, and she will menstruate. A year ago we may have been able to operate, and perform a hysterectomy, but it is too late now. There's no blood available for surgery on a bleeder. Even if you all donated on her behalf at a blood bank, there would be no guarantee of replacement the next time she needed a transfusion."

"What about now, though?" Mrs. Lund asked.

"She's weak. She should be hospitalized, but there's nowhere I can put her at the moment. Everything's full. I can make some calls. Perhaps St. Cloud or Stillwater could take her."

"I think I could get her a bed at the institute," Selena said.

"No," Danny said.

Mrs. Lund looked shocked, and put her hand on Selena's arm.

"I think he means he'd be worried if she was moved," Selena said, looking at him sharply.

"It would be best, if that could be arranged," Dr. Cramer said. "There's more risk leaving her here, where she can't be attended to properly."

"I said no!" Danny repeated.

"What is the matter with you?" Mrs. Lund said in confusion. "These people just saved her. Please, Miss Crockett. Talk to him."

"Danny, come on," Selena said, taking his hand. He pulled it away.

"I just want to talk to you a little. Alone." She stood in the doorway and finally, reluctantly, he followed her out to the kitchen.

"I don't want her in the institute," Danny said firmly.

"Why on earth not?"

"Ask Earl Larsen," Danny said.

"That poor man died of a heart attack."

"Look, Selena, he'd been operated on. All his internal organs were removed. I saw the body. I took *pictures*, for Christ's sake!"

"Obviously because you're still indulging in the preposterous idea that Simon Gray murdered him."

"That's right."

"Why? Why would he murder?"

"Do I have to spell it out for you? Larsen was a witness to that second vampire killing. He saw Gray and—"

"And who?" Selena said, flushing.

"I don't know."

"You've a theory, though, don't you? Something you've sprouted in that reporter's brain of yours? Who did Larsen see that night? Simon Gray and who? Me? Do you think I'm the one who prowls with him? I'm the one who's drinking blood? That *is* what you think, isn't it?"

"I don't know!" Danny shouted. "All I know is there's something you're hiding about yourself. I felt it the first time I laid eyes on you, and I feel it now."

"Look at me," she said.

"I don't want to look at you."

"I said look at me! Look me in the eyes and tell me I'm a killer."

He looked at her. He did feel that secret locked up inside her, and felt vindication hardening him, helping him form the words. But as he looked into her eyes, saw her defiance, and the hurt in them, he couldn't say the words he wanted to say. The words that would have at least made sense of everything. He knew, suddenly, that if he said those words he'd be killing something that was inside both of them, and he couldn't do it.

He closed his eyes. "I just don't want her to die," he said. "It's too much. She's the first person I've let myself love since my . . ." And he shook his head, not wanting to say it.

"I'm sorry about your wife," Selena said softly. "But she's dead, Danny, and you're trying to make it up to her by pretending to be dead yourself. You'd rather have me be a murderer, wouldn't you? That way you could hate me. Isn't that right?"

Just then Mrs. Lund came in uncertainly. "She just smiled at me," she said. "I can't tell you how grateful I am."

"I want her to go to the institute for a few days, Mrs. Lund, if that's all right with you."

"Of course, if you think that's best."

"You'll never see her again, Mrs. L.!" Danny said.

"Danny!" Mrs. Lund cried, deeply shocked.

"It's true. I'm telling you, they'll kill her there!"

"And I'm telling you that she's my niece and if Miss Crockett and the doctor say she should go, then that's where she's going."

"But Mrs. L.!"

"If you say another word, Danny Constantine, I swear I'll never speak to you again!" Mrs. Lund turned away tearfully and went back to the bedroom. Danny stared after her. His head was spinning. How could everything be so crazy?

"Danny," Selena said gently, touching his arm.

"I need some air," he said, pulling away. He went out into the rain and started walking down the alley. Halfway down the block Bing Lockner caught him.

"Connie, for Christ's sake! People get help at the institute all the time."

"Gray hates my guts," Danny said. "When he finds out who Shirley is—"

"Where else are you going to take her, Connie? What the hell else are you going to do?"

"I'll think of something!" Danny said fiercely.

"Goddamn it, Connie!" Bing said, grabbing him. "The kid needs a break. Maybe you're right about Gray. But Dorrie's heard a few things about that place that you don't know."

"Like what!"

"He might have a cure."

Danny stopped.

"That's right. A cure. And maybe it's lucky you're all over him. Maybe he'll fix her up just to prove you're wrong."

"Hell," Danny said, feeling like he couldn't breathe all of a sudden. "Aw, Christ." He stood there wiping his eyes as Bing put his arms around him. "I can't take any more of this, Bing. I can't—"

"You got to, Connie. You're not sick. You have to go on. You owe it to everybody who can't. Including poor Shirley." Bing took a hip flask out of his coat pocket. "Here. Have a slug." Danny took the flask from Bing and drank. "Nothing's gonna happen to that kid, Connie. I promise. Look at me. Did I ever lie to you?"

"No," Danny said.

"And I ain't lying to you now. She'll be all right."

"She's just a kid," Danny said miserably.

"I said she'll be all right. I mean it, Connie. You've got to believe that. You gotta believe it all the way."

Danny nodded.

"Say it."

"All the way, Bing."

"Okay! Why don't you go back down to the office. Don't you have that piece about the shortchange artists to write? You go downtown. I'll stay with Selena and make sure everything's square down at the institute. Okay?"

"Yeah," Danny said numbly.

"Take one more slug before you go. That's it. Drink and go on. That's what you got to do, Connie."

Drink and go on, Danny repeated to himself, numbly, heading for the Ford.

26

That night, Mrs. Lund brought out the food and put the platters straight onto the table without turning on the ultraviolet lights. Everything was overcooked and mis-seasoned, but Kal, seeing how blotched Mrs. Lund's face was, swore it was the best dinner she had ever cooked.

"Where's Lou?" he asked, when they had got to the pie.

"He called and said he had to go somewhere tonight," Mrs. Lund said distractedly. "He said he didn't know when he'd be back."

"Did you tell him about Shirley?" Danny said.

Mrs. Lund shook her head. Then she began to cry.

"Now, Lucille, don't go on that way!" Kal said, getting up and putting an arm around her. "Shirley's in good hands down at that institute. Isn't that right, Dan?"

"Why ask him!" Mrs. Lund cried before Danny could say anything. "He didn't want her to go. He wouldn't even take her there!"

"I want Shirley to be okay, too, Mrs. Lund," Danny said.

"No, you don't!"

"Why don't you go on, Dan," Kal said, giving him a look. "I'll help Lucille clear up."

"Sure, Kal," Danny said softly. "I think maybe I'll take a bath."

"That's a good idea. Take a bath."

Kal had had a crush on Mrs. Lund ever since he'd moved into the house. Well, you couldn't blame him for trying now that she finally had let her guard down. She needed comfort, and Kal could give it to her.

Danny went upstairs and drew a tub of water. He got in and smoked and tried to read a novel, something Michael Arlen had written before he died, but the words just seemed to bounce off his eyes. After a while he gave up and sat in the water listening to the clatter of dishes below him in the kitchen.

Gee, it was funny how people stored up grief like a battery, then shocked you with it later, as if you were the cause of it all. Right now Mrs. Lund hated him. It didn't make sense, and maybe it wouldn't last, but something had broken between them that was going to be hard ever to fix. Maybe they'd work around it eventually, but things were never going to be the same between Danny and Mrs. Lund again.

It's because I let her down, and she knows it, Danny thought. He should have been thinking about Shirley. Of course, he *had* been thinking of her, and maybe if Mrs. Lund knew what he knew, had seen the things he'd seen at the institute, she'd understand. But she hadn't seen them and she didn't understand. All she'd seen was Danny pulling some kind of stunt that didn't make sense, when she needed him to be steady and help pull her and Shirley through. Never mind that he'd showed up with a doctor. Never mind that he'd given two pints of his own blood, never mind that he would have given Shirley all of it if that would have kept her out of that institute.

But Shirley *was* there now, he thought. And maybe that wasn't so bad. Gray was running two operations. There was the institute that people like Selena Crockett and Bing Lockner and even the Archangel saw, the one that helped people, *the one that had possibly invented a cure!* Then there was the other, secret institute, the real one that Danny had been trying to uncover, the dark bedlam-house murder operation. As long as Shirley stayed in that first institute, she'd be all right. They'd take care of her and maybe even cure her, and she would be all right. Shirley would come home and Mrs. Lund would forget about what had happened and everything would be like it was.

But that was the thing. You were always wishing for things to be like they used to be, wishing so hard that you never appreciated that maybe what you were doing *now* was okay in its own way, until something came along and busted that up, too, and then you were wishing for things to go back to the way they'd just been before they busted up. Danny had been living here in the boardinghouse almost two years. Mrs. Lund had taken him in, made him feel safe and at home, fed him, and worried about him, until finally it had been the most natural life in the world for him. She was so warm, not the fussing-over-you kind of warm, but somebody who was just quiet about it, like a stove in the corner. And it seemed that she had built up a new family from pieces that would fit together. She had started out with Shirley, loving her so much that Shirley actually thrived in spite of how sick she was. And then she had brought in Kal, all gruff and smelling like hair tonic, because she thought Shirley needed to know that there were good older men in this world, too. Then came Danny, younger and kind of dashing, running around town after pictures, and finally the crazy little brother, Lou. And somehow, even though five years ago none of them could have imagined living together, it had worked.

So why couldn't he trust Mrs. Lund's judgment now? Why couldn't he accept Bing's advice? The thought of Shirley lying in that institute with Gray anywhere around was too much for Danny. He had to get her out of there! But where could he take her? Where could she get treated, except at the institute?

Then, all of a sudden, he remembered Theo Rostek's offer to help him. Maybe that was a way! Hadn't Rostek told him about the poor couple who'd died up there on Bryant not asking him for help?

Danny shaved, dressed in his best suit, and drove up to the North Side for the second time that day.

There was a big crowd milling around the front of Rostek's Restaurant. Some people were waiting to get in to eat, and even more were lined up in front of the stairs that led up to the dance hall above. It was a dressed-up, mixed-race crowd, the men in sharp linen suits and Dobbs hats, the women in pin curls and fox scarves.

Danny had to park around the block and as he came back to the restaurant he smelled cigars and shoe polish and perfume, mixed with grilled chicken and garlic sausage. There was maybe one white for every three Negroes here, and, as usual in mixed company, the white women outnumbered the men. It was the white men who had the biggest problem accepting this new kind of socializing. There was a lot of nervous and, strange to admit, happy energy radiating off that corner. Danny hadn't figured there'd be a dance here tonight, and in spite of everything, he felt himself cheering up a little.

As he joined the throng, he marveled at the unlikeliness of this old dinner place turning into such a hot spot. Danny remembered old Emil Rostek, with his mustaches and a huge belly straining against a green apron, bringing platters of sausage and kraut and hot potato salad, and schooners of beer from his brother Leo's brewery in New Ulm, to the families out for Sunday dinner. Tonight was Danny's first visit to the restaurant in at least ten years.

There was a big Negro in a white dinner jacket taking names at the door. Danny went up to him.

"I want to see Theo Rostek."

"Sure, you do," the doorman said slowly, after looking him over.

"My name's Constantine. He asked me to come see him tonight."

The doorman looked past Danny and started taking names again.

"Are you going to tell him I'm here?" Danny said.

"I ain't tellin' nobody nothin'," the doorman said. "You want to eat, I'll put your name down. Otherwise get out of the way."

Danny tried to push past him. He didn't get very far. The bouncer caught him by the collar and yanked him back.

"Jerome, let him go!" Danny heard someone say.

The bouncer let go. "Oh, hello, Miss Crockett."

"What's going on?"

"This man's trying to crash his way in."

"He's a friend of mine. I'll take him off your hands."

"Whatever you say, Miss Crockett. I'm just doing my job here."

Danny turned around, ready to tell her he didn't want or need her help. But he wasn't prepared for the sight of her in a silver dress, cut

high in the front and scooped very low in the back, showing off
perfect skin, beautiful bare arms, and the curve that began just
above her hips and rose all the way to her neck. He had never seen
her look so beautiful, not even that day at the Interlachen Club.

"Well!" she said. "You're the last fellow I expected to see tonight."
Her brown eyes grew warm, and her smile melted over him like the
sun on a cold January day.

"Hello, Selena," he muttered in confusion. He hadn't been
thinking about her, but now that she was here and smiling at him,
he felt that cool warmth turning at the top of his stomach. *Stop it*, he
told himself severely. *You're not here for that. . . .*

"Oh, you're angry," she said, reacting to his frown. "I'm
sorry. You all were probably expecting me to call about Shirley. I
did try. But the exchange was out again. I sent a telegram. Did it
arrive?"

"Not while I was there."

"Well, in it I said that Shirley's doing wonderfully well. She's out
of danger, and there's pink in her cheeks now. And she's not
bleeding anymore."

Danny closed his eyes. He felt faint suddenly.

"Are you all right?" Selena asked. "You really ought to be resting.
You gave an awful lot of blood. How much did they take?"

"I don't know. Whatever it takes to fill up two bottles."

"Doesn't he look pale, Amos?" Selena asked a handsome, light-
skinned Negro.

"You're asking the wrong man, Selena," Amos said, with a
good-natured laugh.

"She really is all right, though?" Danny asked again.

"Well, I'm not a doctor, of course. But they definitely stopped the
bleeding. And Simon always says that's ninety percent of the battle."

"Is he . . . he's not attending her, is he?" Danny said.

"Are we going to start that again?"

"Is he?"

"No. He wasn't in the clinic this afternoon."

Danny felt relief wash over him.

"Do you know Amos Bonds?"

"No."

"Amos, this is Danny Constantine. He's a reporter for the *Journal.*"

"How are you?" Bonds said easily, shaking hands with him. "Sorry about your sister."

That felt good, somehow, to think of Shirley like that. Danny didn't correct him.

"Amos is in real estate. He finds properties—or should I say, he finds people with money. Lord knows there's plenty of property these days."

"I'm just a matchmaker," Bonds said.

"What you are is an avaricious and very charming shark."

"Sharks don't make money."

"Oh, money! Don't bore me with money."

"You find flour a bore, too, Selena. Because you don't have the faintest idea how either one of 'em's made."

"I don't want to know. I've got seven elevators full of flour right now."

"And another three full of cash!"

"Oh, bother! What are you accusing me of? I live in a one-room apartment. I don't even own a car. Why, you've got at least six."

"Seven," Bonds said proudly. "Picked up a Stutz last week."

"I warned you if you started bragging about your money, I'd leave. And you didn't listen."

"You didn't expect me to, now, did you?"

"No, I didn't. Now, scoot!" She stood on her toes and brushed her lips against his neck as he laughed.

"I'll see you later, Selena," he said. "Nice meeting you, Constantine."

"Come on, Danny," She took his hand, pulled him inside, and started through the dining room. "Don't you think he's awfully attractive?" she said over her shoulder.

"Sure, I guess."

"You guess. Why, look at that face. Those eyes! He's prettier than John Gilbert and what's even more charming is that he's absolutely dense about it. Women will be swarming around him all night, and all he'll think of is who he can put together with where, with a fat commission for himself in the middle. Such a waste!"

She pushed through the wicket and they were in the kitchen, walking past the line of cooks who were preparing plates of chicken and spaetzle.

"Hullo, Miss Selena," said one of the cooks.

"Hello, Otis."

"Where are we going?" Danny said.

"Upstairs. There's no use clawing through all those people out front."

"Selena, I didn't come here to dance. I came to see Theo."

"Well, he's upstairs. I'll take you right to him. Promise."

"Miss Selena, how are you this evening?" said the headwaiter.

"Just passing through, Ernest."

They pushed through another door and turned at a dumbwaiter loaded with dirty glasses and plates, past an open walk-in cooler, then around to the back stairs. Here there were men and women sitting on the steps smoking.

"Hey, Selena!"

"You going to play good tonight, Max?"

"Aw, Selena, don't I play good for you *all* the time?"

"Depends what you're smoking, brother!" Selena said, laughing. To Danny, she explained, "This is where the boys in the band hide out. The smoke gets awfully thick down here."

At the top of the stairs they came out into a vestibule behind the stage. "He's with me," Selena said to the Negro standing at the door. He smiled and tipped his hat to her, and they went along a back hall, through a coat checkroom, Selena stopping to kiss a red-haired girl who looked Danny over and said something, the two girls laughing and Danny wishing he had heard what they were talking about. Finally they reached the bar.

"What are you drinking?" she said.

"Whiskey sour," Danny said above the noise.

"Whiskey sour, and I'll take a sidecar, Donald."

"Very good, Miss Selena." While the barman shook her cocktail, Danny offered her a cigarette. She took one, and he lighted it for her.

"You certainly know lots of people, Selena."

"Don't I, though?" She laughed. "Actually, I only *remember* lots of them. I try never to forget a name. Whenever I'm introduced to someone, I repeat their name out loud. That way it sticks."

"That kissing you do doesn't hurt either," Danny said, remembering how she had introduced herself to him that day at the Interlachen Club.

"That's for them to remember *me.*"

"It seems to work both ways," he said.

"Well, of course it does. If you make a *special* effort with someone, you're bound to make them do the same, even if they don't realize it."

"Subconsciously, you mean."

"Subconsciously, yes. Now, there's a word. Thank you, Donald; this is a beautiful cocktail."

Danny paid for the drinks and they went out onto the floor of the dance hall. The band was on the riser, tuning up beneath a wooden proscenium that was decorated by a rack of elk antlers at the crown of the arch. On either side of the dance floor was a raised platform with chairs for people to watch the dancing from, and tables lighted by candles set inside blue glass jars.

"Do you mind if we sit upstairs for a bit?" Selena asked. "I prefer watching from up above."

Upstairs in the balcony were the men who worked the spotlights, and several empty tables along an ell. "There!" Selena said happily, claiming a table. "We've drinks and cigarettes, a place to sit, and I've got you all to myself." She crinkled up her eyes at him and Danny smiled back at her. It was a different world inside this hall, and he was starting to feel better.

"Now," she said, "what were you saying about subconscious messages between people?"

"Well, I think it explains why anyone discovers they're interested in someone, even though they've never really talked, or spent any time together."

"Why, Danny Constantine, it is *much* too early for you to be so earnest! Of *course* we're interested in one another. But you mustn't talk about it. The beauty of a subconscious message is that you don't know it. Like having a pebble in your shoe that you don't even find until you finally take it off at the end of the day. 'Why, *that's* what's been bothering me all day long!' "

Danny quickly picked up his drink. He felt embarrassed that she had called him earnest. He felt that, to Selena, being earnest was probably a bad thing, and he did not want her to think bad things about him. Not tonight. Somehow, she had cut him off from that feeling of dread that was chasing him all the time and he felt free, and light-headed, and did not want it to stop.

Watching her look over the rail as the hall was filling up, he said, "You know all *kinds* of people, too, don't you, Selena?"

"I suppose I do."

"Have you always been that way?"

She turned and looked at him. "You mean before?"

Danny nodded.

"I suppose I mixed mostly with my own circle. That was when I was still in school, of course. But you know, it's interesting. The thing about this epidemic is that it's simply eaten away at the foundation of most of the old class distinctions, until they've collapsed and spilled everyone together. Soon, there will only be two classes left: one of them's the living." She fell silent a moment, then brightened. "Oh, there's Theo." She pronounced it *Tee-oh.* "Theo, hello!"

Rostek came over. "Hi, Selena," he said, bending to kiss her, then glancing at Danny. "Hello, Daniel."

"How long have you two known each other?" Selena asked.

"He knew my pop," Rostek said.

"Actually, I was kind of scared of him," Danny said, and Theo laughed.

"Man, me, too! First time I ever saw him at the orphanage, I bawled my head off. I thought he was some big ol' walrus who was gonna drag me down under the ice. And that gravel belly voice of his! When he got mad, you thought he'd blow the head right off your neck." Theo shook his head fondly. "What are you folks drinking? Sidecars?"

"Mine's whiskey sour."

Rostek signaled a waiter. "Bring these folks a bottle of French champagne."

"Theo, I can't let you do that!" Selena said.

"*You* can afford it, girl!" He leaned close to Danny and said in a low voice, "I got some business to take care of. You enjoy yourself. We'll talk later."

"You're always whispering, Theo!"

"Lower I talk, the harder they listen," Rostek said. "I'll see you folks. My, you're looking fine tonight, Selena." He kissed her again, shook hands with Danny, and went off into the crowd.

"So," Danny said, "how long have you known the big man?"

"Two or three years."

"You know what he does for a living?"

"Oh, Danny, it's so boring to talk about what people do. People do what they can, or what they have to, or what other people make them. It's what people *are* that counts. Theo's a sweetheart."

"You sure about that?"

"Yes."

"As sure as you are about Simon Gray?" Danny said.

Selena's smile flickered, then held as she gathered up her evening bag. "Danny Constantine, once in a great while I allow myself an evening out. When I do, I try my best to play the spoiled little rich girl and forget about everything awful that happens in this world. I suppose it's selfish and self-indulgent of me, and I'm sure you don't approve, but I don't care. I have to do it, and I am *not* going to let you spoil things! If you won't allow me my evening, say so, and I'll find other company."

Just then the waiter arrived with an ice bucket and a bottle of champagne. The vintage was prewar. There wasn't anybody left in France to make champagne anymore. Danny looked at the label and twirled the bottle in the ice. *Maybe she's right*, he thought. *Maybe I need a night like this, too.*

He smiled at her sheepishly. "I wouldn't want to let this go to waste," he said.

Selena beamed back at him. "Don't drink it all. I'll be right back."

While she was gone, the band came out again and took its place on the riser. There were soprano, alto, and baritone saxes in the front line, three trombones behind, and three cornet players in back. To their left was the rhythm section: bass, piano, guitar player, and trap drummer. The bandleader was a Negro clarinet player with glasses. The house lights came down and into the spot stepped Theo Rostek.

"How you all doing? I hope you're ready to jump, because tonight we've got a special treat. From Chicago, New York, Philadelphia, Detroit—" he glanced back "—and where else? Oh, yeah, right here. Please welcome the Fletcher Henderson Swing Band!"

Fletcher Henderson leaned into the spot and said, "Thank you. We'd like to start with a new arrangement called 'Don't Be That Way.' " He swung his arms and the horn intro blossomed and settled down above the pulse of the rhythm section. Danny drank a glass of the champagne and watched the dancers bob and swirl on the floor. They looked like tropical fish down there, flashing in the colored lights. He felt the cigarette pack in his pocket. It was empty and he took his glass and went into the upstairs bar to buy more.

Bing Lockner was sitting there. He had his arm around a man who was hunched forward over his glass.

"Say, look who's here!" Bing said. His face was deathly pale. "If it ain't Sherlock Holmes!" He looked at his companion. "D'you know this man, Fitzgerald? This man . . ." He wavered on the stool. "*This* man is a new breed! He ain't just a newshound. He's a newshound with a *conscience!*"

"You don't say!"

"Yup. Uses it, too. He's a reformer. Wants to clean up all the corruption in this town!"

"How long have you been drinking, Bing?" Danny asked.

"Since nine-teen-oh-seven!"

He and Fitzgerald laughed uproariously. Then Bing said, "After you lef' the office I told Walter to stuff it and looked up my frien' here, and went out to his place on White Bear Lake. Me'n Fitz here did a little fishing. Didn't we, Fitz?"

"Not particularly," Fitzgerald said.

"Had to go see him at his place. Tough for Fitz there. He lives in a lodge with three thousand pictures of his wife. We started drinking to them. Some of them twice, eh, Fitz?" He blinked uncertainly at Danny. "D'you know Fitz, Sherlock? He's not a sportsman. He's one of my writer friends."

"Shut your filthy mouth," Fitzgerald said. "I've been a sportsman all my life."

"Well, now I am, too. My career with the dear old *Journal* is over by order of Fitz. Fitz demands we drink to his wife. It's a full-time job. Could take years. Could take longer than that."

"Say, don't I know you?" Fitzgerald said, peering at Danny. He had fine features and a pretty mouth. "Didn't you used to be Jackie Coogan?"

"He used to be Mae Marsh."

"Well, you are a wonderful actress," Fitzgerald said, raising his glass.

"Ssss. Actress. *I'm* the actress," Bing said. "You got no idea how good a one I am!"

"Bing," Danny said, "what's this stuff about quitting?"

"Quit? Did I say quit? No Lockner ever quit! Let us just say I ceased in advance of my colleagues."

"What are you talking about?"

"Crowley doesn't have the stuff to run a newspaper anymore. He's sick! He's out of money! He's through!"

"What do you mean, he's through?"

"I mean he's gonna haveta give it up."

"When?"

"Maybe next week. Maybe the week after."

"Walter hasn't said a word."

"Walter doesn't know it yet. But Dorrie Van der Voort knows. She told me."

"*Fuck* Dorrie Van der Voort!" Fitzgerald said sourly.

"*There* you are!" Selena said, coming over and taking Danny's arm.

"Why, look, if it ain't Selena Crockett," Bing said. "The Flour Queen. Th' angel of Milltown."

"Lay off that, Bing." Selena said frostily.

"Lay off what?" Bing said. Then: "Hey! There's Theo!" He was waving his arm. "Theo, come over here."

"Bing Lockner," Theo said easily. "What's up?"

"Why, your friend Selena and I were just having a little talk. She doesn't like me calling her an angel."

"She's modest," Theo said.

"You were in my column today, you know."

"I saw it," Theo said. "The only thing I understood was Pelican Lake."

"There. You see? That proves it."

"All it proves," Fitzgerald said, "is what I've been saying all along. You're really not much of a writer."

"Dorrie's not much of one."

"I said, *fuck* Dorrie!" Fitzgerald exclaimed.

"Listen, listen," Bing said, grabbing Theo's arm. "I heard a little somethin'. *I* heard that last night one of your runners got caught in an alley by some of the defenders of the White American Race. In fact, th' gentleman in question's standing right over there."

"Is this off the record?" Theo said.

"Do you care?"

Theo sucked on his teeth, then nodded. "I guess I don't. Marquise. Come here." A man with a cut over a swollen left eye that had been closed with some stitches came over.

"These are some nice white people, Marquise. Tell 'em what happened to you last night."

"Well I was minding my own business crossing Bryant when this crazy mother—sorry, ma'am—this crazy white boy takes a swing at me from behind. I look around and he's got another three or four boys with him, riding in the back of a truck, so I take off. Now, ordinarily, they ain't nobody can run with me, no white man, anyway, but I take a look back and this ofay's right behind me. I run into the alley, 'cause I know there's a fence I can jump and lose him on, but I tripped up, and he's got me cornered. They's nothing I can do but pull my razor. I slash with it, get him in the arm pretty good. But then he hit me with something. I woke up later, when it started rainin'. There's my book and my money roll lyin' on top of me. Man, that boy could run! I don't know of any white boys in this town that can run like that."

I do, Danny thought, remembering Lou coming home last night with that blood on his sleeve. "You say you slashed him?"

"Cut him good, right on the arm."

"This man says it was the Klan, Marquise," Theo said. "What do *you* think?"

"They weren't in no sheets," Marquise said.

"Don't matter," Bing said. "Who the hell else rides around in trucks yanking niggers off the streets?"

"The Klan stays out of the North Side," Theo insisted. His eyes hardened. "And I don't like you using that word."

"Why? You're a nigger, aren't you? Now, leave us alone. Fitz 'n I are waxing nostalgic."

"Maybe I ought to wax your white ass."

Bing turned around on his stool. "Klan stays out of the North Side except when you tell 'em to come in," he said.

"Mother*fucker*—" Theo shouted, reaching inside his jacket. Selena quickly stepped between them.

"He's drunk, Theo," she said. "He doesn't know what he's saying. Donald, call these gentlemen a cab, please? And have someone wait with them downstairs until it comes."

"Say! What's the idea of giving us the bum's rush?" Fitzgerald said. He got up and took a swing at Rostek. He only got one. Donald stepped behind and cooled him with a sap. Fitzgerald moaned once and slid to the floor. Theo motioned for some people to come over, and before Danny could say or do anything, Fitzgerald and Bing had been dragged away.

"*That's* bound to be an item now, Theo," Selena said.

"So what? Better the word goes out!" He ran his finger inside his collar, pulled it, composed himself, and smiled at Danny. "I'll see you in a few minutes."

"Jesus," Danny said, when he had gone. "Bing knows better than that."

"He was drunk."

"He knows better no matter how drunk he gets," Danny said. "Maybe I'd better look after him."

"I won't let you go," Selena said determinedly. "He can take care of himself."

"I really don't feel like dancing," Danny said.

"Please, Danny," she said. "Just try to forget about everything for one dance. Please. Then if you still feel like it, you can leave."

He looked at her. She was so damned beautiful, he thought, and there was something in her eyes now that he'd never seen before. She was afraid. And she needed him.

"Okay, Selena," he said gently.

She took his arm and they went downstairs and out onto the floor. Everyone was pressed close to each other, dancing seriously, as if trying to prove there was still some point to it now, that courting was the same thing it always had been. Danny moved with Selena into the swirl, and it was strange, like falling into a river unexpectedly, when you had been walking along the banks thinking about something else. All of a sudden, the river became everything, and all you could think of was how wet it was and whether you could keep your head above water or not. The rhythm section churned and Selena turned to the beat. Danny found himself playing off what she was doing. They swung through the other dancers and came out just in front of the bandstand, where the bandleader stood smiling with his clarinet tucked underneath his arm, keeping time with his other arm.

"Fletcher!" Selena called. "You're swinging tonight!"

"Yeahhhh!" he said, turning to signal the trombones. The players stood and began to drive the song with insistent blasts.

"Isn't it wonderful to dance to?" Selena said. "Fletcher told me that with swing, you take a little breath right before the beat. So you're a little behind, and you can sway in that space, and meanwhile you've got all this urgent breathing going on."

Just then all the lights in the dance hall dimmed and went out. This was something that happened more and more frequently because of how short-handed the power company was. Sometimes a plant would just plain run out of coal or gas, and they would have to switch to another plant on the grid. In the dark and unable to see their charts, the band continued uncertainly.

"Come on, boys, listen to Gene!" Danny heard Henderson yell. Selena pulled Danny closer in the dark and the band kept on, settling behind the drummer and playing what it remembered was on the charts, as the room took on a ghostly, flickering blue glow from the candle jars on top of the tables. Then the cornets pierced through with their corkscrew blast, and Selena suddenly put her arm behind her back, taking his arm with it, pressing them close so that he could feel the front of her hips and the firm mound below it, and the soft curve of her stomach and the warm pressure of her breasts. He felt that warmth spreading to his own chest, collecting until it dropped of its own weight and began to fill him up. For a moment he was embarrassed by his growing hardness and tried to back away, but she used the arm behind her back as a lever and cranked it tighter, so that he was pressing even closer to her.

Her breath caught, and he forgot his embarrassment and squeezed her waist with his other hand, so she did not have to use the leverage anymore and was free to turn with the music along with him, the whole point of dancing now to keep the pressure between them constant and provide an alley of friction after each little breath at the hit of the trap drum. As they came around in the dark, Danny dropped his head to her shoulder, and found it bare. In the candlelight, he saw that her wrap had dropped below the top of her arm, and he pressed his lips against the fragrant smoothness of the base of her neck and sucked in gently, and touched it with the tip of his tongue.

Suddenly, as if in reward, the lights came back, dimmed orange-yellow, then flared and held. The band strained forward again confidently, like a team of horses coming out of a dark tunnel. They turned the lights down again, but Danny, in a moment of self-consciousness, straightened and started to pull Selena's wrap up for her. They were at the edge of the spotlight that was on the band. Danny was looking down, following the curve of Selena's shoulder where it plunged, flaring out, into the soft darkness beneath her slip. He saw the shiny, narrow, and slightly puckered line of a scar that started at her collarbone and fell into those same shadows.

Instantly, he let go of her. She thought he had made a dance move and laughingly turned and tried to take hold of his hands. Then she saw the look on his face.

"Danny, what's wrong?"

The band finished the song as Danny turned away. Selena caught him at the coat check.

"Danny!"

"Your neck," he said.

She flushed deeply.

He took her shoulders and shook her. "When did he do it to you!"

"Danny, it's not important.

"Liar! Damn you, when did he do it!"

"When I was fifteen," Selena said, looking away. "It was right after the first part of the epidemic, and Simon was one of the only surgeons who knew how to operate safely. I had a growth—"

"I don't believe you."

"It's true! Why would I lie about it?"

"It's just like you said before, Selena. We all put on our face to the world, but everything's still a secret inside. And now I know yours!"

"I—I don't know what you mean!"

"Yes, you do. You remember when you ran into me up on the third floor at the institute? I'd just come from the morgue. I saw three bodies with closed-up incisions identical to that scar of yours. Gray fixes people like you up, doesn't he? He changes them so they can drink blood!"

"That's crazy!"

"Is it? What about his secrets, Selena?"

She didn't say anything. Danny took her wrist. "Get your coat," he said.

"What for?"

"We're going downtown to talk to Sergeant Willson."

Her eyes grew hard, and she tried to pull away but that only made him angrier. He wanted to strangle her now for what she had done to those poor people, and what she had tried to do to him.

"Let . . . *go!*"

"What's going on here?" Theo Rostek said, frowning as he came in from the hall.

"Nothing, Theo," Selena said. "We're just having a . . . disagreement."

"Take your hands off her, Constantine," Theo said, pulling a gun. Gradually, and reluctantly, Danny let go.

"Do you want me to take care of this, Selena?" Rostek said.

"No," she said. "He'll leave. Won't you, Danny?"

"Ask her what we were talking about, Theo."

"You've talked enough," Rostek said, jamming the pistol barrel into Danny's back. "Move." He pushed Danny down the stairs and all the way around the corner to his car.

"She's a killer," Danny said. "Three in the last month. Kills them and steals their blood."

"Shut up."

"You don't know what she is!"

"You got no idea what you're fucking with. Scribbling stories for that white-ass newspaper. Murders. There's way more to it than that, brother. Way more. But that ain't none of your business. You understand? This ain't your town anymore. It's *mine*! And I take care of my own. I don't let nobody make trouble for my friends. Got that?"

"You're no different than those bastards at the GNDC."

"Oh, I'm different. They don't even know how different I am. In two years, I'm still gonna be alive. Where are they gonna be?"

"You can't sit by and let people get murdered."

"We ain't talking about that," Rostek said with a hard smile. "We're talking about you messing with a friend of mine. Let me lay it out for you. You go near her again, I'll kill you. Got that?"

"I'm not going to stop what I'm doing," Danny said.

"Then you're a dead man. Simple as that."

Danny cranked the Ford to life and hopped in.

"Simple as that," Theo repeated, watching him drive away.

27

*D*anny drove home and went upstairs. He looked in on Lou first, but Lou wasn't home, so he went into Kal's room instead. Kal was snoring heavily. Danny went up to him and shook his shoulder.

"It's better if I sleep in my own room, Lucille," Kal said.

"It's not Lucille," Danny said. Kal opened his eyes.

"Oh, oh," he said, rubbing his face.

"Never mind that. We've got to bring Shirley home."

"Shirley?" he said, and then remembered where Shirley was. "Are you out of your mind? It's the middle of the night, Dan!"

"Kal, I'm not kidding. I'm going to the institute to get Shirley and bring her home where she belongs."

"The poor girl's sick," Kal said, sitting up.

"She's had transfusions. She'll be all right for a few days. That'll give us time to make other arrangements. Please, Kal. You know I'm not crazy, not when it comes to Shirley. We've got to get her out of there."

Kal snapped on his bedside lamp. The power was very low now, and the light was a muddy yellow. Looking up at Danny, Kal thought he *did* look crazy. But he also knew how much Danny loved Shirley.

"All right," he said, getting out of bed.

In the car on the way to the institute, Danny told Kal everything he knew about Gray, and what he suspected about Selena Crockett.

"I think Gray's perfected a kind of operation that lets somebody take blood directly from someone else without having to arrange a transfusion. He turns them into a kind of mechanical vampire. They drink the blood, but it goes into their bloodstream and not their stomachs. I took a piece of equipment from Gray's desk the day I was down there. Percy Satin said it looked like some kind of valve or pumping system, designed to be sewn inside someone's chest. And Gray's a thoracic surgeon."

"What's that?"

"Someone who specializes in surgery inside the wall of the chest. I think those bodies I saw in the morgue were failed operations, or experiments at perfecting his technique. I think he's offering the operation to anyone who can afford it. That's where he gets the money to finance the institute."

"What about all the people he helps? The children and all."

"Guinea pigs," Danny said. "He experiments on them to find out more about the disease."

Danny slowed, approaching the gates of the institute.

"Is this it?" Kal asked.

"Yeah. I've got to figure out a way to get in."

"I know a way."

"What?"

"I worked here once. When it belonged to the Shriners. I made some repairs in the boiler room. There was a service entrance. Keep going." They reached the end of the fence and a verge of wooded property. "There." Kal pointed out a rusted chain stretched over an overgrown gravel track through the woods. "Where's your tire iron?"

"Under the seat."

Kal got it, went out to the chain, and broke it off.

"Drive through," he said, getting back in. "This goes around past the end of the wall."

They drove ahead, Danny stopping once so that Kal could clear a deadfall out of the way. Finally the drive angled away from the trees and toward the institute grounds. Danny cut his lights, backed up, and turned the Ford around. He got out, opened the rumble seat, and took a blanket.

"Children's ward is on the rear of the first floor," Danny said. He could see orange-yellow lights glowing through the landing windows at the end of the wing, twenty yards away. Everything was quiet. Far away, he heard the moan of a steam whistle coming from the river. They started across the lawn, spongy and wet from the rains, and reached a window. There were night-lights beside each bed, and in their glow Danny could see the bodies of children sleeping under blankets. The window was open a few inches. Danny and Kal pushed it open further, and Danny climbed inside.

"Wait here," he whispered. "I'll get her."

He started moving from bed to bed, checking for size and then for hair color. Once he tapped a shoulder, and a girl turned over sleepily, but it wasn't Shirley. God, he wished he had a truck outside to take all of these kids away from here! But the thing to do, he thought, was to get Shirley away now, then bust the rest of the place up. He'd make Willson and Burns and old man Crowley and the mayor and everybody else listen, all right!

Danny kept checking the beds. Finally, in the corner opposite the window he'd come through, he found her. She was sleeping on her back, breathing heavily, her forehead damp with perspiration. He knelt down beside the bed and whispered her name.

"Danny," she said out loud, waking up instantly.

"Shh, honey."

She was looking around. "What time is it?"

"Late. Listen Shirl, how do you feel?"

"Okay. I've been having awful dreams, though."

"Are you . . ." he hesitated, then made himself say it. "Are you still bleeding?"

"I don't think so. The nurse said the transfusions I got stopped everything okay."

"Good. Listen to me now. I'm here to take you home. Can you walk?"

"I guess so, but—"

"Shhh! We've got to leave now, okay? Here." He took her robe from the hook beside the bed. "Put this on. I'll explain everything to you when we get outside, okay?"

"Okay, Danny," she said, excited, suddenly, by the prospect of sneaking out. She put on the robe and took Danny's arm, padding across the wooden floor to the window where Kal waited.

"Careful," he said, helping her through.

"Hi, Kal," she said cheerfully. "You in on this, too?"

"It's just too quiet at home without you, Shirley," Kal said, hugging her neck.

"Come on," Danny said, jumping outside. They started back toward the Ford. Suddenly the grass lit up. Danny glanced back and saw that somebody had turned the ward lights on. He could hear the stirring groans of waking children and see the long shadows of the two men, with Shirley's in between, pointing toward the dark trees where the Ford waited.

"Keep going," Danny said, letting go of Shirley's arm. "Get her home."

"What are you going to do?"

"Never mind, just run!"

"Come on, Shirley," Kal said, looking Danny in the eye and nodding. Danny turned around and ran back to the window of the ward and crawled inside. The little girl in the bed closest to the window screamed loudly.

"There!" a nurse cried. "I knew I'd heard something!" She and Horace, Gray's security chief, stood in the entrance to the ward. Some of the children were sitting up, others yelling, others hiding under their blankets. Danny raised his arms, causing even more ruckus, and rushed straight toward the two adults. They hesitated, and he slipped between them and ran out into the tower lobby.

"Get him!" Horace yelled.

Danny heard a loud click—the front doors had been electrically locked from the desk. He feinted toward it anyway, turned, rushed halfway up the stairs as a couple of orderlies came out and blocked the way. He came down then, running between the armchairs and tables until finally he was cornered. Orderlies took his arms, and Horace came up to him.

"You," he said, breathing hard. "Snooping around again!"

"So's your old lady," Danny said, listening for the sound of the Ford. It was impossible to hear; he could only hope they had put all of their men on him, and that Kal and Shirley had got away. Horace glanced over his shoulder. Then he stepped up and drove an uppercut deep into Danny's stomach. Danny doubled up, everything going black. He was desperate to breathe but he seemed to have forgotten how.

"Let him drop," Horace told the orderlies. They let go, and Danny fell on his face on the rug.

"One of the patients is missing," Danny heard the nurse say. "Shirley Lund, the one they brought in this afternoon!"

"We better wake up the doc," Horace said. Danny felt a big shoe pressing against his back. "Where's the girl, snoop?"

"Get . . . stuffed. . . ." Danny managed to say.

"Get the lights on outside and search the grounds," Horace ordered. "And get the doc down here now!" He leaned down close to Danny's face. "I was hoping you'd come back, punk. The doc don't like to be disturbed. This time he'll let me take care of you good. Understand?"

"Dr. Gray says to take him to the prep room," the orderly said, running down the stairs.

"The prep room. Are you sure?"

"That's what he said."

"Nuts. Get up."

They pulled Danny to his feet and dragged him through the lobby, back to the hospital receiving room, and through to the prep room. "Strap him to the gurney," Horace ordered, and while he pressed down on Danny's chest, the orderlies fastened leather straps across his legs, chest, wrists, and ankles.

"All right, beat it," Horace told them. When they were gone, he said, "Give yourself a break, Constantine. Tell me what you did with the girl."

"Fuck you," Danny said. There was a burst of white pain in

Danny's head as Horace backhanded him across the mouth, and he tasted his own blood.

"I don't care what the doc thinks he's going to do to you," Horace said. "I'm gonna take what's left. And I'm gonna make sure you're awake to appreciate it."

Just then Gray and a nurse wearing a gown and surgical mask came through the swinging doors. Gray was in a red robe, with a silver satin scarf tucked into the neck. His hair was wet, and combed back.

"Mr. Constantine," he said pleasantly. "So good to see you again."

"We caught him in the kids' ward," Horace said. "And now there's a patient missing."

"I see. And which patient?"

"Um," Horace said. "I heard the name but I was busy with him, Doc."

"And you can only remember so much, can you, Horace?"

"No, that ain't it—"

"I'll refresh your memory for you. Her name was Shirley Lund. She is the niece of Mr. Constantine's landlady. Evidently Mr. Constantine was concerned about the treatment Miss Lund was receiving here. Am I correct, Mr. Constantine?"

"You're a murderer," Danny said.

Gray looked at him coolly. "A murderer. Someone who, for instance, shoots his wife after drinking a bottle of cheap whiskey? Or perhaps a person who stabs a passerby so that he can rifle his pockets? Is that what I am, Mr. Constantine?" He glanced at the nurse. "Would you be so kind as to assist me, my dear?"

Her eyebrows rose, but she nodded and helped him into a surgical gown, and tied on a cap.

"Thank you," he said. "Prepare a donor setup, please." Gray pulled a lamp down from its ceiling mount, switched it on, then pulled down on the bottom of Danny's eyelids. With his thumb and forefinger he felt for the glands beneath Danny's jaw, felt underneath his arms and the inside of his legs.

"A little run-down, but otherwise healthy. Dressed up for the evening. Liquor on the breath. It looks like you've come here directly from a party, Mr. Constantine." He pushed the light away. "I assume you found your courage in a bottle."

A telephone on the wall rang. Horace went over to answer. "Yeah? Yeah? Are you sure? Okay." He hung up and said to Gray, "The boys found fresh tire tracks along that old service road through the woods. They had to stop looking, though, because a shipment just came in."

"How big?"

"Five."

"Five!"

"They've got a new boy who likes the action, I guess."

"You'd better go help them, then."

"Aw, Doc, I was hoping—"

"Yes?" Gray said coldly.

"Nothing, Doc. I'll go see to the new ones right away."

Gray looked down at Danny and smiled. "Your little friend will bleed again, you know. Perhaps not again for several months. But she will, and then what will you do?"

"I'll think of something."

"I highly doubt you'll be thinking of much at all," Gray said. "However, perhaps Mrs. Lund will bring her to us again, and I will be able to finish what I had intended to begin doing tomorrow with her."

"Cutting her up like those others in your morgue?"

"No, Mr. Constantine. *Curing* her. Cut the sleeve away, please."

The nurse took a scissors and sliced the material all the way around just below his shoulder. *My best suit,* Danny thought bleakly as she pulled the material free. Gray pressed two fingers in the crook of Danny's elbow and ran them down toward his wrist.

"Very nice veins," he said. "Good muscle tone, skin smooth and elastic. Tourniquet, please."

"What did you mean you can cure Shirley?" Danny said.

"Just that."

"How? By making her into a vampire?"

"Making her into a vampire. What a hysterical means of expression. But then, you are a newspaper man, aren't you?" Gray tied a length of rubber tubing around Danny's bicep and drew it tight. "As a scientist, I have every right to take offense at that. To compare my work to the lurid imaginings of a Victorian pornographer." He wiped the inside of Danny's arm with cotton dabbed in alcohol, then took an iodine swab and painted the whole area. "You'll note that I am taking the trouble to prepare you properly, although I assure you there will be absolutely no danger of infection in your case. Place the needle, please."

The nurse removed a black stopper at the tip of the needle, felt Danny's arm, then, with a quick, half-turning motion, inserted the needle into the arm vein and removed the tourniquet. She secured the rubber tube—now dark with Danny's blood—with strips of adhesive tape. Danny could see the blood beginning to fill the bottom of a bottle which rested in a rack mounted to the side of the gurney.

"Thank you, my dear. That was excellent. You did what had to be done."

"Thank you, Doctor," she said softly, and left the prep room.

"You're filling that up quickly, aren't you?" Gray said. "The average human body contains approximately eight percent of body weight in blood. You are around a hundred and seventy-five pounds, which would mean twelve to fifteen pints of blood, although I understand from Dr. Cramer that you gave at least two pints earlier today. So perhaps you may be a bit low. You'll get shocky a bit sooner than normal. So ask away! I'll answer anything you like."

"Why did you operate on those people?"

Gray went to the cupboard and got out another donor setup. "In treating chronic HF, there are two approaches to take. One can either devise a therapeutic treatment, meaning a drug or regimen that effects a reduction in bleeding episodes and their severity. Or, there is the prosthetic approach, which can take a number of forms. Anything from the installation of a permanent shunt in the arm, for example, to facilitate ease of blood transfusion in the case of an attack. Or, there are more elaborate means. How do you feel?"

"What kind of means?" Danny said.

"An operation to install certain devices permanently in the chest of a patient. The equipment consists of a series of valves and chambers that effectively link the esophageal tube to the innominate artery and thus the circulatory system. I believe you stole part of that apparatus, did you not? That was the main check valve. It is powered, like the rest of the system, by compressed air. When activated, it enables my patient to *drink* an infusion of blood. It is particularly good for women, who know in advance when they will bleed and can therefore take steps to replenish their blood supply with the necessary blood factors that activate the fibrin-fibrinogen clotting mechanism. It is this mechanism, which is a very complex series of protein triggers and feedback loops, which is devastated by the HF virus.

"Of course," Gray said, "Most people have an aversion to drinking blood. Even though it means their life. And so, along with the valves and reservoirs, I install an *incentive.* Ah! One pint already." Gray clamped forceps onto the tube, and removed it from the bottle, exchanging it for an empty one and putting the full bottle back onto the counter. Danny's fingers were starting to tingle. Gray checked his pulse. "Starting to quicken," he said. Then he released the clamp. "Things will be getting a bit *vague* for you soon, I'm afraid." The blood was filling the second jar.

"You operated on Selena Crockett, didn't you?" Danny said. Gray looked down on him with a surprised expression.

"My compliments, Mr. Constantine. I must admit I've developed a grudging respect for you. And that tenacious policeman who imagines himself to be my nemesis. Both of you have acted, and acted well. You've both uncovered part of the truth about me." Gray leaned closer. "But the tragedy is that neither one of you understands what it is you've found. Do you know why? Because you are blinded by idealism. You oppose me because I do not conform to your ideal of the way things ought to be. But in the end, that ideal filters out much of the world so that you are no closer to the truth than the cynic would be. Yes! You and Sergeant Willson are idealists in an age where idealism is the most incredible luxury. And luxuries must be paid for. You, Mr. Constantine, are paying in *blood.* And Willson will pay in kind as well!"

"What about . . . what about the cure?" Danny said. He felt light-headed now, and it was an effort to talk, to concentrate. He needed to concentrate. If he could concentrate, he could replace the blood he was losing with willpower.

"*That* is an entirely separate line of inquiry, of course. But after nearly six years of research I have succeeding in making a preparation that repairs and regenerates the mechanism in the liver responsible for manufacturing the missing blood factors. Of course, it requires a great deal of, shall we say, raw material, presently, to prepare enough extract to restore a single person to health. A pity, really, you took it upon yourself to remove your young friend from the ward, since I intended to test my latest batch on her."

"You're . . . lying. . . ." Danny managed to say.

"Console yourself with that thought! Although, if you had only left well enough alone, at the very least, your life would have been safe. I had no intention of doing anything with the girl other than treating her. And here you come bursting in, intent on saving her! As though that would make any difference. It's all vanity for you, isn't it, Mr. Constantine? Feeding your egotistic vision of yourself as the Noble Crusader, the man who can live in the age of plague and maintain his humanity, treating everyone with kindness and love. A man who with his vast, invulnerable heart will take on the burdens of the world and ease the pain of all those who suffer. And how? By scribbling *articles*. Hounding me, as though you thought you might actually disturb me. How could you? Nobody can! Certainly not the people of Milltown. Because I am the cold, secret heart of this city! And if I must take a life in order to save two, then let it be so!

"The people here are polite, Mr. Constantine. They understand why it is better to be silent. They mask their true feelings. They let things happen to them and console themselves with the nobility of resignation. It's the old pioneer fatalism, dressed up to look like the modern world. But it's the same: if one child dies, have another. If the flood washes out the fields, plant again when they dry. Keep taking it and taking it, until, of course, you go mad! Yes, and when your neighbor explodes in a bloody burst, thank God it did not happen to you, and paint over the stains on the sidewalk! Oh, yes! This place is perfect for my work! If I had built my institute where people were less sure of themselves, I would never have been able to work in such an exquisite vacuum of secrecy! Death and darkness is where I live, Mr. Constantine. That is my garden! My field!"

Vaguely, Danny saw the nurse, still masked, come into the room. Gray was intent on talking and half turned, unable to get his arm up in time as the nurse struck at him with something.

"You—" he said, eyes wide, trying to pull away the syringe that stuck out of the side of his neck. He didn't reach it. Instead he made a little spin and fell unconscious to the floor.

"How much has he taken?" the nurse asked.

"Tt—" was all Danny could say. He heard a click—hemostats—and felt a dull sting in his arm and a tightness of something being wrapped rapidly around it. Then motion, the door shoving open, the gurney rolling into the dark, and bouncing. Danny faded in and out. He heard keys jingling, felt himself tossing on the gurney, then all was quiet for a moment. He thought he saw red candlelight. Then there was a whir and a dropping sensation that seemed to last for a long time, followed by banging, more bouncing, and then the rush of cool, damp air over him.

"Come on, get up," the voice said, pulling on his arm. Danny tried to make himself sit up, but he couldn't.

"Okay, I'm going to slide you in."

Danny moved forward hard and came to rest on something that rocked. Doing it he hit his elbow on wood, and the sharp pain cleared his head a little. There was a chugging sound, and the smell of gas, and then a deepening roar.

I am on the river, Danny thought. *I'm going up the river.*

He felt a stab in his arm.

"It's something to bring you around. I can't carry you where we're going."

The boat cut against the current. They passed beneath a bridge. It was a high, iron bridge. *Washington Avenue Bridge*, he thought. He closed his eyes and his head began spinning so he opened them again. He turned his head and could see yellow lamplight coming from the shacks out in Bohemian Flats. Rounding the bend now. Ahead the dark wedge of Nicollet Island split the river.

"Where are we going?"

"Someplace safe," the voice said. "But you've got to climb a ladder to get there. Do you think you can do it?"

I can climb a ladder, Danny thought.

The engine slowed, then stopped, and the boat bumped up against a dock. Danny looked up and saw the blackened walls of the Crockett A mill. They looked very high. The woman helped him out of the boat. Then she pushed it away from the dock with her foot and the current took it. Danny stared at the boat turning in the current as it disappeared into the darkness above the falls. He lost his balance but she held him up.

"Hey. I said you have to climb."

I can climb a ladder, he thought. They walked beneath a brick archway. Water trickled somewhere in the dark. A match flared up, the flame holding inside a lamp. The woman was holding the lamp in her hand.

"This is the spillway from the number-three wheel pit. There's a ladder inside to the top of the intake. I'll follow you up. Take your time."

I can climb a ladder, he thought. He wrapped one arm around a ladder rung and squeezed. His body felt like a sack of wet flour. He felt her shoulder pushing below him. He took another rung. He could hear her ragged breathing. The ladder was covered with slick moss and he lost his grip, fell back, and stopped, wedged with his back against cold, slimy brick. His body started to fold inward and he slid down. He didn't care. Falling was the same as climbing.

"Damn you, Danny!" the woman swore, driving him up. He took another rung, and another, and after a long time he lay on his belly and watched curiously as a rat skittered across the bricks at the edge of the lamplight in front of his face.

There was some noise going on behind him. Loud banging, then a rush of water and a rapidly rising whine. A string of lightbulbs flickered above the passage Danny lay in. He could see the woman now and tried to take in who she was.

Instead, he closed his eyes and blacked out.

*E*arly Saturday morning a park worker found a body on the middle overlook of the east side of the falls. The worker quickly left the scene, crossing himself on the way. This was the second time in his life he had discovered a dead body. Once when he was a child in Gallacia he and his brother had found a corpse along a riverbank. The village priest had been called and it was determined that the man had drowned. Anyone who drowned became a vampire, so they had cut the heart out of his body and burned it, and cut off the man's head as well, burying everything separately in unhallowed ground. The park worker's memory of that corpse, and the drained, marble-white, open-eyed face of the dead man now were too close. And here there was no priest to do what needed to be done with the Undead.

He decided to close the footbridge.

Dooley Willson did not arrive at the falls until almost eleven. Four men and a woman had disappeared from the North Side last night. He had been taking statements from worried family and friends, and typing up the reports. When the call about the body at the park had come in he had asked the dispatcher one question: "Negro or white?" When told the body was that of a white man, he decided to finish the paperwork first.

"Send a patrol down to secure the scene," he said.

"There's nobody on shift there today," the dispatch told him.

"There's nobody on duty in Southeast Division?"

"That's right."

"What about Central?"

"Same thing."

He didn't ask about Southwest. He knew they wouldn't touch it. They patrolled the rich white neighborhood west of the lakes. They practically had their own town going there.

Willson called Francis's house. He hated to do it, but he needed the help. When nobody answered he called Francis's mother out in St. Louis Park. She hadn't seen him, though he was supposed to come over that afternoon and fix her kitchen faucet.

There was a second call from the park. Visitors were bothering the caretaker, wanting to know why they couldn't use the footpath over the falls. Willson sighed and got hold of the acting coroner.

"We've got a homicide out in Minnehaha Park," Willson said. "I'll need an ME to meet me on the scene."

"Damn, Dooley. There's nobody here right now," Percy Satin said. "My last guy just went out to Milwaukee Avenue. Some guy went acute in his car. Crashed head-on into a trolley. Six people right there. Twenty-seven last night. All I'm doing is filling out death certificates."

"I need help, Percy."

"Well, I need it, too. We aren't even letting next of kin claim the bodies anymore." Percy had ordered a ban on private burials. All the morticians—and there were only seven left in the whole town—had been deputized and pressed into service processing the victims. The dead were being shipped out to the crematory in Eden Prairie. "It's fired up now, Dooley," he said. "Go up to the top of the Met Building and look west. You'll see that white smoke twenty miles away. All my boys are busy feeding that fire."

"We'll make it quick, Perse," Willson said, and added: "Please."

"All right! I'll be over as soon as I can."

While Willson was waiting, he kept at the paperwork. It was endless. There was more white paper than white people now. You had to do it, though. You couldn't quit. If you quit they'd just be dragging you down with them.

Ten minutes after he called Percy, Theo Rostek and a bodyguard
sauntered into Willson's cubicle. Theo glanced at Willson's holster,
slung on the coat rack, and smiled.

"Morning, chief," Theo said easily, sitting down. The bodyguard
stood at the door.

"What the hell do you want?"

"Heard you were up in the neighborhood this morning," Theo
said. He took a cigar case out of his coat. "Smoke?" The aroma
when Theo opened the case was very fine.

"You've got your fucking nerve coming in here."

"No more than you, coming 'round Plymouth. I figure, we're both
taking care of business."

"I'm gonna throw your high-yellow, numbers-runnin' ass in the
tank."

Theo cut the end off the cigar with a gold cutter.

"You know, I liked it much better when the police was *white*. They
didn't give a damn what we did, as long as we kept to our little old
piece of town. But now you come flying in, stirring people up, giving
folks the idea they can take their troubles to the department." He
shook his head. "They know if they've got a problem, they're
supposed to come to me. But I don't know, Chief. It looks like you've
turned yourself into some kind of hero! All the old ladies talking
about you while they're getting their hair done. Why, they're all sure
you'll be chief one day soon, hallelujah! Our very own Dooley
Willson with an upstairs office in City Hall!"

Theo leaned forward. His eyes turned hard. "One of my boys ran
into trouble the other night. Seems he was cornered by some white
men riding around in a truck."

"So what."

"Yes, thank you, he's fine now. But I started thinking, man, that
sounds like what *Chief* Willson's been working on all these months."

"What the fuck do you want, Theo?" Willson growled.

"Nothin', Chief. I don't want a thing. In fact, I'm here to tell you
I'm taking the whole problem off your hands. You don't have to
worry about those missing people no more. The case is *solved*!" He
smiled. "There! I've just made your life easy."

"What do you know?"

"Sorry. Police matter. *My* police. Although—" He took out a platinum lighter and torched the end of the cigar. "You ever consider quitting the force? They can't be paying you much. Hell, I know for a fact that big Swede partner of your makes fifteen dollars a week more than you do. And him a detective and you a sergeant! Of course, this is a white man's racket here. It will be, too, so long as there's one white man left. Maybe you ought to think about your family. I can use a man like you. We're taking over all their municipal services, replacing them with our own. You want to be chief? I'll make you one, *Sergeant* Willson."

Willson stood up, looking Theo's goon in the eye, reached for his holster, and strapped it on.

"Get out of here. Now."

"You've been notified," Theo said. "I'm taking care of the problem. Don't come around the North Side anymore. Next time I won't be offering no cigars." He took one from the case, ran it slowly under his fine, broad nose, and let it roll off his fingers onto Willson's desk.

"Dooley, I thought you was ready to go," Percy Satin said, stepping into the cubicle just as Theo got up.

"Remember what I told you," Theo said. "How you doin', Percy?"

"Good," Percy said, watching Theo and the bodyguard leave. When they were gone, his eyes widened. "What's he doin' here?"

"Telling me to stay out of his neighborhood!"

"Sounds like a plan to me," Percy said.

"Not to me it don't," Willson said, lighting the cigar Theo had left.

They left City Hall and drove down Hiawatha, Willson fuming with disgust and affronted pride. He felt doubt, too. Some of what Theo said had jabbed him deep. If the white man died, why should the black man cling to the white way of doing things? Why, here was a chance to start clean, come up with a new way that wasn't corrupt, that was fair to everyone. Something that worked.

Of course, Willson thought, *that idea presupposes that our people aren't just as human as the white man.* Greed, selfishness, pride, stupidity—none of *that* seemed to be dying. That was all going to stay, just like Hun, and that's why you needed the law.

He was just settling back in the seat, consoling himself with that thought as he had a hundred times before, when he saw Francis's car on the lawn above the picnic grounds.

"Hey," he said. "Swede's here."

"I thought you said you couldn't find him," Percy said.

"He must have got the message from his mother and checked in," Willson said, as he began to worry about the big man stomping around on the scene. Willson always had to keep Lingeborg out of trouble. He really was a bull in a china shop.

They pulled up to the pavilion. The worried-looking park worker came out of the office. Willson could smell liquor on his breath, but drinking had only made the man more agitated.

"It's on the other side of the bridge down to the second overlook," the worker said nervously.

"When'd the detective get here?"

"What detective?"

"Detective Lingeborg. That's his car up there."

"I ain't seen any detective. And that car was parked there this morning when I came on shift."

Willson went ice cold inside. "Shit," he said, and rushed down past the barrier, over the bridge, and down the steps, the falls roaring in his ears. And saw Francis lying on his back with his eyes open. Willson sank to his knees beside him.

"Man, what—" Percy said, reaching him and taking it all in. Dooley Willson on his knees over the body, shoulders sagging. Was he crying?

"Oh, man," Percy said softly. "That's Francis!"

Willson's arm snapped straight out. "Move back," he said. "This is a crime scene. We're going to go over it right. Go get your kit."

While Percy went back to his car, Willson asked the park worker about the terrace. Was there any other way to reach it? The worker pointed out another bridge, this one below the falls, that led to the opposite bank and a series of steps and overlooks like the one they were on now. Willson began looking around. The terrace was paved in flagstones, with a light covering of rain-spattered mud. The mud was smeared toward the downstream side of the terrace, and the smears were well defined and not washed out. Whoever had surprised Francis had come from the downstream side.

He moved closer to the body. It was crumpled. No blood on the flagstones. There was a shirt button lying to Francis's left. Willson looked down and saw that the material was ripped where the button had been sewn on. Francis's collar had been torn open. He didn't want to move him yet, so he stepped over the body and there, on the neck, were the two puncture wounds. Surrounding them was a red smear. Willson took out his handkerchief and rubbed some of it off. Lipstick.

Percy came down with his bag.

"Got a camera in that?"

"Yeah."

"Take some pictures for me."

Percy got out the box camera, looked into the red window in the back. "There isn't any film, Dooley."

"Is there a thermometer?"

"Sure."

"Then take his temperature."

Percy took the thermometer out of its case. He put on a pair of rubber gloves and attempted to put the thermometer into the corpse's mouth. Rigor mortis had set in, though, and the teeth were clamped tightly together.

"Put it up his ass," Willson said.

"This is *Francis.*"

"Are you the fucking coroner or not?" Willson growled.

"I worked summers in my uncle's funeral parlor," Percy said, shaking the thermometer, unfastening Francis's belt, and pulling the trousers down.

"Damn! *Look* at that."

Francis had been mutilated like Charlie Hayes. His penis had been severed near the tip. There was some blood soaked into his underwear, though not much.

"Take his temperature," Dooley said. He went to the terrace wall. It was built into the hillside and covered over with lilacs and creepers. He pushed the brush aside and looked around, found nothing. He went down the steps toward the river. His eye caught something glittering in a clump of grass growing out of the stairs. He bent down to look. It was a cufflink. Platinum or white gold, engraved with the initials *SG*.

Simon Gray.

He put the cufflink in his pocket. The chill that had descended on him when he had seen Francis's car on the lawn settled, and he felt hard inside, and clear as ice. He went back up to the terrace.

"What's the thermometer say?"

"Sixty-eight."

A body loses heat at the rate of one degree per hour from the time of death. Francis had been dead at least twenty-four hours. Willson knelt again and turned Francis's hand over. The fingertips were blue and curled. In them was a clump of blonde hairs. "You got a glass, Perce?"

"Here," Percy said, handing him a magnifying glass.

"Look at this. See how the ends are bent in a V? These were yanked out of a wig."

"Hey," Percy said. "Like that one there?"

Caught in the thick willows hanging over the creek below the falls was a platinum-blonde wig. Willson put the hair in an envelope, looked around and found a stick, and with Percy holding on to his belt leaned out over the gorge and retrieved it. "Young-Quinlan," the label inside said. Willson put it under the glass. There were brown hairs inside. He put the handkerchief with the lipstick sample on it inside the wig, and shoved the wig into his pocket.

"Let's get the stretcher, Percy," Willson said.

They carried Francis up and loaded him into the back of the van. "I don't know how quick I can get to the PM," Percy said.

"It doesn't matter. I know the cause of death. You just put him on ice downtown."

"What about you?"

"I'll take Francis's car."

Percy nodded. "You okay, Dooley? You don't look so good."

"I'm fine," Willson said.

"I'm sorry about Francis."

"Yeah. I'll see you downtown."

Willson went to Francis's car and got in. It was an Olds, made just after the war. Spotless. There was a metal statue of Saint Christopher on the dashboard. Francis had painted the hair and beard brown, and the eyes blue. Willson stared at the statue, then swore and put the Olds into gear, spinning the tires through grass and into mud, and drove across the river to arrest Simon Gray.

29

The guard at the gatehouse couldn't stop Willson. He drove in, stopped in front, went inside to the desk, and demanded to see Dr. Gray.

"He'll see you in his office," the receptionist said.

"Uh-uh," Willson said. "I want him down here. Now."

A few moments later Gray appeared, walking down the stairs with his hands in his pockets. There was a flesh-colored bandage held to his neck with strips of adhesive tape, half hidden by a scarf.

"Sergeant Willson," Gray said. "How may I help you?"

"You're under arrest."

Gray glanced at the receptionist. "I see. Might I ask on what charge?"

"Suspicion of murder." He took his cuffs off his belt. "Give me your right hand."

"That won't be necessary, Sergeant—"

Willson ignored him, snapped the cuff on, twisted Gray's arm behind his back, and snapped on the other cuff.

"Be so good as to call Frank," Gray said to the receptionist as Willson led him out and put him into the back of Francis's car.

"This isn't the way downtown," Gray said mildly, after Willson turned left on Diamond Lake Road. Willson didn't answer. Once he had put Gray into the car, his interrogation had begun. The first step was to show Gray that he was in complete control of the situation. He drove to the South Central station house, asked the desk sergeant if he could use the interrogation room. When he got the keys Willson put Gray in a chair in the corner farthest from the door. One of the keys worked the light switch on the wall. Willson turned it on.

"I'll be back," he said, and locked the doctor in. He went back to the desk sergeant. "I'm going to the White Castle. You want anything?"

"How about a coffee. Light, sugar."

"Okay."

Willson took the long way. He ordered half a dozen chicken White Castles and ate them slowly at the counter, then ordered three coffees to go, and drove around the lakes to South Central. He gave the desk sergeant his coffee, then took the other two with him to the interrogation room.

Gray sat calmly in the corner, smoking. There were two cigarette butts on the floor beside the chair.

"Want some coffee?" Willson said.

"Thank you. I never drink coffee."

Willson pulled the tab on the cardboard lid of his cup, and sipped it. It was cold. He'd been gone maybe an hour, hour and a half.

"Everything's slow these days," he said. "I had to get hold of a judge out in Wayzata. Sent his little son-in-law over here on a motorcycle with a search warrant. There'll be some cops out at your place about now."

Gray said nothing.

"You look like an orderly man. Everything in its place. Maybe they won't have much trouble at all finding the other one of these." He flashed the cuff link at Gray. He didn't care about Gray's reaction now. All he wanted was for Gray to believe there were men looking for a cuff link at his residence.

"Am I to understand you believe that belongs to me?"

"You can understand whatever you like, Doc. Sure you won't take that coffee?"

"No, thank you."

"Do you remember my partner? Detective Lingeborg?"

"Should I?"

"Lot of people know Francis. He used to patrol Northeast for
years. That was the Polish neighborhood then. Everybody knew
him. It was easy: nobody fucked around because if you did, Francis
would find you sooner or later. He'd wait until you figured things
had blown over, and you'd go out whistling one day and there would
be Francis.

"Francis didn't like making arrests, you know. He hated paperwork, and he didn't like to have to call the Black Marias because it
upset the people in the neighborhood. It reminded them of the old
country, with the tsar's wagons coming 'round and collecting all the
people. The ladies'd be crossing themselves and it was bad for
business because then they'd run home and shut the doors and not
go shopping. So Francis, out of consideration for the neighborhood,
would just take care of a lot of things himself. Sometimes he'd beat
the hell out of them. Just roll their asses down an alley for a block or
two. Sometimes all it took was Francis smiling at them as he walked
by on his beat, and tipping his cap. That's when they knew he had
them, if he touched that cap of his. All those years he worked
Northeast, it was the cleanest neighborhood in the city. Fewest
robberies, fewest murders, fewest assaults, the least petty theft.

"Off the job," Willson said, "he seemed like the dumbest bastard
you ever met. You said something to him and he puzzled it out. You
told him a joke, you might get a laugh next week. He could hardly
write his name, which is probably why he hated the paperwork. But
it was okay, because when he wore the uniform nobody was a better
cop.

"When the city got hit three times real bad with Hun the force was
down to forty-five officers and men. Everything got reorganized.
They couldn't afford to waste cops walking beats anymore. The
people were too spread out anyway. The old neighborhoods were
dead. That Northeast neighborhood around University was all gone
now. High-class man like you probably never went up there much,
but it was a shame. Broke Francis's heart. They pulled him off the
street and gave him desk duty downtown but he couldn't do it; he
was a fucking disaster behind a desk. But when I got promoted to
sergeant in major crimes, which was going to be me and three

detectives down from five, and then it was only going to be one, I asked for Francis, and I got him.

"We didn't like each other at first. He didn't like big black niggers. Never played with them growing up. Kept the few that were in town back then out of Northeast. Now all of a sudden they were coming into town by the trainload, encouraged by the mayor, and the governor, recruited by labor agents, paid bonuses, given houses, given jobs, sent to school at night. Francis didn't think that was right. Francis took it all out on me and refused to work. He would ride along to the scenes, and he would do what I told him to do. But he wouldn't *work*.

"But there was this one case. A little girl found strangled down in Bohemian Flats. It was the sickest crime scene I've ever gone to. Little girl lying there with her dress pulled over her head. And when Francis pulled it down her eyes were popped right out of their sockets. My boys were babies just that age. It was hot and the river stank, and the people down there were dying like crazy anyway; they stood around dull-eyed, like things that had grown out of the mud. And it all just got to me all of a sudden. I went down to the edge of the river and puked myself inside out. When I got done, there was Francis, looking at me.

"Francis still treated me like a nigger after that. Outwardly he never stopped, but inwardly he had, and he started working. The Swede didn't give a fuck about physical evidence. He never talked to witnesses himself. Somehow, though, he was able to take a crime scene in and absorb the truth out of it. Maybe he wouldn't be able to figure out exactly what he knew, or articulate it, but somehow he always sensed the truth. With the little girl, he went over and stood next to the mother's boyfriend. Just stood there, and didn't move, and the boyfriend didn't move either, even after the ME came and took the body away and they were finished with the scene. And then I saw Swede taking a walk with the guy, arm around his shoulder, and he wound up getting a signed confession at the guy's kitchen table. He'd been drinking and the kid was pitching a fit and wouldn't stop and he'd snapped. They hung that guy. And twenty more he caught in the two years we worked together.

"The thing was," Willson said, opening the second coffee now, ice cold, and still drinking it gingerly like it was steaming hot, "we'd been working these mutilation cases. But everything was so damn crazy the last month with Hun coming back and people dropping again that I just didn't do what needed to be done. I forgot that murder's murder. You can't allow it to go on. No matter who it is getting killed."

Willson looked Gray right in the eyes.

"One week ago we found a victim at the Crockett mill. Puncture wounds near the base of the spine. The sex organ of the victim was cut off, and the body drained of blood. You know what Francis said? He said did I ever drink pop from a straw? He knew what was going on. He knew I wasn't seeing it, either, but he left me alone. Two days later, we found another one in the rail yards. I didn't want to deal with it, understand? But I could feel him waiting for me to come around, and finally I made him take a day off. I didn't want to feel that pressure to do what I was supposed to do.

"Anyway, I thought he was at his mother's today. And this morning I got a call about a body out at Minnehaha Falls."

Willson broke it off. "I'll be back in a second," he said, and went out to the desk sergeant.

"Listen," he said, "you got a sweetheart?"

"My wife," he said, giving Willson a strange look.

"What color's her hair?"

"Brown. Say, what do you care, anyway?"

"How soon can you get her down here?"

"She's only a couple of blocks away, if she's home."

"Call her and ask her to come over."

The sergeant shrugged and picked up the candlestick. "You're in luck," he said a moment later, hanging up. "She's just about finished burning my dinner."

Willson waited at the desk until the sergeant's wife arrived, carrying a Dutch oven wrapped in an apron. She was a small woman, which was what Willson had been hoping for.

"Now, just what is so urgent, Matthew!" the sergeant's wife said, trying to sound like she was scolding her husband, while at the same time glancing sideways at Willson with genuine curiosity. There were still plenty of white people who hardly ever saw a Negro. Even when they were looking right at them.

"This is Sergeant Willson," the desk sergeant said. "He's conducting an interrogation in the back."

"What I'd like you to do is wait two minutes and then you walk by the door in the custody of your husband."

"Can I put cuffs on her?" the desk sergeant asked.

"Yeah. I want this bird to get a look. Not too good of one. Just walk her by like you were taking her to the second interrogation room."

"There isn't one."

"He doesn't know that. Two minutes." Willson looked at the Dutch oven. "Say, that smells pretty good."

"And you called it slop!" the woman said to her husband.

Willson went back to the interrogation room. He left the door open. There were now four cigarette butts on the floor next to Gray. *God, I'd like to make him eat those!* Willson thought savagely.

"Would you mind telling me what happened to your neck?" Willson asked.

"I was bitten by a spider."

"You know for sure it was a spider?"

"Yes," Gray said. Was that a touch of impatience? Then: "Where is my attorney?"

"You told your people to call him, right?"

"Yes."

"They usually do what you tell them to?"

"Always."

"Hmm. That's strange, then. Who knows? Maybe he's out of town. Maybe he's at home with a hot piece of ass. Maybe he's down with a case of Hun."

"He's a Negro," Gray said.

"Is that a fact! That's mighty white of you, Doctor. Well, I'm sure he'll turn up eventually, but you know how slow-footed these niggers are! Anyway, it's a good thing he's taking his time, because that gives us a chance to talk. See, we found a number of other items at the scene this morning besides that cuff link. There was a nice footprint, for one thing. My boys'll be coming back from your place with a shoe that fits right in. Then there was something that really caught my eye when I was out there. Damnedest fucking thing. A blonde wig stuck in a tree! Looked like a Hollywood bird's nest. Still had a label inside from the Young-Quinlan store. That's a real old-fashioned kind of place. You ever been in there?"

"No, Sergeant, I haven't."

"My wife's dragged me along a couple of times. There's chairs for men to sit in while their wives try things on, but they're not comfortable. Just straight-backed chairs. See, I think they want the men to get impatient and tell their wives to hurry up and buy something, anything, just to get the hell out of the store. A lot of women just look, but if they've got an uncomfortable man along with them, they'll buy. They got nice salesladies there, though. Some have been with the store for years. They like to keep up on their customers. The one I talked to kept a card file on all her clients. That wig I told you about? It was not a cheap wig. That was one-hundred-percent European hair. Where do you suppose they get European hair these days? Europe's quarantined. You can't even send a cable to Europe now.

"You know what I think?" Willson said, lighting up his cigar. "I think maybe she was lying to me a little bit. Maybe it was one-hundred-percent hair of European descent. It was nice, though. Soft as silk.

"The murder victim had a nice clump of that one-hundred-percent hair of European descent in his hand. There were scuffle marks in the mud around the body. Know what I think? I think the victim fought back a little this time. I think he had a hunch what was really going on, and it scared him to death, and he fought. The others just went down like little lambs, but not this one. I think, in the middle of the fight, the wig got yanked off your friend's head, went into the gorge, and stuck in the branches.

"That lady at Young-Quinlan, she was upset to see that wig tangled up so bad. She didn't sell a lot of them because they're so fucking expensive. You know what she did? She put it right onto a wig stand and started styling it. I hated to stop her, but she had that card file with the names of her customers and what they'd bought."

Willson heard steps just then and turned his back on Gray. The desk sergeant led his cuffed wife quickly past the interrogation room, then through the last door in the hall, which happened to be the bathroom. He closed the door hard, and there was a nice echo. Willson waited a moment, then closed the door of the interrogation room. Now he had to be careful. He really didn't know anything, and so he couldn't say too much. This was where Francis had always been so good. Sometimes he'd just come into the room and stand there, cleaning his fingernails with a knife. Sometimes he'd slap them around. Now, without Francis, Willson would have to be both kinds of cop.

Willson turned around again. Gray sat there smoking. Willson began to speak quietly. "We've got you on the scene last night, Doctor. Your cuff link. Your shoes. Now we've got your partner. You know what? She's one of those remorseful types. She is *filled* with remorse. Sometimes you get them and it's like they never even realized they were doing anything wrong. Then we put the collar on and it hits them. They've been living a nightmare. Everything's all wrong. And the only way they can make it right is to talk. I've seen it a hundred times. She can't wait to sit down with somebody and tell the whole, stinking mess.

"Maybe you'd better get your side of the story down, Gray. Talk to me. I'm the only one who can help you. Your lawyer can't. A jury can't. We're going to tear your place apart out there and when we do, there won't be anything I can do. So tell me now. What happened out there last night, Gray?"

Now Gray smiled. He reached inside his jacket and brought out his cigarette case, took a cigarette, closed the case, tamped the cigarette against the top, all the while smiling at Willson. Willson made a sound deep inside his throat and leapt at Gray, smashing the case and the cigarette away, taking hold of his collar and twisting.

"Let's see that fucking spider bite, asshole," Willson rasped, tearing the bandage off. There was a reddened pinprick. Willson twisted harder. "How'd you get it?"

Gray's eyes betrayed nothing. Incredibly, his expression hadn't changed. He was still smiling. Willson backhanded him. Gray's hair flew. Blood began to trickle from the corner of his mouth. It was bright red and shiny, like fingernail polish or lipstick.

"I'd like to cut your fucking throat," Willson said. "I'd love to see your fucking blood spill out onto the floor. But I'll be satisfied with them hanging you. I'll be there that day, motherfucker. I'll watch you drop."

"You don't know anything," Gray said.

"I'll show you what I know—"

Just then the desk sergeant opened the door. "Willson?"

"I'm busy."

"You'd better come here," he said as a uniformed police captain and a colored man pushed him out of the way.

"My God, Captain, he's being beaten!"

It was Donaldson, head of the special crimes division, and Gray's lawyer. Triumph showed in the doctor's eyes. *See?* they seemed to say. *These men are on my side. And they hate you as much as I do.*

"Get away from him," Donaldson said. "My God, Doctor, are you all right?"

"Where've you been, Frank?" Gray said mildly to his lawyer.

"Downtown," he said. "These bastards gave me the runaround. Then I had to go over to St. Pete's and dig up the lieutenant governor to sign a writ. Everybody else is out of town. They've all run off."

"Have you booked this man?" Donaldson said.

"I'm *interrogating* him."

"Have you booked him?"

"No."

"Then let him go."

"Captain, maybe you and I should have a little talk?"

"I said, he's released!"

"This bastard's a cop-killer—"

"You shut your mouth, Willson, or I'll sue you for slander," Gray's attorney said. Gray smoothed his hair, dabbed the blood from his mouth with a handkerchief, and stood up.

"Sergeant, it has been a pleasure," he said. His lawyer put his arm around him and they left. Willson turned to Donaldson.

"What the fuck are you doing? I *had* him!"

"What do you mean arresting this man?"

"He killed Francis on Friday night," Willson said.

"How do you know? Do you have a witness?"

"It's him," Willson said. "Francis said it was him, and now he's dead. That's all I need to know!"

"You can't arrest Simon Gray. Even if he killed Lingeborg on the front steps of City Hall, you can't do it. He's got to finish his work."

"He's a fucking maniac!"

"He's got a cure for Hun!"

Willson turned away. Gently, Donaldson went on. "Dooley. This town can't take it anymore. If we get hit like we did before we're finished."

"I don't give a shit."

"You heartless son of a bitch, I've lost seven people in my family to this thing. If he can cure it, I don't give a fuck what else he does! You understand?"

"I understand." Willson turned his lapel and took his badge off. "Here," he said. "Take it."

"You can't quit! I need every man now."

"No, Captain. You don't need anyone at all. Because what you just told me is that we don't have laws anymore. That we're making up new ones as we go. That man is a murderer. He should hang, even if he takes that cure to the grave with him."

"You wouldn't talk that way if you were a white man!"

"I ain't a white man," Willson said. "But I am a cop. And I'm following the rules you white men made. That's all I have to do. Follow those rules until every last one of you is gone. I enjoy that. Makes me feel like those rules had a *purpose* after all."

"Us dying won't make this world any better," Donaldson said.

"Does mine," Willson said.

"The sheriff's going to deputize some of Theo Rostek's boys, Dooley. Is that how you want it? You want to leave things to men like him?"

"He's one of us."

"He isn't one of you at all, and you know it. You can't quit."

"Good luck, Captain," Willson said and left the station.

C H A P T E R

30

I t was during batting practice that Lou Ravelli had first smelled the smoke. He could see it rising over the buildings beyond the center field fence. He figured there must have been a house fire going pretty good close along Lake Street, and thought nothing more of it, even though the smoke darkened the sky and his eyes began to smart. The team finished batting, and went back to the locker room. That's when Kelly came in with a pistol shoved into the belt of his uniform. He was wearing his derby instead of a Miller's cap.

"Boys," he said, "there ain't going to be no contest today."

Nobody on the team said anything. They all figured it was more sickness, and they didn't want to hear about it.

"We've locked the gates. We're all going to sit tight 'til this thing blows over."

"What thing, skipper?" Nick Cullop asked.

"There's a mob on Lake Street right now. They're smashing windows and looting."

"What the hell for?"

"How the hell should I know? Maybe because they can get away with it. There ain't no cops around anymore."

Kelly looked Lou right in the eye. "Now, since I know some of you boys got a nose for trouble, I'm telling you again that we're sitting tight right here. They're settin' fires, and we're only a block away from Lake. You know this rat box would go up in a second. So, it's gonna be up to us and the Monarchs to stay here and defend the ball yard."

"Why would they want to do anything to the ball yard?" Sammy Bohne asked.

"Because it's here, stupid. Because it'd make a nice bonfire. Because they want to roast us for th' mess we made o' that double-header yesterday. Because we been losin' to the Monarchs. Because the Monarchs are *in* here. How th' hell should I know? Put your flannels on an' your street shoes, then go see Emil out in the bull pen. He's got shovels and wheelbarrows full o' sand."

"What for, Mike?"

Kelly put both hands over his eyes and pulled on his face. "God save me, there ain't nobody dumber than a second-string catcher! Embers, boy! I want you up there on th' grandstand roof smacking 'em out if they land. And I want th' mob to see you up there, too. They'll think twice before trying anything. Now, get moving."

"What about the bleachers and the seats?"

"That's where the Monarchs'll be. Move!"

Lou finished dressing and went out the dugout to the field. Emil's crew was busy hooking up hoses to the taps around the warning track. There were shovels laid out like bats on a rack, four wheelbarrows, and a big pile of wet sand.

"We'll never get these things onto the roof," Cullop said. "Let's get a couple of buckets, and some rope, and we'll hoist the sand up that way."

They set to work, filling the wheelbarrows and pulling them up the grandstand steps to a place underneath the overhang. In the ceiling of the scorekeeper's booth was a trapdoor that opened out onto the roof. Lou went through first and helped a couple of the boys climb up.

"Crise," Lou said. "Look at that. They're burning up Sears!"

Sears had a big tower store a couple of blocks east on Lake. You could see people coming out of it like ants from a log thrown onto a fire, and gouts of heavy black smoke boiling out of the windows of the upper floors. The block across the street from Sears was burning, too, the dull orange flames shooting into the smoke cloud from the tower. Kelly had been right about the embers. They were starting to fall all around.

"Let's get that sand up here," Cullop yelled, tying rope to the handle of one of the buckets. "Come on, Lou. Start hauling."

"What about them?" Lou pointed to some of the Monarchs, who were lolling in the seats behind their dugout.

"You let Kelly and Rogan worry about them. Get moving."

"Won't even put out a fire in their own house," Lou muttered.

Cullop pushed him, so hard he almost lost his balance. "Look, you stupid son of a bitch. I've been listening to you talk like that all year, and I'm sick of it. That kind of thinking is nothing but trouble. Give it up. There's no point to it anymore! You hating or not hating don't change a goddamned thing up here. Got me? So start hauling that rope. You other boys get after those embers."

Stung by the captain's words, Lou worked quickly. His hands were getting raw from the rope, but he kept hauling sand until there was a pile of it almost as tall as he was. The other boys were throwing it on the embers now, and throwing it fast, because embers were dropping everywhere. A five-block stretch of Lake was burning furiously. The smoke was so thick you couldn't see anyone out on the street anymore, and it was getting hard to breathe. By now most of the boys had taken off their undershirts and tied them around their faces, to keep the smoke out. Hughie McMillen got rid of his shovel in favor of a bat. He stood up there knocking embers apart as fast as they came down.

"Look at that!" McMillen said, pointing to a section of the left-field bleachers that was burning. The Monarchs were trying to put it out with a hose, but the water pressure had dropped.

"Ravelli, Harris, get down there and help those guys," Cullop ordered.

"Goddamn it, Nick—"

"Get your ass down there, Lou, or I swear I'll kick it down!"

They went down the trapdoor. Hughie tossed shovels to them and they ran down the third-base line.

"What's the matter?" Spencer Harris asked one of the Monarchs.

"Beer cups and shit burning underneath the stands!"

It was true. They didn't have enough people working at the stadium anymore to keep up with the trash, and now it was burning pretty good, and starting to ignite the wooden beams that supported the bleacher seats.

"We got to go down there," the Monarch player said. It was Frank Duncan, the catcher who had tackled Lou from behind when he'd charged the mound the first time the Millers and Monarchs played. Duncan had his hat on backwards, and his dark skin was streaked with soot.

"All these stands is burning!" Newt Joseph cried. He was trying to put water on them, but it was coming out of the hose in a pitiful stream.

"Look, Mr. Willkinson's getting the light truck going, so we'll have juice for the well pumps," Duncan said. "You stay on the hoses. I'll go under with these boys." He handed Lou a wet burlap sack. "Come on!"

Lou hesitated. It looked awfully hot down there.

"Listen, Ravelli, I know what I'm doing. Down in Tennessee I'm a volunteer fireman!"

Lou went under with him. It *was* hot. The air was full of sparks and hot ashes, and cups and napkins and peanut sacks were burning in a swirl. Frank Duncan didn't care. He walked right into it, beating at the flames with the sack. Lou watched, and then started doing the same.

"We spread it out, maybe it won't burn so bad," Duncan yelled. He pointed to a big pile that had built up along the clapboards that formed the outer wall of the ballpark. The wind had been shoving everything together for a couple of weeks now, and because it was sheltered from the rain all of it was dry. Flames roared out of the pile. Frank Duncan moved purposely toward it, tripped, and fell in.

He yelled, rolled off, and got up with his arms spread out. He was flaming. He looked like that cross the boys had burned out in that field, Lou thought grimly. When had that been? Just three nights ago. Seemed so long now. Look at him burn, though. All of a sudden Duncan screamed and started running with the flames shooting out of his back. Lou could smell burning wool and hair and then he thought, *This nigger's a ballplayer just like me. He's good. He hits a ton, and the boys on his team look up to him the way we look up to Nick. And here he is running around on fire.*

Duncan ran past Lou, and Lou tackled him and rolled him over in the dirt, smothering the rest of the flames with the wet sack. Duncan still struggled, but Lou wrapped his arms around him and held him tight.

"Ahhgh!" Duncan said, and stopped.

"What's that? You all right?"

"Shit! What the *fuck* you think? My whole backside's fried, you ignorant motherfucker!" Water started pouring down on them. Lots of it. Lou turned over and let it rain down on him. He could hear it sizzling on the fire now. A couple of streams shot through the stands and onto the big pile that Duncan had fallen into.

"I thought you said you were a fireman, Frank."

"I never said I was any good at it," Duncan replied, wincing.

Lou let go of Duncan and started to laugh.

In the end, part of the left-field fence burned, but they let that go. Out on Lake, the fire brigades, such as they were, dynamited buildings and contained the fire, and by six in the afternoon most of the fires had pretty much burned themselves out. Nicollet Field was saved. To celebrate, Kelly and Rogan tapped a couple of kegs of beer at the concession stand and the boys cooled off with that. There were a few burns, some cuts and bruises, and of course Duncan, who had gotten the worst of it. All his hair below where his hat had been resting had burned off, and he had a football-sized red patch on his lower back that Halsey spread with ointment and covered with gauze.

"You probably want to let that air out tomorrow," Halsey said. "Treat it like a strawberry."

"I ain't had no strawberry on my backside before."

"Not since you visited Miss Julene Roberts you ain't," Rogan cracked.

"Aww, shut up, Joe. That wasn't funny that time, either. It hurts like hell!"

"That's a good sign," Halsey said. "If it didn't hurt, you'd be third degree."

Kelly came into the locker room. "Boys, it looks like things have quieted down. I think you can all go home. I'll see you tomorrow morning at nine. We're going to take some extra hittin'."

"Hittin'?" Hughie McMillan said. "What do we need to hit for?"

"To get ready for our contest with th' Monarchs. Right, Bullet?"

"That's right. My boys here at nine, too. We're going to set Frank on fire again and practice putting him out. Just in case."

Lou laughed along with the rest of them, then got his gear together and left the park. His car had a hole burned through the cloth top, but otherwise it was okay. He started her up and drove south to Thirty-sixth to get away from Lake Street. He was feeling pretty good. He'd been a hero down under those bleachers. He'd saved that man's life. Maybe he couldn't erase what he'd done before, but at least he'd done one good thing.

That's what he'd think about, he decided. For tonight, at least, that might be enough.

*E*d Pratt rubbed his eyes.

He was sitting out in the shade of the loading dock on his lunch break, eating a sandwich. It was getting hot again. There'd been record heat all month except for a couple of days of rain, and today, the air was smoky, too. Some of the men who'd ridden in from the west side of town said there were fires along Lake Street, set by looters who'd broken into the stores without being challenged by police, because there weren't any police. There wasn't enough of a fire department left now to fight the fires building by building, either. What they had done was dynamite the blocks ahead and behind the fire to create a break. Now it was burning itself out.

On the rail siding in front of Ed were two boxcars full of paper, the last order delivered from Port Arthur three weeks ago. There wasn't any more paper coming, not that it mattered much. There weren't any print jobs coming in, either. Everything was grinding to a halt. There were only four men working in the plant now. Ed Pratt was bindery foreman, and the bindery crew as well. It was okay, though, he thought. They didn't hire niggers here like some of the other jobbers did. This plant was going to stay white, because Crowley owned it. Pretty soon this latest round of Hun would be over and then only the best, the very strongest would be left. And then they were going to take care of the niggers once and for all.

Ed Pratt took another bite of his sandwich. It tasted like shit. He dropped the rest of it into the bag and tossed the bag into the garbage. Flies and hornets rose in a cloud over it. Nobody was picking up the fucking trash, either. He sighed and went back inside. There was one small four-up job he'd been saving for that afternoon, and he thought he might as well start it now. You had to keep going, even though there was no work and no orders. They were still giving him his pay packet every Friday, and until they stopped, he'd come here and do whatever there was to be done. It was so quiet now, though. The presses were shut down. So were the linotype machines. There were no composers, no pressmen, no strippers. Nothing.

Ed went to the jogger to pick up the flats. On the way he turned the motor on for the guillotine. It started, and Ed felt good hearing the noise. It filled the place up. He was even glad to hear the steel door to the loading dock slide shut with a huge, echoing bang, before it occurred to him that he was the only one in the plant. Everyone else had finished up in the morning. So he turned around and peered at the shadows around the door.

"Who's there?" he called.

"Edward *Pratt*," said a voice in his ear. Ed jumped back instinctively. "How you doing?" Theo Rostek said with a smile. Standing behind Theo were two of his men. They were wearing linen suits. Theo had a yellow bow tie on, and a straw boater.

"What the hell," Ed said, easing up a little. "You shouldn't sneak up on a man like that." He knew who these boys were. They'd done business together. That made it different. Theo was a greedy bastard who sold his own people. You always made use of people like that when you could. It had been a good arrangement.

"I've been meaning to come see you, Ed," Theo said. "How've you been?"

"Good."

"Everybody in the family okay? Ain't nobody springing no . . . *leaks?*"

"We're all fine. How about you?"

"We're busy. Got more work than we can handle. These boys behind me, for instance. Did you know they've been *deputized!*" He glanced back, and the three of them started laughing. "Sheriff of

Hennepin County deputized thirty of my men yesterday. There's a
state of emergency."

"I hadn't heard," Ed said.

"Yeah, well, news ain't traveling the way it used to. Or maybe I
should say, it's gone *back* to traveling the way it used to. Phones are
out, you know. Electricity. Telegraph. I got kids driving around
taking messages back and forth to my *deputies.* It's god-awful to
think about what is happening now! So, naturally, I've been too
busy to attend to things that I normally would see to *right* away. You
understand what I'm talking about, Ed?"

Ed understood, all right. Ever since the night the Klavern had
raided the North Side neighborhood, he'd been hoping that Theo
might somehow overlook what had happened. And with four days
gone by, Ed had almost forgotten about it himself. Forgotten it
enough to have left the gun he'd been carrying at home today.

"No," Ed said. "I don't."

"Ed, Ed, Ed. Why do you lie to me? I thought you and I
understood each other. You look at me and don't see nothing but a
nigger. And I look at you, and I see an ofay piece of shit. We never
made no bones about that. You knew where I was coming from. And
I knew where you were, too. So why don't we start over: Tell me
about Thursday night?"

"Thursday?" Ed said weakly.

"Yeah. Now, I know for a fact that *your* truck came into *my*
neighborhood last Thursday, and tried to pick up one of my runners.
You let him go, which showed you had some common sense, at least.
But then on Friday it was the same thing, only *this* time . . ." He
glanced back at the other two men and walked forward, backing Ed
into the folding machine. "Only this time, you drove out of there
with five of my people. Five! Now, as I recall, when we made our
arrangement I insisted that you could skim off whatever trash you
wanted downtown, but you were to stay out of the North Side. And
you said that was fine. It must have been fine 'cause you never went
there 'til last week."

"It wasn't us!" Ed said.

Theo's men grabbed Ed's arms.

"Ed. My man saw you sitting in the truck. He heard you tell your boys to quit. 'Course, that was just before he got clobbered. Now, why don't you just admit to me you were there?"

"All right!" Ed said, breathing heavily. "It was us. But it was a mistake. We let your man go and I said we had to get out of there, and we did. The next night I had nothing to do with. I didn't want any part of it."

"Who did it then, Ed?"

Ed Pratt hesitated. There was that oath he had taken never to divulge the secrets of a fellow Klansman.

"I don't know. I just know it wasn't me."

Theo snapped his fingers. The two men dragged Ed over to the guillotine. They shoved his arm under the blade and cranked down the clamping bars to hold it there. Theo strolled over.

"Time to get serious now, Ed. Tell me who said to go to the North Side."

"I don't know!"

"Yeah, you do. You're that—what do you call it?" Theo smiled, remembering. "Kleagle? Yeah, that's right! And ain't nobody shits down at that church without the Kleagle smelling it! Now, you talk to me, Ed, and maybe you can make it up to old Theo."

"I said I don't know. Don't you think I'd tell you now if I did!"

"Where's that switch?" Theo said pleasantly. "Oh, yeah. The green button, right?" Theo pressed it with his thumb, and the worm gears above the guillotine began to drive the forty-two-inch blade down. Ed felt it press against his skin, time slowing down until he could scream, "Ravelli!"

Theo pressed the button marked "Release," and the blade popped back to its ready position. A stream of blood trickled down both ends of the deep cut across the top of Ed Pratt's arm.

"That was a name, wasn't it, Ed?"

Ed nodded. He was too scared to talk.

Theo feinted toward the button plate, and Ed screamed.

"Say it again, Ed."

"R-Ravelli," Ed repeated. "It's Lou Ravelli. He's a kid I just recruited, a ballplayer."

"You mean that third baseman? You serious?"

"That's him."

"Shit," Theo said. "And he knows how to play ball, too."

"He's a hothead. I thought he'd be good for the crew but he wasn't satisfied with just taking drunks. He got the other boys riled up. We drove up there and he almost got your man, but I let him loose, Theo, I swear to God. The second night, I didn't know about. I stayed home that night. He must have got the boys together and gone out without me."

Theo nodded at his man, who turned the crank and raised the clamping bar.

"You know, this whole thing's too bad, Ed. That makes one more person I've got to see this afternoon, and the doc's on my butt, too." Ed pulled his arm out of the cutter. Theo let him straighten up. Then he pushed Ed forward hard, turning his head and sliding him forward under the clamping bar. He held him there while his men fastened the bar down on the side of Ed Pratt's head.

"What are you doing!"

"Nice knowing you, Ed," Theo said, pushing the green button.

When Lou came home Mrs. Lund grabbed the sides of his face and kissed him all over until he felt like he was going to drown.

"Oh, Louie! We saw all that smoke. For sure they burned the ballpark down!"

"They didn't, 'cause we saved it," Lou said proudly.

"Are you all right?"

"Yeah, but Jeez, lay off the slobber, will you, Mrs. L.?"

"First Danny, and then you. I didn't think I could stand it. I thought you never were coming home again!"

"It's okay, Mrs. L. It's okay. I'm here."

"I swear I'm going to lock the doors. I'm going to get all of you in here once and for all, and then I'm going to lock the doors and never let any of you out again."

Lou sniffed the air. "What's eats?"

"Meatballs."

"I'll wash up. How's Shirl today?"

"Much better. I let her go listen to the radio with Kal."

"They out there now?"

"Yes. Could you call them for me? Everything's nearly ready."

"Anything you say, Mrs. L.," he said, stopping to kiss her on the way outside. He knocked once at the shack door, and opened it inward.

"Say, Marconi! Mrs. L. says come for dinner."

"Shhh!" Shirley said. "She's talking about Danny!"

They both had their headsets on, staring ahead at the map on the wall with excited eyes.

"What are you talking about? Danny's on the radio?"

Kal held up his hand, then scribbled something in his log book. "I knew it," he said.

"What? What!"

"He shot those pictures of the moon behind the Crockett flour mill. That's where the Archangel broadcasts from! I always thought that would make the perfect spot. Tall enough, anyway!"

"Oh, no," Shirley said, and began adjusting the tuning dials. "Lost it." She took her headset off. She was still pale and thin, but she had been getting out of bed for two days, eating well, and starting to perk up again.

Kal switched the radio off and waited for Shirley to follow him across the lawn. She walked slowly, and finally Lou snatched her up and carried her the rest of the way in. Kal went straight to the phone.

"Hello?" he said, clicking the cradle. "Goddamn it, where's the operator? Hello! Yes, give me the police. Yes, downtown is fine." Mrs. Lund came in from the kitchen. Kal held up a finger. "Hello? What do you mean they don't answer? You mean to tell me there's no police anymore? Try it again!" He waited, then said, "Is there anybody you *can* get me? Never mind, thanks."

"What's going on?" Mrs. Lund said in alarm. "We're just about to sit down to dinner."

"We heard from Danny, Aunt Lucy. He's at the Archangel's aerie! We're going to go meet him!"

"You're not going anywhere. None of you are!"

"Now, Lucille, she was talking about Danny, all right. He wants me to come pick him up."

"I don't know what's come over you, Kal. Kidnapping poor Shirley was bad enough. Why can't you stay home now? It's dangerous out there. They're setting the town on fire, and you heard yourself, there's no police anymore. You've got to stay home!"

"I'll be careful. And I'll have Lou with me, won't I?"

"Huh?" Lou said. "But what about dinner?"

"Dinner can wait," Kal said. "Let's go." He took Mrs. Lund by
the shoulders and kissed her. "I promise we'll be all right. And we'll
come back with Danny! Come on, Lou!"

They got in the car and headed downtown.

"Better stay away from Nicollet," Lou said. "That's where the riot
was on Lake Street today."

"That's what the Archangel said."

"I saved a guy. We were at the ball yard and one of the Monarchs
fell into some fire. I pulled him out."

"One of the Monarchs?" Kal said, glancing at him.

"Yeah. He was in trouble and I helped him out. I didn't even think
about it. Maybe we didn't like each other to begin with, but that was
more because he was on the other team. You get me, Kal?"

"Sure, Lou."

"But then all of a sudden we were on the same team, trying to do
the same thing, and I didn't care what he was anymore. I didn't
think *nigger*. He needed help and I did what I had to do."

"That's good, Lou."

Lou fell silent. The other thing he had done was twisting his guts.
"Oh, God, Kal," he said, his voice breaking.

"What's the matter?"

"All those nights I've been out late. I wasn't playing cards with the
boys like I said I was. I was out riding with the Klan."

"What!"

"This guy came to see me after the game last week and said I
should come to one of their meetings, and I did, and he said they
were doing an important job, and wanted me to come along, and I
did. They had a truck, and we drove around and grabbed people off
the street. Colored people. Last night we got five. Four men and a
lady. We took 'em out to this place and unloaded 'em like cattle."

"What place?"

"I don't know what it was, Kal. This big mansion out on Riverside.
At first I thought this was what I always wanted, rounding up niggers
and putting 'em away for good. But I don't feel right about it!
They're people, like that guy I saved today. And those Klan

boys . . . All they do is hate. I don't want to be like that, Kal! All
twisted up inside. You can't just hate one thing and expect not to
hate everything, sooner or later." He sobbed. "Oh, Christ, what am I
gonna do, Kal?"

Kal was silent a moment. Then he said, "Maybe you already
started doing something about it."

"Yeah?" Lou brightened. "And maybe nothing bad'll happen to
those people—"

Kal slammed the brakes and cuffed Lou hard on the side of the
head.

"Don't be a jackass!" Kal shouted. "You round people up in the
middle of the night and drop them off someplace *like cattle*, and
nothing bad's going to happen?"

"I just—"

"Nothing good can happen from that, you understand?" He hit
Lou again. "*Understand?* I won't sit here and listen to you try to let
yourself off the hook!"

"I understand!" Lou cried. "Just please don't hit me anymore,
Kal. My old man use to hit me."

"Yeah? Well, maybe if he was still around you wouldn't be so
goddamn stupid!"

They were both breathing hard, looking straight ahead through
the windshield. Finally Kal shoved the car into gear and started off.

"I saved that guy," Lou said.

"What's his name?"

"What?"

"He has a name, don't he? What is it?"

"Duncan. Frank Duncan."

"The catcher."

"That's right."

They drove on.

"That was a good thing, Lou," Kal said at last. "It was good you
did that. But it don't make up for anything else. When we get Danny,
you're going to tell the police what you just told me."

"Okay, Kal," Lou said with relief.

They turned onto Second Street from Portland. It was very dark.
The power was out all along the river, and the walls of the mills and

grain elevators were blocked out against an orange glow of fires that still burned on the east side of the city. Kal stopped the car. Lou could hear the river sliding through the dark, making a sound like silk pulled through an ivory ring. They were parked along the rail siding, underneath the trees that made a tunnel against the mill wall.

"Is this the place?" Lou asked uncertainly.

"He took those pictures right here," Kal said, honking the horn.

Ah-oooh-gah! came the sound, echoing off into the darkness.

C H A P T E R

33

*D*anny had slept for almost two days.

It was a draining sleep, sleep like trying to stay afloat in a pool of beckoning darkness, sleep that pulled on you and offered eternal peace. If you wanted to live you could not let yourself sink in that pool, and so Danny's sleep was a desperate struggle from which he woke from time to time, frightened and exhausted, only to fall into it again.

If you slept that way long enough, it would kill you.

While he slept, he heard things. There was a low, bass, vibrating howl that shook his mattress. Banging, sometimes a chorus of banging, that sounded like steel drums. Or the sound of water roaring into some faraway pit. Once he opened his eyes and saw dark walls crossed by melted iron beams that thatched the face of the bright full moon inside a platinum halo of clouds. The quality of light from the moon was familiar. He had been able to capture it once in pictures. Silver grains on glass holding silver light from the sky.

Selena.

Sometimes he dreamed of someone moving near him. She did not walk, but instead changed places instantaneously, like the image on a movie with missing frames. In one part of the dream she shuttled back and forth from the head to the foot of the bed so many times she became a gray blur that colored the walls of the room. Then she vanished and he closed his eyes and sank deeper and almost lost himself again.

Then it was warm and light, but he kept on sleeping.

Finally, with the sky a deep blue over him, he opened his eyes and tried to move. He was very stiff and weak, but he was able to sit up. It was dusk outside, and he was in a small room that had only half a ceiling. There was a doorway with no door and he thought he saw something rush past it. He got up to look, and stopped short. The floor outside it crumpled into darkness. Directly across from the ledge he stood on was a massive limestone wall cut through with tiny windows. The wall was scorched, and through one of the windows Danny could see the river, and the fading glow of the afternoon above the east bank.

He looked up, following the wall to its full height. There was a water tank capped with a conical top tilted like a hat across the rafters of the burned-out half of the roof. Grain conveyors from the big elevators next door ended in nothing. Housed in a rooftop monitor, the drive shaft that had once powered a whole factory now was bent like a candle left in a window. Belts hung raggedly from it, like fringe.

He realized he was inside the burned-out Crockett A mill.

How did he get here? Danny tried to remember, but everything was fuzzy and unreal. He'd been at the institute saving Shirley. Was she all right? Remembering Shirley made him desperate to get out of this place, and he went out along the ledge and saw it ended in midair straight ahead, and on either side. His room was the only thing left on this wall of the building. How did he get here? He remembered rats, but nothing else.

But he was hearing music now.

Faint music that came from the more complete floors on the opposite wall of the mill. It was a song he knew. *"Love by the hour . . ."* The sound faded, and then swelled up again. He heard a trumpet playing the middle eight, and felt his heartbeat quicken. *It can't be*, he thought, looking around and seeing an iron chute that ran from the ledge across the empty air where the burned-out floors had been. He went to it. The chute was fastened by brackets to the floor of the ledge. There was a ladder inside. Danny leaned into it and pushed. The chute wobbled across the space like a huge piano string.

> *Hands in my pockets*
> *I walk in the rain*
> *Making a promise*
> *Not to see you again*
> *I turn the corner*
> *Walk into a bar*
> *Straight to the back booth*
> *Where I know you are*
> *One smile breaks all my willpower . . .*
> *Love by the hour*
> *Love by the hour*

Danny began to climb. The chute bowed sickeningly under his weight as he got halfway across, and he thought of retreating, but then the music ended and he heard a voice—*her voice. The Archangel!* He remembered sitting with her at three in the morning in that room in the Ice Palace, remembered thinking how much he wanted to find out who was inside that bundle of fur and veil, remembered how much her voice had got to him, and how much sweeter it sounded in person, how she had got to him for good that night. He kept going. He didn't give a damn what else happened to him. He wanted to go to that voice.

"We're going back fifty years tonight," he heard the Archangel say. *"'Get a horse!' Remember how your mother used to yell that when a car went by? Although our cars still run, as long as the gas holds out. There won't be any coming from Ohio or Pennsylvania or Texas anymore. They do allow the tanker trains from western Canada, but they're having trouble crewing them out, so . . . Drive carefully! Anyway, as long as there are any of us left there, we will have our entrepreneurs. I hear that the dear old GNDC has put up capital to build a factory in Blue Earth that will brew fuel out of corn. Imagine that! We may go hungry, but at least we will go there by car!"*

Danny stopped. His breath came in ragged gasps. He closed his eyes and collected himself and tried not to think of anything except the fifteen feet of chute left ahead of him.

"*I'm sorry, though,*" the Archangel said. "*I promised myself I'd be comforting and entertaining tonight. The lights not coming on is very serious, I know, but after all, it wasn't so long ago that there was no such thing as electric lights. But I'm sure many of you are starting to wonder, what will become of us this winter? Will there be coal? Will there be oil or gas? My friends, there will be trees. This is the City of Trees, so perhaps the best thing you could do now is sharpen your ax and lay in your fuel yourself. No one will blame you for chopping them down. More than likely, nobody will stop you, either. I'm afraid we can't ignore the fact any longer of how thin the ranks of our police force have become.*"

Danny reached the end of the chute, rolled over, and listened. It was hard to tell whether the voice was real or coming from a radio speaker.

"*Oh, bother! How unconscionably boring of me to repeat the things you already know. Much better I should play records that you probably can't find here anymore. For instance, here's a recording of Paul Whiteman. Those of you who visited New York right after the war should remember him fondly. The song is 'Nickel in the Slot.' The Archangel saw the rotund Mr. Whiteman and his orchestra at the Aeolian Hall the last time she went East, which was 1924. All that's left of New York now is a piece of Harlem, of course, which I suppose would have suited Paul Whiteman just fine. Anyway: 'Nickel in the Slot.'*"

Danny heard the needle come down on the spinning record. The song was very loud. He stood up and went through a crumbled doorway that opened into a hall. There had been offices here, he thought, looking right, seeing a narrow strip of light spilling out beneath a door that was covered by a heavy carpet held in place by a strip of wood nailed to the transom. Danny went to it, and slowly pushed the carpet aside, and saw *her.*

The Archangel sat at a wooden table. There was a microphone in front of the horn of the Victrola, and the glowing tubes of her transmitter, shining like the towers of some fantastic miniature city, and cables snaking across the floor. The Archangel was looking through a wood crate of records on the floor next to her chair. *She doesn't have blonde hair!* was his first thought, not believing it at first, because he had so strongly imagined she was a blonde all this time. Her voice was blonde. . . . He came forward and touched her shoulder gently, so that he wouldn't scare her, but she jumped and turned, letting out a scream that burst out of her and drove a shaft of cold, icy sound right into his heart.

The Archangel was Selena Crockett!

"Y-You're up," she stammered. "You shouldn't be up. You're very, very ill!"

He couldn't say anything. All he could feel was bitterness welling up inside him. The Whiteman record ended. Quickly, she put another disk onto the spindle, cranked the player, and dropped the arm. Danny took one step toward her. She swiveled the chair all the way around. He stopped, because she was pointing a pistol at him.

"Out in the hall," she said. "We can't talk here."

"There's nothing to say."

"This" she said icily, "is *her* place. Do you understand? You can't come in here."

Danny still didn't move.

"Please, don't make me hurt you, Danny," she said, her eyes pleading with him. "I have to protect *her*, and I will!"

Reluctantly, Danny raised his hands and backed out through the carpet.

"Go ahead," he said when they were out in the hall. "Do it. Shoot me right in the goddamn head. Make yourself a nice hole to drink from."

Selena let her hands drop to her sides. There were tears in her eyes. Again he thought how much she looked like Sonja, and viciously, he put that thought down, hard enough to kill it for good.

"I should have strangled you at the dance," he said.

"Please, Danny—"

"You went straight to the clinic after I left, didn't you. You went there to warn Gray!"

"Yes!" she cried. "But you don't understand—"

"I understand plenty," Danny said savagely. "You've got yourself quite a life going, don't you? Playing the rich philanthropist, and the voice of the angel, and then when that gets a little dull, going out and killing for kicks."

"But I haven't killed anyone!"

"Save it, Selena. I've seen the scar. I know what it means. Gray explained it all to me before . . ." And then he stopped, because he remembered Gray going down, and a masked nurse holding a needle.

"*You* stabbed Gray," he said.

"Yes."

"Why? *Why!*"

"That night at the dance, all I wanted to do was forget everything. I just wanted to have one night with you, a night where I could be happy . . . the way people used to be, before all *this!* I suppose I was wrong to think it was even possible. But there was a moment, when we were dancing together . . .

"Then you changed so fast. I didn't know what happened at first. One moment we were together dancing and then all of a sudden I felt you hating me. Then you were yelling about my scar and I just . . . I just went all to pieces after you left. I was so angry, and upset. And I thought you were crazy and might do something to hurt Simon.

"So I went out to the institute. I told Simon what had happened. And that you'd be coming for him. He didn't seem worried about it at all. He just thanked me, and asked me to gown up, that I might be needed down at the clinic.

"I heard the commotion when they caught you. Then Horace came back and asked me to get ready to assist Dr. Gray with a transfusion. I started for the clinic as I usually did, but Horace said no, we were going to the locked ward. I'd never been in the locked ward before.

"Horace opened the doors. The inner one was heavy metal, like a prison door. Just inside was another receiving room like the one for the regular clinic. Simon was waiting for me there. He took my hands and looked me in the eyes and said that he had a secret he was going to share with me. He said I might see things in the ward that would confuse and upset me, but that I must be strong. He said we were fighting a war, and that I had been a help to him in the rear, but that now he needed me on the front lines. He asked, 'Do you trust me?' And this feeling came over me. I *wanted* to trust him. I felt that anything he might do had to be the right thing.

"Then he told me he'd developed a cure for hemorrhagic fever. One that had to be prepared from large quantities of fresh, African blood. That had been the key all along. Hun is a variant of an *African* pestilence, and the African genotype developed a natural resistance to it. He said he reduced the blood to this essence, but that it was costly. To prepare enough serum to save a white woman required nearly five hundred pints of Negro blood!

"I asked, stupidly, whether that was the reason for the locked ward—that he had so many Negro donors and did not wish to upset his white patients. Lots of them would have objected; I've seen it plenty of times. They ask whether there's any Negro blood going into them. They ask it even when they're dying, when their lives could be saved by the very blood they think they're too good to get!

"Simon said no, his regular donations were collected by the vans. What I was about to see was different. He took hold of my hands . . . said I must realize that only a few people at the institute and in the GNDC knew the type of research he was conducting in this ward. He was taking a chance, trusting me, but he felt I was up to it. He had wanted to show me these things for such a long time. . . ."

Selena wiped her eyes. "Oh, Danny, what I saw! There were six men strapped down and being bled. All had passed out. There were three others who looked like they were dead. All Negroes. Dr. Gray was explaining to me how they bled them twice, first when they came in, and then, after they were allowed a few days to build up their strength, a second time, for good.

"He told me that the real work of the institute was the perfection of this serum. Soon doctors would be coming from all parts of the world to learn his technique. He would teach them to become the saviors of the white race. It was hard, and might seem cruel, he said, but it was not meant that the white race should perish. Science had injured her. It was science that was going to have to save her. And he wanted me to help him. He said that he knew what it had cost me to see my whole family die. That was what had made me strong. He said he knew I understood him completely, that I was the only woman who did or ever would.

"Oh, Danny, looking into his eyes I believed in him. I could feel how noble he was, how he had suffered because of what he had to do! I *wanted* to help him. He made me understand that being strong meant that I was going to have to put my old scruples aside. That I had to be loyal to my own kind. That I was taking life so that others like myself could live. He said it was no different from eating, or breathing, and that it would be easy. The men on those beds weren't suffering. They only drifted away. And that their sacrifice had made them noble, too, because they had given their lives so that others could live.

"He had me, Danny! I would have done anything for him then! He knew it, too, because he said, 'And now, Selena, you must show me how strong you are. I am going to ask you to assist me now. The work is the same as you've been doing with the donors. But there is a white man who is a threat to us, and a traitor to his race. He wants to stop our work. He wants to stop it because he is weak. Too weak for our race to tolerate any longer. Do you understand?' I remember saying that I did. I don't know why! I ought to have been confused, or afraid, but I wasn't. He has a way of making you think what he wants is right. You forget everything else. All I wanted was to show him I could be strong for him.

"So I got everything ready, and they brought you in. I knew it was you and I didn't care! Simon looked back at me and I could see he was absolutely sure that I belonged to him now. And maybe I did. I was hurt because of how you left me at the dance. I thought I hated you!

"I said to myself, 'Let him do what has to be done.' If you were in Simon's power now, it must be because you deserved it.

"So we began the transfusion. He used me so perfectly. He did the prep work and asked me to stick you. I was in a fog, Danny. When I pushed that needle into your arm it was as though I was fixing everything with one motion. A prick of a needle and the whole world would be cured! How happy I was for that moment. But then I looked down at you. Our eyes met and . . .

"I went into the assistant's dressing room and sat down and tried to smoke. I tried not to think about anything. But the harder I tried the more I kept seeing your face. And I thought of you lying in that ward with those other men. I didn't know them. They were just bodies strapped down to beds, but I knew you, and suddenly through you, Danny, I knew them! And I knew Simon was killing people. I asked myself over and over if that was what I wanted, and I thought, no! Three times a week I come up here and talk on the radio to try to wake people up. And it is so hard, Danny, because nobody ever talks back. I never knew whether I was doing any good or not until I met Shirley Lund that afternoon. She was so upset about missing my show. Here she'd almost died, and that's the first thing she thought about. And oh, God, Danny, everything just seemed to crash in around my head, and I realized how tired I was of going it alone. That's why I wanted to put everything into Simon Gray's hands. He's a genius at finding people who are at the end of their rope, and using them. That's what he does. That's what makes him a vampire!

"I couldn't let him do it to me, Danny. I had to try to stop him somehow. So I went to the dispensary and found some sodium pentothal and filled a syringe, and came out and stuck it into his neck. He collapsed. I stopped your transfusion and rolled you outside on the gurney to the pavilion. There's an elevator there that goes down to the boat landing. I stole Simon's launch and brought you here."

She looked at him.

"Maybe you couldn't bear the thought of all that blood going to waste," Danny said. "Maybe you wanted me for yourself!"

"Oh, Danny, think! If I wanted to kill you I could have done it anytime. I've been feeding you, trying to help you get your strength back."

"You've got the scar," Danny insisted.

"But I wasn't even here when that first man was killed! I was in Chicago, broadcasting from the Blackstone Hotel!"

And then, suddenly, Danny remembered that night he had been taking moon pictures on the rail siding outside the mill. How he had moved his aerial, to pull her broadcast better. How the music and the sound of the Archangel's voice had lulled him to sleep.

"You could have said you were there. You were right here all the time, and came down and killed that man."

"The bartender said the blonde woman was talking to that poor man *for three hours,*" Selena said. "You told me that yourself. And you said you were listening to the Archangel's show the whole time you were exposing those plates. How could I have been in the bar and up here broadcasting at the same time? I couldn't have! I was in Chicago, I swear to you! I wouldn't do anything so awful. I couldn't! That's why . . ."

"Why what?" Danny said.

"That's why I've always gotten treatments from Simon!" She reached up and unbuttoned the top of her blouse and pulled it open. "This is what you saw the night of the dance. Yes, I'm a bleeder! I've been one since I was seventeen years old, and yes, Daddy did take me to Simon Gray when he was practicing in New York. He operated on me and installed something inside my throat to make it easier for him to treat me."

"To drink blood, you mean."

"No! I've never done that! But every six months I went to Simon, and he washed my blood. I'm not sure what he does, exactly. It's always done under anesthetic. And it keeps my bleeding under control. I can live normally. I forget I even have chronic HF most of the time, except when I'm about due for another wash. That's what the scar's all about, and yes, I *am* ashamed of it! All the time I think it's only my money that's saved me, that I have no right to be alive when so many other people have died. That's why I try to do so much. That's why I created . . . *her.* The Archangel doesn't have a past. She's a voice without memories, or obligations, or sins on her soul! She's what I want to be, what I really wish I was, and oh, the record's finished. Let me go, please. Let me be her again. Just once more. You can do what you want after that, but let me at least tell the people what I know!"

Danny closed his eyes and leaned against the wall, fighting the dizziness that swept over him. "I have to get out of here," he said. "Where's your car?"

"I don't have one. You know I don't drive."

"How do you get here, then?"

"I've a chauffeur. But there's no way to call him from here."

"Look. My friend Kal never misses your program. Tell him to meet me here."

"I won't give *her* away!"

"You don't have to. Just say to meet the man who interviewed you at the spot where he took pictures of the moon. He'll understand. Say the message is for Kal Hromatka."

"How do you know he'll hear it?"

"Because he's in love with you, too!" Danny said softly.

"What?" Selena said, wonderingly. "What did you just say?"

"Just tell him, Selena!"

She nodded and they went back into the studio. Selena lifted the arm from the record player, and slid into the chair in front of the microphone.

"Pardon me, friends," she began.

Her voice is changing! Danny thought.

"It's not like me to let you alone for so long. It's because—well, I suppose there's no other way of putting it—your Archangel's had a visitor. A young gentleman, actually."

Selena glanced back at him with a dreamy expression. She didn't look like Sonja anymore. She seemed to have changed somehow, her form less physical, as if there were a halo surrounding her now.

"I know what you are probably thinking, and I don't blame you. When a lady such as myself entertains a gentleman in her rooms alone, naturally the eyebrows will go up. And if you could see this gentleman, I'm sure at least the ladies, and some of the men, would find it difficult to believe what I'm about to say, but here's the truth: I've stayed chastely away from him, despite all temptation. Romance, alas, is a luxury we can't afford in our present circumstances. We can think about it, though, and I'm afraid this young man has no idea of the kind of thoughts I have had about him since we first met in a very cold room in the Ice Palace last February. And that, listeners, I must leave to your imagination as well!

"This young man tells me that Mr. Kal Hromatka is a devoted listener. Kal, if you are listening, hello! Can you hear me clearly? If so, listen carefully, Kal. My visitor wants to see you right away. Please come, with a car, to the place where he shot pictures of the

moon. Do you understand? He'll be waiting nearby. Please hurry,
Kal, as a special favor to the Archangel.

"*In the meantime, while we're waiting, let there be music!*"

"Selena," Danny whispered, as the record started.

"Shhh," she said, putting her fingers to her lips. And then, softly, gently, and finally, touching them to his own.

C H A P T E R

34

*A*t that moment, Dooley Willson was cutting into a piece of squirrel roulade in the back room of Rostek's Restaurant. Theo sat back and watched the big cop eat.

"How is that?" Theo said. "Tender enough for you?"

"It's good," Willson admitted grudgingly.

"Man's got to eat now and then," Theo said. "You want anything else? More bread?"

"I'm fine, thanks."

Theo nodded to the waiter, who left and shut the door behind him. He poured himself a drink and filled the rest of the glass with a siphon.

"I'm glad you came to see me, Chief. I know you're a proud man. Everybody up here thinks the world of you. We got to take care of those people now. Folks here would feel good knowing you had your hands on things. I got associates in Chicago, Cleveland, Philly. They all are trying to get organized, but I want to show them the way to do it! This is a good town, if you don't mind the cold. Me, I don't mind. I got me a nice fur coat!"

He laughed, opened a cigar box on the desk, and offered it to Willson. Willson shook his head.

"I know it's hard," Rostek said softly. "We been looking at each other from opposite sides of the law. But that was the white man's law, and it's gone now. We got to have our own. Now, up here, I've always provided protection, a little enforcement now and then, when people sometimes lost respect for the situation, if you know what I mean. But we've got to be more organized from now on.

"You know, you'd think folks would be overjoyed that this happened. Finally God rained down punishment on our oppressors! We're free, but most folks ain't looking at it that way. Bad as the white man treated them, they still felt comfortable having him around. Know what I mean? You, for instance. I know you got no use for a white man, and yet there you were working with him every day. And now that he's gone, you don't know what to do with yourself! That's the way lots of folks are taking this. 'Specially up here, where the white man pretended to welcome us. 'Come on up! We'll give you a house, and a job, and pat you on the shoulder and say you're an Upper Midwesterner just like me. Weren't no slaves here, no sir! We fought for the *Union* up here! Why, we're open-minded and tolerant, and we like you! Yes, *suh!*'

"And see, it's all a *lie.* They wanted us here so they could live off us, just the way they always have. Nevertheless, folks is worried. You can smell all those people dying out there now. Don't matter what color they is. Puts a man in mind of his own time coming. And thoughts like that have a way of making people reckless. That's why we had that fire out there on Lake today. It'll get only worse, unless we show folks that we got our own institutions in place. We'll make our own law, Dooley. And we'll need somebody like you, good and strong, to enforce it."

"What's your offer, Theo?"

"I'm proposing a police force. *Our* police force. Uniforms. Badges. Officers. And you running it all." Theo smiled warmly. *"Chief."*

Just then a waiter came and whispered something to Rostek. "You sure?" Rostek said, and when the waiter nodded, Rostek got up.

"I got to take a call," he said. "Bring Sergeant Willson some more coffee, will you, Eddie."

"I'm fine," Willson said.

"Bring him some. I'll be right back."

Willson pushed his plate away as the waiter poured him coffee. He

hated being lectured to by this hoodlum, even if what he said did
make sense. Willson wasn't even sure what had possessed him to
come up to the North Side in the first place. He'd sent Della and the
kids out to her sister's in Chaska, and he'd hunkered down in the
house waiting for Gray to come after him. For two days he'd waited,
sure he would see that son of a bitch step out of the long green car
and straighten his tie, looking up and down Willson's street like he
owned the place.

But Gray hadn't come. And Willson had got more and more
restless, and then hungry, too, because Della had taken most of the
stuff from the pantry and the icebox with her. Finally, Theo had
called him and asked for a meeting at the restaurant, and he told
himself it was hunger, more than anything, that got him to go. So
he'd sat there and eaten Theo's squirrel and listened to his smooth
proposals, even though he knew it wasn't any good. Theo Rostek had
been a crook when the world was white, and he'd still be a crook
when all of the white folks were gone. You couldn't work for a crook
and pretend you were operating inside some kind of moral armor. It
was bad enough he'd sat there eating his fucking cabbage roll!

He was getting up to leave just as Theo came back from his phone
call.

"I don't think it's gonna work, Theo," Willson said.

"Hold on, Chief," Rostek said. "You remember our talk the other
day?"

"What about it?"

"Well, it came to my attention that the *Klan* has been pulling some
of our folks off the street."

Willson sat down. "Spill it," he said.

Rostek smiled. "I thought you might be interested." He sat on the
edge of the table. "Now, I personally went over to see one of those
white-sheet boys yesterday, and he told me what I was hearing was
true."

"Who did you see?"

"That really doesn't matter, anymore, Chief. I'm afraid I had to
put a little—how should I put it?—*pressure* on him. And now, I
guess you might say he's in no shape to wear his hood." Theo

laughed. "But what's really good is that I just found out that one of the other boys who was in on it happens to be a roommate of that reporter friend of yours."

"Constantine?"

"That's right. Danny Constantine."

"Constantine doesn't have anything to do with the Klan," Willson said flatly.

"Oh? And how do you know that?"

"Because I know him. He's a fair-minded man."

"Whooo! Listen to that! Mr. Constantine, why, he's a *fair*-minded man! He would never do nothin' to hurt us colored folks! No, *sir*!" Theo's smile faded and he leaned close to Willson. "You listen to me, *Chief*. That man has one of the Klan living under his own roof. You think he doesn't know about it? *Bull*shit! He knows, and he knows something else that you'd better start learning, too. He knows how to take care of his own!"

Willson tried to look away, but Rostek came around to face him. "Look here, Willson. I know you been working on these disappearance cases for a year now. And I'm telling you, this boy, Lou Ravelli, was part of the gang that kidnapped four men and a lady Saturday night. I'm also telling you that I had some people looking for him, and I know where he is right now! You say you know how to take care of your own? Prove it. Put your high and mighty attitude aside and come with me right now."

"I ain't going *nowhere* with you!"

"Oh, *fuck* you, Dooley! I'm just trying to get by, just like you. You ain't any better than I am. It's all about pushing people around, and there's the ones doing the pushing and the ones getting pushed. You and I push. Stop hiding behind the law! At least I'm honest about what I do. These people been murdering, Chief. *You want 'em or not?*"

"I want 'em," Willson growled.

Rostek clapped his hands together. "Damn right!"

"But I'm going to make an arrest and see he's booked."

"You turned in your badge."

"I can still make a citizen's arrest."

"You gonna keep hiding 'til you can't hide anymore."

"That's the way it's got to be, Theo."

Rostek shrugged. "Okay. Won't make no difference. You want to ride with me?"

"We'll take my car."

"Won't make no difference, either," Theo said.

"Where are they?"

"The old Crockett Mill," Theo said.

Downtown in the offices of the *Journal,* Bing Lockner was working the baseball ticker. He sat with his feet up, pulling the yellow tape through his fingers. Only two scores had come over, one of them a Negro league game in Pittsburgh between the Crawfords and the Homestead Grays. The other contest had been played in Pawtucket, where what was left of the Red Sox had played their minor league affiliate for the eighth day in a row. That was all he had to go on today.

Under his feet, on the desk, was the chart he had been keeping since the start of the season, showing the games that, according to the schedule, ought to have been played, and the standings. Bing had Philadelphia ahead in the American, and St. Louis in the National. St. Louis had already won forty-seven games this year. Bing had felt, before the season began, that 1930 would be a good year for the young, scrappy St. Louis team with their hillbilly pitchers, young Dizzy and Daffy Dean. And they had got off to a great twenty-and-four start before the league shut down for good. Bing thought it was only right that they should keep it up, even though he'd given them an awful streak of eight losses in a row the week before Memorial Day. They'd come out of it, though, like he knew they would. They would have taken that doubleheader with the Cubs today, he thought. Four to three in the opener, and then pounding Chicago for nineteen hits and twelve runs in the capper.

He pulled the chart out and marked the line score on it carefully. He wasn't in any hurry. Walter still didn't know whether that boxcar of paper would arrive from Port Arthur or not. There were rumors that the Canadians had sealed the border at Grand Portage, and that their gunboats were blockading the lake around Superior and Duluth. Bing thought that was probably true, but sooner or later, Crowley would dig up enough paper for the *Journal* to go on for another week or two, anyway. After that, well, the people of Milltown could always read the *Defender.*

The sports ticker was quiet. All of the tickers were. It was too quiet in the office, too, had been ever since Danny Constantine had disappeared Saturday night.

Bing felt a chill, got his feet off the desk, turned a piece of paper into the platen of his typewriter, and began to type the baseball copy. The noise from the typing comforted him. The stories were all off the top of his head, but Bing shuffled the names and details from the thousands of baseball games he had covered during his career and came up with an entire day's action.

"Copy!" he yelled, yanking the last page of his story from the Corona and holding it up above his head. Nobody came to take it, though. After a moment Bing turned around and looked out over the city room. It was deserted.

"Jackie!" he called, walking out from his desk to see whether Walter Burns was in his office. Then he heard footsteps.

"Sorry, Mr. Lockner!" Jackie said, running up breathlessly.

"What the hell's going on? Where is everybody?"

"Up in the plant," the copy boy said. "They got the radio on up there, listening to that lady."

"What lady?"

"The Archangel! She's saying folks is being held prisoner out at that institute. That Dr. Gray's killing 'em!" Jackie's dark eyes shone. He was very excited. "You ought to go up and listen to her. She's yelling like a preacher!"

The phone rang at Bing's desk. Bing half turned, and stared in the direction of the sound.

"You want me to get that, Mr. Lockner?" Jackie said.

"No," he said. "You take this."

He let go of the copy and walked back to his desk. The phone kept ringing. He looked at it, then picked up the candlestick and put the receiver to his ear.

"Bing Lockner," he said.

"Please hold the line," an operator said. A moment later came a cold, steady voice Bing knew.

"I need some information," the voice said. "There is a woman on the radio. Where is she?"

"Gray?" Bing said. "Why are you calling me here!"

"I don't have the time or patience to respect the subconscious territory you've carved for yourself anymore, Mr. Lockner. Tell me where the Archangel is. *Now.*"

"You . . ."

"Shall I come down there? Is that what you want? Should I wring the truth out of you with my bare hands?"

"Nobody knows where she is," Bing insisted weakly.

"You know *exactly* where she is. More than that, you know *who* she is. In February you arranged an interview with her for Mr. Constantine."

"Mrs. Van der Voort handled that."

"*You* are Mrs. Van der Voort, Mr. Lockner. Among other people. Shall I go further? *Or will you tell me now!*"

Bing sat down. "She broadcasts from the flour mill," he heard himself say. It must have been he, although he didn't feel as though he could possibly have been speaking those words. They came from somewhere very far away. "The Crockett mill."

The line went dead. Bing clicked the cradle and got the switchboard. "Hello? I was just cut off."

"The party hung up, Mr. Lockner," the operator said. "Do you want me to try to connect you again?"

Bing stared at his baseball chart.

"Mr. Lockner? Shall I connect you with someone?"

"No," he said. "That won't be necessary."

He got up, went to the coat rack, and put on his coat and his hat. He lighted a cigarette, took it from his mouth in order to pick a piece of tobacco off the tip of his tongue, and then started for the stairs.

"Lockner!" Walter Burns called from the mezzanine. "Where the hell do you think you're going?"

"Home," Bing said.

"You can't do that! I need you! I just got off the phone with the

paper company. There's three carloads of newsprint on a siding out
in Hopkins, and we can have all of it!"

"Good for you, Burnsie. Congratulations. But my work's done."

"Lockner! You can't walk out on me like this. Who's going to
write my copy! Lockner! Bing!"

Bing walked downstairs. "Good-bye, Reno," he said to the old
guard as he signed out.

"Good-bye, Mr. Lockner," Reno said. "You be coming back
tonight?"

"No, Reno," Bing said. "I don't expect I will."

"Well, you be careful," Reno said. "It's not a good night to be
out."

Bing looked at him. "You ever blow the whistle on a pal, Reno?"

"I don't even think I own no whistle, Mr. Lockner."

Bing smiled. "That's the way. If anyone asks, tell 'em I'm home
taking a long nap. Twenty years ought to do it."

"I will do that, Mr. Lockner," Reno said.

35

*U*sed to work here when I was a kid," Kal Hromatka was telling Lou. "All along this stretch of river these mills were going twenty-four hours a day. I worked in the machine shop. I was a skinny kid, so sometimes if a drive belt snapped, I got the job of running a stringer up through the courses. Sometimes you'd be in there nose to nose with a rat. See this scar?"

"Yeah?"

"One of 'em took a chunk out of my cheek. Damn near tore my face off. Scared me to death. Nose to nose with me, hissing like a cat!"

"I don't think anybody's up there, Kal," Lou Ravelli said uneasily. "You sure this is the place, Kal?"

"It's the place," Kal said firmly. He got out of the car, opened the trunk, and found his flashlight. He turned it on and shined it toward the wall of the mill. "Come on, Lou," he said. "We're going in." He started slogging over the deep limestone-flake gravel that covered the ties of the rail spur, the beam of his flashlight trained on a door beyond the line of trees at the corner of the wall. It was swinging open and shut.

"Wait up, Kal!" Lou called.

"For Christ's sake, will you come on!"

"I don't think I can go in there, Kal," Lou said weakly.

Kal stopped. "You're going in, all right. You're going to shut your puss and follow me."

They went up a crumbled sidewalk, and Kal swung the door open with his foot. Inside it was dark and silent. Lou aimed the flashlight beam up into the vast empty space above them.

"Jeez, where *is* everything?" Lou said, looking up at it.

"Down there." Kal pointed the flashlight at the mounded pile of blackened timbers, shattered porcelain grindstones, bricks, and twisted machinery. There were weeds and a couple of small trees growing out of the rubble.

"This building was wood floors and timbers. When it burned, the whole factory dropped down into the basement. And it's all honeycombed with waterworks. Listen."

Water gurgled from somewhere down below the rubble.

"Do you think Danny's down there somewhere?" Lou asked.

Kal trained the beam on the skeleton of an exposed stairwell. "No. Look where there's still parts of a floor. You need height to put out a good radio signal. Up's where they are."

They went to the stairs. With the outside wall of the stairwell gone, the stringers no longer had any support and the whole structure shook with every step Kal and Lou took.

"I tell you, I don't like this," Lou said.

"Stay close to the wall," Kal said. "We'll be okay."

"Did I tell you I had to put out a guy who was on fire today, Kal?" Lou said, testing the landing with his foot.

"You told me. Go on."

They turned the corner and started up the flight leading to what had been the fourth floor. They were almost to the top when a big man with a crew cut stepped out of the shadows.

"Well, ain't this cozy," he said, leveling a gun at them. "I was hoping somebody would come along." He peered down at Lou. "Hey. Don't I know you?"

"No," Lou said.

"Yeah. Yeah, I do. You were one of the boys with the shipment the other night. What the hell are you doing here?"

"You know this slob?" Kal said.

"Who you callin' a slob, old man? Get up here. That's right. Nice and slow. My boss'll want to talk to both o' you."

He backed up against the landing wall as Lou and Kal came up, then realized too late that the landing was too small for him to cover both men with the pistol. Kal shined the flashlight into his eyes, and Lou, chopping down on the big man's wrist, knocked the gun away. Kal drove his shoulder into the man's chest and tried to wrestle him down. They rolled against the wall, Kal trying to hold him, then lost their balance at the top of the stairs and fell. Lou heard them crashing down the stairs together in the darkness. There was a sharp crack of breaking concrete and a short, violent scream. Then silence, except for the faraway sound of running water.

"Kal!" Lou yelled, picking up the flashlight and the gun.

"Down . . . here."

Lou shone the flashlight down the stairwell. Kal was pulling himself on the stairs above the snapped-off landing.

"Jeez, where'd he go?"

"What the hell do I care? Help me. I think my goddamn ankle's broken."

Lou went down and tried to pull Kal to his feet.

"Oww! Yeah, it's broke all right. Son of a bitch!"

Carefully, Lou helped him get to the landing and leaned him up against the wall. With his legs stretched out, Kal's left foot was turned at a funny angle. Looking at it, Lou fought a sick feeling that rose in his stomach.

"Should we try to set it or something?"

"Just find Danny," Kal said, wincing and breathing hard.

"What if that guy comes back?"

"He ain't coming back," Kal said. "Go on. Two floors up. It's the only place they can be."

"Okay. Okay." Lou closed his eyes a moment, then started.

Willson had driven fast and took the shortcut down Royalston across the Glenwood Bridge over the rail yards and then through downtown until he reached the rail spur behind the line of mills. He set the brake and then reached under the seat for something.

"They're here," Theo said, as they got out of Willson's car. "My boys are never wrong. Looks like we're gonna have us a little party tonight. Bake us a *cake.*"

"Stick 'em up, Theo," Willson said, coming around the front of the car with his pistol drawn.

"Chief. What do you think you're doing?"

"I said put 'em up!"

"You're the boss," Rostek said, turning.

"Hands on top of the car." Willson reached for the cuffs on his belt. He snapped them on Rostek's right wrist, and pulled his arm down around his back.

"Got to hand it to you, Chief. You follow that code of yours all the way to the end."

"Shut up."

"And you know, that would be all right if it all was ending out here tonight. But you know what, Chief? It ain't ending here. Not unless you kill me."

"I said shut up!" Willson snapped the other cuff on and turned him around.

"See, 'cause it's a problem now. What am I gonna do with somebody who refuses to do business with me? I can't let that slide, Chief. Gives too many other people ideas. The kind of people who don't follow no *code*—"

Willson saw Rostek's eyes widen then, an instant before he heard the crunch of footsteps on the gravel behind him, felt something hard smash against the side of his head, saw the burst of light and then nothing.

"*My* kind of people!" Theo said with a big smile. "How you doing, Marquise?"

Marquise looked down at Willson. "You want me to take care of him?"

"Now, that's what I like about you, Marquise. You *ask*. Some of the other boys woulda just shot him. Come on. Get me out of these cuffs."

Marquise found Willson's key ring and unlocked Theo's right wrist. When he tried to unfasten the other manacle the key wouldn't turn.

"Jammed," Marquise said.

"Hell, never mind. You stay here and keep an eye on him. I don't
want to lose the chief. We're gonna have to work on him a little when
this is all done with, but I think he'll come around."

"Okay. You be careful, Theo."

Theo smiled. "Shit," he said, and headed for the mill.

I don't care who she is or what she's done, Danny thought, as he
listened to the Archangel tell the whole city about Simon Gray and
the real work of the Hematological Institute. As he listened he
marveled at the change that had come over her. It was as though she
had taken on all the pain and suffering of Milltown, and replaced it
with understanding and love. Even though the truth was so hard to
hear.

*"Oh, darlings! I can't blame anyone for trying to go on with his or
her life. What else could you do? We still don't know what's killing us.
Even after all this time we don't know if the poison's in the air, or in
the water or the food, or even whether it's the sunshine, or some
terrifying pestilence sent from another world. We can't see it, we can't
taste it or smell it. So, maybe the only way to protect ourselves from it
was to pretend that it simply wasn't happening, that Hun did not
exist.*

*"And that has worked here for almost twelve years. We have
suffered as great a loss proportionately to our white population as any
other city. And yet something in our determination and character
made it possible for us to go on, where other places gave in and
destroyed themselves. We brought in outsiders, healthy outsiders who
would not get sick, and we taught them to help us run our town.
There was nothing wrong with that. It was the only thing our stoic
character would allow us to do. But in the end we ignored certain
things that we ought to have paid attention to.*

*"For instance, did you know that for the past year someone has
been kidnapping Negroes off the streets? Usually derelicts or newcom-
ers without family or strong local connections. We might have asked
ourselves why this was happening, and determined that, if it was a
reaction to the policy of encouraging Negro settlement, that it was
ultimately dangerous and not in our best interests to allow it to
continue!*

"But we didn't care that 'they' were disappearing. It wasn't happening to 'us.' And as we well know, whenever something horrible and incomprehensible happens to someone, there's a part inside our minds that says, 'Well, he must have deserved it. Otherwise it never would have happened.' And, after all, wasn't it only right that 'they' should suffer, too? So we were quite willing to let these kidnappings go on.

"But people, I tell you tonight—all of you, Negro and white—that these people have been kidnapped and taken to the Hematological Institute, where their blood is stolen from them and given to patients who have no idea where their transfusions have come from. Those of you who have put your faith in the institute, who have hoped that the rumors that a cure was being developed there were true, must realize your faith has been abused. The institute is a lie, and its founder . . . Its founder is a murderer.

"I'm sorry to be the one to tell you these things. Because hope is so very precious now, it is very difficult for me to do it. I'm afraid I have suffered a death of my own recently, perhaps the most terrible death anyone can face. I have experienced . . . quite vividly, the death of something I held very dear. The thing that allowed me to continue, and live, and hope. I experienced . . . the death of an illusion.

"You see, I admired Simon Gray very much. I saw him as a great man, doing great things. Someone who had the intellectual and moral strength to heal the world! And he does in fact have the talent and strength to do this, except that it has been twisted into a force that mocks and destroys all those around him! Yes, even now it is difficult to speak of. I hesitate, when I ought to be exposing him for the monster he is, and yet something of his personality holds me back!

"Well, I must go on. Later will be time enough for all of us to grieve for the loss of our illusions. Later we can curse ourselves for our weakness and stupidity, for our willingness to believe, not in truth, but in what we wanted to believe. But now is the time to find this man, to smoke him out, to stop him, to go to the institute and free those prisoners who wait to be drained of their blood in the locked west wing. That is the only cure that is possible now, darlings. Go there! Go—"

The glow of the transmitter's tubes suddenly broke and faded.

"What happened?" Danny said.

She didn't speak at first. Then Selena struck a match, held it, trembling, to the wicks of candles that were stuck into bottles. "The power's gone off," she said, in a voice that was diminished, and sad. She turned and looked at him.

"Can you fix it?"

"I don't know. It's never happened before." Selena turned. "I could feel them out there tonight, Danny," she said. "I could feel them listening to me. It was as if they were hungry and I was feeding them, and then suddenly they were gone." She closed her eyes and shuddered. "Oh, Danny. I've been alone for so long. . . ."

"No," he said, going to her. "You're not alone."

"I lied to you. I've lied to everyone. You knew I was a liar. That's why you thought . . ." Her voice broke. "God, who am I kidding! I'm every bit the killer he is."

"You didn't know," Danny said.

"But I should have figured it out! I was right there, giving tours, while those poor people . . ."

"Selena, look at me."

"No."

"Look at me." He tipped her chin with his finger. "Selena, you've helped thousands of people at the mission, and here, too. You gave people hope. They believe in you, and they still do. You can't blame yourself for wanting to live. That's what I did when Sonja died. Don't you see? I wouldn't let myself really see you or feel anything for you because I thought I didn't deserve to. Because of her."

"Because of Sonja," she repeated.

"Yes. Because of Sonja. Do you remember how I once said you looked like her? You don't, really. I said that instead of what I really thought, which was that you were like her because of how you made me *feel*. Like I was worth something. Like I was the luckiest guy on the face of the earth. That's what I felt, the first time I ever laid eyes on you."

"At the club that day?"

"No, Selena. I felt it that night I interviewed you at the Ice Palace. Under that veil, and covered in furs, and you know, I didn't even wonder who you really were. I just thought you were wonderful. But I didn't want to know your name. That way I didn't have to worry about being unfaithful to Sonja. Do you understand?"

"I think so," Selena said, hugging his waist.

"I fell in love with you that night. And I was in love with you that night at the dance, and even when I thought you were a murderer. I hated myself, but that's how I felt."

"I love you, too, Danny," she said, looking up at him. He knelt down and kissed her.

"Oh, Danny," she whispered. "We mustn't do this now. Not here. Your friends are coming—"

"Shhhh." He kissed her again, with everything he had, trying to pour his whole soul into hers. But he felt her tense up suddenly, and he opened his eyes and saw the candles all flicker at once, and then something sharp jabbed his neck. He went numb almost instantly, and fell on his back on the rug.

"What a tender scene," Simon Gray said contemptuously.

He looked down at Danny. In his hand was a syringe, with a drop of thick, red-brown liquid gathering at the tip of the needle. Danny saw Selena jump up, Gray catching her wrist and forcing her to sit again. Danny tried to cry out, but his body would not obey his mind.

"Did I do it correctly?" Gray said. "A jab to the neck, was it not? Admittedly, your stabbing me was the more dramatic, having as it did the additional element of betrayal." He glanced down at Danny. "Of course, I took extra trouble with this particular injection. I want him to be fully conscious for what I'm about to do to him." He took a small morocco-covered box from his coat pocket.

"Leave him alone, Simon," Selena said. "If you want to punish someone, punish me."

"Oh, I will punish you, my dear. Don't worry about that." He let go of her wrist suddenly and reached for her face and stroked it with the back of his hand. "Can you see her face, Constantine? Even now, she trembles like a canary at my touch. Perhaps you'd like to see more? You'll kiss me, won't you, my dear." He leaned toward her, drawing closer as her eyes widened.

Selena slapped him. Roaring with fury, Gray slapped her back and turned, blood dribbling from the side of his mouth.

"Don't think your sudden conversion will do you any good,

Selena! Your money always kept you insulated from the unpleasant-
ness of your condition. Well, your money isn't any good here." He
turned toward Danny and held up a scalpel.

"You want to know about the details of my operation? How I
installed the valves and the filters that allow people like her to drink
blood? How I place electrical probes deep into the brain stem to
make sure the blood-drinking's the most excruciating pleasure
they'll ever experience? Look at her, Constantine, she grows faint
just remembering! Well, you shall know how I do it firsthand! You'll
be able to watch me take your heart out of your chest and hold it
beating in my hand! And you'll see that she won't do a thing to stop
me—"

Selena screamed and threw herself at him. They struggled,
turning, then Gray backhanded her hard once more. Selena crashed
against the transmitter, moaned, and slumped to the floor.

"Get up," he snarled, forcing her to her feet. Her hand was cut
where she had tried to take the scalpel from him.

"No—"

"You are going to watch me operate. And what's more, *you will
like it!*"

He pushed her into a chair, then, reaching behind the transmitter,
ripped out a length of wire. He wrapped it around her wrists and the
spokes of the back of the chair.

"Now let us begin," he said, lifting the scalpel again, he turned
toward Danny Constantine.

Dooley Willson came to beside his car, fighting a wave of pain from
the blow to his head. He opened his eyes. There was a black man
sitting on the running board of a long green car. The man took a
toothpick out of his mouth and nodded.

Willson began to stand up.

"No, no. See, you're gonna stay right where you are, Chief."

"What did you call me?" Willson said, shaking his head to clear
it. "Did you say *Chief*?"

"Theo said to cover you," Marquise said in alarm. "You sit back
down."

"I asked, what did you call me?"

"I'm serious, now. Don't make me shoot you."

Willson used his left hand to slap the pistol out of Marquise's hand. A straight right put the numbers runner down for good.

"Chief," Willson spat, collecting the gun and starting for the doorway, following the footprints in the gravel. Just inside the door he heard a crash and a short scream that cut off suddenly. Then, above, the muffled sound of voices. He cocked his revolver and moved toward the stairway, shining his flashlight down into the collapsed subbasement. Then he stopped.

There was a dead man impaled, spread-eagled, on a length of pipe. Blood flowed from his mouth, red and shiny as a candy apple. The man's eyes were open. Willson recognized him. It was the goon from the institute.

Willson took a cigar from his shirt pocket, shoved it into the corner of his mouth, and started up the steps. On the third landing his flashlight went out. He shook it, then swore and tossed it into the darkness. Somewhere far away, a steam whistle blew. He started up the stairs, then light dazzled him and he felt the stairs giving way underneath his feet. Instinctively, he jumped forward, landing hard on his belly on the steps above, clawing with his hands to keep from being sucked down and away and finally reaching the solid landing.

"Who's there?" he said to the light. He had lost his pistol.

"Who're you?"

"Police."

"Thank God!" Kal Hromotka said. He looked at Willson the way a lost kid looks at his father.

"I'm Sergeant Willson." He knelt beside him. "What's the matter with you?"

"I busted my ankle," Kal said, wincing.

"I'll get you some help soon," he said. "Where's the kid you came with? Ravelli."

"Up there."

Willson nodded.

"You're here to arrest Lou, aren't you?"

"Yeah."

"He didn't know what he was doing. He ain't a bad kid. He's just mixed up because of all the rough time he's had."

"We've all had a rough time, Pops. He ain't no different than anybody else."

"I know," Kal said. "Here. Take my flashlight."

"Thanks."

"Bring Danny back, too."

"Danny? You mean Constantine's here?"

"Yeah."

"Okay. You sit tight. I'll bring 'em both down."

"He didn't know what he was doing," Kal repeated.

"Nobody does," Willson growled, starting up.

Lou Ravelli found the transmitter room by the candlelight spilling through the partially open door. He came up and looked inside and saw a tall man pressing a knife against the bare chest of someone who was lying on the floor.

It was Danny.

"Hold it!" Lou said.

Gray did not appear to hear him. He pressed the point of his scalpel against Danny's skin. Lou could see it making a little depression. Danny did not seem to be aware of what was happening to him.

"I said stop and get away from him!"

"No," Gray said mildly.

"I'll blow your damn brains out!"

"I wouldn't advise you to do that, Mr. Ravelli. His throat will be slit before I fall."

"How do you know who I am!"

"Because we've done business. You're one of the men who brought me five *donors* Saturday night."

"Don't listen to anything he says!" Selena cried.

"These people are my enemies, Mr. Ravelli," Gray said, looking back for the first time. "*Our* enemies. You know the work I do. I have invented a cure for Hun, and these two are trying to keep me from giving it to the world."

"He's lying!"

"Lying?" Theo Rostek said. "We got *lying* goin' on up here?" He clucked his tongue and stepped in around the heavy curtain. "Look at this! Who we got here? Doc! And Selena Crockett, and you," he said, pointing his pistol at Lou, "you're that boy plays for the Millers. And Danny Constantine! Shit! We got *everybody.*"

Lou turned uncertainly toward Rostek. Instantly Theo's eyes hardened. "You better put that down, boy."

"N-no," Lou said. "You drop yours!"

"Listen to me, both of you," Selena cried. "Don't you see the real enemy's right in front of you? He's been killing your people, Theo! Don't you understand? That clinic of his is nothing but a front for a blood farm. He's been doing it all along. Urging the GNDC to bring in more and more Negroes from out of state, knowing he'll get his share of them and no one will say a word. He hates you! All of you! All those people streaming up from the South with their belongings tied inside sheets. All those black faces replacing the white ones. He knows he can get away with it because everyone looks the other way. You can stop him, Theo! You can stop him right now!"

"You're bleeding pretty bad, Selena," Theo said, pulling his handkerchief from his coat pocket and, keeping the gun on Ravelli, helping Selena to wrap her cut hand. He stepped back and nodded at Gray.

"What about you, Doc? You holding that little knife, and Danny boy just lying there without his shirt. You ain't going bugs on me, are you?"

"In comparison to whom?" Gray said.

Theo laughed. "That's a tough question, Doc. But I think I've got it sorted out." He looked at Lou. "See, the doc and I have an understanding. It's business. I don't pry into his personal business, and as a matter of fact, I've seen more than I want to right here. We had an arrangement and he always stuck to it. Which is more than I can say for my good friends in the *Klan.* See, I had an arrangement with your lodge brothers, Lou. They were supposed to stay out of my neighborhood. And they always did—until you joined up."

"I'm warning you," Lou said. "Drop it—"

A shot cut him off. Lou let go of the gun, falling to his knees with a quizzical expression on his face. Then he collapsed face down next to Danny.

"I never warn anybody," Theo said. "Sorry, Selena. It's business. Not black business or white business. Just business."

Gray took a deep breath. "Perhaps," he said, "it would be better if we take Miss Crockett back to the institute."

"What about Danny-boy?"

"Kill him," Gray said.

"Shit," Rostek said, poking at Danny with his toe. "Already looks dead!"

"Drop it, Theo!" Dooley Willson ordered from the doorway.

"I ain't dropping nothing," Rostek said, without looking back.

Willson gave out a roar and went at him. As the two men struggled, Gray ran past them out of the studio.

"You lousy, murdering crook," Willson said, trying to squeeze Theo's gun loose. "You *work* for him. You sell your own people to him!"

"I protect my people. Anybody else . . . *fuck 'em!*"

Willson turned Rostek around and punched him hard in the gut, yanking the gun out of his hand as Rostek collapsed.

"Where the hell did Gray go!" Willson yelled, running out to the hall.

"There's a ladder to the roof," Selena said, pointing the way.

Willson came back in and put Lou Ravelli's pistol in her good hand. "You keep this bastard covered. If he blinks an eye, shoot the son of a bitch!"

He ran out to the ladder and started up. His head hurt like hell, and for an instant he felt dizzy, but he forced himself to keep going and came out onto the roof. Most of it was gone, except for the beams and the part above the stairwell. Willson could see the dull glow of scattered fires burning across the city and the few electric lights that remained on the west side of town. Gray was standing on the ledge overlooking the river. He turned, and smiled ironically at Willson.

"Have you read the Bible, Sergeant?"

"I ain't in the mood to talk religion."

"I could offer this city to you," Gray said. "Everything you see now. Would that be enough to tempt you?"

"Shut up, Gray. You're all done."

Gray's eyes narrowed. "What are you going to do? *Arrest* me?" He tossed his head with icy contempt. "Please do so, by all means. I want to be arrested. Do you have any idea how quickly I'd be acquitted? You haven't a shred of evidence against me. Moreover, when I tell the world I've developed a cure for Hun, you more than likely will be lynched. So please—" He held his arms out. "By all means take me into custody. Do your duty, Sergeant Willson."

Avenging two hundred and fifty-three people was his duty, Willson thought, as he squeezed the trigger.

Gray glanced down at his coat. He flicked at his chest as though he was brushing off a bit of lint. Then he looked up at Willson again.

"Jesus merely refused the offer, you know," Simon Gray said. Then he fell back into the darkness, toward the river.

CHAPTER

36

*D*ooley Willson slowly climbed the ladder back down to the hallway. He was angry at himself, angry because he had let Gray goad him into pulling the trigger. That's what that crazy mother wanted all along, he thought. Pull him out of line. Make him a killer, too.

He went back into the studio. Constantine was sitting up now, trying to put his shirt back on. Theo Rostek was facing him, sitting cross-legged like an Indian and smoking a cigarette with his free hand.

"Well, well," Theo said when Willson pushed through the carpet. "If it ain't the chief!" He looked past him. "Where's Gray?"

"In the river," Willson said.

"In the river? He jumped in the river?"

"I shot his ass."

"Shot his ass," Rostek repeated. "Not good, Chief. Not good at all."

"Shut up."

"You folks hear that?" Theo said pleasantly. "This is the man who said he had to play by the rules. That he believed in the *law*. And what's he do? Shoots down a doctor like a dog. Judge and jury, just like that! Something *I'd* do."

"I said shut up!"

"You made a big mistake, Chief."

"He deserved it." He glared down at Rostek. "Just like you."

"Yeah. That's right! Maybe I do. And maybe he did, too. But tell me if I'm wrong, here, Chief. Didn't you just shoot the one man who could tell you who killed your partner?"

"Maybe you know," Willson said menacingly.

"Shit. Like I *care.*"

Willson kicked him in the face. Danny put his arms around him and tried to pull him back, but Willson gave him an elbow and sent him sprawling.

"Sergeant!" Selena cried. "That's enough!"

Willson turned, anguish distorting his face.

"You're not like him. Don't let him drag you down to his level. You're not like him at all."

He closed his eyes a moment. And then he stepped around and pulled Danny to his feet. "Sorry, Constantine," he said. Then he turned back to Theo Rostek.

"You're under arrest," he said.

Taking Rostek down to Willson's car, they found Kal Hromatka on the landing. Selena looked him over, and determined that his ankle was probably fractured, and said she could get Dr. Cramer to set it at the Lutheran Mission.

"Where's Lou?" Kal asked.

"Lou didn't make it, Kal," Danny said softly. Kal nodded. He had heard the shots.

"He was trying to do right today," Kal said.

"I know," Danny said.

They rigged up a blanket stretcher and brought Kal outside. As Danny drove downtown to the mission, Kal tapped Selena on the shoulder.

"Pardon me," he said. "But you're the Archangel, aren't you?"

Selena smiled. "I'm Selena Crockett," she said.

"But I mean, you broadcast that message to me from the mill. I heard it. That's why me and Lou came down in the first place. I've listened to you every night, Miss Crockett. I've heard all your programs. Me and Shirley, well, that's what we do every night. Find you and tune you in. If you don't mind me saying so, you're every bit as beautiful as your voice. I mean your voice sounds as beautiful as . . . Oh, hell," he said, face reddening with embarrassment.

"I understand," she said kindly. "Thank you."

They reached the mission and got Kal onto a gurney. Dr. Cramer was there tending to patients at the walk-in clinic. He quickly determined that Kal's fracture was not a compound one, and set it. When the cast dried, Danny drove Kal home. The yellow glow of an oil lamp shone through the front windows.

"Lucille's waiting," Kal said grimly.

"I'll tell her what happened tonight," Danny said.

"You let me do that," Kal said.

"You sure?"

"Lou and I talked things out on the way there," Kal said. "I think I can make her understand how he got himself into trouble. And got out of it."

"Okay, Kal," Danny said. "But at least let me help you inside."

"I got to get used to these crutches," Kal said, getting out of the car.

"Tell Mrs. Lund I'll be back later. I'm going to the office for a while."

"You going to write about Miss Crockett?" Kal asked.

"She's part of the story."

"Could you leave her name out of it, Dan? She's the Archangel. That's all anybody has to know. If you tell who she is she won't be able to talk to us anymore. You understand? We need her to talk to us. We need to know she's watching over us."

"I'll try, Kal."

"You go on. I'll take care of Lucille and Shirley."

Danny drove downtown through the dark streets. He parked in front of the narrow *Journal* building, and found the door was locked. He knocked on it until Reno appeared.

"Evening, Mr. Constantine," he said, unlocking the door.

"Hello, Reno." He began signing his name to the book, and then stopped. The place was absolutely silent. No clattering typewriters. No low rumble from the presses upstairs. "Where is everybody?"

"Ain't you heard? Paper's shut down. On account of Mr. Crowley killing himself."

"What?"

"Yeah, early tonight. Took strychnine or something. Anyway, Mr. Burns went around and told everybody to go home. Said there wasn't gonna be a paper tomorrow on account of Mr. Crowley's memory!"

"Is anyone here at all? What about Mr. Lockner?"

Reno scratched his head. "Mr. Lockner? He quit!"

"When?"

"This afternoon. Guess it don't make no difference now, but Jackie said Mr. Lockner told Mr. Burns he was quitting. I guess it's true, too. He was acting awful strange when he signed out that last time."

"What do you mean, strange?"

"He asked me if I knew what it was like to, how did he say? Whistle at a pal?"

"Blow the whistle on a pal?"

"That's right! That's just what he said! He looked mighty low, too!"

"Thanks, Reno."

"You not going up?" Reno said. "Your name's in the book."

"Keep it there. I'll be back," Danny said.

He jumped in his car, drove the three blocks to the courthouse, ran inside up to the second floor, past empty cubicles to Dooley Willson's office. Willson was sitting at his desk with a pair of reading glasses perched on the end of the nose. He was scowling at his typewriter.

"Jesus!" he said, startled, when Danny came around the half wall. "What the hell are you doing, Constantine?"

"Bing," Danny said, leaning over with his hands on his knees, trying to catch his breath.

"What?"

"Bing Lockner. He's the one who tipped off Gray."

"What are you talking about?"

"Didn't you wonder what Gray was doing at the mill tonight? How did he know where I was?"

"He heard Selena's broadcast, just like your friends did."

"But she talked in code. There were only three people who knew I'd taken pictures outside the mill the night of that first murder. Kal, Walter Burns—and Bing Lockner."

"So?"

"Bing *knew* Gray in Detroit. And in New York. They moved in the same circles. In fact Selena told me that's where she met them both the first time, when she went there to get treated for Hun nine years ago. And Bing knew who the Archangel was."

"How do you know that?"

"Because he got me the interview with her last winter! I'm right about this, Willson! I just came from the paper, and the guard told me Bing left late this afternoon after saying something about blowing the whistle on a pal. He told Reno he'd just blown the whistle on me!"

Willson got up and put on his hat. "You know where he lives?"

"Yeah. The Zier Row. Ninth Street and Fourth Avenue."

"Let's go talk to him," Willson said.

here's nobody home," Danny said, pulling the bell one last time before standing back to look at the dark windows of the second-floor corner flat of the Zier Row house.

"We break in?"

"I know where there's a spare key."

Danny reached underneath the stand of the ornamental pot next to the landing. Bing's key was still there. They went in and Danny used it to open the door of the row house and the one to Bing's apartment on the second floor.

The apartment was small and very neat. There was a green table in front of the window with a typewriter on it and a kerosene lamp, a pack of cigarettes, an ashtray from the Chicago World's Fair, and a silver lighter. The window overlooked a corner park and a church with a broken-off steeple. There was a sheet of paper in the typewriter, and a stack of blank sheets beside it.

Willson tried the lights. They were weak, but at least they were working over on this side of town. He opened the closet. Inside were six or seven jackets, neatly hung trousers, and in the back, dresses. Silk ones.

"Shit," Willson said. He pulled down a hat box and lifted the top. In it was a wig stand.

"Sergeant? Come here." Danny was in the bathroom. There were rinsed-out elastic wraps hanging from the shower-curtain rod. On the floor, a big, soft-leather bag lay open. Willson pulled the shower curtain back. The tub was full of pink water and soaking, blood-stained pillowcases.

"He's a bleeder," Willson said.

Danny turned away and closed the door. He didn't want to believe it.

"Where the fuck is he?" Willson said.

Danny went back to the typewriter, and pulled a half-typed sheet of paper from the platen.

A Caddy's Diary

June 29th

Anybody who says that lugging golf bags is no kind of life for a fella never had the chance to carry for the likes of Mrs. Selma Wannamaker. She is one swell-looking dame as well as being sweet as they come. Maybe she don't tip so good, but she sure knows how to shame the other ladies in her foursome into dropping an extra dime.
Particularly she is fond of working on Mrs. Gray, who never pays for anything and who is known in the caddy shack as the Vampire, because she has been observed to put the bite on her own servants. Jump Hurlee, who is my best friend and the boy who taught me all I know about the game of golf, says Mrs. Gray's chauffeur has to go to a shylock every Monday just to cover the expense of working for her. So when Mrs. Wannamaker gets Mrs. Gray to cough up her share, you are certainly grateful, but you feel a little funny about it, wondering whether her parlor maid will go to bed hungry that night on account of you. Jump always says the only cure for a cheapskate is a loaded pistol and he is certainly right about most things, but that Mrs. Wannamaker sure's got a pistol built into her

voice when it comes to squeezing the coins out of
Mrs. Gray. And, of course, when she comes out of
the clubhouse in her sweater sets, it never occurs
to anybody that Mrs. Wannamaker never pays for
nothing either.
<u>Until today</u>

"What are you looking at?" Willson said.

Danny picked up the phone. The exchange was open. "Yeah, can
you put me through to the Lutheran Mission? Thanks." He handed
the typed sheet to Willson. "This is the story he was working on.
Look at the names, and what he underlined at the end—Yes, is Miss
Crockett still there? I see. How long ago? Look, do you know
whether anybody else has telephoned for her this evening? Okay.
Okay, thanks." He threw the phone down onto the bed. "Come on!"

"Constantine! Where the hell are you going!"

"He's at Selena's!" Danny yelled back.

"Oh, Bing," Selena Crockett said, sitting propped up in her bed.
"It's sweet of you to call on me." She had just got home in a cab, and
had made herself a cup of tea, when Bing had arrived.

"Well, I was worried," he said. "You went off the air so suddenly
tonight." He pulled a chair up to the side of the bed, wincing slightly
as he sat down.

"Is something the matter?"

"I've been a little off-kilter lately," Bing said. "I think maybe I've
got an ulcer."

"No!"

"Imagine that. A relaxed fellow like me. I've been drinking
buttermilk."

"Buttermilk! Where do you get buttermilk?"

"Soybeans. Can I let you in on a little secret about buttermilk?"

"What's that?"

"It curdles gin."

Selena laughed. It felt so good to laugh, after everything that had
happened. She'd been surprised to see Bing, but glad he'd come
over. Bing had always been able to make her laugh. And she'd been

worried about what had happened to him after Theo Rostek had
thrown him and Fitzgerald out of the club that night. It seemed so
long ago, now. . . .

"I'm glad you're cracking jokes again. I hated seeing you so down
the other night."

"Well, Selena, to tell you the truth, I was down about . . . you."

"Me? But why?"

"Dorrie told me something that worried me very much. She said
you were sweet on a certain young reporter from the paper." He
shifted a little in his chair, wincing, and then got out a silver
cigarette case, opened it, and offered Selena a cigarette.

"No, thanks," she said.

"What happened to your hand?" he said, eyeing the bandage
on it. He took a cigarette for himself, tapped it on the case, and
lighted it.

"Nothing. It's a scratch."

"Did it stop bleeding?"

She nodded.

"Good. Now, it's very strange," Bing went on. "This guy's been
missing four days. Almost the same amount of time that you've been
away from the mission, Selena. That's not like you. That's not like
you at all. In the meantime, the Archangel's been on the air almost
constantly, and quite the rabble-rouser. She's gone beyond her usual
gently biting satire. I listened and said to myself: that girl's changed
somehow. Something," he said, drawing deeply on the cigarette and
blowing the smoke toward the ceiling, "something has made her
reckless. Made her forget about the people who have looked out for
her for so long."

"Are you asking me for an explanation?" Selena said.

"Of course not. I'm just telling you the way I figured things. When
people fall in love they somehow think it's their duty to air out all
their secrets. You want your lover to know everything that you know,
so that he'll love you every bit as much as you love yourself. And so
you say things you'd never dream of telling anyone else. To shock
them . . . The more shocking the better, isn't that so? Because if
they know the absolute worst, and won't run away, why, then the
love is true."

"What is it you're asking me, Bing?"

Bing smiled. "We've known each other for a long time now, Selena. And we've had a certain amount of trust between us. You let me in on your radio thing, and I never told anyone, did I? Even when there were plenty of people who'd have given their right arm to know who the Archangel was, and where she was calling from, I never let you down."

"I know."

"Do you remember when you and I first met? At that party in East Egg? You'd got away from your father the day before and had your hair bobbed, and he'd insisted you wear that great, droopy hat and a wool jumper that probably suited you in the fourth grade. And you were so cross with him, and didn't want to talk to anyone, certainly not with me. We were introduced and of course you'd never read anything I'd written, didn't care that I'd just come from Paris, even though that very piece of news had nearly caused a stampede among the other ladies present. Your daddy had brought you to the party to meet someone, and you weren't keen on that either. Do you remember? And I happened to be in a good position, sitting halfway up that ridiculous staircase in the main hall, when he practically dragged you over in front of Simon Gray."

He stubbed his cigarette out. "You know, Selena, I'm quite a student of human behavior. I've seen a lot, even for a man my age. And I have to confess that I have never seen anyone change in the presence of another person the way I saw you change when your eyes lit on the good doctor. Why, it was as though he'd melted and recast you right on the spot! You straightened up, you flushed, those wonderful eyes of yours got so wide! I can't tell you how jealous I was."

"I was only a little girl, Bing. You know how fond I've always been of you."

"But you don't get it yet, do you? Not even after all these years. You changed, yes, you were obviously taken with the doctor, the way most ladies were that day. Charm came out of him like heat from coals. It cost him no effort; in fact, I'm sure he never thought about it at all. It was just a power of his, like vision, or the skill he had with his hands. So while I felt a bittersweet twinge watching the effect he'd had on you, imagine what I felt seeing what you did *to him!*"

"What do you mean?"

Now, for the first time, Bing's expression hardened. "Don't pretend, Selena. It's unworthy of you. Even now, after all that's happened, you still want reassurance. Still want someone to tell you how special you were to him. You were the only person he was kind to. Do you realize what that means? He used everyone else he knew. Made them do things they'd never imagined doing before. Made them do things, and *like* it!"

"Maybe you had better go, Bing," Selena said, trying to gather herself. "We can talk about this later."

"No. We'll talk about them *now.* How is it you have no appreciation for the gift he gave you! You and I were the same. He operated on you just as he did on me. We've the same equipment inside, only he took pity on you. He loved you enough to make sure you didn't have to do the things that I did in order to live! He gave you four or five serum treatments a year, enough so that you could live normally. And he made sure you didn't remember the operation, or even what he did to you while he was treating you."

"No!" Selena said, putting her hands to her ears. "You mustn't—"

"He gave you life, and he spared you the cost. And how did you repay him, Selena? What happened at the mill today? Where is he? *Where is he, Selena!*"

"I don't know!"

Bing leapt to the bed and pinned her arms back. "Damn you! Tell me the truth!"

"He's dead!"

He let go of her. Bing's face went deathly white. "No," he said.

"He and Sergeant Willson both arrived at once. The sergeant tried to arrest him, but he ran to the roof. I don't know what happened, except that the sergeant came back alone."

"You're lying," Bing said. "How can he be dead? He isn't dead!"

"Yes," Selena said.

Bing nodded. "All right. I just wanted to hear you say it. As soon as I heard your voice on the telephone I knew. He went there to kill

you, and he failed. And now . . . now I can't do anything to help
him."

"He was murdering people, Bing—"

"What's that to you? He saved your life, and that's how you
thanked him? By betraying him and destroying everything he was
trying to do? He had the cure, Selena! He was going to give it to the
world. But you didn't want that, did you? You wanted to keep it for
yourself!"

"That's not true!"

Bing took off his coat, and opened the bag he'd brought with him.
In it was a blonde wig. He slipped it over his head, went to the
mirror, straightened it.

When he turned around he was not Bing Lockner anymore.

"You!" Selena said in horror.

"You wanted truth, luv?" He was speaking with some sort of an
accent. "All right, then. He made me into quite the little predator.
Partly to keep me quiet. Partly because he saved all his pure thoughts
for you. With me, he liked to watch. He'd sit there smoking while I
did them in. Christ, I hated him for that! But I couldn't help wanting
to do it. Maybe I wanted them to catch me, though. The one I killed
by the mill, I left a calling card. Or maybe I should say I left the poor
bloke without one! Hoo, Simon had a fit! Threatened to strangle
me with his bare hands. And maybe he would have, too, except
for the papers I have in my safe-deposit box. The whole thing's
there. All the details of what I did in Chicago, and in Detroit, and
New York, too. That very weekend in East Egg, I took one of
the wives out in a rowboat on the sound at midnight. She never
came back. Killed the old man, too. Oh, I killed plenty with Simon
right there at my side. And now, I guess I've got to learn to do it
alone."

He took an instrument that looked like a chrome stapler from the
bag.

"What are you doing!"

"I told you, luv. I'm in a bad way tonight. You might be a bleeder,
too, but I'm taking the chance that his last treatment on you took
permanent. That's what he said he'd done and I'm going to take him
at his word."

"Bing. Don't you see this is your chance to stop this? He's gone. You don't have to do it anymore!"

"You're the one that don't understand. Gray made me want it more than anything. He made it so I get all shivery inside, and I've got to do something about it." He smiled. "Don't worry. I'll try not to hurt you. In fact, I'm a bit nervous tonight. I ain't never done no girl before. Though I must say I've always fancied you a little—"

"*No!*"

He rushed the bed and she rolled off, and heard an explosion come from the other side of the room. Bing straightened up, reached for his head. The wig came off in his hand. He blinked his eyes, turned.

"Hello, Connie," he said.

"Bing—" Danny said, moving toward him.

He coughed, blood bubbling from his mouth, wavered, and fell face forward across the bed.

"Selena!" Danny cried, going to her. "Are you all right?"

"Yes," she said, putting her arms around him.

Willson knelt down and looked in the bag Bing had brought with him, pulling out the canister of compressed air. "What's this for?"

Danny lifted Bing's shirttail. There were the metal nipples protruding from the skin just below the ribline. "It's power for the pumps inside his chest," Danny said. "Once the tank was attached he could drink anything and it would go straight into his own bloodstream. He'd kill somebody whenever he needed a transfusion, and drink it straight."

"Jesus," Willson said. "That was Gray's cure? I wonder if there's any more like him running around."

Danny and Selena looked at each other.

"I am one, Sergeant," she said.

"No, Selena!"

"What are you talking about, Miss Crockett?"

"I've got the same equipment inside me. My father paid Dr. Gray to operate on me when I was a kid."

"You've killed people?"

"No. Or maybe I have, indirectly. Gray used to give me treatments. . . . He'd knock me out with a drug and do something to me. Probably he gave me complete transfusions. He'd never say. And I never was sure where the blood came from, although now . . ." Her voice trailed. "I guess I do."

Willson nodded.

"Now just a minute, Willson," Danny said. "You don't think she's responsible for any of this—"

"We're all responsible, Danny!" Selena said. "That's why we're in this mess. We've got to stop pretending!" She looked at Willson. "Do what you must, Sergeant. I'll understand."

"I'm not going to arrest you, Miss Crockett. I need your help. You know the institute. We'll need help going through the records," Willson said. "Find out what's in there. Get some real doctors. Maybe there really is a cure."

"And what if you do find it," Danny said. "Then what?"

Willson looked at him. "We get it out to the folks that need it," he said. "Is your telephone working?"

"Yes."

"I'll call Percy, then."

He made the call and the three of them waited in Selena's kitchen for the coroner to arrive. Danny got his cameras out of the car and took pictures of the crime scene. Willson collected the evidence, and wrote up the notes. It was hard for Danny to look at Bing, but he got through it all right by squeezing the reality into the viewfinder. He was doing his job again. Bing would have approved.

Later, when the coroner had taken the body away and Willson had left with the evidence, Danny and Selena went out to the porch to smoke. Dawn was just beginning to color the eastern sky, and from Selena's building Danny could see the old, empty mills standing like a row of dark teeth guarding the slow, muddy river below a bright morning star.

Selena rested her head against his shoulder, and soon she fell asleep. She really was some kind of angel, he thought, though maybe she had fallen a little. Danny put his arm around her and she sighed, and he decided he would go see Walter Burns later on.

He had a feeling that maybe now he might be able to write a good lead.

Acknowledgments

In conjuring up my version of 1930 and the events of the Hun epidemic I did my best to immerse myself in the newspapers, films, books, and magazines of the period, as well as history, medical, and sociology textbooks. But I would also in particular like to thank Audrey Canelake and the staff of the History Department of the Minneapolis public library for providing source material about the Minneapolis Millers baseball team, and especially for recommending Larry Millet's fascinating architectural history, "Lost Twin Cities," which showed me the look and flavor of Minneapolis before the ravages of "urban renewal." I also greatly appreciate the assistance the staff of the Downtown Center of San Francisco's Irwin Memorial Blood Bank gave in researching the details of blood-collection procedures during the twenties and thirties, and Ann and Diane Cassidy's advice about sources of hematological and antique medical information.

Special thanks also go to my old, old chum and personal historian Neil Trembley, who lent me valuable materials from his private collection, and who took me on a tour of the ruins of the Washburn A flour mill at two in the morning one ghostly moonlit night. Thanks, as well, to my equally old friend Alan Mathiowetz, for his assistance with the technical details of 1920s photography, and to Jan Borene, for the use of her truck while she was on her honeymoon.

Beyond the research, I am grateful for the day-to-day support and assistance in countless psychological and material ways of: my agent, Richard Curtis; my editor, David Hartwell; Frances Collin, Jim Kelly, Lisa Goldstein, Kevin Anderson, Ed Ferman, Kris Rusch, Kip Conner, Ryan Conner, Linda Sackett, to Amira Alvarez, for her excellent proofreading, Peet's Coffee, the MIS departments of TMJB and P&M in San Francisco, Pat Ryan and Pat LaForge of Automation Partners, the Columbo Accordion Company, and, to my cool bandmates in the Naked Barbies, Dan Lashkoff, Evan Eustis, Dan Vickrey and Hans Raag, and in particular to my songwriting partner Patty Spiglanin without whose friendship and wry observations I would surely die. Thanks very much to all of you for helping to bring *Archangel* to life.